Vargul let out a hideous shriek.

The beast plucked off his opposite leg and did the same thing. Vargul's shriek died to a mere whimper, and then the merchant mercifully either went unconscious or was already dead.

Ran heard the sickening crunch of bones as it chewed and then swallowed. His stomach turned over, but he managed to bite back the surge at the back of his throat.

"The best part is coming," said Kan-Gul. "Now watch."

Ran felt forced to look, like Kan-Gul had somehow taken control of his body. Down in the pit, Vargul's body lay on the floor minus one arm and one leg. He looked like a rag doll. But the creature still hovered over him.

Vargul's body jerked. As it did, the creature opened its jaws and sucked in a huge gulp of air. The air in the pit went incredibly hot, and Ran heard Vargul's screams again and again and again, despite the fact that his body showed no signs of life.

"Yes, my lovely, feast on his soul. Take it all in and consume him entirely. Yesssss."

This was what Kan-Gul's creations did to the people they killed. They ate their souls so they couldn't journey to the afterlife. Ran shook his head and only stopped when Vargul's screams finally ended several minutes later.

When Ran opened his eyes, the creature was gone from the pit.

Kan-Gul's voice was hushed. "You will now be taken back to your cells. I believe you have much to discuss."

BAEN BOOKS
BY JON F. MERZ

The Shadow Warrior
The Undead Hordes of Kan-Gul
Slayers of the Savage Catacombs (forthcoming)
The Temple of Demons (forthcoming)

To purchase these and all other Baen Book titles in e-book format,
please go to www.baen.com.

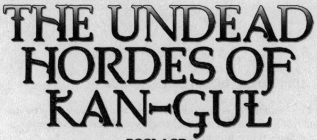

THE UNDEAD HORDES OF KAN-GUL

BOOK 1 OF
THE SHADOW WARRIOR

JON F. MERZ

THE UNDEAD HORDES OF KAN-GUL

Copyright © 2013 by Jon F. Merz

A Baen Books Original

Baen Publishing Enterprises
P.O. Box 1403
Riverdale, NY 10471

www.baen.com

ISBN 13: 978-1-4767-3675-4

Cover art by Sam Kennedy

First printing, November 2014

Distributed by Simon & Schuster
1230 Avenue of the Americas
New York, NY 10020

Library of Congress Cataloging-in-Publication Data
2013015994

Printed in the United States of America

10 9 8 7 6 5 4 3 2 1

DEDICATION

❈❈❈

For my son William—born with the spirit
of adventure and daring, yet gifted with
compassion for all souls.

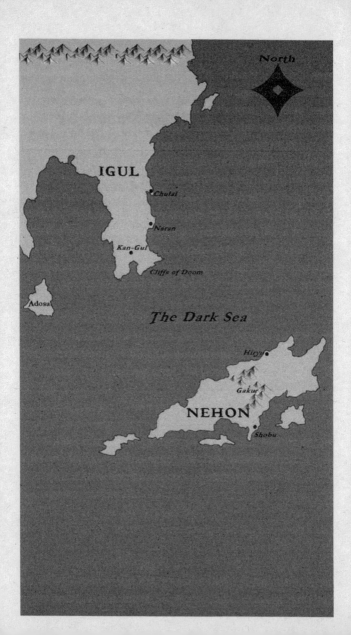

THE UNDEAD HORDES OF KAN-GUL

BOOK 1 OF
THE SHADOW WARRIOR

CHAPTER ONE

Tucked away in the corner of the bar, Ran attracted little attention. Over the last few weeks, he'd allowed his beard to grow out, giving his face a decidedly shaggy appearance. His hair, longer than it had been when he'd left the mountains of Gakur, draped about his face, cloaking the majority of his features. But his keen eyes peered out through the loose strands, watching everyone who came into the tavern.

A bowl of rice and fish sat before him, and he ate by burying his face into the mixture using his chopsticks to shovel in his food. Bits of briny morsels clung to his beard, and flecks of rice spattered the wooden bar top, drawing a frown from the tavern owner, watching this strange customer who had entered his business looking poor and unkempt but had paid with a single gold coin for food and drink. Then there was the fact that he wore a curved sword that commanded respect despite his appearance. Few would be foolish enough to wear such a blade unless they knew how to use it

Ran read the tavern owner's facial expressions and body language, not to mention the guttural noises the man made when he glanced in Ran's direction. These betrayed far more than if the man had simply spoken.

The tavern owner probably didn't think Ran was Murai—the warrior class that dominated this region—but he could be a former Murai who had left service or been on the losing side of a clan war and had taken to wandering in search of money. He'd no doubt seen such men before. And while they might have none of the honor and grace of a proper Murai warrior, they were nevertheless lethal and deserved a wide berth.

It was even more obvious the tavern owner thought Ran was a slob. The sooner he could get Ran out his tavern, the better.

It was exactly what Ran wanted. Tavern owners were notorious gossips, and Ran wanted no one asking him questions and digging for information about who he was. His safety depended on people avoiding him or, even more preferable, not noticing him at all. In a tavern, Ran had to make himself as unapproachable as possible. Places like this usually had a few braggarts about who would bother you if you simply tried to be unobtrusive. So Ran had adopted an appearance that kept civilized people at bay while adding a hint of potential danger.

He hoped it would work.

The docks outside the tavern were busy: scores of ships were moored, gathering supplies or unloading trade goods from across the Dark Sea.

Ran hoped to journey west—far west—all the way to the kingdom of Valrus, home of Princess Cassandra. Ran had rescued the princess from an evil sorcerer. But after rescuing her, Ran had not been able join Cassandra on her long journey home, for he had an obligation to his clan—the Nine Daggers. So, after an awkward parting, he had returned to his clan's domain amid the misty peaks of the Gakur. Even as he did so, Ran longed to journey with the princess, to see her safely returned to her people.

After informing his clan leaders of his encounter with the sorcerer, Ran was sent on a *shugyo*, a wandering quest meant to prove he was actually ready to become a full member of the clan, to put its needs before his own selfish desires.

Ran had departed almost immediately, for he knew his destination. And the next step in this long journey would be to cross the Dark Sea.

Ran returned his gaze to the *Aqaria*. This unassuming trading vessel would be his means of leaving Nehon, would deliver him to Igul and the lands beyond.

The door to the tavern opened and two women walked in. One of them was draped in a dizzying array of silks that wound around her body and tucked into her curves. Her almond-colored skin offered a contrast to the swirl of colors. Her sharp eyes, tilted up at the corners, drew Ran's attention as did the intricate tattoo that covered part of her face. She was so beautiful, for a moment Ran forgot all about Cassandra.

But then his training kicked in, and his eyes were quickly drawn to the woman at her side. This woman moved like a warrior. And her appearance left little doubt about that fact. Half a dozen throwing knives sat in horizontal sheaths running obliquely from her left shoulder to her right hip. A sword rested at her side, shorter than most of the ones Ran had seen before. Judging by her gait, the way she wore her weapons, and her shifting gaze as she took in each of the occupants of the tavern, she was well trained as both a warrior and a bodyguard.

They were an interesting pair, Ran decided. He belched once, which instantly drew a sidelong glance from the warrior woman. He grunted once approvingly. The young pretty one would need looking after in a place like this, no doubt.

Ran washed a mouthful of food down with a swig of rice wine from the small porcelain cup in front of him. He didn't like the idea of drinking and risking his awareness, but if he did something out of character, it might stand out in the memory of the tavern owner. Ran's teachers at his clan had been most insistent about the need to completely throw oneself into whatever disguise one attempted. Partial attempts never succeeded; Ran had to look and act the part. Most importantly, he had to believe he truly was who he appeared to be.

The two women sat at one of the smaller tables close to the hearth. For the moment, Ran tucked them away because his attention was drawn to another newcomer who had just stormed into the tavern.

"Barkeep! Serve me some of that tasty rice wine you make so well. I am parched from a day of business." Rotund and tall, with flaming locks of red, the man stood a few stools away from Ran and proceeded to down several cups of the rice wine. Ran busied himself with eating, but he made sure to catalog the foreigner's movements.

It was certain he was from the northern lands far from

the shores of Nehon. A trader, no doubt. Ran noted that his hands seemed free of the heavy calluses that would have marked him as a warrior or a laborer. No, Ran decided, this one would do battle with sums of money, not with the edge of a sword or axe, nor with the tools of a craftsman.

The Northerner swung his ample girth onto a stool and spent several moments adjusting himself until he managed to achieve some degree of balance. Then he put both hands palms down on the bar and smiled at the tavern owner. "The name is Vargul."

The tavern owner gave him a small grin, but it was clear he cared little for the boisterous man. Still, when Vargul laid several gold coins on the counter, the tavern owner's eyes gleamed. The coins vanished and were replaced by several more cups of rice wine that Vargul downed immediately.

Ran frowned. The trader was out of his element. Displaying that sort of wealth wasn't wise at the docks. Ran had already noted at least three scroungy men paying far too much attention to the red-haired foreigner now that they had seen his money. Ran set his chopsticks down and swished a bit more rice wine into his mouth.

It wasn't a question of if one of the men would move on Vargul. It was only a question of when and who.

Ran didn't have to wait long. From his right side, he sensed movement and saw a tall, lean figure cut across the room. He wasn't even trying to be subtle. Instead, he sat down next to Vargul at the bar.

Vargul turned in his seat, a broad smile spilling across his face. "Hello!"

The man grinned and showed no teeth, causing Vargul

to pull back. But then the man grabbed hold of Vargul's left hand and pulled him in closer. "You seem to have a lot of gold, my friend. How about giving me some of it?"

Vargul sputtered and looked at the tavern keeper for help. But the owner wasn't interested in getting involved. Ran knew the type. They would only get involved if they themselves were threatened. Otherwise, they had to remain above the fray if they had any hope of staying in business.

"He won't help you," said the man. "Give me your purse."

Vargul shook his head and sputtered something that sounded unintelligible to Ran. It did little good, because in the next breath, the wiry man moved suddenly and had a knife at Vargul's throat.

"I could slice your throat open and take it myself."

Vargul froze.

Ran sighed. The merchant obviously had no common sense hiding anywhere about his voluminous proportions. And because of that, Ran now faced a decision: get involved or let Vargul lose all of his money.

Out of the corner of his eye, Ran noted that the pair of women were watching the exchange closely. The warrior in particular sat motionless. But Ran noticed that one of her hands had strayed toward her throwing knives. If she acted, the entire scene in the tavern could explode into a bloodbath. That would result in the local authorities coming in to break it up, asking all sorts of questions. Ran certainly didn't want that to happen.

As Vargul shied away from the knife beneath his chin, Ran shoved his bowl away suddenly. As he did so, the door to the tavern opened and a man stood in the light. He was heavy, but much of his bulk seemed to be muscle. It was Malkyr, the captain of the *Aqaria*.

"The *Aqaria* sails in ten minutes. Anyone who has secured passage should get aboard now. I don't wait for stragglers."

The pair of women immediately rose and moved toward the door. Ran saw his opportunity. He rose from his seat, and, while everyone's attention was focused elsewhere, he came up behind the ruffian and jammed the tip of his left thumb into the area right above the cutthroat's kidneys, boring it in to create maximum pain. As the thug reacted by arching his back, Ran used his right hand to knock the knife arm to the left and away from Vargul's throat.

Even as the ruffian stumbled off the bar stool, Ran plucked Vargul from the stool and shoved him toward the door. "Our ride awaits." Ran hustled him outside before Vargul could even comprehend what had just happened.

Ran didn't want to wait around for the thug to regain himself and come back for revenge.

Outside, the sun had vanished behind gray clouds. Ran frowned. It had been bright and sunny earlier. The prospect of traveling during a storm didn't sit well with him. Especially since he disliked boats. But reuniting with Cassandra meant crossing the Dark Sea, so that was where his path lay.

Vargul managed to find his voice. "How—what did you do back there?"

Ran shook his head as he moved them through the throngs of people clogging the docks. "Saved your life and your purse, near as I can figure. Do yourself a favor: from now on, don't go showing off your wealth around the docks. It's a damned foolish thing to do. I know up North, people seemed a lot more civilized and you obviously felt free to flaunt your wealth. But down here, that will get you killed and your body dumped into the sea."

"Then I am indebted to you, my young friend." Vargul clapped him on the back. "And I always repay my debts."

Ran led him down toward the gangplank of the *Aqaria*. "I'm glad to hear you say that. You see, I haven't purchased a fare yet for this trip."

Malkyr stood at the top of the gangplank and welcomed Vargul aboard. Then his eyes turned to Ran and narrowed. "What do we have here?"

But Vargul was true to his word. He wrapped an arm around Ran's shoulders and smiled at Malkyr. "My friend. You don't mind if I bring him along, do you?"

"Are you paying his way?"

"Of course."

Malkyr stepped back to let them both pass. "Then he is most welcome."

As Ran passed by, Malkyr put one hand up. "I certainly hope you have no reason to use those swords during this trip."

Ran glanced down at the twin blades he wore in his sash—one long and one short—that marked him as a warrior. He smiled at Malkyr. "So do I."

Malkyr stepped aside as Ran felt his feet touch the deck of the *Aqaria* for the first time. The ship lolled gently at its mooring and Ran's stomach rolled with it. He grimaced and wondered whether eating had been wise.

Still, it had been a long journey, and it was better to have a full stomach than not. He glanced overhead and saw the gray clouds had been joined by darker ones.

"Don't let them bother you," said Malkyr as his gaze also turned to the darkening clouds. "The gods always throw us a party when we sail."

"Do they?"

Malkyr winked. "I've ridden out far worse storms than the one that seems to be brewing now. And this ship is the finest I've ever sailed. She'll get us where we need to be."

"I hope you're right," said Ran. He moved farther aboard as Malkyr began calling out orders to cast off. Ran watched the deckhands scramble from bow to stern, throwing lines back toward the docks. Malkyr called for one of the sails to be raised. As the wind caught hold of it, the *Aqaria* pulled away from the dock, into the deeper part of the channel that led to the open sea.

Ran headed for the midships and braced himself. Ahead of him, the Dark Sea stretched like a hungry maw. It looked capable of swallowing the entire land. The *Aqaria* wouldn't even be a single bite. With a final look, Ran turned and descended into the bowels of the ship to wait out the coming storm.

CHAPTER TWO

The spray of salt water lashed across the bow of the *Aqaria* as it cut its way through the trough of another wave. The unending up and down as waves rose and fell under the keel made Ran's stomach heave. As the bottom of another wave dropped out, Ran bit his tongue to stem to rising gorge in his throat. His knuckles were white as he gripped the bulwark with his right hand and the hilt of his curved sword with his left.

"We couldn't have waited until the storm subsided?"

His question produced a loud bellowing laugh from the stern of the boat, where Malkyr handled the wheel with nonchalance as he faced the storm. "Too rough for you, then?" He ran a hand through his thick, coarse beard, where briny droplets glistened. "The Dark Sea is always like this. It doesn't matter when we set sail. So best to get on with it, eh?"

Best to get us back on to dry ground, thought Ran. Ahead of the boat, he saw only dark clouds and darker waves. The ship on which he sailed seemed terribly small in comparison to the brewing tempest. He'd started the journey belowdecks, but when the waves had started tossing the *Aqaria* about, he'd decided it was better to at least have fresh air while he convulsively emptied fish and rice into the surging sea.

He forced himself to grin; the fact that he was seasick humbled him. A recent graduate from the many arduous years of shadow-warrior training, Ran had seen a fair share of combat. Yet despite his fighting prowess, the sea had beaten his formerly iron stomach. If his teachers could see him now, they would undoubtedly dispense a lesson about Ran's need to keep his ego in check. They would lecture him that his ego would grant his enemies a way to control and manipulate him.

But the teachers and the school of the Nine Daggers itself were many leagues to the east, hidden away behind a veil of perpetual fog in the mountains and valleys of Gakur. There, the Shinobujin had trained for generations, perfecting their abilities far from the prying eyes of those who would wish them harm. Famed for their ability to steal secrets, infiltrate impregnable castles, and hide in plain sight, the shadow warriors bore a fearsome reputation for their cunning and guile as well as their use of both traditional and unorthodox weapons. And if those failed, their skills in unarmed combat were also legendary.

Ran didn't feel particularly legendary at the moment.

He bit back another tidal surge of vomit and steadied himself with a deep breath. He allowed his legs to spread and then sank his hips a bit more, giving him a better base of support.

So far, his wandering quest—what his clan called a

shugyo—wasn't as thrilling as he'd hoped. Certainly not as much as his final test before graduation. But the end result of that test had been that Ran had passed and simultaneously violated one of the school's rules. His punishment was to embark on a *shugyo* where he would test himself and his skills while journeying abroad. This wasn't so unusual in itself: the school normally dispatched its agents all across the lands near and far. It was how they kept tabs on what everyone else outside their secluded world was up to. The masters at the school could then decide if certain events required their intervention or not. Sometimes interventions took the form of subtly applied misinformation. Other times the actions were much more direct.

Ran's best defense while he was outside the protection of the school was to never let anyone know that he was a shadow warrior. Certain rulers offered a huge bounty for the death of anyone found to be from the school. Others sought to employ them to their own ends, despite their distaste. So Ran simply adopted the manner of a wandering warrior looking for opportunities to sell his blade to whoever could afford him. To help his disguise, Ran had stopped shaving and now sported a stubbly growth all over his face. His hair had grown longer, but he didn't pull it back off of his face the way the warriors of his homeland did. Despite his obvious youth, the overall effect of the ruddy, unkempt appearance gave him an edge that made people slightly wary when he approached.

Which was exactly what he wanted.

"Where are you headed?" asked Malkyr.

"West. To find work."

"What—there aren't enough lords in Nehon who could use your blade alongside theirs?"

Ran shrugged. "Perhaps I'd like to see the world."

"Indeed," said Malkyr. "You're young enough, and adventure awaits. Is that it?"

"Perhaps." Ran eyed the clouds. "This storm doesn't seem to be helping matters, though."

"We'll get through it," said Malkyr. "The current is being a bit troublesome, but the *Aqaria* is strong enough to handle it."

Ran nodded. "You keep water below?"

"Yes. Try not to drink too much, though. We're only a few hours into this journey, and we won't see landfall for another day."

Ran ducked belowdecks and found the barrels of water. He sipped at the ladle. As the cool water touched his throat, it removed the sting of bile. He found a berth near the other travelers and settled himself as best he could. In seconds, he was asleep.

Hours passed before he heard heavy footfalls clomping down the ladder. He cracked an eye and saw Malkyr looking around at his passengers. "This damnable storm is worse than any I've seen. We're not going to make the port of Chulal."

"Where are we headed?" asked Ran.

"Hopefully to Naran." Malkyr spat on the deck. "But I wish we weren't."

The old drunk sat up at the mention of Naran, but quickly tried to hide his attentiveness.

Ran was fully awake now. "Why?"

"Because it's a lawless place. Smugglers, thieves . . . they dominate the area. There's no real ruling warlord. And the reefs nearby are deadly to ships like the *Aqaria*."

Nearby, the female warrior grunted. "Kan-Gul."

Malkyr whipped his head around and frowned. "I'd prefer you not speak that name, Neviah."

Ran sat up. "What is Kan-Gul?"

"Not a what," said Malkyr. "A who." He frowned. "I need to get back up on deck."

Ran watched him leave and then turned to Neviah. "He doesn't seem too eager to talk about things."

Neviah cursed and then yanked one of her throwing knives out of its sheath, running her eyes along its honed edge. "I'd hoped to give that area a wide berth."

"What's the problem?"

She eyed him. "You've never heard of Kan-Gul?"

"No."

She shrugged. "Some say he's a sorcerer. That he employs the undead to do his bidding. He controls that area, and the land is said to be rife with evil magic."

"You believe it?"

Neviah frowned as she slid the knife back into its sheath. "I believe it enough to want to avoid the land and anything to do with Kan-Gul."

The ship lolled to one side, and Ran's stomach rolled with it. He swallowed quickly and tried to concentrate on dispelling his nausea. "I need some air."

He climbed topside and was immediately drenched as a wave crashed over the bow of the ship. Ran sputtered and stumbled toward the rail and spat the salt water out of his mouth. Still, the cold water refreshed him.

A full day had passed, and dawn was close. The dark clouds overhead were lighter toward the heaving horizon. Malkyr stood by the tiller, and Ran wondered if the captain had even slept. Another wave crashed over him, and Ran steadied himself, watching the roiling seas, and he forgot his queasiness for a moment.

Mostly because he'd noticed something moving out of flow with the surging waves.

"Malkyr?"

"What is it?"

"I've heard stories of creatures that live in the seas. Have you ever seen them?"

Malkyr laughed. "There are things that swim in these waters that will eat you in one gulp, my boy. Huge, dangerous beasts that don't care if you have a sword on your hip or not." He paused. "Why do you ask?"

Ran pointed just as the ship rose on another swell. "There appears to be something following us. Just under the surface."

"Probably a pod of dolphin," said Malkyr.

But Ran heard the uncertainty in his voice and saw a ripple of concern crease his forehead. Malkyr turned and barked an order to his first mate in the strange tongue that the seafarers used. Ran didn't understand the language— if you could even call the short, guttural utterance that—but he understood that Malkyr was concerned enough to order the first mate to stand ready with a large harpoon. Even as the storm clouds drew closer to the ship, the polished, folded-steel tip of the harpoon gleamed like an eye, searching for prey.

The first mate hefted the harpoon with scarred, tanned

arms. A broken nose jutted out from under his brow, but his eyes were keen as they searched the waters around the ship. He said nothing to the captain but stood ready to hurl the giant spear.

The fingers of Ran's left hand rested just below the guard of his sword. Normal warriors in his country often used their thumbs to ease the blade forward in its scabbard. But Shinobujin preferred using their index fingers underneath to accomplish the same motion. It often gave them the barest moment of advantage. In battle, you took whatever advantage you could get. Ran wasn't sure how effective the edge of his folded steel sword would be against a leviathan from the deep, but he felt a measure of confidence anyway.

"Are you certain you saw something?" asked Malkyr.

Ran kept his eyes on the churning swells. "I did. It moved out of time with the flow of the water around us. We are definitely being stalked."

Malkyr grunted and aimed the bow of the ship into another wave, keeping a firm hand as he fought to keep the *Aqaria* from turning and taking a potentially mortal wave broadside. Ran was grateful for his experience. He wouldn't have wanted to go overboard in seas like this, regardless of the beast stalking the depths below them.

A sudden boom overhead tore open the skies, and rain dropped down in sheets. Ran heard Malkyr laughing and found the man's behavior strange. "How can you find this funny?"

Malkyr pointed at the heavens. "The gods love to make the lives of mortals miserable. This weather, these waves, and even now the presence of some watery behemoth . . . But I'll show them. Never let them see the fear that threatens to squeeze your heart. I'll face whatever they throw at me. And more." He shook a fist at the sky as more thunder roared. "You can't kill me!"

Ran's frown deepened. He wasn't certain what the gods might or might not have to do with his present situation, but he saw no use in angering them further. Why ask for more trouble when there was no guarantee they'd outlive their immediate circumstances? It just didn't seem wise.

He stared out over the waves and then saw a flash of movement again out of time with the rest of the flow of the sea. A shadow streaked horizontally across the waves in front of the bow. Ran was about to say something when he felt the breeze of the harpoon shooting past him, its silver barbed tip almost buzzing as it cut through the rain and streaked out beyond the ship. Ran watched it arc and then fall into the waves and the dark bulk just beneath.

Malkyr laughed again. "How's that for a shot, eh?" He nodded at the first mate. "Excellent job."

But the answer from the first mate was drowned out by a sudden screech as something rose up out of the waves ahead of them, spraying red foam across the bow and the deck. Ran caught the stench of brine and blood mixed together. The harpoon may have struck the creature, but just as Malkyr might have done with the gods, it had merely angered the beast.

And now the creature seemed intent on attacking the ship.

Ran glanced back at Malkyr. "Do you have other weapons on board this ship?"

"Another harpoon, and then we have our swords."

"Any spears?"

Malkyr frowned. "No."

Ran unsheathed his sword. "I suggest you call your men to arms." As he said this, he felt the ship shudder. Ran turned and saw a massive tentacle come over the side of the ship. It crashed on the foredeck and shattered a wooden crate, spilling grain all over. Ran immediately rushed forward, swinging from high to low and severing the tentacle as far up as he could reach. The finely honed edge of his sword sliced through the muscled limb. Blood spouted from the stump, and the beast screeched again.

Ran didn't stop. He spotted another tentacle rising out of the surf. Even as more rain slashed at him, he leaped high and cut horizontally, shearing another piece from the leviathan. He heard shouts behind him and risked a quick glance. Another tentacle had entangled one of the crew, its suckers already attached to his body. The man howled over the roar of the storm as his friends desperately tried to free him.

But in another blink, the tentacle vanished back into the sea, dragging the crewman to his death.

Malkyr shouted orders at his crew, but it was obvious that panic was setting in. The first mate tried to keep some measure of control, but then a rogue wave tossed the ship, and the first mate went over the side and vanished. Another tentacle appeared and smashed into the mast in the center of the boat. Ran heard the splintering of wood and looked up to see the mast breaking.

"Look out!"

Even as he shouted a warning, the timber crashed

down onto the deck, crushing another crew member. Ran dodged the ruffled and drenched sail and the lines that threatened to spool around his feet. He'd spotted another tentacle lashing at the midships and struck out with his sword, cutting deep into the flesh and muscle of the suckered tendril. Dark blood poured from the gaping wound, spilling onto the already slippery deck. Ran jerked his blade free, and almost instantly the tentacle slid back into the deep.

His breath came in spurts now, and the adrenaline flowing through him made his pulse drum in his ears. He took several deep breaths and managed to calm his heart rate. He turned and saw the crew still trying to clear the wreckage of the mast from the deck. Men worked feverishly to cut the lines and toss the timber overboard.

Movement in his peripheral vision made him turn in time to see a massive tentacle streaming straight at him. Ran ducked and then heard the song of steel as another sword cleaved through the tentacle. He looked up to see the old drunk launching a series of lightning-fast cuts that severed the tentacle in several places. The wounded stump shrank back over the side of the ship.

Ran rose on his feet, steadied himself, and waited for another tentacle to appear.

But no new attacks came.

The beast's screeching had given way to the howling wind and thunder of the storm.

The older man grunted and nodded once at Ran. Ran smirked. When he first saw the old man on board the *Aqaria*, he'd thought the man was a mere drunk. But the way he wielded his sword clearly indicated a warrior of great skill.

Ran looked at his own blade and saw that the rain had already cleaned most of the blood from it. He flipped it over and performed a quick move to flick away the rest before resheathing it again.

"Is it gone?"

He glanced back at Malkyr. "Seems to have disappeared, yes."

"Gods be praised. I wasn't sure we'd survive that encounter."

"You've lost your mast and sail," said Ran. "How will we ever reach land now?"

Malkyr frowned. "The current is strong and pulling us to the west. With any hope, we should reach landfall by night."

"You're certain of that?"

Malkyr grinned. "Much more certain now than I was a few moments ago."

"Why so?"

"Look."

Ran turned and felt his stomach drop. A huge wave was headed right for the ship.

CHAPTER THREE

If Ran thought Malkyr would panic, he was sorely mistaken. Instead, as the huge tidal surge lifted the boat beneath its keel and carried it like a piece of driftwood, Malkyr let out a long and deep laugh that seemed to echo off the storm clouds above. Ran, who had finally warded off the effects of seasickness thanks to the combat, now felt himself becoming queasy again as the boat surged through the water on the back of the wave. *This can't be real, he thought*. The boat would probably capsize, but still Malkyr would laugh at the gods for this.

He's mad, thought Ran. As he watched, the captain's hand never left the tiller, and Ran could see how hard his grip was on the piece of wood that enabled him to keep on course. They were headed west, no doubt, but in what condition would they reach land?

Ran steeled himself on the bulwark, one hand never far from his sword. He gritted his teeth and willed that their journey be a swift one. While he had studied many techniques used for fighting on ships, Ran had never felt at ease on the bucking beasts and preferred having his feet on solid ground.

"The man might well be the death of us."

Ran glanced behind him and saw the old drunk who had helped him fight off the monster a few moments earlier. He was squatting and wiping his blade clean, his eyes never leaving the prized two-handed curved sword. "And if that happens, then all of this will be for naught."

Ran sank on his haunches close by and watched the old man work for another moment before responding. "You're quite adept with that blade."

The man's eyes lifted and held Ran's gaze. "Are you asking me a question or simply stating the obvious?"

"I thought I was paying you a compliment."

"Compliments are for women. You fought by my side when we faced that creature instead of running or acting like a damned fool. That's enough."

"I'm Ran."

"Kancho."

"You've used that sword a lot," said Ran. His eyes had spotted several nicks along the edge of the blade. "You haven't had time to put a whetstone to that edge."

Kancho shrugged. "I left my home rather unexpectedly. I didn't have time to get it fixed. But there's nothing too serious about them. The blade still cuts like a sharp tongue."

"A tongue eager for blood," said Ran. "Why did you leave your home so suddenly?"

Kancho regarded him for a moment and then went back to wiping his blade. "You ask a lot of questions for someone so young."

"I apologize if I offended you." Ran started to stand.

Kancho held up one hand. "Don't worry about it. I keep to myself mostly. It's a bit out of the ordinary for me to have long conversations."

Ran glanced away, but kept Kancho in his peripheral vision. There was a lot more to this old man than met the eye. Not only had he handled himself like a seasoned warrior during the melee, but he knew how to care for his sword. That skill alone marked him as something more than what he appeared. No, Ran decided, this was no regular man. He was most likely a member of the professional warrior class in Gakur, the Murai. Judging by the reverence he showed for his blade, there was little doubt.

But why was he disguised? Murai were a proud class of expert warriors who would never conceal themselves the way Kancho was.

Unless . . .

If Kancho had dishonored himself, then that might be cause for a false identity. But just as quickly as the thought had occurred to him, Ran dismissed it. If Kancho had dishonored himself or the lord he served, then Murai tradition mandated that he commit suicide through ritual disembowelment. That was the only way to remove the shame that he would have brought upon himself and the lord he served.

Ran took a breath and looked out over the horizon. The storm clouds, dark and streaked with charcoal gray seemed never-ending. And Ran wasn't sure where the clouds stopped and the land they traveled to began. Even if they were close to the coast, they might never know it.

But Malkyr looked every bit as confident as he had

when the sea monster had attacked them. His hand was still firm on the tiller, and his eyes never wavered. Ran found his presence almost unnerving in its nonchalance. To Malkyr, this sort of thing might happen on a daily basis. Ran hoped it was a once in a lifetime event.

"You're fair with a sword as well," came Kancho's voice again.

Ran smiled. Clearly the old man was making an attempt at communicating. "Thank you."

"But you're not one of the Murai."

"How would you know if I was?" asked Ran.

Kancho chuckled. "I would know."

"I could be, though."

"You're young," said Kancho. "And judging by how you wielded that sword, you've been trained in other lineages than what the Murai study."

Ran frowned. "I was taught by my uncle, whose father had once served a lord in the far north."

"So why didn't your family continue to serve?"

Ran looked away, trying his best to affect deep concern. "My uncle's father . . . left service, and became a wandering warrior for hire. He gradually found his way south and married. He taught his sons everything he knew about fighting."

"But you didn't learn from your father?"

"My father was killed when I was very young," said Ran. "I have no memory of him. I was raised by my uncle and infused with the knowledge that had been shared by their father."

Kancho looked up from his work and stared at Ran for another moment. Then he grunted and looked back at the sword in his lap. "Well, you're a credit to them, at least. Good balance. You seem to understand distance. Overall, I'd say with a little seasoning, you could become a true warrior. But why are you out here on this accursed vessel? Why not stay in Gakur?"

"I'm not of the Murai," said Ran.

"It's in your blood," said Kancho. "You could ask to have your family name reinstated at the capital."

Ran smiled. "I would never be able to serve as well as the Murai. I've been brought up to make my own decisions, to steer my own fate."

Kancho grinned. "If that's so, then why take a chance on this damned boat?"

"I want to sell my blade on the mainland."

Kancho frowned. "There's little honor in being a sword-for-hire, Ran."

"True, but there are lots of riches to be had."

"Is that why you fight? For money?"

"If I say yes, will you condemn me for it?"

Kancho finished with his sword and slid it carefully back into the scabbard. Then he got to his feet and placed one hand on the bulwark. "Men fight for many reasons. Some for honor. Some for the love of a woman. Some for money. As long as you can deliver on the promise that your sword carries with it, what difference does it make?"

Ran wasn't sure he trusted that statement as a true account of how Kancho actually felt, especially if he was Murai. "So, why do you fight?"

"I fight for my daughter," said Kancho. And then he disappeared belowdecks, leaving Ran alone amid the heaving swells that carried the ship farther westward.

Ran thought about going after him, but decided it was best to leave him be. When Kancho felt like talking again, Ran felt certain he could get him to open up and give some more indication of why he had taken to disguising himself.

The giant wave that had picked the *Aqaria* up and carried her seemed to be subsiding now. *Thank the gods*, thought Ran. If they could make dry land before nightfall, his feet would never leave the ground again.

Ahead of him, he watched as Malkyr ordered two deckhands to fit a smaller spare mast where the main one had been torn apart. They did so and then ran up a fresh sail. Instantly, the wind took hold and the *Aqaria* resumed making good speed. The deckhands tied the sheet off and then busied themselves with other tasks up on the deck.

Ran's queasiness subsided as he made his way along the starboard side of the ship and looked again at Malkyr. This time, the captain of the *Aqaria* took his eyes off the horizon to nod at Ran. "You'll have to watch yourself around that one."

"Kancho?"

Malkyr smirked. "There's not a person on this ship that believes he's just some harmless old drunk. No matter how much rice wine he spilled on his clothes to affect the stench he carries. It's not enough. If you're going to disguise yourself, you have to be convincing about it."

"Do tell," said Ran as he climbed toward Malkyr.

"Kancho's disguise is superficial. It'll fool some of the people some of the time. But it won't hold up to real scrutiny. His bearing, his skill with weapons, even his weapon itself tell a tale all the rice wine in the world cannot wash away. As you've clearly noticed."

Ran smiled. "Was I that obvious?"

Malkyr shrugged. "Maybe I've been around the rat-infested docks too long. Everyone at the edge of the sea carries a tale. And everyone's always one step away from jumping a ship bound for anywhere but where they are right then. You can't trust appearances."

Ran nodded and then pointed to the horizon. "Are we closer to land?"

"Unfortunately, we're much closer than I'd like."

"How can you tell? All I see is a huge bank of clouds. I can't fathom if it's mist, fog, or the clouds themselves. We could sail right for the very edge of the world, and I wouldn't know it until we fell off."

"Aye," said Malkyr. "Which is exactly why you should always trust your captain. He knows best." Malkyr pointed. "There. You see that break in the mist? The area where it's darker?"

Ran looked at where he pointed and saw how the darker mist seemed to be increasing. "Yes, what about it?"

"That should be Naran," said Malkyr quietly.

But as the fog shifted, Ran suddenly saw that it wasn't a port at all. Sheer imposing cliffs jutted out of the water.

"Blast it," said Malkyr. "This cursed storm blew us even farther south than I expected."

"Where are we?"

"They call those the Cliffs of Doom because if you're not careful the reefs around here will gouge a keel and you'll sink in twenty fathoms of water before you know what even hit you."

As he said this, Malkyr leaned on the tiller, pushing it to the starboard side. The boat responded by veering to port, away from the dark rock cliffs. "This is where it gets tricky." He whistled, and one of his crew appeared on deck. Malkyr spoke quickly in the sailing tongue, and the man nodded, moving up to the bow of the *Aqaria*. There, he planted his feet and held his arms out in front of him.

Malkyr nodded at him. "We'll seek shelter in calmer waters, drop anchor, and ride out this storm. Chung will guide us into the mangrove swamps that line the coast. It's a tricky process since the entrance that we need to find is a mere spit of clear water. On either side are the reefs that will grind up my keel if we're not careful." He shouted to more deckhands and they came up and took down the sail. The *Aqaria* slowed and then eased forward, carried on the current.

"Have you ever lost a boat before?"

Malkyr stared at Ran. "Never ask a captain that."

Ran smiled. "Seafarer superstition?"

"That," said Malkyr. "And he might just throw you off his ship."

"My apologies," said Ran. "I didn't mean to imply you weren't capable."

Malkyr shrugged. "When you sail these waters for as long as I have, you realize that stuff is mostly routine."

"Being attacked by sea creatures is routine?"

Malkyr pointed at Chung. "It is when you're headed into the Dark Sea and toward Iyarul. The sea is lousy with the stuff of nightmares. And some say the lands of Igul are even worse."

"We'll see," said Ran.

"You'd better get down below and tell the others that we're going to be moving slowly from here on out as we try to thread our way through this mess. I don't want anybody up on deck. But stand by in case I need you all to abandon ship."

"Will do," said Ran. He started down and then turned back toward Malkyr. "But you've done this before, haven't you? Brought a ship through here?"

Malkyr smiled. "I've plied this sea for thirty years. This isn't my first time seeking shelter in these waters. But the sea never stays the same. She changes as she pleases. And sometimes, she likes to spring surprises on even the wisest sea captains there are."

CHAPTER FOUR

Ran ducked beneath the deck and bumped his head as he did so. He'd never get used to the cramped conditions aboard a ship, he decided. But if he could manage to escape with only a bump on his head, he'd consider it well worth the price. He rubbed his head and made his way past the crates that were stacked and held in position with thick hemp cords. Beyond them, the *Aqaria* housed a small passenger section that was in effect little more than a hollowed-out section with a few cushions in it.

Kancho looked up as he approached. "And just what is the situation topside? We seemed to have picked up speed. But now we're slowing again."

"We have. Malkyr let out a new sail, and it was carrying us faster. But we're approaching the coast, and he dropped it."

"Why would he do a thing like that?"

"Reefs," said Vargul. "I've heard this coastline is rife with the things. If Malkyr's not careful, he'll smash us all to pieces."

Neviah frowned, but as Ran looked at her, he thought it only enhanced the beauty of her blue eyes and high cheekbones, which ran nearly parallel to each other. "I am not interested in being dashed on the rocks of some forsaken coast. I have places I need to be." She turned and spoke quietly to her young woman.

Neviah turned and caught Ran staring at them. "Do you always stare at women that way? It's rather blatant."

Vargul guffawed. "He's just being honest. And I don't blame him one bit. Both of you ladies are a sight for sore eyes."

Neviah regarded him. "You'll want to show proper respect. I assure you that I could make things very unpleasant for you if you were to even try anything improper, Northerner."

"My name is Vargul. And it's true I'm from the north. But so what? Vargul travels the world over seeking goods to bring home and sell to his kinsmen. And I have an eye for ravishing women. Which both of you are. I mean no disrespect by stating that."

Neviah frowned at him a moment longer and then looked back at Ran. "You have something to tell us?"

"Malkyr says to keep yourselves here but be ready."

Kancho looked up. "Be ready for what?"

"I don't know. He says the sea floor shifts in these parts, and the reefs could well wreck the ship. If that happens, then we'll have to get out of the boat quickly."

Jysal blinked at Ran. He found the effect pleasant. "Are we to swim then?"

"If it becomes necessary," said Ran. "The other option is to stay here and drown."

Neviah shook her head. "I am Jysal's protector. She will stay with me at all times."

Kancho glanced over. "Protector?"

Neviah nodded. "You find that unusual?"

"I wonder why Jysal needs protecting," said Kancho. "There's nothing unusual about a woman being a warrior. Nor a beautiful warrior."

"She is on her way to a temple to the north of here. Once there, she will continue her education. But the road to the temple is a dangerous one, so I was hired to make sure she gets there intact."

Vargul rubbed his enormous belly and sighed. "I wonder if Malkyr has any more food aboard this floating tub? It's been several hours since my last meal."

Ran felt a spike of nausea at the thought of food. Kancho noticed and smirked.

"Not hungry, Ran?"

"Not even remotely."

Ran turned to head back up to the deck, when he felt the ship suddenly rise. He heard Malkyr swear loudly. Ran grabbed at one of the ropes hanging overhead to keep his balance, but then the entire ship seemed to turn over. Vargul cried out as he lost his balance and fell from the seat to the floor. Kancho stayed where he was, and Neviah clutched at Jysal like a mother hen.

"Ran!" Malkyr's shouts brought Ran to the deck in time to see that another giant wave had taken the boat up and lifted it high on a swell. Sea spray lashed at Ran's face as a deluge opened up from overhead.

Malkyr was pointing to one of the deckhands already in the wake of the boat. "Can you get a rope out to him?"

Ran judged the distance, but he saw it was already too great. There was no way he could reach the man. And then another wave covered him up and sucked him beneath the swells. He turned back to Malkyr to tell him, but in that next second, the *Aqaria* turned on top of the wave, and the stern now shot toward the coast. Malkyr was shouting orders to the remaining deckhands, but chaos overwhelmed them.

And then Ran saw the ominous black shapes beneath the water rising up like so many teeth. "Reef!"

Malkyr looked, and his eyes widened. "Hang on! Everyone hold on to something!"

The wave smashed them right down into the reef. Ran heard the awful sound of splintering wood as the reef tore into the keel of the boat, shredding the planks that ran horizontally. Water gushed up from belowdecks. The *Aqaria* spun once more and then came to rest atop a pointed shard of reef.

Almost instantly, Kancho shoved his way onto the deck from below. He was drenched through with seawater. Behind him came Jysal and Neviah. Vargul came last, trying to heave his girth up the ladder leading to the deck. He frowned when he saw Malkyr. "Damn you, Malkyr! You've gone and lost my cargo because of this. I'll see you ruined."

Malkyr waved him off. "I'll replace your blasted cargo, you damned fool! Now, if we don't get off of the ship, we're all going to drown."

Ran looked out into the swirling mist. "How far is it to shore?"

Malkyr shrugged. "Perhaps three hundred yards. No

more, I'm sure. The reefs lie at a pretty fixed distance from the coast."

Kancho waited no longer and leaped into the surf, narrowly avoiding impaling himself on a shard of reef. Neviah looked at Jysal and then nodded. Jysal jumped into the waves, followed by her protector. Vargul shook his head and eyed Malkyr. "I'll see you ruined for this, mark my words." Then he jumped as well.

Malkyr gave his remaining crew the order to jump, and they did so, leaving only Ran and himself. Malkyr grinned mischievously at Ran. "Some journey so far, eh?"

"I could do without all the excitement. I'm more tested in battle than I am in swimming around reefs."

Malkyr clapped him on the back. "At least you're not losing your boat over this. The *Aqaria* has been very good to me. Losing her hurts."

Ran frowned and then searched for a spot in the water to land. Already the other passengers and crew were swimming in the direction of shore. Ran picked a patch of water and then stepped off the boat. His masters back at the school in Gakur had taught him several techniques for entering the water without making a big splash. Ran employed one of those techniques now, keeping his feet together. At the last second, he grabbed a breath before he hit the water and sank. Once beneath the waves, he scissor-kicked back to the surface.

He grabbed a fresh breath as rain pelted him from above. *Some trip*, he thought. He saw Malkyr's head break the surface several yards away. Malkyr spotted him and pointed in the direction of the shore. Ran started swimming toward the coast, with Malkyr behind him. As he swam, Ran spotted a crew member about twenty yards ahead of him, off to the left and swimming hard.

He looks scared, thought Ran. Then he saw the reason why.

A huge fin broke the surface.

And Ran heard Malkyr swear behind him. "Reef sharks!"

Ran had no idea what the beasts might be like, but he knew they had rows of teeth they'd like nothing better than to bite into a fresh bit of swimmer. He redoubled his efforts and saw a glimpse of land through the mist.

A terrible scream from the crew member punctured the air. Ran turned, saw a spray of bright red blood explode from the waves before turning frothy pink as it fell and mixed with the sea water. A giant mouth reached up out of the waves and took the crew member down. The surf churned, and Ran saw a hand stab through the surface before being jerked back under. Then it was gone.

As Malkyr swam past him he shouted. "You'd better swim like the gods of death are on your heels."

Ran needed no further encouragement and piled on the effort. His legs were strong from years of training, and he used that strength to his advantage now, pushing past Malkyr. He felt something swim past him, brushing against his tunic as it did, but then it flashed off toward Malkyr.

Ran turned to call out but then felt his feet touch the bottom. At last! He saw a fin emerge behind Malkyr and waved him on. "One behind you! Swim!"

Malkyr didn't waste time turning his head, he merely swam even faster toward Ran. Ran kept moving toward the shore, feeling the depth of water recede as he did so. And then Kancho was there, his sword out. Ran unsheathed his and together they stood in the thigh-high surf as Malkyr stroked toward them.

Just as it appeared he was safe, Malkyr cried out in pain. Ran searched the water, and then Kancho pushed past him. "We need to help him."

Ran waded out, not sure how they could hope to help Malkyr. But Kancho didn't stop, and then Ran watched as he slashed through the waves at the shark. Again and again, Kancho cut down through the water. Ran saw a movement of gray under the surface and stabbed at it with his blade. He felt a moment of resistance before his blade slid deep into the belly of one of the ravenous beasts. The water around them was stained a deep, dark red. Malkyr had stopped screaming, because he was unconscious.

Kancho nodded at Ran. "Get him out of the water."

Ran grabbed at Malkyr beneath his armpits and hauled him back toward the shore. As they came into shallower water, he could see that Malkyr had suffered a large bite to his left calf. There was a lot of blood loss from the shredded skin and muscle, but otherwise he was unharmed. Still, if they didn't stop the bleeding, he would die quickly.

Neviah rushed into the surf as Ran approached. "Let me help."

Ran nodded and allowed her to take an arm. Together, they dragged Malkyr's body to the black sandy beach. Ran collapsed, huffing as he sought more air for his exhausted body. Neviah peered into Malkyr's eyes. Then she spoke to Jysal in a strange tongue that Ran had never heard. Jysal reacted immediately, tearing a section of her dress and handing the strip of cloth to Neviah. Neviah tied it around the upper part of Malkyr's leg.

Kancho struggled out of the surf, his sword dripping blood. He glanced at Malkyr and then at Neviah. "Will he live?"

Neviah shrugged. "I don't know. He has lost much blood. But if the gods are kind, they will help stop the bleeding."

"And if the gods aren't kind?"

Neviah shrugged. "Then we are lost in this land with no guide."

Ran watched as she turned back to tend to Malkyr. Around them, the black sand extended only so far before a mass of mangroves clogged their path. There seemed no easy way out of the tiny beach they lay on. The *Aqaria* lay offshore. Between them, packs of hungry sharks patrolled. And the only other way was to venture off into the swamps in front of them.

As he thought about their options, Ran saw a creeping mist coming down. The sky grew darker as night started to fall.

Whatever their prospects for survival, one thing seemed certain: tonight was going to be very uncomfortable.

CHAPTER FIVE

Ran woke just after dawn. He had no memory of the previous night. He had no recollection of posting a guard to watch over them while the others slept. He had nothing at all. All he could remember after they pulled Malkyr from the bloody surf was watching the darkness fall and the mist surround them. He'd naturally been exhausted, of course, but he still should have established a rotating system of watch.

He turned to his right and felt the stiffness in his joints. Kancho lay a few meters away from him, one hand on his sword. But he let out a snore and then started to turn over. Ran looked beyond and saw that Neviah and Jysal were bracketing the injured Malkyr.

Vargul was gone.

Ran sat up, his left hand grabbing for his sword. He rolled over and nudged Kancho. The old man's eyes blinked a few times and then opened. "It's morning?"

Ran nodded. "Did you stay awake last night?"

Kancho rubbed his eyes, seemed unsure of himself for

a moment and then shook his head. "No. I don't think I did. I remember seeing that mist come through the mangrove trees. I remember thinking it looked so fluffy. So comforting. The next thing I remember is you waking me up."

"That's about what I remember as well," said Ran. "We all fell asleep without anyone to watch over us."

Kancho eyed him. "You say that like—"

"Vargul's gone," finished Ran. "I don't see him anywhere."

Kancho stretched his arms overhead. "He could have gone to look for provisions. He does seem to require an ample supply of food, after all."

"I hope you're right," said Ran. "But I have a feeling it's nothing so simple as that."

Neviah had woken Jysal. They were tending to Malkyr as Ran walked over to them. He noticed that Malkyr was awake. He looked a bit pale, but otherwise he seemed in good spirits.

"How is he?"

Neviah looked up from where she had taken off the strip of cloth that Jysal had supplied yesterday. "The bleeding has stopped, but I'm worried about the discoloration of the skin around the wound. It may be infected. I'm not sure about that yet, though."

"How will you know for sure?"

Neviah nodded at Malkyr. "He will develop a fever."

"There is a way," said Jysal. "If we can locate a cherul root, that should take the sickness away from the wound and leave him able to heal." She glanced around. "But I do not know if such a thing grows in these parts."

Ran squatted next to Malkyr. "Feeling any better?"

Malkyr grinned. "You saved my life. You and that old drunk."

Ran grinned. "Just doing the same for you that we would have wanted someone to do for us."

"I owe you my life," said Malkyr. "I won't forget that debt."

"Good," said Kancho's voice behind them. "You can start repaying us by not swimming with the sharks any longer."

Malkyr looked up and smiled at Kancho. "Thank you for saving me."

Kancho grunted and looked across the water at the *Aqaria*. "A shame your crew didn't make it."

Malkyr replied. "They were good men."

Kancho nodded. "I don't think the sun is going to come out today. But it's getting humid. I already feel wet enough."

Neviah glanced at Ran. "Where is the portly one?"

"Vargul?" Ran shrugged. "We were just wondering that ourselves." He stood and walked to the edge of the trees that bordered the black sand beach. A few yards in, he spotted a broken branch. Judging by the color of the broken part, it had happened only a few hours previously.

He looked back at Kancho. "I think Vargul went this way."

Kancho approached, his hand always on the hilt of his sword. "Show me."

Ran pointed. "Through there. The broken branch."

Kancho stayed quiet for a moment and then grunted. "It's muddy. Shouldn't be too difficult to follow him. Shall we?"

"What about them?" Ran pointed back at Neviah, Jysal, and Malkyr. "Can we leave them behind?"

"It's either that or we drag along an injured man who can't walk," said Kancho. "You and I can make better time. If we're lucky, we'll also be able to get some sort of game to eat. We're going to need food if we have any hope of figuring our way out of this mess."

Ran glanced back at Neviah. "We're going to follow Vargul's tracks. It might be a good idea to make a fire and look for freshwater. But stay within earshot of the camp."

Neviah frowned. "I would prefer to go with you. We are in a foreign land. There may be enemies all around us."

Kancho sighed. "You've got your backs to the sea, and you're hemmed in by thick forest on either side. You're as safe as you'd be with us. And you've got to look after Malkyr. We can't bring him along or he'll die."

Neviah nodded. "Very well. But if you find the cherul root, please bring some back with you."

"What does it look like and where does it grow?" asked Ran. He'd studied herbology at the shadow-warrior school, but he couldn't reveal such knowledge in front of people he didn't know.

Neviah told him the plant's appearance and where to look, and then Ran nodded to Kancho. "Let's get going. The sooner we find him and bring him back, the better. None of us ought to be walking this swamp alone."

"Agreed," said Kancho. "And I wonder just what he thought he was doing by going off on his own in the first place. He doesn't strike me as the type to take risks unless he's certain of some greater reward."

Ran pushed into the forest and instantly felt his feet sink into several inches of mud. The ground sucked at his boots, squishing and creeping in to touch any bit of exposed skin with its clamminess. Ran heard the whine of bugs around his head. He waved one of them off, but several more joined in the assault and he soon gave up.

Vargul's tracks were more difficult to follow than Kancho had led him to believe. Because the ground was so muddy, as soon as Ran removed his foot, the ground would swallow the prints up. He frowned and turned to Kancho. "Tracking isn't going to be easy." He grimaced. "And it stinks horribly here."

"You'll get used to the smell." Kancho frowned. "Look for top sign. Branches and the like. He'll have to push them out of his way to make any sort of progress. And the plants won't be able to make that type of abuse disappear."

Ran was an expert tracker, but maintaining his cover meant not allowing Kancho to see his skill at following people. As it was, Ran had already noted the bent branches and mud scuffs on logs and roots ahead of him. Still, as he moved through the swamp land, he made his progress appear unsure. That meant it took longer to move through the area and search for Vargul, but Ran needed to make sure Kancho did not suspect him of being a shadow warrior.

Ran also felt a lot less armed than when he'd been back aboard the *Aqaria*. Jumping into the water, he'd been forced to ditch his throwing blades, the flat plate metal with sharpened edges that he'd been concealing in his inner tunic pocket. The metal weighed him down, and it had to go. He'd also been forced to part with his length of chain that he'd been fond of using to tie up opponents he didn't need to kill outright.

At least I managed to hold on to my sword, he thought as he eased over another log and put his feet back into the swampy ground. But it was only one weapon. Not the usual assortment another operative from his school might carry. Of course, Ran could always rely on his unarmed combat skills if need be. But choosing to use them would run the risk of compromising his disguise.

Vargul's trail led them out of the swampy bog that surrounded the beach and onto higher ground. Ran marveled at the lack of life in the forest. Even the tree trunks seemed devoid of new leaves, their withered, twisted branches seemingly incapable of supporting life. Around them, Ran heard no birds. And there was no sign of any animals in the area. Just bugs and trees.

He pulled up and waited for Kancho to approach.

"Is there a problem?"

Ran frowned. "This place feels strange."

"How so?"

"You haven't noticed the lack of animals?"

Kancho shrugged. "They could be holing up for the day. Maybe they come out only at night."

"It's not just that. There's no real sound here. No birds. No breezes. It's just . . . still."

Kancho looked around them and picked out a break in the trees. "There's a path there. Maybe it will lead to Vargul."

"Or perhaps not," said Ran. "I don't like this place."

"Nor I," said Kancho. "But we owe it to Vargul to at least look for him. There's no telling where that oaf could have blundered off to. And if he's in danger, it will be up to us to help him."

"He could already be dead," said Ran. He knew that Kancho's upbringing as Murai would obligate him to search out Vargul and assist him, even at the expense of his own life. Ran wasn't so ready to throw his away that cheaply.

Kancho laid a hand on his shoulder. "I'll take the lead for a while. Just watch my back."

Ran moved back a few paces and watched as Kancho threaded his way down the trail. It wasn't much of a trail in reality, more of a game run. That fact cheered Ran a little. If there was a game run, that meant animals. Perhaps Kancho had been right. Maybe the animals only came out to hunt at night. If that was the case, then they would need to set up a system of hunting to get some food. Already, Ran's stomach was grumbling noisily.

Kancho looked back at one point. "You're as bad as the man we're looking for."

Ran smirked. "I don't think I'm quite *that* bad. But I am hungry. Aren't you?"

Kancho shrugged. "You learn to make do without."

Typical Murai sentimentality, thought Ran. They would forsake every ounce of their own comfort in order to live up to the ideals set forth in their warrior code. It was a noble gesture, he supposed, just not a very practical one. Why suffer through hunger and deprivation if you didn't have to? Still, Kancho seemed to have little problem quelling his hunger pangs. There was some value in that, Ran knew. He thought back to his own wilderness survival training, spending days on end searching for berries and small game. He wasn't looking forward to the constant gnawing hunger pangs in his gut.

They traveled several miles, and then Kancho abruptly stopped. Ran approached him. "Something wrong?"

"The trail has vanished."

Ran looked around them and saw that Kancho was right. The bent sticks and various other top sign they'd been following seemed to have been erased. The two men stood in the midst of leering trees, scarred trunks, and very little else. The effect was almost completely disorienting. Ran glanced back the way they'd come and nodded. "Maybe we should head back to the beach."

Kancho frowned. "We can't just leave Vargul."

"We're not leaving him behind," said Ran. "We're going to come up with a better plan than the one we have right now. There's no point in searching blind. And we've got a wounded man back at camp who is also our responsibility. Besides, Malkyr knows this territory better than us. Once he's recovered a bit, we can try again."

"Neviah said something about a root. I haven't seen a damned thing that even resembles it."

Ran shrugged. "Nor have I. But that doesn't mean she and Jysal can't forage a little closer to camp." His stomach grumbled once as if to underscore the point.

"And what about food?" asked Kancho. "We've seen nothing that we can hunt."

"True," said Ran. "But maybe we can trap some small fish in the tidal pools close to the shore."

Kancho nodded. "All right, but I'm not setting foot back in that water to try my hand at fishing. Not with those sharks out there."

CHAPTER SIX

It took them much longer to return to the beach, even though they followed their own obvious trail. On the way back, Ran and Kancho were forced to battle a never-ending assault from the mosquitoes that called the swamp home. Swatting the annoying pests as they whined in their ears and tried to fly into their mouths sapped their energy, and by the time they reached the beach, both men were exhausted. Kancho went to fall asleep under the shade of a tree. Ran noticed that Malkyr was sitting upright.

"You look a whole lot better."

Malkyr smiled. "I feel better. Neviah and Jysal took care of me. Seems they found a root, and its medicinal properties have staved off any rot."

Jysal sat nearby. Ran watched her as she ground up some strange roots between a flat stone and a round one. "Nice work. I take it you found what you were looking for?"

She smiled at him. "It's not hard if you know where to look. Neviah is making a soup down the beach."

Ran turned and noticed the thin plume of smoke for the first time. Neviah had gotten a fire started and found a few shells on the beach that she was using to boil water. Ran frowned. Where had she found water? He wandered over to ask. "Our search didn't go so well."

"I noticed."

Ran pointed at the shells. "You found water?"

She shrugged. "I am quite adept at looking out for myself. Survival has been something I've been taught since a very young age. Even in the most inhospitable places, you can usually find what you're looking for."

Ran's mouth watered as he caught a sniff of the herbs she'd added to the water. "It smells delicious."

Neviah nodded. "Truthfully, there's not much. But it should give us some energy while we wait for Malkyr to figure out a way to get us home."

"You think he will?"

Neviah shrugged. "He says he can probably work out a way to get us over to that seedy harbor."

"That would be welcome news."

Neviah looked up at him. "And what are you on this trip for?"

"Work," said Ran. "I thought perhaps some warlord would be interested in hiring my blade."

Neviah smiled. "There's no work in Nehon?"

Ran frowned. "I get bored easily." But he wondered about the real reason he'd come on this journey. Princess Cassandra was truly a beauty, and the idea of bedding her at some point down the road wasn't unappealing to him. Of course, he had to find her first. During their final meeting, she'd told him to journey west and find the kingdom of her father. Perhaps Ran would find something interesting to do there. He was on his own, after all. And despite the fact that his masters back at the hidden mountain temple had tentacles everywhere, they might not mind if he vanished altogether.

He frowned. No. They would come after him if he abandoned the network. Loyalty was what they demanded. It was how they ensured their own survival. And it was why they'd invested so much time in training him for his eventual journeys around the world.

"You look troubled."

Ran erased the frown on his face and shook his head. "Just tired. First the swamp and then the woods beyond. They're filled with bugs. I'm tired and hungry."

Neviah motioned for him to sit down. "Come. You can try the first batch of soup and tell me what you think."

"I'm too hungry to complain." He waited while she used some leaves to handle one of the deep sea shells filled with boiling soup and pass it over to him. Ran peered into its steaming depths and was immediately struck by the variety of herbs and plants that it contained. He spotted something opaque floating in the broth and pointed. "What's this?"

"Crab meat. We found some down the beach in a tidal pool."

Ran's mouth watered even more, and he took a tentative sip. He had to blow and force himself not to slurp the entire mixture up. "It's delicious."

Farther down the beach, he heard Malkyr's shout. "Hey, you going to leave any of that for the wounded guy or what?"

Neviah smiled at Ran. "There's plenty. You take that and I'll see to my patient."

He watched as she rose easily on her well-muscled legs and padded down the beach bearing another shell full of soup. Ran had encountered a lot of warriors before, but nothing like Neviah. She seemed almost unreal with how easily she affected her role of protector and yet still maintained an ability to whip up a delicious soup and tend to Malkyr's wounds. Whoever trained her, thought Ran, they did one amazing job.

He wondered about Jysal as he continued to sip the soup. She was far younger than Neviah. Perhaps she wasn't even out of her teens yet. And there was an air of innocence about her that seemed so delicate. Yet beneath the innocence, Ran could sense something else. It reminded him of how a beautiful day in the mountains could be shattered by a sudden storm. You might have a crystal blue sky one moment, and in the next the clouds would form and a deluge would follow. He watched her and wondered what her storm clouds might be.

"You keep staring at her, and people might wonder if you're going to marry her."

Ran had heard Kancho approach by the grinding of sand beneath his feet. "I thought you were catching up on some sleep."

"I was, but there's food to be eaten."

Ran eyed him. "Didn't you tell me earlier not to pay attention to my stomach?"

"Only because you were letting the entire forest know we were there."

"I doubt that."

Kancho helped himself to a shell full of soup and squatted next to Ran. "The real question is what we're going to do about Malkyr. He's wounded. Which means his ability to travel is seriously affected. If he can't make his own way out of here, then we're all in trouble."

Ran chewed on the crab meat. Already, he could feel the effects of the soup hitting him. He felt more energized and at the same time, his body wanted to rest. Overhead, the sky had brightened, but not enough to let the sun shine through the darker clouds. "I suppose we can see how he is tomorrow morning."

Kancho slurped some of the soup. "Vargul is most likely dead."

Ran looked at him. He thought about asking why Kancho thought so, but decided against it. They were both warriors. And Kancho seemed pretty sure of it. "We can't say we didn't try to reach him."

Kancho shrugged. "Of course we can. We went as far as was prudent. But my reason for coming on this trip was not to have to save some fattened merchant from the northlands."

"Why are you here?"

Kancho slurped more soup and shook his head. "Not yet, Ran. I don't know you well enough. And something tells me that you're not being entirely honest about who you are. So I'll keep my secrets as well."

Ran smiled. "Fair enough."

The afternoon passed uneventfully. Malkyr ate more than his fair share of the soup, but Neviah didn't complain. Jysal ventured into the periphery of the swamp a few times and returned with more roots and herbs whenever she did.

These were added to another soup that Neviah created for supper. Bits of driftwood kept the fire fed, but Ran wondered how long they would be able to keep that up. The swamp would yield far less dry firewood than the beach.

As the sun started to set, the band of travelers gathered around the fire, trying to stay warm. Despite the flames, the fire seemed incapable of warding off the night chill. Jysal drew close to Neviah to share warmth. Malkyr complained about the cold.

Ran waited until the daylight had vanished before asking Malkyr. "How are you going to get us out of here?"

Malkyr smirked. "Not much I can do about the situation right now, what with this bum leg of mine and all."

Kancho shook his head. "We cannot stay here. We are exposed to the elements. We cannot venture into the water to reach the *Aqaria*. That means our only option is to take to the swamp tomorrow and make for the woods beyond it." He eyed Malkyr. "Tell us what you know of this area. Who lives in these parts?"

Malkyr's smile vanished. "This is the land of Kan-Gul."

Ran looked up. "The man you spoke of on the boat when we were at sea?"

Malkyr nodded. "The same. But he is no man. Some say he is beholden to some strange dark lord, the likes of which very few have even heard of."

"What of this dark lord?" asked Kancho. "If he is a god, why trouble himself in the affairs of mortals?"

"Kan-Gul seeks to appease him through terrible

sacrifices." Malkyr shrugged. "Of course, this is all hearsay. Legends that drunken sailors spout in the taverns that line the docks. Still, no one I've known of has ever ventured here and returned home before."

"If he offers sacrifices to his god," said Neviah, "then what does he get in return?"

Malkyr fixed her with a hard stare. "You should be careful of asking questions that might earn you an answer you wished you'd never heard."

Neviah shook her head. "I am the sworn protector of Jysal. It is my duty to know of and understand any and all threats that may arise to confront us. The whims of some strange lord in a foreign land do not frighten me."

"They should," said Malkyr. "It is said that Kan-Gul has an army of the undead at his command. Terrible soldiers who have risen from death to serve once more under their lord. They are unfeeling creatures devoted only to killing and eating that which they kill."

Kancho gripped his sword a little tighter. "I have never seen a man with his head taken from his shoulder rise and walk again."

Malkyr's smile danced in the firelight. "Perhaps you have not seen all there is to see in this world then."

"Perhaps, but it will be a strange day indeed when my blade severs a head and yet that foe remains alive."

"Words are just that," said Malkyr. "And when given around a warm fire, they are little more than sound. We will see if you are as good as you claim if we encounter Kan-Gul's hordes."

Kancho nodded slowly. "And I look forward to that day."

"Well, I don't," said Jysal suddenly. "I have no interest in claiming the thought of such creatures does not terrify me."

Malkyr bowed his head. "Forgive me, my lady. I never meant to scare you with such tales."

Neviah frowned. "I'll bet."

"They are just stories," said Malkyr. "Legends, if you will. As I said, they are the fodder that drunken minds conjure up in the sweaty mead halls. Pay them no mind."

Jysal eyed him a moment longer and then moved a bit closer to Neviah.

Kancho cocked an eyebrow. "It would appear that our story time is now concluded."

Ran nodded. "It's better that we sleep anyway." He looked at Malkyr. "Are you tired?"

Malkyr shook his head. "Not even faintly. I've been resting all day, and, frankly, I'm tired of sitting on my backside."

"You'll do well to stay on that backside," said Neviah. "If you start the bleeding again, you may die."

Malkyr sighed. "You changed the dressing on it earlier and there was no blood."

"Yes, but you could do something to start it again. Stay where you are."

Ran sighed. "You can still take a watch. The rest of us will sleep while you take the first shift. Wake me in two hours and I'll relieve you. We're not going to lay about like we did last night."

"Agreed," said Kancho. "We're lucky we're all still alive and weren't killed during the night."

Malkyr stretched his arms overhead. "Very well. You lot rest. I'll take my turn same as any other."

Ran and the others arranged themselves around the fire. As he peered into the trees, Ran saw the mist descending once more.

CHAPTER SEVEN

It was not Malkyr but the warmth of the morning sun that woke Ran finally. He sat up immediately. Malkyr hadn't roused him for his shift last night. Ran glanced around. Aside from the still slumbering form of Jysal, the beach was deserted. Even the embers of the fire had died down to nothing but cold bits of charred wood. Ran's hand went immediately to his sword, which he was relieved to see was still by his side. He got to his feet and scanned the sand for any signs that would tell him where the others had gone. He frowned at the sight of the smooth beach, undisturbed except for where the waves of the sea gently licked at its shoreline.

Ran moved to Jysal and paused to gaze at the curves of her body. She was exquisitely beautiful, but Ran shrugged the thought from his mind and squatted next to her. "Jysal. Wake up."

Her eyelids fluttered open, and it reminded Ran of a butterfly flicking its wings in the lazy summer. She smiled. "I don't suppose it's breakfast?"

Ran frowned. "I wish it was. But I've got bad news. We're the only ones here."

Jysal jerked upright. One glance told her everything she needed to know. "Where did they run off to?"

Ran shook his head. "I have no idea, truly. I only woke up a few moments ago myself. The last thing I can remember is telling Malkyr to wake me up in two hours so I could take my shift on guard duty."

"That's all you remember?"

Ran frowned. "I remember seeing the fog last night. Right before we fell asleep."

Jysal nodded. "I remember that fog, too. It was with us the first night as well."

"The night we lost Vargul," said Ran.

"Do you think they're connected?"

"They have to be," said Ran. "There's nothing else that could really explain it. It's not as though our fellow castaways are going to abandon us. Neviah would lay down her life for you. That's fairly obvious."

"She is my protector," said Jysal. "Her job is to make sure I get to the temple. She takes her role very seriously."

"She seems like a formidable warrior," said Ran. No sense in annoying Jysal with useless platitudes. And Ran could see that Neviah would be a handful if it ever came to combat with her. Better, Ran decided, to treat Neviah with the respect she deserved rather than try some of the silly machismo he'd seen during the course of his travels. He sometimes found himself wondering if it wasn't just insecurity that made men think less of women. As if admitting they were equal would somehow disrupt the essence of who they were as men. To Ran, such sentiment made no sense whatsoever. If your opponent was a good warrior, then the least you could do was respect them for their prowess. Better to give them the respect they'd earned than underestimate them and find yourself on the end of their blade.

But Ran knew that logic was often in short supply when it came to the mind of a fighting man. It was a weakness his elders at the school had often taught him to exploit for his own purposes, whether in combat or in the art of gathering information.

"Where could they have gone?" asked Jysal. She patted the sand next to her. "I mean, Neviah was resting not more than a few feet from where I lay. I would have heard any sort of noise, wouldn't I?"

Ran knelt and examined the sand again, but, apart from a shallow impression where Neviah might have lain, there was no sign of a struggle. "I think we have to operate on the assumption that they were taken in a way that would not wake us. Or them."

Jysal shook her head. "I don't understand."

"I think they were all still asleep when it happened."

"The mist."

Ran nodded. "Fog, mist. Whatever it is, I think we can also safely assume it's not natural. And given the tales Malkyr spun last night, the likely culprit would seem to be that man Kan-Gul."

Jysal shuddered despite the warmth of the encroaching day. "I don't know what it is, but the thought of him unnerves me."

"We don't know what he's like aside from Malkyr's description," said Ran. "But he's got our friends, hasn't he?

And I don't much like the idea of him being able to pluck people while they sleep and drag them away as captives. Seems like an unfair fight to me."

Jysal got to her feet and brushed a few clinging particles of sand from her tunic. Ran tried to keep his eyes from watching her. He didn't succeed.

"Do you think that this Kan-Gul character sent his minions to the beach and had them carry off Neviah and the others?"

Ran pointed at the sand. "I doubt it. There are no tracks anywhere."

"Might the wind have blown them away?"

"Some perhaps, but not all. And it would have needed to be strong wind to do that." Ran glanced skyward. "I think the answer is probably that Kan-Gul sent something flying this way. They could swoop in and pluck them right off the sand and be gone without making much noise. If the mist somehow subdued us all like a drug, the others wouldn't be in much shape to battle them off."

"Their weapons are gone as well," said Jysal. "Do you think that was intentional?"

"I slept with my hand on my sword," said Ran. "It's likely that Kancho did as well. And Neviah would be armed." He sighed. "But I doubt it matters. Once they wake up from their slumber—assuming this happened during the dark of night—then I'm sure they won't have their weapons on them by now. Kan-Gul will have made sure of that."

"We've got to get them back," said Jysal.

Ran smiled. "A minute ago you were telling me that you didn't want to meet him."

"Yes, well, whether or not I like the idea, it's got to be done. I can't leave Neviah to some awful fate. I'm not even certain of the way to the temple I'm headed to, especially now that we're so far off course."

Ran nodded. "We'll get them back." He felt certain that the universe in its infinite wisdom would consider the removal of Kan-Gul necessary so as to better promote harmony. At least, he hoped it would.

Jysal was looking at him oddly. "You're a difficult man to figure out."

Ran felt the weight of her stare and looked away. "What do you mean?"

"I mean you talk like a warrior, yet you don't appear to be as forthright as Kancho. He's a professional warrior even if he thinks he's hiding it. Whatever agenda he's got, it seems to be something he won't likely share with anyone anytime soon."

"Especially if we don't find him in time," said Ran.

"Don't dodge the question, Ran."

He smiled. Something about her tone reminded him of Cassandra. He sighed, seeing the image of the princess in his mind. The two of them could no doubt find many adventures to occupy their time. And who knew? Perhaps something else might develop between them in the meantime.

Ran would never escape the reach of his clan, but if he chose to settle elsewhere, he could continue to serve them by sending information from time to time. And if they sent any operatives into the area, he could provide them shelter and security.

"Ran."

He blinked. "I'm afraid I'm not sure what you mean."

Jysal frowned. "I see Kancho isn't the only one keeping secrets on this trip."

"Secrets keep you alive," said Ran. "If you're too exposed, then your enemy will know the means by which your death can be brought about."

"Spoken like a keen strategist," said Jysal. "Which, of course, doesn't even come close to answering my question."

"Exactly," said Ran. "And I have a better idea, anyway. Why don't we concentrate on finding our friends, and then later on you can worry about who I am?"

Jysal seemed about to protest that idea, but then stopped when she looked in Ran's eyes. "You and Kancho explored yesterday. Are we heading back that way?"

Ran frowned. "It's a muddy swamp, and then the ground climbs up into a dense forest. Can you handle wading through muck for a while?"

"Of course, I can."

"Mosquitoes, too," said Ran. "They're thick under that canopy. I'm afraid there's not much I can suggest unless you want to coat your skin with mud."

"Do you think that would make me look better?" Jysal smiled at him.

"It would be a shame to cover up your beauty," said Ran. "But if you would be more comfortable that way, I would certainly understand."

Jysal laughed. "Thank you for the compliment, I think."

Ran bowed his head. "We can take the path Kancho and I started yesterday. Stay close while we're in there. We didn't go too far before the trail went blank and we were forced to turn around and come back."

"We're not turning around this time, though, are we?"

Ran glanced at the waves battering the wreck of the *Aqaria*. Their choices were limited. Stay here and wait for the mist tonight, swim out to the *Aqaria* and risk death, or venture into the swamp and forests trying to find their way to Kan-Gul's lair. Ran thought about the words from one of his teachers. Whenever the options facing you are equally bad, any choice will be the best, provided you are not immobilized by indecision.

So be it, he thought. "We'll head through the swamp and the forest. Kan-Gul must make his home somewhere within a short distance of the coast. Something tells me he will need to have supplies brought in from time to time. And any traders will need to pass through the harbor that Malkyr had been aiming for after that storm blew us off course. We'll go as far as we can before making camp for the night."

From inside her tunic, Jysal produced a slim dagger. She hefted it in one hand and then slid it through the belt of her tunic. "I'm armed, just to let you know."

Ran nodded. "Where did you hide that?"

Jysal smiled. "That's one of my secrets."

"Fair enough. Let's go." Ran led her into the trees at the edge of the beach. They walked a few hundred yards, and then the land sloped down into the mud and grime of the swamp. Behind him, Ran heard Jysal take a breath and mutter something. "Are you all right?"

"This smell," she said, wrinkling her nose. "What in the world makes such a stink?"

"Decomposition," said Ran. "With all of this water, the

roots and plants tend to decompose and give off swamp stink. You'll get used to it if you try not to let it bother you."

"I feel like I can't take a breath without vomiting," said Jysal.

"I know the feeling," said Ran. "Now come on. The sooner we're through this part, the better."

They walked another twenty minutes through the knee-and-thigh-deep stagnant water. Twice Ran heard the hissing of a snake in the nearby area, but they were not accosted as they plowed on. Each step Ran took seemed to suck at his legs, and given the lack of food they'd had, he was worried about becoming too exhausted to be much good in case they ran into danger.

For her part, Jysal seemed to not complain too often. Ran found himself surprised that she did not protest much as they made their way through the swamps. He heard her slapping her skin from time to time as mosquitoes hounded them both with ravenous appetites. But otherwise, she was as quiet as she could be, a fact Ran appreciated as he tried to sense whether there was danger around them.

The entire locale seemed even more ominous than it had yesterday when Ran had trekked through here with Kancho. Again, the lack of life made him wonder what could have snuffed out the essence of the place so easily. Certainly, he would have expected more than just snakes.

Gradually his feet found firmer footing as the land started to ascend out of the swamp. Ran took a final step out of the water and then collapsed on the grassy bank nearby, trying to draw more air into his lungs. He was soaked with sweat as the sun overhead heated the entire area into a humid sweatbox.

Jysal fell to the ground nearby and wiped a hand across her brow. "I thought that would never end."

Ran smacked a mosquito and nodded. "The only thing that seemed to be alive in there were these damned bugs. Otherwise, the place was almost completely void of life."

"Almost?"

Ran shrugged. "I heard some hissing. May have been snakes."

"Lovely," said Jysal. "I hate snakes."

"Well, we didn't run into any, so we can't complain. And now we're out of the swamp. This part, at least, is somewhat easier. We'll have firm footing from here on out."

Jysal sighed. "I must look a frightful mess."

Ran grinned as he stood. "You still look beautiful, have no worries." He ran a hand along the hilt of his sword and made sure it was still snug against his side. "We can't stay here too long. I'd like us to be well away from the swamp before we need to make camp for the night."

"Why? I'm exhausted. Between the heat, the water, and those insects . . ." her voice trailed off.

"I'd rather not be around here to see what might come awake when night falls," said Ran.

Jysal pulled herself to her feet and stared at him. "And you think being in the forest will be any better?"

"Probably not," said Ran. "But with firm ground underneath my feet, I can at least be sure that I'll be balanced if I need to fight."

They moved off, and Ran found the lack of life unsettling. More than that, it was as if the entire forest had been muted by some unseen force. Ran heard no animals.

He heard no bird calls. Every so often, a twig would break in the distance and he would nearly yank his sword from its scabbard.

He stopped and took several deep breaths to calm himself. Gradually, his heart slowed.

Then Jysal shrieked.

Adrenaline flooding his veins, Ran pivoted and drew his sword. Three paces behind him, Jysal looked absolutely terrified.

"What is it?"

She pointed at her thigh. There on her skin, Ran spotted a thick, bloated leech. He took a breath.

"I thought we were under attack there for a moment."

"I am," said Jysal. "Do something."

Ran sighed and used the tip of his blade to nick the leech neatly in two. Dead, it fell from Jysal's thigh, and bright red blood stained her skin. She used a swath of her tunic to wrap the wound.

"Thank you."

CHAPTER EIGHT

After they'd spent five minutes scraping off mud and drying out, Ran insisted they keep moving. The trees that loomed in on the game trail they walked along helped stave off most of the blazing sun overhead, but even without the swamp water nearby, the humidity still plagued them, making their clothes stick to their skin. Ran's breath felt heavy and congealed every time he breathed. He longed for the crisp, cool air of the mountains of his homeland. Behind him, he could hear Jysal having similar problems. He glanced back a few times, and she managed a weak smile each time he did so, but Ran knew she was struggling to keep up.

For his part, Ran wasn't too bothered by the strain, although he marveled at how much more taxing the walk was on him when the sun shone rather than under the blanket of gray clouds yesterday. He would have gladly swapped the weather for that of the previous day, but he knew that was impossible. He saw a thick pine tree and slowed to a stop.

Jysal seemed grateful for the break. "I would take all of my clothes off and walk naked if I thought it would help."

Ran smiled. "As uplifting as that would no doubt be, the mosquitoes would hound you mercilessly."

Jysal sighed. "I thought we'd leave most of them behind at the swamp, but I guess I was mistaken about that."

"They can be just as bad under the trees as in the swamp," said Ran. "There's really no escaping the buggers except to keep going and hopefully see the landscape change."

"They were not a nuisance at the beach, though."

"The salt air keeps them away," said Ran. "Trust me, I wish we were walking along the shore right now."

Jysal said nothing for a moment but glanced around. "How much farther did you get yesterday with Kancho?"

Ran pointed a few hundred yards ahead. "That's where Vargul's trail went cold. It was as if he was simply lifted off his feet and carried away. Which, bearing in mind what we discussed earlier, now seems all the more likely."

"What do you think would have the strength to carry away a fully grown man like that?"

Ran's hand went to his sword without his conscious volition. "I don't know. But something tells me we'll find out before too long."

Jysal smirked. "I don't know how much of a threat I'll be with my dagger."

"Better than nothing," said Ran. "Just what are you on your way to this temple for, anyway? And why do you need a bodyguard for the journey?"

Jysal shrugged. "I am promised to the temple. Once there, I'll start my education."

"In what?"

Jysal continued, ignoring Ran's question. "Neviah's job was to make sure I got there intact. The roads are dangerous for a single woman traveling alone."

"The roads are dangerous for anyone," said Ran. "But I can see why having Neviah along would make you feel safer."

"She's a blessing," said Jysal. "And I miss her dearly."

"But you won't tell me what you're going to learn at the temple," said Ran.

Jysal smiled at him. "Didn't you just tell me how dangerous it is to reveal too many secrets about yourself?"

"Maybe."

"Well, maybe you'll get some answers. Eventually." Jysal looked up at the sky through the trees. "I'd kill for a breeze right now."

Ran nodded. "It's still pretty hot even in the shade. But we should keep moving."

Jysal pushed off of the tree trunk and held her hand out toward the trail. "Lead on and I shall follow. I'm tired but I will keep going until you say it's time to stop."

"We won't be stopping until sunset if we can hold out. I want to put as much distance between us and the beach as possible."

"Why?"

"Well, for one thing, I want to find our friends. And for another, if we are indeed being hunted, then I want to make it difficult for those who would capture us to find us. If we're not at the beach, that makes their job that much tougher."

"Unless Kan-Gul has the ability to see where we are.

Then he could simply direct his minions to come here instead of the beach."

Ran nodded. "True, but I still hope that we can make it tougher on them than it has been." He turned and started down the game trail once again, picking his way over the twisted and gnarled roots that looped up out of the ground to turn an unwary ankle. But Ran's steps were sure-footed, garnered from his years of training. He could steal across a roll of wet rice paper without causing any breaks or crinkles in the surface. He could even glide across nightingale floors designed to creak when weight was applied to them.

Jysal hadn't had such training however, and it wasn't long before her foot caught in one of the roots and she went down hard. Ran was by her side instantly, helping her back to her feet. "Are you all right?"

Jysal put some weight on her foot and after a second nodded. "I think so. I didn't see that root."

"They're all over the place. Just try to mind them and we'll be fine."

Jysal leaned into him. "Thank you."

He looked down into her eyes and found himself almost falling into the darkness contained within. Jysal's smile was bright, and her breath warm on his neck. But then Ran saw the image of Cassandra's face in his mind and eased back away from Jysal. "We should keep moving."

If she was upset by Ran's move, only her eyes widened in surprise, as if Ran had done something so completely unexpected, she didn't know how to process it. "I think that's the first time I've seen a man turn down an invitation like that," she said quietly.

"I mean no offense," said Ran. "But we really need to keep moving."

Jysal tested her foot again and then nodded. "It feels all right. Let's go."

Ran turned back to the trail, grateful she couldn't see the blood rushing into his face. He took a few deep breaths to get himself back under control. It was tempting—far too tempting—to grab her up in his arms and lie with her right then and there under the trees in this strange place. But who knew what might be lurking nearby? If Kan-Gul was everything Malkyr had tried to make him out to be, it was conceivable he knew where they were, as Jysal had suggested. It was also possible he could send his minions to attack them while they were in the throes of passion.

No, he decided. It was far better to keep to the task at hand. If they got through this land and away from Kan-Gul, then perhaps he would take Jysal up on her invitation. She was far too beautiful to ignore, and Ran felt his pulse quicken at the thought of what they could do to each other.

He checked the ground and saw that the sign that Vargul had left behind as he'd walked this trail was deteriorating even more as the elements sought to erase it. And there, just a few yards ahead, Ran could see where the sign ended abruptly. He stopped for a moment. *He was taken here*, he thought. His hand was on his sword, when he heard Jysal breathe sharply.

"Ran!"

In an instant, he had his sword out, eyes already up and scanning the landscape. "Where?"

"Ahead of us. In the brush."

Ran heard Jysal pull her dagger out and continued to

search the brush ahead of them. The trees formed pockets of shadows that kept things hidden quite well. But as Ran narrowed his eyes and scanned left to right, he caught a glimpse of movement and then zeroed in on the location.

There.

With both of his hands on his sword, he moved farther ahead of Jysal. "Stay where you are," he said to her quietly.

The eyes watching him were yellow and stood out from the surrounding brush. Ran wondered how Jysal had spotted the creature, but then it moved and Ran no longer cared. He was simply grateful that she had.

The beast lumbered around the side of the tree trunk and then stretched lazily, as if pondering what to kill first. Ran watched its muscles shudder and ripple beneath the taut mottled fur. It looked like an overgrown dog—possibly a wolf—but there was something far more sinister about it. Its eyes roved over Ran, and then its tongue snaked out and licked its muzzle. It sniffed the air and then moved a few steps closer to Ran.

Ran never took his eyes off the beast. He felt certain that doing so would prompt it to attack. And clearly, the beast used its apparent nonchalance to lull prey into thinking it hadn't seen them when it certainly had. Was this the reason there was so little life in the forest? Had it killed everything? For that matter, had it killed Vargul?

No, Ran decided. If it had, there would have been signs of a struggle. Vargul would not have gone down without battling for his life. There'd be blood spatters on the trees and other indicators that they'd fought a savage duel here. But Vargul's tracks simply vanished.

This creature hadn't killed him.

Ran eyed the beast. It must have been close to eight feet long and perhaps five feet high at the shoulder. Ran wished he didn't have to kill the creature. But he would if it left him no choice.

"What does it want?" Jysal's voice was a quiet whisper in the woods.

Ran kept his eyes on the beast. "I don't know. It's not behaving like it wants to attack. But I'm not about to let it know I think that."

"Can you kill it?"

Ran almost smirked. "Can I? I hope so. Must I? I hope I don't have to."

The beast eyed Ran and then let out a single low-pitched growl. Ran's eyes narrowed even more. The beast compacted its haunches and then edged around them, always pointed right at Ran. He saw its eyes flick over to Jysal only once before coming immediately back to rest on Ran. *It knows I'm the threat*, he thought. The fact he had a nearly three-foot-long razor-sharp blade in his hands had probably clued it in.

Another growl bubbled up from the beast's throat. Ran felt his heartbeat increase but willed it to slow back down. He couldn't stave off the effects of his excitement completely, but he'd been taught to use his breathing to calm himself as much as possible prior to combat. That training helped him now. The danger of adrenaline was that it narrowed his awareness and tunneled his vision. By maintaining proper breathing, Ran could keep his wits about him and be ready for anything that tried to surprise him.

When the beast launched itself, there was no warning.

If Ran hadn't kept his breathing going, he would have been caught off guard and hesitated a fraction of a second. In that time, the beast would have clamped its jaws around his neck and finished him with one awful attack aimed at tearing out Ran's throat.

Instead, as Ran exhaled smoothly, he stepped to the side and brought the single-edged curved blade up in a tight arc that slashed through the beast's underside, slicing neatly through its belly and into its vital organs. Ran kept moving as he cut and the beast fell heavily to the ground, staining the earth dark with its blood and innards. It uttered one whimper and then lay still.

Ran flicked the blood from his blade using the quick motion that he'd practiced so often it was ingrained and then returned his sword to its scabbard.

Jysal rushed over. "Are you hurt?"

Ran shook his head. "No."

Jysal looked at the beast and then back at Ran. "I don't think I've ever seen anyone make a cut like that. You were so precise and so effortless at the same time. Where did you learn to handle a sword like that?"

"Just a lot of practice," said Ran.

But Jysal wasn't convinced. "I've seen men who practice with swords before. And I've known warriors with a lifetime of experience who could never make such a precise cut like you just made." She shook her head. "If you don't want to tell me, that's fine. But don't lie and feed me some line about practice. What you did there was far more than just practice."

Ran glanced overhead. The sun was starting its arc toward the horizon. "We should keep moving." He pointed at the dead beast. "We'll lose daylight sooner than we think, and I don't want to imagine the woods filled with those things."

"That's all we'd need," said Jysal. "Is it likely there'll be others in the forest?"

"Probably," said Ran with a sigh. He was concentrating on his breathing, willing his stomach to combat the effects of the adrenaline as well. "Come on."

He led them farther down the game trail, past the point where Vargul had disappeared. This was now new territory. He stopped every few feet to check his direction of travel, but the game trail seemed to be the only available route to take. Unlike other forests he'd been in, this one only had the one game trail and not a whole bunch crisscrossing each other. Ran wondered if that meant there were fewer animals that lived here. Perhaps Kan-Gul had scared them all off.

Or perhaps there was a more evil reason for the game trail's existence. If someone got lost in these woods, they'd be tempted to do exactly what Ran and Jysal were doing now: stick to the only likely path through the forest in the hopes of finding civilization.

And that would make them far easier to ambush.

We're being led exactly where he wants us to be led, Ran thought. *Well, if that's his game, we're not going to play it.* He turned and waved Jysal up to him.

"What's the matter?"

Ran explained the situation and then pointed through the trees. "I think we're going to take a different direction now."

"Are you sure that's such a good idea?"

Ran nodded. "Absolutely."

Jysal's eyes widened again. "I think they might disagree with you."

Ran's hand went for his sword, but Jysal stopped him. "No."

As Ran turned, he saw what she had seen behind them and on either side of the game trail: more beasts exactly like the one Ran had just killed. And they didn't look nearly as nonchalant as the first one had.

CHAPTER NINE

"Don't move," said Ran, slowly drawing his eyes across the multitude of beasts before him.

He heard Jysal snicker. "What on earth gave you the impression I had any intention of moving?"

"Fair point," said Ran. He'd foolishly resheathed his sword after dispatching the first beast. He wished he had it back in his hands now. But the movement of drawing the blade would no doubt spur the beasts to attack them. And Ran didn't want to draw them into that sort of action. The odds were not good they'd survive.

But the beasts seemed uninterested in attacking right away. What were they up to? They hemmed Ran and Jysal in on either side and then straddled the game trail behind them. In front of him, Ran could still see the game trail, and it was free of any of the beasts. He thought back to what he'd been pondering: the obviousness of the game trail. It had led them here to this point before Ran had considered that it could be used to ambush them very easily. And now, upon reaching that conclusion and resolving to go off into the bush, the beasts had shown up.

Shepherds.

Ran almost grinned at the realization. It was already too late to do anything about it.

"Jysal."

"Yes."

"They're not going to attack us if we stay on the game trail."

"How do you know?"

"Think about it," said Ran. "They only showed up when we thought about going off the trail on our own. They're here to make sure that we don't leave the trail and keep going forward." He pointed behind them. "See? We can't go back. And either side of the trail is hemmed in."

"You really think so?"

"I'm betting our lives on it, apparently." Ran put his hand on his sword, but none of the beasts moved. Their eyes never left Ran, however. Ran could have pushed the issue, but he chose not to. Better to let them think he was being compliant for now. That way, when the time came to escape, they'd be surprised.

He hoped.

"We're going to keep walking on the trail. Do you understand?"

"We don't appear to have much choice in the matter."

"Not unless we want to end up as dinner for these guys," said Ran. "Otherwise, no, we don't."

He felt Jysal's soft touch on his back. "I trust you, Ran. Remember that."

He nodded. "All right then. Let's keep moving."

Ran might not have drawn his sword, but he kept his left hand on the scabbard as they walked. Ahead of him, the game trail climbed slowly through a copse of trees that shrouded the area ahead in deep shadow. Ran frowned. Not being able to see clearly made him wonder what might be waiting for them. He slowed down and glanced back again at Jysal. "Can't see ahead. It's dark under those trees."

But even as he said it, Ran heard the unmistakable growl of beasts from all around them. Jysal's eyes widened, and she looked at Ran. "I don't think they like you slowing down. They've been keeping pace with us as we walked, and now you're not moving."

Ran frowned. "I don't like walking into an area like this."

"As you said before, we don't seem to have a say."

Around them, the growling continued. Ran saw the hungry eyes staring him down, daring him to try to make a move. Whatever they were, the beasts seemed supremely confident of their ability to kill Ran and Jysal without too much effort. Ran sighed and then motioned for Jysal. "All right then." He turned and walked into the tunnel of trees.

Under here, it was significantly cooler. And the farther they traveled, the colder the air got. The thick humidity they'd experienced for the majority of their hike through the swamp and forest was now gone. In its place, Ran could see his breath as he exhaled. The shadows all around them made seeing clearly a difficult task. But Ran knew enough to use his peripheral vision instead of trying to look directly at something. As he did, he saw shapes and movement. But he resolved to keep his head down and keep moving ahead. The memory of the growling beasts still filled his head.

The ground continued to slope upward, forcing Ran to bend slightly forward and put the strain of exertion on to his thigh muscles. Behind him, he could hear Jysal breathing hard. She was clearly struggling to keep up. He looked back, but she only gave him a close-mouthed smile and pointed for him to keep going. One thing was certain: Jysal might have the appearance of a beautiful woman, but she was pretty tough as well. The hike would have taken a lot of sturdier warriors down. But Jysal was still gutting it out. Ran respected her for that.

The air lightened around them as they plodded up the hill. On either side, the trees still loomed close, their twisted, gnarled trunks a slate gray wall. But ahead, the shadows retreated. Ran could see things now.

He stopped.

Waited.

But no growls chased him.

Ran smiled and then turned as Jysal stumbled into him. "Why did you stop?"

"They're gone."

"What?"

"The beasts. They've left us."

Jysal took a big gulp of air into her lungs and then turned, looking around, but then looked back at Ran. "When did they vanish? I could have sworn they were with us every step of the way."

"I think that was their job," said Ran. "To make sure we didn't stray from the path and to make sure that we entered that tunnel of foliage."

"But why? What was the point? And why did the first one attack us?"

Ran turned back and stepped forward. He waved Jysal closer to him. "Perhaps it thought we were easy prey, and once we killed the leader, the rest came to herd us."

"Herd us where?"

"There," Ran replied pointing to the west.

In front of them, the ground broke into an open plain devoid of any sort of cover for hundreds of yards in every direction. As Ran scanned the ground, he could see no place where they could hide and observe the massive stone fortress resting in the center of the plain.

It might have been built from giant stone bricks, but from the distance they stood it looked as if it had been vomited straight up out of the earth in some sort of molten geyser before cooling to a dull, lifeless gray appearance. Spires jutted toward the sky, which had grown as gray as the fortress. Arrow slits pockmarked the walls, and the ramparts looked more like rows of serrated teeth than they did proper fortifications.

"It's terribly ugly," said Jysal. "Who would have created such a terrible castle?"

"Kan-Gul," said Ran simply. "I think we've arrived at his home." He shivered unintentionally as a cold breeze blew over them.

"And what happened to the warm air?" asked Jysal. "It's gone frightfully cold."

Ran set his jaw. The answer was as obvious as everything else that had happened to them since they'd been cast ashore in this horrible place. "Sorcery." He spat on the ground.

"You don't like magic practitioners?"

Ran edged his sword an inch out of its scabbard. Just being in this place reminded him of another sorcerer he'd dealt with recently. "Their quest for power has a tendency to corrupt their souls. And they forget their place in the universe, seeking instead to dominate all those they consider beneath them."

"Not all sorcerers are like that," said Jysal quietly. "Some of them help people."

Ran's frown deepened. "I have yet to see any evidence of such things. The sorcerers I have known have all been cruel men, best put to the sword before their evil ways could fully manifest."

"Would you see all sorcerers put to death so readily?"

Ran eyed her. "Until such time as I see proof that not all magic users are evil, yes."

Jysal glared at Ran. "Well, perhaps you shouldn't make such sweeping generalizations. You might be surprised to learn that there are good sorcerers in this world. And you might also be surprised to learn that the good sorcerers are just as disgusted with the evil ones as you are." She pushed past Ran and stepped out onto the plain.

Ran grabbed at her arm, but she twisted away and walked on.

"Jysal, wait," said Ran. "We don't know what's out there. They could have spotters looking at us right now."

"I don't really much care," said Jysal. "The company I currently keep isn't exactly up to my standards."

Ran frowned. She'd obviously taken great offense at his opinion of sorcery. But that was his experience so far. He didn't think it was entirely fair that she judge him on it, considering he didn't know all there was to know about the field of magic.

Jysal strode on across the plain and then abruptly stopped. She raised her right hand and held it palm out toward the fortress. Ran heard her chanting something under her breath, a type of singsong series of words he could not understand. After a moment, Jysal's body swayed slightly, and he thought she might fall to the ground. But she managed to stay upright and then finally turned to stare at Ran.

"Our friends are inside."

Ran cocked an eyebrow. "And just how do you know that?"

Jysal sighed. "You know, for a warrior as adept as you are, you certainly seem to lack an ability to grasp the obvious."

"Now you're insulting me?"

Jysal lowered her hand and shook her head. "I am a sorceress."

Ran felt like she'd punched him in the gut. He swallowed. "Oh. Sorry about what I said back there. It's just that I've only known—"

Jysal's hand came back up. "Forget about making excuses. You said what you said." She took a breath. "And honestly, it wasn't fair of me to act like that. In truth, I'm not a full-fledged sorceress yet. That's what the temple is for. I'll get my full training there. That's why Neviah was accompanying me. It's her job to make sure I make it to the Temple for my education."

"I had no idea."

Jysal smirked. "Obviously."

"So . . . what can you do?"

"What can I do?"

"Yes, what sorts of spells or incantations are you able to do?"

"Didn't you just hear me? I'm going to school at the temple to learn how to do that sort of thing. For now, my power is just raw and untempered. I don't have any real control over it."

Ran pointed at the castle. "But you just told me that you could somehow tell our friends are inside there."

"They are."

"Yes, but how do you know? Exactly, I mean."

Jysal shrugged. "It's a basic technique I've been able to do since I was a very young girl. I can close my eyes and see things. That's really all it is."

"And what about that spell you just muttered while you were doing it? What was that all about?"

Jysal smiled. "Oh, that."

"Yes, that."

"That was me making you feel bad while I stood there saying a bunch of nonsense."

"That was nonsense?"

Jysal nodded. "Total gibberish. I don't have any idea what those words meant."

"And the upraised hand?"

Jysal laughed now. "Did you like that part? Was it effective?"

"Very."

Jysal sighed. "Well, that was fun. But really, I can see our friends in my mind's eye. I'm confident they're in there."

"You're sure about that? I've often heard that desires and ego can sometimes interfere with what we think we see or feel."

Jysal eyed him. "Have you really, now? That's not the sort of thing I'd expect a warrior of common background to know much about."

Ran said nothing.

Jysal grinned after a moment. "Still not going to share it with me, hmm? Very well." She nodded. "But you're correct about our personal whims sometimes impacting what we can sense. Those who are able to acknowledge and then subjugate their ego will find their vision is truer than it would be otherwise. That's one of the hardest things to attain, mind you, but it can be done."

"And you've done that, have you?"

"I have," said Jysal. "Not that it was easy. It was, in some ways, the most difficult thing I'd ever attempted while I was growing up. But eventually, I found the clarity that I sought."

Ran squatted by the ground and ran his hand over the dirt. Particles of hard, packed earth came away in his hand. He peered at the castle, and his eyes went to the walls themselves, trying to spot a weak point he could exploit to somehow gain entrance.

He saw nothing.

The single portcullis of thick, spiked iron barred their way. Otherwise, the shortest distance from the ground to an arrow slit was at least forty feet. He would be hard-pressed to find a way in. And from this distance, the walls themselves seemed almost marble smooth. He couldn't free-climb that without risking injury, perhaps death if he fell from too great a height. If he died, what good would he be to his friends trapped inside?

"It looks quite impressive," said Jysal.

"It is," agreed Ran.

"Can you find a way inside it?"

He glanced at her. She only smiled at him.

Ran shook his head. "Not from this vantage point. As far as I can tell, it's largely impenetrable." His teachers had always stressed that even the most impregnable fortresses still had weaknesses. But he didn't want to reveal that to Jysal. At least not yet.

"There's got to be some way inside," said Jysal. "But I suppose it's a matter of getting up close and seeing for ourselves, eh?"

"We've already been seen," said Ran. "There's not much point in trying to hide and observe the structure in secret. They know all too well that we're out here."

"Who does?"

"Them," said Ran, pointing ahead at the castle. And even as Jysal turned to look, he could see that if the beasts had seemed wholly unnatural, the warriors striding toward them across the plain seemed even more so. But one thing seemed certain: Ran and Jysal were going inside the castle.

CHAPTER TEN

"What are they?" Jysal's voice was hushed and draped with fear.

Ran watched the warriors marching toward them with a mixture of revulsion and wonder. Each wore padded leather armor reminiscent of the type worn by Murai warriors in Nehon and strode with purpose toward Ran and Jysal. But if their armor was new and crisp looking, their faces were anything but. Gray skin covered their heads, and milky white opaque eyeballs rested in their sockets. Ran wondered if they were even able to see, but judging from how well they moved, he guessed that sight was not the issue. If these warriors were undead, how can they be killed?

"I can't look at them," whispered Jysal.

"Don't turn away," said Ran. "And don't make any sudden movements. Let me handle this."

Jysal nodded.

Ran smirked in spite of the situation. The warriors continued to approach. When they were but twenty feet away, the line of them suddenly stopped. Ran's left hand rested on his scabbard. His right hand stayed at his side. He hoped his body language conveyed the fact that he was ready for a fight but not yet posing a direct threat. Still, if he suspected that he and Jysal were in immediate danger, he would act without hesitation.

One of the gray-skinned warriors stepped forward. Ran looked directly into what might have once been eyes full of life but were now blank milky white orbs. The warrior raised his right hand toward Ran and then uttered a single halting sentence tainted by an accent of some sort.

"You will come with us."

Ran thought about replying, but then decided against it. What was the point? He doubted the warriors would be able to tell him anything useful. And if Kan-Gul was the man behind the state of these dreadful men, then Ran definitely wanted to meet him and see for himself what else he was capable of doing. Ran had seen the effects of sorcery before, and he didn't relish the thought of battling another evil wizard so soon. But then again, he didn't think he had much of a choice. If the universe had put him here, then Ran was determined to see it through to the end.

Whatever end that might be.

So instead of saying anything, Ran merely nodded once and then waited as the warriors all turned around in unison and started walking back toward the castle, their footfalls echoing in perfect time as they did so. Ran glanced at Jysal, and then they fell into step behind them.

"Do you have a plan?"

"Of course," said Ran.

"And what is it?"

"My plan is to get inside and see what's going on. Then I'll come up with some type of a plan to free our friends and get us out of there."

"That's not much of a plan. There are dozens of these warriors here. And as good as you are, I don't think you're a match for all of them." Her voice trembled as she spoke.

Ran frowned. "Thanks for the vote of confidence. I really appreciate that." He shook his head. "Look, the fact is we have no information about Kan-Gul, so doesn't it make sense to see what he has to say?"

"Only if that means he's not going to kill us."

"If he'd wanted to kill us, we'd already be dead," said Ran. "He might only want to kill you. In which case, I'll just leave him to it and be gone."

Jysal looked horrified. "You wouldn't."

"I wouldn't," said Ran with another grin, hoping he'd broken her growing panic. He nodded at the warriors. "We need to find out more about these creatures before I try anything. Otherwise, I'd be a damned fool. And I don't like to think of myself as a fool."

A stiff wind blew across the slate gray plain as they walked toward the castle. To Ran, the gray features of the landscape matched that of their escorts. He tried hard to remember what his teachers had told him about sorcery and its uses outside Gakur. But even then, their experience was somewhat limited. What his elders knew of magic, they had only been able to piece together from reports from their network of spies throughout the lands. Or at least, that's all they had taught him about it.

There were, of course, the rumors that high-level shadow warriors could employ a certain type of magic as well. But those claims came mostly from people who had never set foot into the training halls that Ran had. So what they thought they knew came from their own fertile imaginations. The leadership at his school had always been content to let such myths and legends propagate themselves. It helped add to their fearsome reputation.

Ran had also been exposed to enough of the school's teachings to know that more often than not what others saw as magic was in reality simply a new perspective on something that no one else had yet thought to see. Skills that had gone dormant in other people were reawakened through the shadow-warrior training and honed to the point of becoming a tool for use instead of one that gathered only rust.

But then again, Ran had heard other whispers of levels far beyond his own that hinted at the potential for even more unusual skills. Whether they were magic or not, Ran didn't know. But he wanted to live long enough to see if they were.

The warriors seemed to be headed for a wall that had no gate in it. Ran wondered whether or not they would be asked to walk right into the side of the castle. He hoped he was wrong and that a gate would suddenly appear. But so far, nothing had. When he'd first gazed at the castle, Ran's keen eyes had seen only one way into the castle: through the portcullis. But the warriors showed no signs of heading for that entry point.

Where would they enter?

"They expect us to walk through stone?" Jysal's voice was quieter still.

"I don't think they will do that."

"Funny way of showing it. How come we're not heading for the main gate? Doesn't that make the most sense?"

Ran shrugged. "Ours is not to question, just to obey." He winked. "For now."

Jysal shook her head.

"That's all we have right now," said Ran. "I suggest you simply relax and see where things take us."

"Do you really believe that? Is that what all of your training has taught you?"

"Some of my teachers would probably tell you that they're convinced I've learned nothing in my time with them." He shrugged. "But the truth of the situation is this: there's no point in doing anything rash at this point. We need to see what type of man this Kan-Gul is and what he's done with our friends. If there is action to be taken, it will be only if we're in immediate danger."

"I hope you're right about this."

Me, too, thought Ran.

The warriors suddenly stopped marching and fell silent. The one who had addressed Ran stepped closer to the fortress wall and placed his withered gray hand on the smooth surface and uttered something unintelligible. Ran could make no sense of the words, but the effect of the utterance was immediate.

The smooth surface instantly slid back and in, revealing a secret entrance to the castle, one no doubt guarded by powerful magic. Ran glanced at Jysal. "Apparently, there is more than one way into the castle."

"What did that thing say?"

Ran shrugged. "I have no idea. Aren't you supposed to

be the sorceress in training? I assumed you all spoke the same language."

"Don't be daft," said Jysal. "Magic isn't some universal tongue. There are as many different types and varieties as there are people in the great lands. What works for one sorcerer may not work for another. Each type of magic is unique."

"Apparently," said Ran. He had little trust in such things anyway. He trusted his training and his cunning a lot more than he did the arcane words spoken by mages and warlocks. But even he had to admit that the sudden appearance of the entryway was impressive.

Kan-Gul was probably trying to manipulate them psychologically. If they were impressed with his magic before they even met, then that would put them on an unequal level. Ran and Jysal would naturally think of Kan-Gul as being more powerful.

Even if he was not.

Ran grinned. Crafty stuff, but then again, Kan-Gul had probably never dealt with a Shinobujin before. Ran's teachers had always stressed that deception, manipulation, and clever strategy were far superior to merely wielding a sword or breaking bones. At times, Ran could appreciate that sentiment. But at other times, there was nothing better at solving a problem than simply relying on the folded steel of his curved sword. If that meant he lacked finesse, then Ran was comfortable with that assessment. He could always become more refined, provided he lived long enough.

Kan-Gul was clearly trying to intimidate them. Perhaps that was why they hadn't been taken with the others. For some reason Kan-Gul felt he needed to impress them, keep them intimidated and cowed by his almighty powers.

Ran had a choice to make: either he could let Kan-Gul think he had bought into it by pretending to be suitably impressed, or he could simply appear bored by the whole thing. One reaction would almost certainly guarantee that Kan-Gul would grow angry, while the other might cause his vanity to swell to the point that he showed a weakness to Ran.

One that he could exploit when the time was right.

The warriors all moved into the secret entrance. Ran looked at Jysal. "Seems rude of us not to accept the invitation."

Jysal pointed at the castle. "You do realize that once we're inside, there's a distinct chance we won't ever come back out?"

"There's always that chance," said Ran. "But then again, there are very few certainties in life. And I've always preferred trusting the universe to put me where I'm most needed."

"You think you're needed here?"

"I don't know just yet," said Ran. "But our friends are going to need my help. Our help, for that matter. And if we stay out here, then there's truly nothing we can do for them."

"Well then," said Jysal ducking into the opening. "I guess we'd better go and see this man Kan-Gul, eh?"

"Indeed," said Ran. And he, too, ducked into the opening.

It was dark inside. For a moment, Ran's stomach dropped at the thought that he had misjudged the situation and they'd suddenly stepped into an ambush. Then he heard the wall slide back and out, sealing the entrance from the outside world.

As soon as the wall had closed the entire way, a soft, warm light filled the room. Ran heard something like the snap of a whip and smelled some sort of burning in the air. He looked around but saw only that the gray-skinned warriors were moving away and arraying themselves against the wall on the far side of the room they now stood in.

"Ran . . ." Jysal's voice was once again quiet.

"Yes?"

"Your sword."

Ran looked down and frowned at the sight of his blade missing from his belt. "Well, that's odd."

"Odd?" Jysal shook her head and sighed. "You're entirely unarmed. Kan-Gul can now do whatever he wants to do to us and there's not a thing you can do to stop it."

"Has anyone ever told you that you are far too much of a pessimist?"

"No."

"Well, I'm telling you now," said Ran.

"Oh," said Jysal. There was no mistaking the disappointment in her voice. Ran smiled. In her place he might have felt the same thing. But he knew what he was capable of even if Kan-Gul did not. Ran had his own surprises he could play out at his leisure. And they were surprises he doubted Kan-Gul had ever experienced.

The warrior who had addressed them out on the field now came walking back over to Ran. "You will follow me."

Ran nodded, and he and Jysal fell in behind him. The warrior led them out of the room and down a twisting corridor that sloped ever upward toward a grand entrance pavilion made of white alabaster. Far above them, the ceiling arched and looked tall enough to pierce the very heavens themselves.

"It's beautiful," said Jysal quietly. "I've never seen anything quite like it."

"Nor I," said Ran. The spectacle was indeed awesome, and he couldn't help but feel like this was another act by Kan-Gul to load the dice in his favor upon meeting them.

The warrior led them through the pavilion and into a throne room with blazing braziers at the four corners. In front of them sat a throne made out of what looked like one huge crystal. Ran wondered what the cost of such a thing might have been. He couldn't fathom it.

"Welcome."

The voice was different from any he'd ever heard. When Ran turned, he finally got a chance to lay his eyes on the sorcerer known as Kan-Gul.

CHAPTER ELEVEN

Ran blinked, and the figure in front of him vanished. Ran whirled around and saw that Kan-Gul had somehow managed to make himself reappear seated on his throne. The smile he wore seemed friendly and inviting enough, but he was doing everything in his power to impress Ran and Jysal with his abilities. Ran narrowed his eyes and stared at the sorcerer, trying to figure out what sort of man he would be.

Judging by the few seconds he'd seen him standing upright, Kan-Gul must have been at least six and a half feet tall—easily a head over Ran. But he was ridiculously thin, and the layers of robes he wore only had the effect of making him look like a skinny man wrapped in a huge amount of blankets. Ran noted that Kan-Gul's eyes seemed to reflect serious power. They were bright and green and glittered. Ran felt himself drawn to those eyes, pulled into their shimmering depths. He shook himself and turned to Jysal.

She stood transfixed before the throne, a dull smile on

her face even as her eyes still radiated life. Ran nudged her, but she didn't respond. He glared at Kan-Gul. "What have you done to her?"

"We haven't been properly introduced," said the sorcerer. "I am the warlock Kan-Gul. You are in my home. And it is my utmost pleasure to welcome you here to my humble residence."

Ran narrowed his eyes. "I am known as Ran. I hail from Gakur."

"Gakur? Across the Dark Sea in Nehon?"

"The same."

Kan-Gul fingered the tuft of hair at his chin. "Interesting. Are you Murai?"

Ran kept his hands near his belt, even though he no longer had his sword. "No. I am a wandering warrior."

"You're unemployed," said Kan-Gul. "How interesting. And yet you wear clothes that are in good condition."

Ran shrugged. "I wear what was on my back when our ship went down at the coast. Nothing more, nothing less."

Kan-Gul shook his head. "Ah yes, the coastal storms that plague this land are truly awful at this time of year. I must apologize for the tempestuousness of our local environment. I would hope it hasn't caused you too much suffering."

Ran thought about the crewmen who had been taken by sharks. But he didn't say anything about it. They were gone, and nothing Ran would say could bring them back. Better to try to help the others, if they were still alive. "I'm not so concerned about the weather. I'm more concerned about my friends."

"Your friends?"

"Four of them washed ashore with us. One vanished the first night, one disappeared in the swamp, and two more on the second night."

"Yet you and this lovely creature were not taken? How interesting."

Ran had wondered why they weren't all taken that second night. He was more certain than ever it was all part of some elaborate attempt to intimidate himself and Jysal. Ran shook his head. "I don't find it interesting. I find it annoying. I want to know what you've done with them and why they were taken in the first place."

"You think I have them?" Kan-Gul leaned back in his throne. "I must say, leveling accusations at your host isn't exactly the best way to start a relationship. I'm a bit taken aback by your lack of civility, Ran."

"You are the only person we've seen since entering this strange land. No one else could have done it. No one else has the power to do it."

"And what sort of power would you imagine I have?"

"The creatures in the forest. Those warriors."

Kan-Gul smiled. "My men. They are called Chekhal. Do you know the word?"

"No," said Ran.

"It means 'without soul.' Those warriors were once living, but now they are not. They have been restored from the dead. Unfortunately, they no longer possess souls."

"Necromancy," said Ran. "You should have left them in the ground."

"Why on earth would I do a thing like that? They are more useful serving me than decomposing and being food for the worms. And with me controlling them, they can satisfy their lust for the flesh of the living."

"Flesh?"

Kan-Gul nodded. "They do, of course, need sustenance. Not even my magic can sustain them indefinitely. So I send them forth to hunt, and whatever they find, they are entitled to devour, bones and all."

"No wonder you have no one living nearby."

Kan-Gul smiled. "Was that a joke?"

Ran shrugged. "More a statement of fact. Did you kill everyone who used to live around here?"

"Me?" Kan-Gul put a hand on his chest. "By the gods, no. But the Chekhal did. It was most necessary for them to be rewarded for their loyal service. And frankly, a bunch of fisherman living on the coast were more of a bother than they were an asset to my little kingdom here."

"You're just as guilty of murdering them," said Ran. "You can't just put a crime like that off on your undead henchmen."

Kan-Gul said nothing for a moment, choosing instead to run his eyes over Ran from head to toe. Finally, he shifted in his seat and cleared his throat. "And what makes you think that it's even a crime to kill a worthless human in my kingdom? Perhaps the greater crime is to trespass through my lands without asking permission from me first. Perhaps that is the more egregious transgression. After all, Ran from Gakur, you are in a foreign land. You are a long way from your home, wherever that may be. And as such, you are subject to the laws of the land that you travel through."

Ran smiled, but he held no mirth in the gesture. "I

would ask you to look kindly upon any perceived transgressions that may have resulted from our being shipwrecked on your shore. Surely that will count for something."

Kan-Gul looked at his hand as if studying his nails. "Tragically, such things as being shipwrecked do not normally enter into consideration of crimes here. I'm afraid my laws are quite stringent. Otherwise, I would have chaos in my court, and I simply could not tolerate that."

"Your court?"

Kan-Gul waved his hand lazily. Behind him, the room shimmered for a moment. Then a half dozen other chairs appeared. None of them matched the grandeur of Kan-Gul's throne, but they were opulent enough to suggest that the people now occupying them were aristocrats of some type. Ran eyed them individually and then collectively. There were men and women seated there, each with their eyes locked on to his. None of them said a word. They simply sat there, unmoving.

Every few moments, the air around them shimmered. Ran frowned.

Illusion.

He'd seen this before. The effect was sometimes good and sometime obviously not real. From what he could judge, Kan-Gul had some ability, but not nearly as much as he probably thought he had. Perhaps, Ran thought, his more powerful skills lay in the realm of necromancy instead of illusions.

"Do they talk, or do they just sit there?"

Kan-Gul smiled. "They will speak if I ask them to. If I command it."

"Otherwise, they will say nothing. They'll simply sit there until you make them disappear again."

Kan-Gul yawned. "Sometimes I find their conversation uninspiring. I decided they should only speak when spoken to."

"That must lead to some great conversations." Ran pointed. "I think one of them is getting ready to fall asleep."

Kan-Gul glanced over at the shimmering figure of a heavyset man on the end. Then he looked back at Ran. "Perhaps he did not get enough sleep last night."

"Perhaps," said Ran. "Good rest is seemingly very hard to come by in your lands."

"No doubt exacerbated by sleeping on the beach."

Ran nodded. "I've had better rest than what I got laying on sand."

"No doubt." Kan-Gul spread his hands. "You are more than welcome to spend the night here in my castle. I can assure you that your rest will be more enjoyable than any you have had of late."

Ran felt certain that any sleep he got in this castle would probably be his last. "You've taken my sword from me."

"Indeed," said Kan-Gul. "I've found that weapons tend to complicate otherwise enjoyable conversations."

"What have you done with my blade?"

"It is safe, have no worry. I do know that people from Gakur tend to be very protective of their swords. Some, I've heard, even believe they are imbued with the souls of their creators. And many tell me that the blades produced in your country are among the finest anywhere throughout the world."

"The blades are indeed exquisite," said Ran. "As for the blades holding souls within them, I find that many people tend to be more superstitious than practical about such matters."

"You don't believe that a sword can hold a soul?"

"I believe that a sword can cut. That it can take a life as surely as it can protect a life. I believe that a finely made blade is one of the best things a man can own in this dangerous thing we call life. But otherwise, I have little use for superstitions and legends."

"You are a pragmatist, then?"

"I believe in what I can see. What I can feel."

Kan-Gul smiled. "In that case, here." He waved his hands.

Ran felt the reassuring presence of his sword in his belt and let his left hand drift to the scabbard. "Thank you."

"It is a trifling matter." Kan-Gul waved his hands again, and the members of his court vanished. "We have more important matters to discuss anyway."

"Why did you get rid of the court?"

"They were boring me," said Kan-Gul. "Besides, I can tell you never bought into the illusion."

Ran smiled. "It was an admirable attempt."

"But you saw through it."

Ran shrugged. "I see through many things. But that doesn't mean I see all there is to see."

Kan-Gul folded his arms across his chest. "You are an intriguing man, Ran from Gakur. I have met others from your lands, yet none have impressed me the way you have."

"Flattery?" Ran cocked an eyebrow. It seemed beneath the sorcerer to pay him such lip service.

"Think of it more as a compliment," said Kan-Gul. "Perhaps an acknowledgment that you are not nearly as boring as many of your countrymen."

Ran shifted, aware that he'd been standing during the entire conversation. "You've had many here in your court?"

"A few. One very recently, in fact."

Could he be referring to Kancho? Ran frowned. "My friend who went missing was from Nehon. He's Murai."

"Is he? Interesting. Did you know he was also most ungrateful for my hospitality? He kept insisting on his freedom and how he would strike me down if I did not let him and the others go, and on and on and on. I must say, it got extremely tiresome dealing with him."

"He is Murai," said Ran. "They tend to be rather inflexible about such things as that. Did you take his sword as well?"

"I did."

Ran nodded. "No doubt that made him all the more agitated. Murai do not like to be without their swords even during lovemaking."

Kan-Gul chuckled. "Is that how they are? Truly?"

"So I've heard," said Ran. "But I am not Murai, so I can't say for certain."

"Well, regardless," said Kan-Gul. "He is now locked up elsewhere and doesn't really matter to the extent of our conversation."

"He is still my friend," said Ran. "And I would see him released, if you would grant such a thing."

Kan-Gul yawned again. "There will be a time and place to petition me about granting freedoms, have no worries. But for now, we have other important items to discuss."

"Such as?"

"Such as the state of this lovely woman you are traveling with. Who is she?"

Ran glanced at Jysal, but the young sorceress was still staring right at Kan-Gul. Clearly, the sorcerer had put her under some sort of incantation. Ran looked back at him. "Her name is Jysal."

Kan-Gul licked his lips. "She is utterly exquisite."

Ran nodded. "She is indeed beautiful."

"She is beyond mere beauty," said Kan-Gul. "I can sense an energy flowing within her that renders even her appearance insignificant. I can almost taste the spirit of her essence on the air itself."

Ran shrugged. "She was on the ship when it went aground. Her protector was also taken during the second night we were on shore."

Kan-Gul nodded. "And I can certainly see why such a wondrous creature would require the assistance of a bodyguard. Something as delectable as this should not be wandering around these lands without a savior of some sort."

"Neviah was a very capable protector," said Ran. "She would give her life to save her charge, I have no doubt."

"Nor I," said Kan-Gul. "And unlike the Murai, she was far more graceful, despite her reluctance to speak."

"You have them both?"

"I have all four of them," said Kan-Gul. "They are safe for the moment. But whether they remain so is entirely up to the outcome of our conversation."

"What is it that you want?"

Kan-Gul blinked and then reappeared next to Jysal.

He moved his hands in a very strange fashion while muttering something guttural in a language Ran could not understand. Then he ran his hands over the surface of her tunic, cupping her breasts slightly and licking his lips as he did so. Ran felt his blood boil at such a show of disrespect but kept his temper in check. It would do him no good to lose control. At least not yet.

"Isn't it obvious?" said Kan-Gul after he had finished running his hands all over Jysal's body. "I want this one to be my queen."

"And what of what she wants?" asked Ran. "Does that matter?"

"Why should it? Women rarely know what they want until they are placed in a situation. It is only then that their true skill—that of adapting to a situation—becomes apparent."

"So you're saying that Jysal will learn to love you?"

"Exactly." Kan-Gul clapped his hands, and in the next instant he was seated on his throne once more.

"I don't think she would like that very much."

Kan-Gul sighed. "Well, it's either she become my queen or you all die. And honestly, either option will no doubt provide me with a great deal of enjoyment." He grinned at Ran. "Who knows, if she refuses to be my bride and I have you all put to death, I may still force myself on her."

Ran frowned. "I would not let that happen."

"Really?" Kan-Gul's smile spread even wider across his face. "And just how would you do that? You do not even have a sword."

Ran looked down, but the sword on his belt shimmered

and then turned into a limp piece of rope that fell by his side. Another illusion, only this one had fooled him completely.

CHAPTER TWELVE

"I'm afraid," said Kan-Gul, "that our time grows short. I must therefore ask you to accompany my warriors to a special holding cell. But fear not, I think you will at least enjoy some company for a short time." He waved a hand, and two of the Chekhal stepped forth from the wings to stand near Ran and Jysal. "Please do not attempt to escape. I assure you that this fortress has been designed specifically to thwart any attempt in that regard."

Ran smiled. "What are you doing now?"

"I must tend to some business," said Kan-Gul. "But fear not, we will see each other again very soon. I have a demonstration in mind that may make you reconsider my previous offer."

"I'm not in a position to agree to your offer," said Ran. "You're talking about a grown woman here. She should be able to make her own decisions. If she decides to stay with you, then so be it. But I cannot speak for her."

"Perhaps not, but you can certainly persuade her to consider my offer. And I would be so very glad if you would. It would make things a whole lot easier than the alternative."

Ran frowned. A demonstration. The alternative. None of it sounded good. But until he could figure out a plan of attack, there seemed little point in trying to kill Kan-Gul. Twice during their conversation, Ran had noticed the sorcerer himself appeared to shimmer. It was likely his image was nothing more than an illusion as well, with the real necromancer hiding somewhere close by. This first meeting was probably as much about gathering information about Ran and Jysal as it was about trying to intimidate them.

The Chekhal were real enough, however, and Ran felt one of their hands close over his biceps. The grip was like a steel vise, and he almost winced at the pressure exerted on his arm. Fighting these things would prove to be a challenge, no doubt about it. But surely they must have some sort of weakness he could exploit. He would need more time to study them. It was likely he would end up battling them at some point soon.

Jysal allowed herself to be led away without so much as a peep of protest, but then again, she still seemed to be under Kan-Gul's control. Ran hoped it would wear off as soon as they were out of the throne room.

The Chekhal steered them down twisting, winding passageways. Torches lit the way, fitted into brackets that seemed set unnaturally high into the walls. Who could have reached them? Then Ran realized that Kan-Gul didn't need to reach them. They were probably magical, and one of his spells would be enough to replenish their light if need be.

They reached a spiral stairway built of huge stone blocks leading downward into darkness. But as they descended, more torches flickered into existence. As they passed, the flames diminished and eventually vanished altogether. That must have been part of Kan-Gul's plan to thwart escape. He probably thought that without light, most people would stumble about lost. Ran had been memorizing every detail that he could since they'd entered the keep.

They gradually descended into the bowels of the castle. Ran sniffed the air. It was cold down here. And a variety of scents tickled his nostrils. One of them was unmistakable: fresh blood. But whose? He hoped it wasn't from one of his fellow travelers.

They reached the bottom of the stairway, and the Chekhal led them down a narrow passageway. Smaller torches cast dancing shadows on the walls as they passed what looked like prison cells. Heavy stone doors set with inlaid bars prohibited escape. The Chekhal guiding Jysal reached a cell and placed a key into the lock, turned it, and opened the door. He shoved Jysal inside and then stepped aside.

The pressure on Ran's arm increased, and he, too, was placed into the cell. He expected it to be cramped, but once inside, he could see that it was larger than he'd originally thought.

It was also occupied.

"Ran!"

Malkyr lay slumped against the far wall, one hand clasped over his injured leg. Beside him sat Kancho, Neviah, and Vargul. Ran grinned in spite of their situation. "It's good to see you all alive."

Neviah moved immediately to Jysal's side. "What happened to her?"

"Kan-Gul placed some sort of spell over her. She never moved, never uttered a word the entire time I spoke with Kan-Gul."

Kancho got to his feet. "Spoke with Kan-Gul? You saw him?"

Ran nodded. "We just came from his throne room, actually. He's a necromancer. And he's fairly adept at illusions as well. He even had me fooled into thinking he'd given me my sword back."

Kancho grumbled. "I wish I had my sword back. I'd make short work of him and his band of thugs."

"What happened to you guys?" asked Ran. "We were on the beach, and then in the morning you were gone."

Kancho shook his head. "No one knows. We fell into some sort of sleep. When we awoke, this was where we found ourselves."

Ran gestured to Malkyr. "How is his injury?"

"Better, actually," said Kancho. "He'll probably be able to walk within a day."

"If we have a day," said Vargul. "I've heard tales of this sorcerer. I know what he does to those he captures."

Kancho waved him off. "You're still alive, Vargul. We don't know anything about this man yet. It would be foolish to make predictions at this point, don't you think, Ran?"

Ran sighed and slumped down against the wall. "He seemed to know exactly what he was doing. He wants to take Jysal for his queen."

"What?" Neviah looked up, horrified. "There is no way I would ever permit that."

Ran held up his hand. "I told him as much. But he insisted that he would have her one way or another."

"I'll die before she stays here with such a monster," said Neviah. "How can he simply assume that she would ever consent to such a thing?"

"Apparently," said Ran, "that's where I come in. He wants me to help convince her to stay here and marry him."

"Of course, you'll do no such thing," said Kancho.

"Obviously," said Ran.

"There is only one option," said Vargul. "We need to figure out how to escape. Did you see anything on the way down here, Ran?"

Ran nodded. "Some. Kan-Gul uses a great deal of magic to make this place seem like a labyrinth, but I think there may be a way to get ourselves out of here."

"The sooner the better," said Neviah. "His magic is apparently quite strong. I can't seem to bring Jysal around."

Ran frowned. "I had hoped that once we were out of the throne room, she would snap out of it."

Neviah shook her head. "Not yet, at least. Perhaps if she sleeps."

But they heard a stomping of feet from outside their cell. Ran held up a hand. "It doesn't sound like any of us are going to get any sleep right now."

Malkyr struggled to get to his feet. "What's going on?"

Kancho shushed him. "We don't know."

The empty face of a Chekhal warrior appeared at the bars of their cell. "Stand back against the wall."

They all did as he told them, and then Ran heard the key jangle in the lock. He listened intently as the key turned and the lock opened. Then the door swung out into the corridor. The Chekhal waved them to exit. "You will follow me."

Ran led them out of the cell, following behind the Chekhal. Being this close to the soulless warrior allowed him to see if there was anything he could exploit to his advantage. Each Chekhal warrior seemed to wear some sort of special leather armor that moved and flexed very easily so they weren't encumbered by any sort of bulk. Ran supposed that was good, since it would only offer limited protection.

Unless Kan-Gul had bestowed additional properties on the armor. But there was no way of knowing that without getting into a fight with one of them.

They moved past the stairway that led upstairs and down another long passageway. The air here felt warmer, and torches flickered brightly. In this passage, there were no prison cells, but Ran noted the existence of bunks along the wall. Was this where the Chekhal had their barracks? He glanced back at Kancho and pointed at the bunks. Kancho nodded.

The existence of a barracks meant an extra bit of trouble for them during any sort of escape, Ran thought. If there were guards nearby, they would easily be reinforced by any of their brethren sleeping in the barracks just down the hall from where the prisoners were. That sort of close proximity meant that stealth would be absolutely essential if they were going to successfully escape. For Ran, that wasn't a problem. But his other companions might find it much harder to be quiet and move slowly when all of their instincts screamed at them to run.

Ran shook the thought out of his head. He hoped they'd have time to properly plan things out. For right now, he contented himself with simply noting as much information as he could about the layout of the dungeon.

Ahead of them, Ran could see more torches illuminating the way. But then they turned to the left, and the Chekhal warrior led them into a small room before turning to them and saying, "Stay here."

Then he walked out and closed another door behind them. Another lock slid into place. This cell was much more cramped than the previous one. Vargul pounded on the door and shouted, but it did no good.

Ran glanced around the cell. There was nothing here. Kancho came up next to him. "What do you think?"

Ran shook his head. "I don't know. I don't think we're going to be here all that long. It doesn't look like a holding cell. It's too . . . temporary."

"What makes you say that?"

"No toilet, for one thing," said Ran. "If we were meant to be here for long, they would at least have a hole in the ground."

"Perhaps they intend to kill us within the next few minutes and there's no need for a toilet."

"Good point," said Ran. "Either way, this isn't where we're going to stay."

Kancho sighed. "I hope you're right. The bunks along the wall back there didn't give me much hope about escaping."

"Perhaps," said Ran. "But it might also be another

tactic that Kan-Gul uses to intimidate his guests. Show them something that sinks their morale when the reality is far less than the illusion."

"I don't follow your thinking."

"Kan-Gul seemed intent on making an impression from the moment his warriors took us inside the castle. But it might just be to make us think he's more powerful than he might be. His warriors are reanimated from the dead. They have no souls. Does it make sense that they would need a barracks? Why would they even care about such things? They're dead, after all."

"Maybe we don't know all there is to know about the undead. Perhaps they like having a comfortable bed each night after they're done doing whatever it is they do."

Ran grinned. "You could be right. If that's the case then all we need to do is tempt them with downy pillows and we should be able to walk right out of here."

"Something tells me it's nothing as simple as that."

"Agreed," said Ran. He nodded toward the others in the cell. "How are they all holding up?"

"Fair, given the situation," said Kancho. "But Vargul seems to be the most unstable. He hasn't shut up since we got here. Claims that the Chekhal told him they were going to suck his very soul out through his marrow."

"That must have had quite an effect on him."

"He's not a warrior, that one," said Kancho. "All he knows are the pleasures of the money he hoards. He's never known the thrill of combat or the idle talk that can infect a spirit during times of stress."

Ran sighed. "We have a formidable task ahead of us. You, Neviah, and I are the only trained warriors here.

There are an awful lot of Chekhal to deal with, and I'm not even sure they can be stopped."

"If we can get our swords back, I'll find out just how unstoppable they are. But without our weapons . . ." Kancho's voice trailed off.

Ran agreed. If they couldn't locate their missing arms, there was little point in trying to fight. Their only other option would be to simply flee the castle and hope to find a way to get free of the lands that surrounded them. Ran thought about the beasts that had herded them toward the castle. Facing those things without weapons would prove nearly impossible.

But he would tell Kancho about that particular problem later. No sense getting worked up over it before they had to face them. Better to keep him focused on the task at hand: escaping and locating their weapons.

They heard another key in the lock and turned in unison. The door swung open, and Kan-Gul appeared in the doorway. "How is everyone doing? Are you all well? Have you been enjoying my hospitality?"

Vargul launched himself at Kan-Gul, but the sorcerer merely held up a hand and it was as if Vargul had slammed into some sort of wall. He stumbled back, dazed and confused.

Kan-Gul sighed. "There is always one unruly guest at any party. Tragically, the best thing seems to be to get rid of them rather than have to endure their rude and boorish behavior any longer than absolutely necessary." He stepped back into the passageway and nodded. Two Chekhal warriors came in and dragged the stunned Vargul out of the cell. The door slammed shut behind them.

Ran moved to the door. "What are you going to do with him?"

Kan-Gul's voice floated back in response. "Have no worries, Ran of Gakur. You will see soon enough."

CHAPTER THIRTEEN

A few minutes later, the door of the cell reopened. This time, four Chekhal warriors waited for them in the passageway. Filled with uncertainty, Ran stepped out of the cell. He guessed that Vargul had been killed already and that the presence of four Chekhal couldn't mean good things for them. He reflected briefly on whether or not the decision to come to Kan-Gul's fortress had been a wise one, but then realized they hadn't had much choice in the matter—only the illusion of choice. He frowned. Kan-Gul was certainly better at subtly manipulating events than doing it overtly. That would bear remembering if he had any hope of getting out of this place alive.

He wondered whether other Shinobujin who had been dispatched on *shugyo* had found themselves in similar situations. His elders back at the school had noted that Ran, for all his skill, was inexperienced in the ways of the world. A *shugyo* was usually deemed the best way to see who had the tenacity and ability to survive beyond the protection of the school's walls.

So far, thought Ran, *I don't think they'd be too pleased with my performance.*

He followed the lead Chekhal warrior around a bend in the passageway that led them up along a spiral path that eventually deposited them into a balcony overlooking a wide-open, high-walled pit.

Vargul stood in the center of the pit, still looking as dazed and confused as he had been immediately after Kan-Gul had stopped him in the cell.

Kan-Gul stood in the balcony and turned to the travelers as they filed in. "Welcome, my friends, welcome. Please seat yourselves. The festivities are about to begin."

"Now we're friends?" whispered Kancho to Ran as they sat down in the stone chairs.

"Doubtful," said Ran. He looked at Kan-Gul. "What are you going to do with Vargul?"

"It's not me that has chosen this path," said Kan-Gul. "It was your friend Vargul who made the decision to attack me. This is merely a delayed form of self-protection, if you will."

"Let him go," said Ran. "You don't need to do this."

Kan-Gul smiled. "Oh, but I'm afraid I do. You see, I want there to be no mistaking my intention. Or my desires. And I've found that it's often helpful to illustrate my resolve through demonstrations like this." He winked. "Plus, it's fun."

Ran frowned but turned around to face the pit below them. Vargul seemed completely unaware of his surroundings. In fact, he seemed mercifully ignorant of the entire situation. *Perhaps that's a good thing*, thought Ran. He glanced at Neviah, but the protector wore a grim expression on her face and kept her eyes locked forward. Jysal, still semi-stunned, leaned against Neviah.

"Not to worry," said Kan-Gul from behind them. "While Vargul is a bit confused right now, the spell will wear off shortly. I wouldn't want him to go through this not feeling every exquisite bit of agony."

Ran bit his lip. He felt certain there was no way Kan-Gul could have read his mind, but he would have to be on guard for such a thing anyway. He looked at Vargul and wondered exactly what the sorcerer had in mind for him.

He didn't have long to wait. From somewhere underneath the balcony, Ran heard the sound of chains being pulled back and a gate being hoisted. And then Vargul screamed.

"Ah, you see? The spell has now worn off, so Vargul can appreciate his immediate future," said Kan-Gul. "Such as it is."

"This is cruel," said Neviah quietly.

"That's the point," said Ran. "He wants us to see this and realize we're totally at his mercy."

Neviah took a deep breath and then covered Jysal's eyes with her hand.

Ran looked down into the pit. Vargul was at the far side, scrambling for any sort of purchase he could find on the wall, but the sides of the pit were smooth marble, and they offered nothing that the portly merchant would be able to use to climb out of there. Ran shook his head and hoped this demonstration would be quick.

Underneath the balcony, the ground shook. Behind them, Kan-Gul laughed and clapped his hands. "Now you will all see my favorite thing in the whole wide world."

Ran leaned forward and caught sight of a giant head directly beneath the balcony. Ran didn't blame Vargul for screaming. The thing beneath them was huge. And when it stopped a few paces farther on in the middle of the pit and turned to face the balcony, Ran got a better look at Kan-Gul's pet.

The head of the beast was similar to what he'd killed in the forest. But the four limbs jutting out from its side gave it an almost arachnid appearance, despite the fact that it walked on two heavily muscled legs. Padded leather armor like the type worn by the Chekhal covered its entire body. It carried no weapons that Ran could see, but then again, with something as terrifying as this, it didn't seem to need any.

"What do you think, Ran?"

Ran glanced back at Kan-Gul. "It looks like you've stuck a few pieces together and created a monster."

"Indeed. Do you recognize the parts of the beast you killed in the forest before coming to the castle?"

Ran nodded. "Yes, but this is far larger than what I killed."

"True enough. Size is always an issue for me. I could have probably achieved similar results with something far smaller, but I do like to see the effect that size has on my audience. It's somehow more gratifying this way."

Ran couldn't fault him for that. The sheer enormity of the beast would terrify anyone. Ran was safe on the balcony, but even he felt vulnerable sitting at the edge in the stone chairs.

"Where do you keep it? Down below?"

"It has its own cage, yes," said Kan-Gul. "I've also taken

the liberty of adding a few enhancements to it. The extra appendages give it increased dexterity. And it has some of the same features as the Chekhal. Specifically, this creature has no soul. It therefore requires the same type of sustenance."

The distinct lack of population in the surrounding lands made even more sense to Ran now than it had earlier. Kan-Gul must have taken as many of them as he could prisoner and fed them to his creatures. The ones who hadn't fled were no doubt dead by now. Ran shook his head. Kan-Gul had to be stopped. If he was allowed to continue living, many others would perish. And Ran couldn't in good conscience allow that to happen.

He was sure his elders back at the school would agree.

Vargul's shrieks were now mere whimpers. So far, the creature had remained in the center of the pit, completely still. Kan-Gul no doubt had the thing under his control. Ran frowned. The evil sorcerer was letting the tension and fear build to a proper pitch before releasing the thing on Vargul. Ran sighed. Neviah was right: this was inhumanly cruel.

"So, my friends, are we ready to witness the power of what I've created? I can assure you that it is most exhilarating."

"Not for Vargul, it won't be," mumbled Kancho.

"Get on with it," said Ran. "Vargul doesn't deserve this."

Kan-Gul frowned. "But he does deserve it. You see, he attacked me. How would you have me respond?"

"Not like this," said Ran. "But if this is the way it has to be, then be quick about it."

"Quick is exactly what this will not be," said Kan-Gul. "In order to extract the deepest and best part of his essence, Vargul needs to be completely terrified of what is about to devour him. The anticipation of his death heightens the energy my pet can gain from eating his soul. Interesting, wouldn't you agree?"

"Just get on with it," said Ran. He glanced down at Malkyr, but so far the captain hadn't said anything. The expression on his face was grim, but his jaw was set. Ran guessed he wasn't going to say anything that might land him in the pit to face a similar fate.

Incredibly, down in the pit, Vargul had come away from the wall and was approaching the beast. Ran shook his head. Did Vargul think that because it wasn't moving that he was somehow safe? Or was he trying to work up a strategy for dealing with it? Without weapons, there seemed little the merchant would be able to do. And even if he was armed, his background wasn't in fighting. At best, he'd manage to wound the creature before it killed him.

"Your friend surprises me," said Kan-Gul. "He's not crying out in fear."

Ran smirked. Vargul was as good as dead, but at least he'd managed to inflict some level of disappointment on Kan-Gul.

"Well, allow me to remedy that situation," continued Kan-Gul. He clapped his hands three times, and the beast suddenly let out a tremendous roar. This had the effect of making Vargul scream and once again flee for the nonexistent safety of the wall. Next to Ran, Jysal jumped as well. She wiped her eyes and looked around.

"What's going on? Where are we?"

Ran groaned. He'd been hoping she might be spared the forthcoming spectacle. Neviah whispered in Jysal's ear while Vargul's screams filled the air. Jysal took one look at the beast in the pit and then turned and buried her face in Neviah's shoulder, weeping.

Kan-Gul started laughing. "Now, that's more like it. You see? The fear is almost palpable. Can you imagine how much it must drive my pet crazy to have such essence on the air? He's salivating at the thought of it."

The sorcerer was right. Even as he said it, the beast's jaws gaped and spilled strands of saliva on to the floor of the pit. The stench of its breath made Ran wince. He had to bite back on his tongue to keep from retching.

Malkyr wasn't quite so disciplined. He leaned over the edge of the balcony and vomited into the pit.

"Did I forget to mention the peculiar aroma of my pet's breath? It's invigorating, isn't it? Certainly wakes you up."

Ran glanced back and saw how much glee was plastered across Kan-Gul's face. *He's enjoying this far too much*, he thought. "What are you waiting for? Do it already."

Kan-Gul glared at him. "Don't spoil my fun, Ran of Gakur. Otherwise I might not look so favorably upon you."

Ran turned back around. The longer this went on, the worse it would be for all of them, but most especially Vargul. Ran was comfortable with the idea that he would die one day, most likely in battle. It was a fate he'd resigned himself to and made peace with. Accepting his own mortality had been the first key step toward becoming a member of the Nine Daggers. But people like Vargul, who made their living on trade and commerce, had no inkling of what real pain was like. They didn't know the bite of steel. And they never imagined they might end up having their soul devoured by some otherworldly beast manufactured by an evil sorcerer.

The beast now turned and fixed its gaze on Vargul for the first time. Vargul screeched and clawed at the wall desperately. Ran saw streaks of blood and realized that Vargul must have broken his nails trying to scratch his way to freedom. But he didn't seem to even feel the pain, as scared as he was.

"Now watch, my dear guests. Watch and understand the nature of what awaits you all unless you agree to my demands."

Kan-Gul clapped his hands once more. The beast moved, lumbering across the pit, its limbs all in motion. Vargul pleaded for mercy, but Kan-Gul only continued to laugh. Vargul tried to run to the creature's left, but it simply changed direction and blocked his path. Vargul ran to the right, and the beast blocked him again.

Vargul backed up until he could go no farther.

The wall stopped him.

And then the creature roared again and plucked the merchant right off of his feet, hoisted him in the air, and used its extra appendages to grab Vargul's arms and legs at the same time.

Jysal's sobs grew louder.

Ran took a breath and watched as the creature plucked one of Vargul's arms off at the shoulder. Blood spurted from the now empty socket. The creature let it spill into its mouth, slurping hungrily as it did so.

Vargul let out a hideous shriek.

The beast plucked off his opposite leg and did the same thing. Vargul's shriek died to a mere whimper, and then the merchant mercifully either went unconscious or was already dead.

But that didn't stop the creature from continuing to slurp up the merchant's blood. Then it crunched into the arm and leg it had ripped off of Vargul's body. Ran heard the sickening crunch of bones as it chewed and then swallowed. His stomach turned over, but Ran managed to bite back the surge at the back of his throat.

Malkyr vomited again.

"The best part is coming," said Kan-Gul. "Now watch."

Ran felt forced to look, like Kan-Gul had somehow taken control of his body. Down in the pit, Vargul's body lay on the floor minus one arm and one leg. He looked like a rag doll. But the creature still hovered over him, like it was waiting for something to happen.

And then Ran saw it. Vargul's body jerked. As it did, the creature suddenly opened its jaws and sucked in a huge gulp of air. The air in the pit went incredibly hot, and Ran heard Vargul's screams again and again and again, despite the fact that his body showed no signs of life.

"Yes, my lovely, feast on his soul. Devour every delicious bit of it. Take it all in and consume him entirely. Yesssss."

Vargul's screams echoed over and over again in the pit and in the air all around them. This was what Kan-Gul's creations did to the people they killed. They ate their souls so they couldn't journey to the afterlife. Ran shook his head and only stopped when Vargul's screams finally ended several minutes later.

When Ran opened his eyes, the creature was gone from the pit and only Vargul's torn-apart corpse remained.

Kan-Gul's voice was hushed. "You will now be taken back to your cells. I believe you have much to discuss."

CHAPTER FOURTEEN

"That was a pretty horrible thing to have to witness," said Kancho back in the cell.

Neviah sat in the corner with Jysal. Jysal had stopped weeping on the way back, but the effect on her was obvious. Ran looked at Kancho. "We don't have many options to work with here."

"Escape is the only one that I can see," said Kancho. "We certainly can't wait around for that madman to kill us all one by one. I don't know about you, but I've never seen my death coming at the hands of a beast like that while I'm unarmed. Even if we don't make it out of here alive, I'd rather go out on my own terms than Kan-Gul's."

"Agreed," said Ran. "We just have to make sure that we choose our moment carefully. Kan-Gul is no fool. He'll be expecting something from us. I don't want to get out of here only to walk into a trap."

"As long as we don't wait too long," said Kancho. "Because I don't think he will."

Malkyr sat nearby. "Who will?"

"Kan-Gul. He'll kill us all if we don't do something."

Malkyr shrugged. "Seems like our destinies have already been cast. I don't see a way to get out of this place. Did you see that pit Vargul died in? There was no escape from there, either. Kan-Gul seems to have thought of everything."

Ran frowned. "I don't think your attitude is going to help us very much. If you'd rather stay here, then be my guest. But I'm not going to stop trying to find a way to get free."

"Suit yourself," said Malkyr. "I'm going to get some sleep."

Kancho aimed a kick at his head. "I can't believe I entrusted my life to you aboard that so-called ship of yours."

"You leave my boat out of this," said Malkyr rubbing the spot where Kancho had kicked him. "I did what I was paid to do."

"You were paid to get us safely to the other side of the Dark Sea," said Ran.

"Exactly. And here you are. You're welcome." Malkyr shifted his position and moved away from the rest of them.

Ran watched him go and frowned. Malkyr's attitude was disturbing. And Ran didn't like the fact that he wasn't anxious to escape. Who would willingly choose to stay here?

"Forget him," said Kancho. "We've got things to figure out. He'll only get under our skin and make us less productive."

"You're right," said Ran. He walked over to Neviah and crouched down. "We're going to figure out a way to get out of here."

Neviah eyed him. "How will you do this?"

Ran glanced at the door. "I'm not sure just yet. But we're not just going to sit here and give up."

Neviah nodded. "When you are ready, let me know. If it's my destiny to die here, I will at least take many of the enemy with me."

"Hopefully it's no one else's destiny to die here," said Ran. "Try to get some rest for the moment." He nodded at Jysal. "How is she?"

Neviah looked at Jysal and then back at Ran. "She's never seen anything so terrible. So horrifying."

"Probably not."

"But she'll be okay. Once her nerves calm down, she'll be well enough to travel."

"Good." He moved back to Kancho. "Think of a way out yet?"

Kancho cracked a small grin. "Any plan will first have to start with that door. But I'm afraid lockpicking skills were not in the curriculum I was taught as a Murai."

Ran eyed him. "I thought you might be Murai, but wasn't sure given your appearance."

Kancho sighed. "I was forced to adopt a disguise in order to escape Nehon. Otherwise I would have been hunted down and killed before I could get across the Dark Sea."

"Why would that be?"

"I disobeyed a direct order from my lord. Such a thing is considered treasonous and punishable by death. My death, in this case." He smiled. "It would seem that my karma is proving rather unescapable at the moment. But I'm resolved not to die before I can exact my revenge."

Ran frowned. "What vengeance do you seek?"

"My daughter was taken by a band of pirates off the northern coast of Nehon. I haven't seen her in months. There's been no word of ransom. For all I know, she's already dead. But I won't stop until I find the people who took her and make them pay for their crimes. Naran was my real destination, but nobody would sail there, so I sailed with Malkyr, trying to get as close as possible to the port before heading south on foot."

"How was your daughter taken?"

"She was sailing on a sloop to visit family and a coastal raider took them just offshore. But they turned toward Igul and disappeared into the fog. I asked leave of my lord to pursue the men who took her, but he denied my request." Kancho shrugged. "I've spent weeks planning my escape. And my eventual vengeance. But now I've been delayed. And I've dishonored my clan at the same time."

Ran clapped him on the back. "You've accomplished a lot, it would seem."

Kancho looked at him incredulously and then broke into a smile when he saw Ran was kidding. "I suppose I rather have."

"Let's take care of this mess first," said Ran. "And I promise to help you when we get out of here."

"Why would you do that?"

"What?"

"Risk your life for someone you don't really know." Kancho shook his head. "That path is mine to walk alone. I could not ask you to come along."

Ran said. "There are other people in Gakur who place value on family and making sure wrongs are righted. I happen to be one of them."

"But you're not Murai," said Kancho.

"No," said Ran. "I'm not. But Murai don't have a monopoly on honor."

"Having a nice talk are we?"

Ran and Kancho turned at the sound of the voice at the door. Through the bars they saw Kan-Gul's smiling face. He looked gleeful, and it sickened Ran.

"What do you want?"

"Just curious as to whether you've had an opportunity to discuss my offer."

"It's not an offer," said Ran. "It's a demand."

Kan-Gul shrugged. "Semantics don't matter to me. Have you convinced Jysal to marry me yet?"

"No."

Kan-Gul frowned. "Did you see the manner in which your friend was killed? The act of killing his physical body was awful enough, but the truly horrid aspect is that the man once known as Vargul now has no soul. He is well and truly dead, unable to journey to the afterlife or come back in another body. He no longer exists on any plane. Can you imagine the terror of such finality? Do you appreciate the final fate you all face?"

"You made it abundantly clear what would happen to us," said Ran. "Why is she so important to you, anyway?"

Kan-Gul smiled. "Surely you have sensed her power. She is percolating with unbridled and untrained magical energy. It drips from her pores like some delicious wine. I can taste it emanating from her any time she is near me. Such power will prove useful to me." He licked his lips. "She has other amenities as well and I will certainly avail myself of those. But her magic . . . that is power I shall have, and it will come in handy once my friends from the far north arrive."

Ran frowned. "Friends from the far north?"

"Didn't I tell you?" Kan-Gul smiled. "I've made an alliance with the large army massing up there. They are looking forward to conquering the lands in these parts, including Nehon and your beloved Gakur. With my magic magnified, it will be much easier."

Ran couldn't recall hearing any reports about large armies to the north. As far as he knew, the lands to the north were sparsely populated frozen wastelands. "What happens if Jysal refuses to marry you?"

Kan-Gul stared at Ran. "You will all die the same way Vargul did." His face vanished from the bars.

Ran moved closer to the door and peered out. He couldn't see much, but he sensed that Kan-Gul was gone. Ran looked back at Kancho. "I really cannot wait to kill that man."

"You may have to wait in line," said Kancho. "Is what he said even possible? Could he actually use Jysal's power to complement his own?"

"It's possible," said Neviah from behind them. "It's not an easy thing to do, but I've heard of others who have done it successfully. And as a result, their power was magnified exponentially." She shook her head. "What such power would do for Kan-Gul is something I would prefer not to even think about."

"We're not going to let him do it," said Ran. He looked back at the door. As much as he would prefer to not do what needed to be done, he saw no other way to get them all out of there and escape to freedom. And given that

Kan-Gul had ably demonstrated his preference for death and mayhem, Ran knew he would have to be the one who led them out of this place.

He reached into his belt and extracted the only other thing that had survived the shipwreck and Kan-Gul's magic: a long thin wire that had been sewn into the belt he wore around his waist. Ran felt Kancho's eyes on him and looked up. "This might just work."

Kancho's mouth was grim. "You can pick the lock on the door?"

"I haven't done it in quite some time," said Ran. "But the skill was taught to me when I was a young boy." This was a lie, of course; Ran was an expert at picking locks. But he hoped to stave off any questions from Kancho about his own background for as long as possible.

He moved closer to the door and peered out through the bars. Torches still flickered in the passageways, but he couldn't see much beyond the cell door. And that was the truly risky part. If he got to work on the lock and a Chekhal guard happened by, they would take the wire and then Ran would have no other options left. But as risky as it was, Ran believed he had no other choice. So he set to work, snaking the wire first through the bars and then down to the lock itself, testing to see if it would reach.

He felt a moment of relief when he was able to reach the lock with the wire. He quickly withdrew the piece and nodded at Kancho. "It will work, I think. Provided I haven't forgotten any of the things I was taught."

"Who taught you how to pick locks?" asked Kancho. "Such skills are normally reserved for thieves and other criminals."

Ran busied himself with fashioning the requisite type of pick he thought the lock would need. "My father's brother was a common thief at one time. He hid out in our home after a robbery that he'd committed, and while there he took me aside and showed me the skill. Perhaps he wanted his nephew to become a thief like him, I don't know. I was only a boy."

"What happened to him?"

Ran shrugged. "He was caught by the Murai and boiled alive for his crimes."

Kancho nodded. "Justice was served."

Ran eyed him. "He was still family. I would have preferred justice be swift and deliver him to the afterlife a little quicker than six hours of torturous pain and eventual death."

Kancho frowned for a moment and then nodded. "It is a rather barbaric form of punishment. He must have done something truly awful to warrant such a sentence, however."

"I never knew," said Ran. "Once he was dead, my family never spoke of him again." He bent the wire again, forming it into the intricate shape that would perform the action. He held it up in the dim light and tried his best to eyeball it. Training had taught him a lot; back in Gakur, the teachers had made students pick locks while being suspended upside down over the side of a mountain. The ability to focus and shut out discomfort and danger ensured they could pick a lock confidently and in any sort of bizarre circumstance.

"Is it ready?"

Ran nodded. "I hope." He felt another measure of relief that Kancho seemed to have accepted his explanation about his ability to pick a lock. Kancho might have been on the run and with his own death sentence hanging over his head, but if he knew there was a shadow warrior in the same cell with him, his honor might take over, and he might try to kill Ran with his bare hands.

It was not a fight that Ran wanted.

Fortunately, he was a very good liar. During his training, the teachers had taught all of the trainees how to lie convincingly, act, and disguise themselves. All of the skills were intertwined with each other. You couldn't disguise yourself completely unless you truly believed in the role you were adopting. That took an extra bit of psychological skill to pull off, but eventually all of them had succeeded. Ran could almost believe Nakadai, the instructor who had taught him how to pick locks, was really his uncle. Even now as he worked with the wire, he saw Nakadai's face in his memory, the older Shinobujin sitting on the stone floor surrounded by all manner of locks and picks, scattered metal bits and filings.

Back then, Ran had doubted his ability to ever pick a lock. Nakadai had first demanded to see his fingers.

"Show me what you have so I may know what I am working with."

Ran had splayed his fingers, and Nakadai took each in his hands, prodding and eventually nodding to himself. "They are sufficient." He had turned and picked up a padlock from the ground, before tossing it to Ran. "Open this lock."

"I don't know how," Ran had replied.

"You don't know how because you don't try to see how it works in the first place," Nakadai had scolded him.

"Before you can pick a lock, you must understand how all locks function. Once you know this, opening them becomes a simple matter. Even for the most complex mechanisms. There is no gray in this skill. A lock is either locked or open—never sort of open or sort of locked. You must learn as many locks as possible and store that information in your head for when you need it."

It had taken him years to absorb everything that Nakadai had to teach.

Ran held up the wire. The majority of it was still the long, slightly curved bit that he would fish out through the bars and down to the lock. But toward the end, the wire was bent into a series of peaks and valleys. "Time to test this out and see if it works."

Malkyr came over when he saw the wire. "Do you think that will really work?"

Ran frowned. "What do you care? I thought you were just going to sit here until Kan-Gul feeds your soul to his monster."

Malkyr shrugged. "I didn't know you actually had a plan for escape."

Ran sniffed. "I wouldn't call this any sort of plan. At this point, it's still very much a bad gamble."

Kancho grinned. "I'd rather gamble on you than wait for a certain death."

Malkyr nodded. "As would I."

"Very well," said Ran. "Then we will see if I've been able to remember my teachings." He smirked. "Or else our future does not look as enjoyable as I would hope."

He again checked the bars and the passageway as best he could. But he saw nothing and sensed nothing out there that might compromise him. He glanced back at Kancho. "I'll need you to stay by the bars here with me. Let me know if you see anyone coming, all right?"

Kancho nodded and moved to the door. "Good luck."

"Luck is exactly what we're going to need," said Ran. "But it's not the only thing that might get us out of here."

"I think you're clear," said Kancho after a moment.

Then Ran slid the wire out of the cell toward the lock.

CHAPTER FIFTEEN

Ran maneuvered the wire into the lock and felt the end of it bite into the pins. This was where it would get tricky. From his position, he could only exert so much pressure on the lock and trying to do it from an obtuse angle meant the wire might bend in the wrong way and not rake the pins properly. Ran took his time, just as he had been taught over the years, and kept working the wire back and forth, trying to find the optimal position for it to work.

He thought back to just before his final exams at the school—a series of missions that would stretch over three months. His lockpicking teacher, Nakadai, had taken him aside after Ran had failed a practice exercise designed to simulate sneaking through a castle. Ran had nearly breached the door but rushed the final step and dropped his pick. The sound echoed through the room, and Nakadai had called a halt to the exercise. "Just remember, picking a lock is a skill that is usually done under great haste, but you must act like you have all the time in the world when you do it. Otherwise, in your rush to do it quickly, you will fail to open the lock. This failure will lead to more delays and more anxiety on your part. So as tough as it is to do so, force yourself to slow down and do it right the first time."

Ran hadn't believed in the advice at the time. And one of the missions he was sent on involved picking several locks. Ran rushed through all of them and had to pick the lock several times to get it open. Each time, he swore that he would slow down and do it properly, but the stress of the assignment made him hurry. And inevitably, he made mistakes.

He felt the wire rake another pin, and put it into the proper position. A deft touch helped him feel the slightest push back from the pins. He would have liked to be able to hear a bit more of the clicking that was happening several feet away from him, but the sound was muffled by the thick door. Ran would have to settle for doing it by touch alone.

"How's it going?" Kancho's voice was quiet but anxious.

Ran didn't move his head, knowing that doing so might cause the wire to slip out of the lock, and he'd have to begin again. "Give me a few minutes, will you? I haven't done this in a long time."

"Sorry."

Ran grinned as another pin clicked into position. By his reckoning, there would only be a few more of them to rake. But then, as he pushed the wire deeper in, he felt it stop. Something was blocking the wire.

"Damn."

"What?"

Ran sighed. "I need to adjust the wire. It's not properly formed and ran into the side of the lock." He withdrew the wire, sank down to the floor to relieve the strain on his legs, and examined the tip. The lead portion was bent just a fractional increment away from where it should have been.

Kancho squatted beside him. "Are you going to be able to do this?"

Ran eyed him. "Like I said, it's been a while."

"We may not have much longer. Kan-Gul doesn't strike me as someone who has a great amount of patience."

"I agree," said Ran. "But rushing this is only going to screw things up. I've got to take my time and do it properly. It's extremely difficult working the lock from behind a closed door, standing up and unable to see or hear what's going on."

Kancho held up his hands. "Sorry. I know you are doing your best."

"Thanks." Ran finished bending the wire back into position. "There. This should work." He stood back up and checked the passageway again. "Ready?"

Kancho moved into position. "Do it."

Ran slid the wire back out of the cell and once again worked it into position. The tip scraped the outside of the lock, and Ran cursed himself for speeding up the process. He closed his eyes and took a deep breath, willed himself to slow way down, and then exhaled smoothly as he opened his eyes with renewed focus. "Here we go."

He felt the wire enter the lock. Keeping his breathing steady, Ran tried to avoid knocking any of the pins he'd already raked out of position. But the tip of the wire seemed to slide right past them and kept going until Ran could feel pushback. He was at the next pin. He let his mind reach out, trying to visualize how the interior of the lock would look. In his mind's eye, Ran could see the pins magnified and the tip of the wire nudging them out of the way ever so slightly. The pressure released, and he was past the first pin.

"One down."

Ran continued working on the lock, and with each new pin that he successfully raked, he increased the pressure just so to make his way deeper into the lock. The trickiest part would be after he was through all of the pins. He'd have to turn the locking mechanism using the wire. Ordinarily, he would have two tools for this purpose, but here he only had the one. If he'd been closer, he could have bent the wire in on itself and used both ends to do the work. But if he did that here, he never would have been able to reach the lock in the first place.

He felt the wire slip past another pin and nodded to himself. Almost there. He felt the pressure of the last pin and worked it into the proper position. Then he was through the lock.

Ran allowed himself a moment to take a deep breath. "I think I've got all the pins moved. Now I've got to turn the entire lock assembly without knocking any of them out of alignment."

"Is that difficult?" asked Kancho.

"Ordinarily? No. It would take but a second. But with only a flimsy piece of wire, it's going to take a bit of a miracle to get it done."

Kancho eyed him. "I think I speak for everyone when I say we have faith in your abilities."

Ran grinned. "Thanks. But save your praises until I get this done. Otherwise, you might find your faith misplaced."

Ran took another breath and reset his position. "Okay, let's get this done."

He withdrew the wire ever so slightly, until he felt he had it in the right position. Sticking his other arm out as much as he could through the bars, Ran tried to get the necessary position and then, when he had it, started twisting the wire within the lock. The bolt was heavy, and it took a lot of energy to make sure he kept a steady pressure on the wire.

A little bit more, he thought. *Just a bit more.*

Clunk.

Ran exhaled in a rush. Then he quickly withdrew the wire back through the bars and looked at Kancho. "We're through."

Kancho's face broke into a wide grin. "That might be the best thing I've heard since we ran aground."

"Agreed." Ran slumped down the wall next to the door and gave himself a few moments to rest after getting the lock picked. In the meantime, Kancho let the others know that the cell was now open. When he was done rousing them and keeping their excitement in check by insisting they stay quiet, he moved back to where Ran was.

"Are you all right?"

Ran nodded. "Just needed a moment."

Kancho eyed the door. "I think our first priority has to be getting our hands on weapons. Otherwise, any guards we meet will just hack us to pieces. And I don't fancy the notion of taking on those Chekhal without my blade."

"Nor I," said Ran. "But we don't have the slightest idea where Kan-Gul will have stowed our gear."

Kancho smiled. "Actually, I might be able to help in that regard."

"How so?"

"When they escorted us past the barracks, earlier, I saw a side room. Not sure what it was, but weapons are usually stored near barracks."

"Or it could be empty . . . or full of Chekhal warriors."

Kancho grinned. "I suppose it could. But it's worth a look."

Ran nodded and stood back up. "Let me go first and check it out."

Kancho's eyes narrowed. "Why you?"

"I can certainly move quietly alone than with the whole group."

Kancho didn't seem to buy it. "Is this another skill you were taught by your uncle the criminal?"

Ran shrugged. "Nah, I've always been comfortable skulking about in the shadows. Maybe that's what drew my uncle to me and made him attempt to corrupt me with his thievish ways."

He'd meant it as a joke, but the expression on Kancho's face told Ran that the older Murai wasn't deriving any mirth from the statement. Ran put a hand on Kancho's shoulder. "Just give me two minutes, and I'll be back."

"Fine."

Ran checked the passageway and then pushed the door of the cell open, praying it wouldn't squeak as he did so. But fortunately, the hinges seemed well-oiled and they didn't make a sound as the door opened. Ran exhaled and moved out into the corridor, closing the door behind him. He took a moment in the middle of the passage to acclimate his ears to the ambient noises that he could catalog. He sniffed the air but found nothing out of the ordinary. And there seemed to be no one around that might have presented a threat.

On deeply bent knees, Ran kept his back to the stone wall and his arms spread for balance and support, as well as for the sensory feedback they could provide. Using an ancient cross-stepping technique, he moved down the passageway, scanning with his eyes and making sure his feet didn't accidentally brush anything that would make noise and potentially alert the guards.

As he came abreast of the barracks room, the torches high up on the wall were barely generating any light whatsoever. But Ran didn't mind. He could see very well in the darkness. Moreover, the lack of light in the magic torches told him that his presence hadn't been detected yet. Had it been, they would have certainly flared into life.

Still, he'd have to be careful. The torches were like an early warning system. And Ran couldn't afford to have any alarms go off.

He moved to the opposite wall in one slow fluid motion, adhering himself to the stones and willing himself to remain calm and relaxed. He again paused, listening for anything that might cause him to suspect that he was in danger.

But he heard and sensed nothing.

Creeping farther into the barracks, he saw rows of beds but no Chekhal warriors sleeping in them. Ran frowned. Had it been an illusion as he'd suspected earlier? Was Kan-Gul trying to make them think there was more going on here than there was? The deeper Ran got into the barracks, the larger it became. Rows upon rows of beds were here, and they seemed to stretch on forever.

Ran paused. What was it that Kan-Gul had said earlier about the large army to the north? That they were coming to the fortress? He frowned. There was certainly plenty of room in the castle to accommodate them. And if Kan-Gul had the amount of magic at his disposal he believed he would with Jysal, then it was possible that this wasn't an illusion after all, but preparation for a coming invasion.

Not good, Ran decided. He needed to get word back to his superiors in Gakur about the potential invasion. It would probably be the first they'd heard of it. And if it was, then they would need to work their manipulations on the warlords in Nehon and convince them to band together to prepare for invasion.

Ran knew what that would mean: he'd be assigned to scout out the potential threat posed by the army to the north.

That meant there was an even greater reason for escaping from this place. He couldn't delay. As he moved through the barracks, he saw a small room to the left. Was this what Kancho had noticed? Ran was impressed. The room was barely noticeable, and he himself had failed to spot it earlier. But when Ran looked inside, he was extremely glad Kancho had seen it.

He was standing in an armory. There were racks filled with swords, including the two curved Nehon blades that belonged to Ran and Kancho. There were straight swords as well as other blades of types that Ran had never seen before. He wondered if this was where Kan-Gul stored all the weapons from the people he'd murdered. With a frown,

Ran realized the sheer number of weapons in the armory meant that Kan-Gul must have murdered hundreds, if not thousands, of people.

He took his sword and Kancho's back with him to the cell. Neviah, Jysal and Malkyr would have to wait until they got out to arm themselves. Ran couldn't risk carrying a bundle of blades back that might make noise or compromise his ability to stay undetected.

Back in the passageway, he moved as quickly as he could and returned to the cell. He handed Kancho's sword through the bars. Kancho's eyes lit up when he grasped his treasured weapon. Ran motioned for him to stay quiet and then pulled the door to the cell open.

Kancho came out and put his cupped hand over Ran's ear. "Was it an armory?"

Ran nodded. "We'll need to go back so Neviah and the others can get weapons, too. I couldn't take a chance on bringing back too much."

"Understood." Kancho moved back into the cell and explained the situation to the others. They nodded in agreement, and then Kancho looked at Ran.

With a nod, Ran waved them out into the passageway one at a time. Kancho came out first and went to one side so he could keep watch for the guards. As the others filed out, Ran positioned them near the stone wall and told them to stay still.

Malkyr was the last to hobble out of the cell. His leg was still causing him to limp. Ran frowned. An injury like that could compromise the entire escape. But he couldn't leave him behind. That wouldn't be right.

Slowly, the five of them moved down the passageway

toward the barracks. Ran led them inside one at a time, figuring it would better that way so they could minimize the chances of being spotted. He took Neviah in first. After briefly searching for her own weapons amid the piles of gear, she finally shrugged and then outfitted herself with a slim sword and several daggers that she tucked into her belt. She smiled at Ran and exited. Malkyr came next and chose a thicker straight sword. Jysal came last and chose three daggers that she dutifully tucked into her belted dress.

Back in the passageway, Ran eyed them all. They had weapons. They were out of the cell.

Now they needed to get out of the castle.

CHAPTER SIXTEEN

Ran took the lead and Kancho brought up the rear. Neviah came after him, then Jysal, then Malkyr. Ran figured this was the best way to maximize their fighting ability. He motioned Neviah over for a quick hushed chat. He realized he wasn't fully aware of her capabilities.

She squatted next to him while the others kept a lookout. "Yes?"

"Can you wield magic?"

She smiled. "Unfortunately, no. My job has always been to protect the sorcerers, not to actually cast spells. It's beyond my ken, frankly."

Ran nodded. "All right, I wanted to be sure before we moved out. It occurred to me I'd never asked."

She touched his arm. "Do not worry yourself about such things. You've already done more than any of us had a right to ask you to do."

"What—breaking us out? How could I leave you all behind?"

"Yes, the escape, but also the leadership you've shown.

You might try casting yourself as a wandering blade for hire, but I think there's more to you than meets the eye." She smiled. "But do not fear. If you have secrets that you wish kept, I will not say a thing."

"Thank you." Ran glanced around. "Now let's get moving." He stood and nodded to the others, and they got into position. He took a moment to say one last thing to them all. "I will scout ahead first." He looked at Neviah. "If I signal for you to stop, make sure you pass it down the line. I don't want anyone bumping into each other. Metal swords and daggers tend to make a lot of noise when that happens."

"That's the last thing we need," said Neviah. "I will keep watch for your cues, Ran."

"All right then, let's get moving." Ran resumed his place at the front and led them out of the barracks area and back down the passageway toward the staircase they'd used when the Chekhal initially brought Ran and Jysal to the cell. Ran slid his sword forward and across his front, put his back against the wall, signaled for Neviah to hold where she was, and then used the same cross-stepping technique he'd used previously to ascend the stairs with his back to the wall. In this way, Ran could see what was happening in both directions. With his hands outstretched again, he could easily feel for any problems before he bumped into them.

Keeping his breathing even, Ran climbed the steps. He allowed his focus to soften in the dim light and listened for any noises up ahead of him. As he did, something registered in his subconscious, and he froze.

Listening.

Smelling.

There. He heard a shift. It was a tiny sound, but it was out of the flow of other noises he'd become accustomed to. Someone or something was up ahead of him on the staircase.

But what?

Ran eased up another step. From his position on the winding staircase, he could see back down to Neviah and in the direction above him as well, but not enough to register what might be making the sound.

Rather than risk it, Ran descended again. As he came to Neviah, he removed his sword and gave it to her. "Hold this for me and give me one of your daggers."

"Why?"

"There's someone or something up there at the top of the staircase. I'll need to get a lot closer before I can determine what it is. My sword might scrape against the wall at the wrong time. I don't want to risk it."

Neviah took out one of her daggers and gave it to Ran. He tested what it took to pull it free of its scabbard and then tucked it away in his belt; he needed both hands free to negotiate the stairs. "I'll be back as soon as I see what the threat is. Pass it down the line quietly."

As she moved off, Ran began his slow, careful ascent of the steps again. As he moved, Ran eased his body forward in a rolling motion that brought his weight down evenly and never compromised his balance. If the steps had been wooden, they would have presented even more of a challenge because they might creak at the worst possible time. Ran had methods for dealing with that eventuality, but a big part of him was grateful the steps were made of stone. Wood took a lot longer to cross without making any noise.

But even though they weren't made of wood, Ran still needed to exercise the utmost care and focus now that he knew there was someone at the top of the stairs. He figured it might be a guard, stationed there in case of escape. But what if there were two of them? Taking them both out without anyone raising the alarm would prove nearly impossible.

Then there was the inevitable question of what it would take to kill a Chekhal warrior. Kan-Gul had mentioned they were reanimated dead warriors. But were they still vulnerable to attack in the same way that humans were? Ran had an idea of how he would attack, and felt fairly confident it would be enough, but he still had to keep his breathing under control, because the butterflies in his stomach were fluttering like mad.

Ran realized at that moment that it wasn't so much the idea of fighting that had him nervous. It was the thought that he might end up like Vargul if he wasn't careful. Ran had never formulated much of a belief system about the afterlife and the whims of the gods and goddesses. He was usually too focused on the real world and learning how to be a shadow warrior. But he liked to think there might be something after all of this.

If he was caught and his soul devoured, however, it wouldn't matter if there was an afterlife.

Failure, he decided, was simply not an option.

He paused again at the spot where he'd heard the sound a few minutes earlier. Waiting, Ran closed his eyes and opened his mouth to allow his ear canals to better grab at sounds floating in the air. And sure enough, he heard something again. This time it was a bit more substantial: the sound of metal scraping against the wall. Ran pictured the scene in his mind and saw a guard leaning back against the wall. He waited to see if there was any conversation and heard none. Then again, he cautioned himself, the only time he'd seen Chekhal talk was when they were addressing the prisoners. Ran had no idea if they spoke to themselves or shared some sort of hive communication.

He hoped they didn't have the ability to send their thoughts over distances. If that was the case, they would all be in a big heap of trouble.

Ran took another step up and stopped again, trying to see if he'd been detected. He was now out of sight of Neviah at the bottom of the stairs, but he was growing ever closer to the top of the staircase. Any moment now and he expected to be able to see the threat.

As such, he sank even lower, hugging the wall with his arms and keeping his knees deeply bent. Each cross-step brought him ever closer to the top. Then, as he rounded the next turn, he saw it.

A lone Chekhal warrior stood at the entrance of the stairway with his back to Ran but turned just enough so that if Ran wasn't careful, the Chekhal might notice movement in his peripheral vision. Ran watched to see if the Chekhal had any sort of pattern to his movement, but after ten minutes, he guessed the Chekhal would stand there until the end of time without much movement.

So be it.

Ran sank back down the staircase a few steps and moved to its inner wall. Then he reascended. In this way, he would come out at the top and be farther behind the sentry, hopefully more in his blind spot.

Ran sank as low as he possibly could and moved into position about ten feet behind the sentry. Looking around the body of the Chekhal, he tried to view the hall they had passed through before descending the stairs. Torches flickered and cast enough light to see across the room, but Ran saw no other guards. Perhaps Kan-Gul felt secure enough in his layout of the fortress that he didn't think he needed to put more guards around.

Satisfied that the guard was seemingly all alone, Ran shrank back and slowly pulled Neviah's dagger from its sheath. The blade was about eight inches long and single-edged, which meant he would have make sure he cut in the right direction. It would have to be quick and as quiet as he could manage.

Ran came up in one fluid motion, covering the distance between him and the sentry in the space of a mere second. He aimed the dagger at a spot just to left of the spinal cord at the base of the sentry's head and then stabbed straight in and cut to the right, severing the cord and brain stem in one single slash.

Dark, viscous blood dribbled all over him, but there was nothing he could do about that now. As Ran had made the cut, his other hand had come up under the Chekhal's left arm and across his chest to get better leverage for his cut while pulling the Chekhal back and down the staircase, using the shadows within to conceal the kill.

Surprisingly, the Chekhal immediately went limp. Ran let the body down as quietly as possible, making sure that his sword didn't bang into the floor. Then he raced back down the stairs and got Neviah to help him move the body down to the barracks, where he asked her to move one of the Chekhal's arms out to the side.

"What for?" she asked.

Ran unsheathed his sword. "I need something." And he made a quick cut, cleaving the Chekhal's hand off at the wrist. He grimaced, but scooped up the grisly trophy and stowed it in his tunic.

Neviah frowned at him. "I never figured you for being that sort of man."

"I'm not," said Ran. "You'll see when we get there." He shoved the rest of the Chekhal under one of the bunks. "Hopefully, by the time they notice he's missing, we'll be long gone."

Neviah had taken her dagger back. "I hope you're right."

"So do I," said Ran. They went back, and Ran led them up the staircase. At the top, he sniffed the air. The stench of blood was apparent, and there was a lot of it on the stone floor and parts of the steps. He frowned. Ordinarily, he might have tried for a bloodless kill by breaking the neck of a target. But given that the Chekhal were a different breed, he'd felt that severing the spinal cord was the only way to go. Apparently, he'd been right. But there was still evidence of the kill on the floor. And it was evidence he wished he could erase.

Speed now became essential. Once the guard was noticed missing, the alarms would no doubt sound. Kan-Gul would bring his full power to bear on them, and he doubted they'd have much of a chance at escape if that happened. But outside the fortress, with their wits about them and steel in their hands, there might be a better chance.

Provided they could make it out.

In his mind, Ran knew the route they would take. They would try to go out the same way they'd come in: through the secret entrance.

He sighed. Thinking about the situation he was in, Ran would have had a better chance of success if he left his companions behind. Duty dictated that he escape and get word back to the Nine Daggers about the potential invasion. And without any of the other travelers hindering his progress, Ran could escape and reach friendly territory much faster than he would otherwise. No doubt his old instructor Senno, who had taught all of them the principles of escape and evasion, would yell at him for dragging along the others.

Ran smirked. Senno would have suggested killing them all and then leaving. But that wasn't feasible. While Jysal and Malkyr would be easy enough to dispatch, Kancho and Neviah were another matter.

And then there was the fact that Ran didn't think he could simply kill them in cold blood. Even if it would be more merciful than leaving them to a fate Kan-Gul had in store for them.

Ran looked back at the column of escapees and nodded. It was time to go.

They moved quickly across the open area of the hall, and then beyond they passed through the throne room. At each point, Ran checked ahead to make sure they were not about to run into a horde of guards or Kan-Gul himself. But thus far they had seen little activity in the fortress.

Perhaps Kan-Gul was elsewhere? Ran had little doubt he could probably use all sorts of magic to make that happen. Still, it had been a while since the sorcerer had checked on them. At any moment he might decide to come see if they had made a decision. Ran didn't want to wait around for that to happen.

From the throne room, they moved back down the hallway and finally Ran felt his spirits lift when he saw the room ahead of them where he and Jysal had initially come into the fortress itself. He motioned for Neviah to wait and then stalked ahead, his feet barely brushing the floor as he did so. At the entrance to the room, he stopped. Then he sank down to the floor and eased his head around the entrance ever so slowly.

The sight that greeted him made his heart sink.

A dozen Chekhal warriors stood along the walls with their arms crossed over their chests. Ran watched them for several minutes, but he could detect nothing about their state of readiness. Were they awake or asleep? Or were they in some sort of suspended animation until Kan-Gul called upon them?

It was risky. If he assumed incorrectly, they would walk right into the sort of battle they were trying hard to avoid in the first place. But they couldn't stay here. Once the guard was found missing or Kan-Gul detected that his precious trophy had managed to escape, these Chekhal would probably be the first ones to respond. And they would blunder right into the escape party.

Ran licked his lips and slinked back to where the others waited. He motioned Kancho up to where he stood with Neviah.

"There are twelve Chekhal in the room. I don't know if they're awake or asleep or what. But they are in there. And the problem is, we can't stay here. Nor do I know the way to the main entrance."

Neviah shrugged. "I think this is our best bet anyway. Who knows how many more guards might be waiting by the main gate?"

Kancho nodded. "I agree with her. We're here already. We'll take them down hard and fast and then get out." He stared at Ran. "Are you sure you can get the door open?"

Ran patted his chest where the Chekhal hand was stowed. "I'm pretty sure I can."

"All right then," said Kancho. "We attack."

CHAPTER SEVENTEEN

Ran and Kancho considered the scene before them. With twelve Chekhal warriors, there would be enough action for everyone. But the task was to make sure they had the advantage for as long as possible. If the Chekhal were able to raise the alarm, there would be too many reinforcements to handle.

"We need to make this quick," said Ran quietly.

Kancho pointed. "I'll go in first and take out those two closest to the far wall. That will draw the attention of the others to me and enable you all to get behind them. And hopefully make quick work of them."

"That's a pretty big risk you're taking."

Kancho grinned. "Just don't be late. As soon as I launch the attack, be on my heels and get killing."

"I will."

Ran relayed the commands back to Neviah and Jysal. He didn't waste time trying to fill Malkyr in on the attack. With his wounded leg, Malkyr was more of a liability than an asset. Ran motioned for him to stay well back. Malkyr only shrugged and then nodded.

"We're ready."

Kancho eased his curved blade out of its scabbard and smiled once at the honed edge. Ran knew the feeling. Kancho was appreciating the fact that he had a weapon worthy of battle in his hands. While Ran wasn't Murai, he nevertheless appreciated the craftsmanship of the blade he wielded. It had seen him through some truly harrowing encounters.

"You can count on a sword," said Ran.

"And it will never betray you," said Kancho. "I have seen the deaths of many men at the edge of this blade. I'm grateful for its service. Sometimes I think I have no right to ask any more of it than I already have. But here once more we enter into the fray like two old friends. Blessed be its existence, for without it, I would be half the warrior I am when I hold it."

Ran gave him the moment. After a few seconds, Kancho took a deep breath to flush himself with fresh oxygen. Then he stood and eyed Ran.

"Remember: as soon as I hit them."

"Done."

Kancho took another breath, and Ran saw his face change into a grim mask. Then he charged into the room, his sword already swinging at the head of the closest Chekhal warrior.

Ran came in quickly behind him.

As expected, the instant Kancho entered the room, all of the Chekhal turned to face him, but Kancho was moving so fast that he was already past most of them before they had a chance to register the attack and attempt a defense. The first two Chekhal on the far wall fell to Kancho's blade

kick slam into him from his side. He fell to one side, aware that the last Chekhal was coming toward him with its sword raised overhead. Ran had one chance. He rolled toward the Chekhal as the sword arced down at where his body had been a moment before.

Instead of cutting Ran open, the sword bounced off the stone floor with a tremendous clang. Ran brought his sword up and plunged it deep into the bowels of the Chekhal. There was an awful stench, and Ran bit back the flood of bile in his throat. He jerked his sword loose and then came up, cutting horizontally and severing the head of the last Chekhal.

With a final gasp, the Chekhal fell forward on its face and was still.

The air buzzed around them. Ran surveyed the scene. The entire battle had taken perhaps a single minute. It had seemed at once incredibly slow and lightning fast. Ran could feel his heart thundering in his chest and willed himself to calm down. He flushed himself with more oxygen and looked at Kancho. The older warrior was sucking down gulps of air. He smiled at Ran.

"Well, that was something."

Neviah was retrieving her dagger and wore a tight grin on her face. "I needed that."

Ran knew the feeling. He'd been wanting to battle these guys since they'd been taken into the castle. And it felt good to at least partially avenge Vargul's death. It would've felt better, Ran decided, if they had killed Kan-Gul.

But they needed to escape.

Kancho came over. "Everyone all right?"

Ran glanced around. Malkyr had entered the room and looked amazed at the scene before him. Perhaps he'd never witnessed such carnage before or maybe he'd never seen death dealt with such speed and skill as what Ran, Kancho, and Neviah had managed. Either way, Ran could see he was impressed.

"Remind me never to upset you lot."

Neviah grinned. "We will."

"Much as I'd like to take a moment and rest," said Ran, "there's no time. I fully expect this encounter will soon be felt all over the castle. And Kan-Gul will send his legions after us."

"You have the key to get us out of here?" asked Kancho.

"Indeed," said Ran. He reached into his tunic and brought out the dismembered Chekhal hand. "I think this is how they enter and exit as they please." He walked to the farthest wall, careful to avoid the widening pools of gore that sopped the floor. It wasn't blood, per se, but rather some other liquid that looked every bit as foul as it smelled. Once at the wall, Ran held the hand up before it and then touched its dead flesh to the surface.

There was a single clicking sound, and then the entire wall started to move. First it slid in toward Ran and then to the left. Then he felt a rush of cool air on his face and knew they'd managed to breach the castle.

His relief was short-lived, however, as in the next instant, a shrieking wail arose within the castle. Ran winced and looked at Kancho. "So much for us leaving unnoticed."

Kancho smirked. "We knew they'd find out eventually. Let's get out of here."

Ran dropped the Chekhal hand and looked back, ushering Malkyr, Jysal, and then Neviah out of the castle. Ran took a final glance around and then stepped outside for the first time in nearly a full day.

The night greeted him like an old friend. While he would have preferred daylight for ease of movement and speed, Ran appreciated the fact that the night would potentially enable him to use the darkness to his advantage. He could lead them nearly as well as if the sun were high in the sky. He had no idea what the capabilities of the Chekhal were and how they operated, but he was willing to guess the darkness might be something of an equalizer for them as they made their escape.

At least he hoped it would be.

Jysal tugged on his sleeve as they made their way out across the barren plain in front of the castle.

"Are you all right?"

She nodded. "Fine, thanks to you and Neviah. But I wanted to remind you of something."

"What?"

"The Chekhal won't be the only dangers we face out here. There are still those doglike things prowling the countryside. And you can bet that Kan-Gul will exert his influence over them. They'll probably pick up our trail without much effort."

Ran frowned. He had indeed forgotten about the dogs. Their presence would no doubt complicate things, perhaps fatally so. But they couldn't wait here. Already sounds of war cries echoed off of the castle walls behind them. Kan-Gul would not like losing his prized possession. And he would spare no effort to haul them back inside and put them to death in ways probably more terrible than what had befallen Vargul.

"Press on," said Ran. "We will deal with those creatures if it comes to it. There's no sense worrying about them now."

Kancho stood back as Ran passed by him. "I think it's probably best if you lead us."

"Why?"

Kancho grinned. "You are more likely to be comfortable stealing through the night than I am. My skills are on the battlefield and are therefore limited. You don't seem so encumbered."

Ran wondered if Kancho had realized what sort of warrior Ran was, but there was no time to ask. He only nodded. "Very well, stay close. The woods are likely full of dangers other than the Chekhal we left behind."

Ran led them across the plain and then spotted the trees that had led them here. He knew the game trail would be there and they plunged into the woods on the other side of the plain. Ran sniffed the pines as they entered and felt a measure of security wash over him. It reminded him of the game trails he'd snuck down back in the mountains of Gakur and the concealment offered by the boughs made him feel safer than on the open plain.

He chose his steps carefully, his eyes scanning left to right, using his peripheral vision to see instead of staring directly at something where his eyes would not function best in the low light conditions. His nostrils flared as he moved the group off at a brisk pace. And his ears took in every sound.

They descended into the forest proper, where Ran and

Jysal had first seen the dog creatures. But the woods seemed as empty of life as they had on their arrival. Perhaps the creatures were sleeping? Or perhaps Kan-Gul hadn't unleashed them yet? Part of Ran wondered if they might have been another illusion, but then he remembered that he had slain one of them. That kill had been real enough.

Behind him, Ran could hear the footfalls of his party. Kancho walked as quietly as he could, but Malkyr was making a tremendous amount of noise. Ran called a halt to their march and moved back. Malkyr's face was streaked with sweat. He looked up as Ran approached.

"Sorry. I'm trying my best to be quiet."

"Try harder," said Ran. "You're making so much noise that every creature in these misbegotten woods will have no trouble tracking us."

"What's the point? Where are we going to go? Back to the beach? Then what? Kan-Gul will just send his minions to deal with us. Or that accursed fog. Sooner or later, we will end up back in his clutches. We should just give him the girl and be done with it."

Ran never saw Neviah creep up behind Malkyr, but the edge of her blade gleamed once in the night air as it came to rest on Malkyr's throat. "I will tolerate no discussion of us surrendering to Kan-Gul or giving him my charge. That is not up for debate."

Malkyr's eyes looked completely white as he struggled to clear his throat. "I only meant that our options might improve if we considered all eventualities."

"Do you remember what you said back in the castle?" asked Neviah.

"N-no."

"'Remind me never to upset you.' Well, you're upsetting me now. I strongly suggest you shut your mouth, do as Ran says and be quiet, or else I will dispose of you for the creatures in this forest to consume at their leisure. Do you understand?"

Malkyr's head nodded ever so slowly as Neviah's blade rested against it. She waited one more second and then pulled her blade away. She nodded at Ran. "I believe we are ready to continue."

Ran returned the nod. "All right then. Remember what I said: speed and stealth are essential. We know Kan-Gul will be after us, so we need to make sure we are prepared for the coming attack as best we can."

He turned and looked out into the night. Somewhere out there, Kan-Gul's forces were preparing to marshal against them. The question was, where was the best place to defend themselves?

Chapter Eighteen

Ran recalled a lesson in strategy from one of his teachers back in Gakur. The elderly man they called Taba was a veteran of countless campaigns and in his heyday had been a seasoned agent for the Nine Daggers clan. In his advanced years, he puttered around the sprawling compound and seemed content to spend his days sipping rice wine and marveling at the progress of the seasons. Underneath his nonchalance, though, lurked a keen mind unfettered by the assault of time.

"When one is being chased—be it figuratively or literally—you have but two options: go where the enemy expects you to go, or go where they least expect you to go."

"But one choice is better than the other," Ran had insisted.

The older man had only smiled. "Is it? Which is the better?"

"To go where they least expect you. In that way, you may surprise them."

"Perhaps, but while it does gain you the element of

surprise, it does not gain you the opportunity to use their assumption of superiority against them."

"I don't understand."

The older man had taken a sip of rice wine before continuing. "Picture it this way: if I am chasing you and you go where I least expect it, I will pursue you with all my senses alerted to the possibility of ambush. I will move slowly and you will then be worn down by the wait."

"But . . . ?"

"But if you go where I expect you to go, then I proceed with a certain degree of confidence that you are now in my trap. As a result, my awareness is less and your chance of surprising me grows even greater. Both options therefore have their own unique strengths and weaknesses."

"And how will I know which is the better choice?"

"You will only know that when you are in the situation itself. Even then perhaps you will not know for certain if you are choosing correctly. But as we have talked about already, indecision is the cause of more death than is making a choice and following it through."

As the night air made his skin prickle, Ran smirked. Far easier to espouse such things in the comfort and security of the compound in Gakur than out in the real world. Still, the lesson on indecision was certainly easier to understand. Ran considered his choices. They could proceed back to the beach. Once there, they would be hemmed in with their backs to the ocean full of marauding sharks and other possible dangers. They would have limited mobility in the sand and limited room with which to operate and maneuver. But those same limitations would also affect their enemy.

The other choice would be to go off the path and enter unknown terrain. They might well find themselves a better place to make a defensive stand against Kan-Gul's hordes. They might be able to escape. Or they might well find themselves in an even worse place than before.

"Why have you stopped?"

Kancho's voice jerked Ran out of his mind and back to reality. "Sorry, just considering our options."

"Stop considering and make a decision. Already, the woods behind us are filling up with movement and noise. The longer we stay here, the more danger we will face—regardless of your decision."

Ran nodded. "You're right, of course. Forgive me."

Kancho gave a curt bow. "Lead us out of here, Ran. You know how to do it better than any of us."

Ran took a final glance at the game trail in front of him. Staying on it would bring them back to the beach. Veering off would take them into the unknown. Ran took a breath, closed his eyes, and let his gut guide him.

He stepped off of the game trail and into the deeper forest. The party stayed with him, and they soon found themselves in a shallow valley hemmed in by trees on all sides. Ran led them up the slope on the other side, passing through tall dead grass that brushed against their exposed skin like the coarsest wood. But Ran pressed them on, increasing his speed. He wanted to be as far away from the Chekhal as possible when they chose the location for their defensive stand.

There was also the chance that they could get far enough away to escape Kan-Gul's borders. Ran had no idea if he manned those borders with more Chekhal, but if they could get that far, then they might stand a chance. They might even find some friendly forces that would align with them against Kan-Gul.

Maybe.

Such things were off in the future, and Ran couldn't waste time and energy on them. He needed to safeguard his party. And so they kept climbing the steep slope.

Malkyr dragged on them with his injury, however. Ran glanced back and saw the captain dragging his bad leg. Behind him, the tall grass was already smashed down in places where Malkyr had passed. Ran frowned. He was leaving far too much sign that they'd gone this way. Even if the Chekhal were undead, they would be able to see the clear trail left in Malkyr's wake.

It was unacceptable.

Ran called a stop and switched the order of march. Malkyr looked concerned. "Why are you switching things around?"

"Because you may as well send a messenger back to tell our enemies which direction we're traveling. Your injured leg is compacting all the grass around you, and that leaves a very telltale sign of our passage through this area. We can't have that."

Malkyr frowned. "There's nothing I can do about it. My leg is throbbing with pain."

Ran nodded and looked at Neviah. "Can I ask you to bring up the rear from now on?"

Neviah frowned, and Ran knew she was hesitant about not staying next to Jysal. He held up his hand. "It's just for a little while. As we travel, I'd ask that you occasionally reach back into the grass and tuft it like this." Ran showed her the action that would spring the stalks back up rather than leave them compressed. "It should help mask our presence."

Neviah sighed. "All right. But if he continues to be a problem, I have a better suggestion on how to correct his behavior."

"I'm sure you do," said Ran. Ran had to admit it was a valid suggestion—one which would've met with approval by several of his former teachers. But just as he rejected turning Jysal over to Kan-Gul, he didn't want to sacrifice Malkyr. "For now, we're all in this together."

He turned back, and they continued up the slope. At the crest of the hill before them, Ran paused and looked back. Neviah was doing her part admirably, stopping every few steps and ensuring the grass behind her looked as undisturbed as possible. Ran realized that she knew the exact technique for doing it and hadn't needed him to show her at all. He made a note to ask her where she'd learned the technique. Apparently, Shinobujin weren't the only ones trained in such matters.

A stiff breeze blew in from the southwest, and Ran tasted the brine on it. They were still reasonably close to the coast, despite the fact they traveled in a northeasterly direction. He would have to make sure of their direction of travel or run the risk of walking around in circles. People tended to favor one foot over the other, and, left alone without landmarks, they would invariably eventually circle around on themselves. Such a thing would be disastrous to them at this point, with the Chekhal on their heels.

A rustle in the trees to his right made Ran turn around and sink down, eyes scanning the underbrush. No movement caught his eye, but a quick sniff of the air told him there was something else out there with them in the dark. Was it a lone Chekhal? Or one of those dog creatures?

Kancho came up next to him. "What is it?"

Ran pointed off in the distance. "There's something else out here with us. I don't know what it is, but it's close."

Kancho eased his sword out and squatted down, crossing in front of Ran. He entered a dense copse of trees and Ran heard a single slash of his blade. Two minutes after, Kancho reemerged with his sword resheathed.

"Some type of ground bird, with wings like I've never seen before."

"Did it attack you?"

Kancho shook his head. "No, but it meant to take flight and I figured it was better to not have it flying around. It might well have alerted Kan-Gul as to our presence."

"Fair enough," said Ran. "Let's keep moving."

Overhead, the sky showed no moon, and the darkness was nearly absolute. But using his peripheral vision and years of training Ran was able to discern a route across the terrain. Their journey took them through more valleys and atop more ridges. The height of the trees grew shorter with each valley they passed, and Ran realized they were entering more mountainous country now.

Behind him, Malkyr had started complaining about the travel. "We've had no rest in ages. How are we supposed to keep up this pace?"

Kancho frowned and nodded at Ran. "He is holding us back. Even the young girl moves without complaint."

"Malkyr is obviously unused to this type of thing. He is at home on the sea but a mess on land."

"Rather the opposite of you," said Kancho with a smirk.

"You'll get no argument from me there," said Ran. "I suppose we should take a quick break." He drew them up to a large cypress tree and waved them all in. "We can't risk a fire, but take a few minutes to sort yourselves out. I wish I had food and drink to offer, but all I can give you is time to rest."

"It's more than enough," said Jysal as she collapsed and leaned her back against the trunk of the tree. "I felt certain my legs were going to fall off."

"You've acquitted yourself well," said Neviah to her younger charge. "And it speaks volumes about you that you didn't waste your breath complaining about the trip thus far."

Malkyr dragged himself under the canopy of the tree. "Bah, say what you want about me, but at least I speak the truth. This is a waste of time. Kan-Gul will find us easily enough. It doesn't matter if we've taken another route. His magic is too strong for us to overcome."

"You say that with a certain amount of confidence," said Ran. "How would you know how powerful he is?"

Malkyr shook his head. "What—you didn't see what I saw him do to Vargul back at his castle? Surely that was enough to convince you of his power."

Ran shrugged. "Most men in this world have power of some type or another. But they aren't invulnerable—even a sorcerer like Kan-Gul. As much as he appears to be unbeatable, he no doubt has his own weaknesses. All we need to do is find out what they are and exploit them."

Malkyr waved his hand. "As if it's that easy. You're a fool if you think you can deal with him."

"I never said I thought I could deal with him, but together, we might just have a chance."

"Save your breath," said Kancho. "Malkyr has obviously decided that his fate has been predetermined already."

"And haven't you?" asked Malkyr. "Kan-Gul knows these lands too well. And no matter what we might try to do to him, he will no doubt find us and inflict a horrible death upon us all. Except perhaps for Jysal. She can use her physical charms to ensure that she at least has the hope of some sort of afterlife. The rest of us are doomed."

A dagger embedded itself in the trunk next to Malkyr's head and quivered for a moment before coming to a complete stop. Malkyr nearly jumped out of his skin. "Wha—?"

Neviah's face appeared in the darkness. "I'm tired of listening to your stupid talk. You need to shut your mouth and remember that there are five of us here. And we are all relying on each other to get through this. If you don't think you can do that, then tell me now and I'll cut your throat and leave you here. I can make it quick and painless. You won't even know it's coming."

Malkyr eyed her and then turned to Ran. "She wants to kill me."

"She's not the only one," said Ran. "You need to either accept that we aren't simply going to give up, or you can go off on your own and take your chances without us. Either way makes no difference to me. But if you stay here, you're going to keep your mouth closed. I'm tired of listening to you bemoan our fate before we've even had a chance to write it."

Malkyr shook his head. "You're all living in denial."

"Perhaps," said Neviah. "But I'd rather live there than dwell in the pessimism of your world. Remember what Ran said to you, because I won't give you another warning."

Ran took a breath and looked at Jysal. She was watching him carefully. She smiled once and then closed her eyes completely. Ran yawned. He would have loved to spend the next few days sound asleep. But they needed to keep moving.

"All right, let's get moving again."

"Already?" But Malkyr said little else when he saw the look Neviah was giving him. Instead of continuing to complain, he got to his feet and leaned against the tree trunk. "Very well, then. Let's see where we can go."

Ran held his hand out to Jysal. When she put her hand in his, Ran was surprised at how warm it felt. It was like Jysal had untouched energy coursing through her very veins.

"Thank you," said Jysal as she got to her feet.

Ran nodded and then let go of her hand quickly before Neviah had a chance to plunge a dagger into his chest. Kancho led them out of the canopy and looked overhead.

"There are no stars in the sky."

"It doesn't matter," said Ran. "We must keep moving. Eventually, we will exit from Kan-Gul's lands and find ourselves elsewhere. A man's power can only extend for so far. Kan-Gul can not have limitless resources."

"I hope you're right," said Neviah. "I would hate it if that blundering oaf behind us actually manages to be right about something."

CHAPTER NINETEEN

They continued for another half mile before Ran felt something in the air. At first, he wasn't sure if it was just his mind playing tricks on him or if it was, in fact, real. But then he heard a terrible screech from somewhere behind them and felt the air move with an almost throbbing sensation. As if the very fabric of night itself were being beaten.

Ran turned and saw a vague dark shape flit across the expanse of sky overhead. But given the night was already so dark, he was unable to get a clear picture of what was flying above them. He felt Kancho's presence next to him.

"What is it?"

Ran shook his head. "I have no clue. But it seems fairly large. And its wings are clearly capable of producing a tremendous amount of wind."

Kancho frowned. "Is it possible that the bird I slew earlier in the trees was its offspring?"

Ran eyed him. The realization had also occurred to him, although he wasn't keen to share it until Kancho had made the statement. "Anything in this land seems possible.

But if it is indeed the parent of what you slew, then odds are good that it will seek justice for what you did. I expect it will attack us before too long."

Kancho looked around in the dim starlight. "There is sparse cover nearby."

Ran saw that he was right. They were currently atop a hill and the ground leading down into the closest valley was threadbare with more dead grass and little else. If this creature meant to attack them, then they would probably be better off here, where they could at least fight it on solid footing instead of being picked apart farther down in the valley.

Another screech filled the air as the beast flew overhead creating a wind that nearly took Ran off his feet. Kancho held on to him, and Ran shook his head. "That's one large creature."

Neviah drew Jysal close to her. "How have we angered this beast? What does it want with us? Does it serve Kan-Gul?"

"It's irrelevant now. The thing seems intent on attacking." He eyed Jysal. "Is it possible for you to use magic against it?"

Neviah looked horrified. "She is not supposed to use magic at all before she has had a chance to be properly trained."

"We need every asset we can muster here," said Ran. "If Jysal has any ability at all, then now would be a good time for her to use it."

Neviah looked at Jysal. "I forbid its use. You know the consequences of attempting any sort of invocation without the proper training."

Jysal nodded and looked down. "I'm sorry, Ran. Neviah is right. If I try and fail, I could end up killing myself."

Ran frowned. Jysal hadn't mentioned that before when it had been just the two of them. Was it really possible for her to jeopardize her life using magic? Ever since Kan-Gul had cast his spell on her, Ran could sense the energy swirling about her. Surely it was powerful stuff. And they could definitely use her power.

But another screech jerked him back to the present as the creature screamed overhead again.

Then Ran heard another screech.

An echo?

"No."

Kancho's voice was quiet, but Ran knew what he meant. There was another beast in the air.

"What are these things?" There was no mistaking the fear in Malkyr's voice as he spoke. The dark of night worked against them, concealing the creatures. They were effectively blind against them.

Ran heard another screech.

Three.

"There are three now," he heard himself say to no one in particular. None of them was armed with a projectile weapon. No arrows, no spears, no nothing that could be fired at the targets. If these creatures attacked, it would be down to close combat with swords. Ran wasn't sure he fancied the idea of engaging the giant claws of whatever sort of beast this was.

He ducked instinctively as one of the creatures screamed in and beat the air with its wings. Ran felt the raking talons barely miss his back as he dropped to the ground. With a single breath, he ripped his sword free and cut up at the creature as it flew past. His sword cut only empty air.

Kancho helped him up. "Maybe this is the wrong place to be."

"What do you mean?"

Kancho pointed down toward the valley. "If we get lower into the bowl of the valley, they will have no choice but to enter it if they wish to fight. If we stay here, they can pick us off by dropping down out of the sky. Down there, we can fight them with our backs to the downward slope. It's a bit more secure."

"Not by much."

"Do we have a choice?"

Ran shook his head. "Everyone head for the valley."

The air filled with more screeches and screams now. The party ran for the valley. Malkyr tripped twice, and each time one of the creatures barely missed plucking him from the ground. "Don't leave me!"

Kancho ran back to help him and dragged him farther down the valley. Ran's peripheral vision caught movement streaking toward him from the right side. He spun and cut up with his sword. This time, he felt the edge of his blade cut deep into flesh. A horrible shriek filled the air, and he felt a torrent of liquid fall on him, its odor distinct and foul.

The creature flew off, and Ran had no inkling of how badly he might have injured it. Although he felt certain that he had managed to at least wound the beast. Was it a mortal injury, however? Or was it merely enough to enrage the beast further?

He didn't want to stick around to find out. As much as

Ran would have preferred holding his ground and fighting the beasts, there seemed little point in doing so. Reason was important, and fighting an airborne creature in the pitch dark seemed foolish to Ran. He knew Kancho agreed. As much as the Murai might never dream of running from a foe, surely this was a good example of being smart in battle.

The party stumbled down the slope, harassed by the creatures as they flew in again and again. Each time they made a strafing run, Ran felt certain one of them would feel the bite of talons entering their skin and then the sensation of being plucked from the ground. Briefly, he wondered if these were the very things that had kidnapped everyone from the beach when they'd first arrived.

There was no way to tell, however.

Ran saw another dark shape zip past overhead aimed right at where Kancho stood. There was a flurry of movement he couldn't see, and then he heard another shriek. He ran over to where Kancho stood and found the older warrior down on one knee, his sword hanging from his other hand.

"Are you all right?"

Kancho brought his hand away from his shoulder. It was dark with blood, and Ran could smell the copper on the air. Kancho frowned. "It must have managed to rake its claws across my back as I cut at it."

"Did you wound it?"

"I might have. It certainly seems to have gotten me."

Neviah came over and tried to look at the wound, but shook her head. "I can't see a thing. If I'm to properly treat his injuries, we need to find some place where we can make some sort of light. Otherwise, this might be a mortal wound and I'm powerless to stop it."

Ran glanced around. The slope continued down to the valley floor. There was little down there but a copse of trees at the base of the slope. Still, it might offer them some degree of shelter if they could reach it in time. He pointed. "Aim for the trees down there. If we can reach them, we should be safer than we are right now."

Neviah looked at Jysal. "Go. Run like the hounds of hell are on your heels, for surely they are."

Jysal took off, and Ran watched her zip down the slope. The creatures that flew overhead tried twice to attack her as she ran, but each time, she seemed to blink in and out of Ran's vision. Had she actually vanished? Or was it merely the darkness playing tricks on his eyesight? He'd worked in the night often enough to understand the illusions that darkness could play on a man.

He glanced at Malkyr. "You're next."

"Me? I'll never get halfway down there before those things grab me up and feast on my innards."

"Stay here then," said Ran. "I'm tired of dealing with you." He and Neviah grabbed Kancho up under his armpits and hauled him to his feet. Together they stumbled down the slope. Kancho's head was already lolling from side to side as they moved farther into the valley.

Ran heard the screeching of the beasts overhead and tried to see where they were in the sky. But he couldn't pinpoint them and decided that it was better to keep focused on getting Kancho downhill than waste energy on spotting the beasts.

Malkyr lumbered past them at one point, and as soon

as he was twenty feet ahead of them a creature flew in sideways. Malkyr screamed and dropped to the ground. Ran saw a massive gaping maw open and close on the space Malkyr had occupied a moment previously. Then he heard the beast screech in frustration as it beat its wings and took off again.

Neviah eyed Ran. "It's huge."

Ran shook his head. "Never seen anything like it before."

"D-dragons," said Kancho quietly. "Dark as night."

Ran frowned. He'd heard rumors and legends of dragons before, too, but while the world certainly had an extraordinary number of foul creatures, he had yet to see an actual dragon. Still, he didn't discount the possibility. But if Kancho had killed a baby dragon, then there was no way the parents would tolerate it. Suddenly the copse of trees they were aiming for looked pitifully small and weak.

They had little choice.

Ran wondered about the eyesight of the beasts. They had made repeated attacks, and yet, each time, they had failed to kill any of the party. Kancho had been wounded, but it could have been far worse than it was. Ran thanked a number of gods and goddesses and hoped that their luck would somehow be able to hold until they reached safety.

Malkyr had picked himself up and continued to tumble down the slope toward the trees. Neviah grunted under the weight of Kancho's body, and Ran struggled to keep his end up. "Kancho?"

He got no response from the older warrior. "How bad do you think it is?" he asked Neviah.

"I have no idea of how bad it might be, and I won't

until I can examine him without being harassed by the likes of these beasts. Let us hope those trees offer more than shade."

Ran and Neviah had to duck three more times as they stumbled down the slope. The beasts—dragons, or whatever they were—continued to plague them the entire way. Ran saw Malkyr finally manage to disappear into the trees and almost grinned. Then they were forced to drop to the ground as another aerial assault lashed by overhead.

"Come on," said Ran. "We're nearly there."

Neviah nodded, and they got Kancho up and moving. Their steps became clumsy, and they nearly fell again. The copse of trees was but twenty yards from them. They were so close.

Another screech filled the air, and this time when Ran looked up, he saw what looked like a blanket of absolute darkness descending for them fast.

And then he saw a bolt of brilliant blue energy shoot in from somewhere ahead of him. It struck the creature, illuminating it for a split second and causing the creature to flip over and fly away. But Ran had seen enough of it to know how huge it actually was. If this was a dragon, he decided, then he never wanted to see one again.

They tumbled into the trees and saw Jysal standing there, a faint glow still surrounding her hands. Neviah let Kancho droop to the floor. "I told you no magic!"

Jysal shook her head. "If I hadn't done something, that thing would have killed all three of you. And then where would I be? This clod can't protect me," she said, nodding at Malkyr, who huddled near a tree trunk. "Only you can."

Neviah sighed. "Very well, but no more magic."

"Fine."

Ran looked down at Kancho. The older man was unconscious. Ran tried patting him on the back to wake him up, but it did no good. He looked up at Neviah. "Tell me what you need to make him better."

Neviah frowned. "I need light. That's the most important thing."

From outside the copse of trees, a huge breeze blew in and rustled the limbs like a hurricane. "Something tells me those things aren't exactly happy we're in here," said Malkyr.

Ran glanced around. The trees abutted the edge of the slope, and he made his way over to them. If he could find a bit of kindling, they might be able to make a fire, and hopefully that would be enough for Neviah to see how bad Kancho's wound was.

He felt around the base of the slope, finding nothing but loose rocks. Then he stuck his hand into an opening.

And kept going.

He pitched forward into deeper darkness and nearly lost his footing. Had Neviah not grabbed at his arm, Ran would have fallen all the way in. Neviah hauled him back and frowned. "What is that?"

Ran felt around the opening and then nearly grinned in spite of the danger that surrounded them all. "I think it's a cave."

"Are you sure?"

"No, I'm not. But it seems to be large enough to permit access to it. And I think our chances are better inside than if we stay out here. There's no telling how long those things will wait before they decide to rip these trees apart."

Neviah looked at Jysal, who only nodded. Neviah turned back to Ran. "Lead, we'll follow."

"All right," said Ran. "Let's gather up Kancho and see where this will take us. If nothing else, it might offer a chance to light a fire away from seeking eyes."

"Good," said Neviah. "Then perhaps I can help Kancho before it's too late."

CHAPTER TWENTY

Ran led the way into the small cave, helping Neviah carry Kancho in next. Jysal came after, followed by Malkyr.

"This is what we left the outside world for?" Malkyr's voice came out of the darkness.

"You could always go back," said Neviah.

Malkyr replied. "I'm the only one here speaking the truth about our situation. The rest of you are choosing to believe in some fantasy escape that will never happen."

Ran shrugged mostly to himself, since they couldn't see each other in the blackness of the cave. "So, if that's true, you should be all the more willing to step back outside and take your chances with those beasts. I'm sure they'll be very open to discussing things with you right before they devour you."

Neviah said. "I need a light if I'm to help Kancho."

"I'll get a fire started," said Ran. He managed to find a bit of dry wood by the entrance where some starlight filtered in. He removed a handful of lining from inside his tunic and rubbed it until the small strands came apart and produced a fluffier mixture. Then he found a small stone and struck the end of his sword pommel against it, producing a spark that he aimed into the fluffy bundle. It caught, and Ran held it under the dry wood until it started to smoke and then burst into flame.

Malkyr coughed. "Wonderful. Now we'll all die from breathing smoke. Brilliant."

Ran eyed him. "I'm almost ready to suggest that Neviah kill you so we can be done with listening to your incessant complaints. Kindly shut your mouth."

"Or leave," said Jysal. "We would welcome the peace."

"Maybe I should leave," said Malkyr. "But you'd soon miss me."

"I doubt that very much," said Ran. "But you're welcome to test that theory." He walked over to where Neviah was still bent over Kancho and held out a flaming bit of wood. The flames cast dancing shadows all along the walls of the cave. "How is he?"

"Still unconscious," said Neviah. "Which, given the quality of conversation, might just be something of a blessing."

Ran grinned in spite of their situation. He liked Neviah and her sense of duty. She had a keen sense of humor as well. He peered closer and saw the blackened edges around Kancho's wound. "What is the cause of that?"

Neviah shook her head. "I don't know. It looks like infection has already set in."

"But he was only wounded a few minutes ago. It can't be infected already, can it?"

"I'm at a loss," said Neviah. "I've never seen infection set in this quickly. I can try to treat it with some of my herbs, but there's no guarantee that any of it will work. It might all be for nothing."

"Do your best," said Ran. "That's all Kancho would ever ask of you."

"All right."

Ran left her to it and moved closer to Malkyr. "You and I are going to have a talk. And it goes like this: shut up."

"I don't take orders from the likes of you," said Malkyr. "You're too young to give me commands."

"Would you prefer to fight me over it?"

Malkyr frowned. "Time was, I would have gladly beaten the snot out of you. I knew how to fight, growing up on the docks the way I did."

"Time was you were a lot younger," said Ran. "Time is you're nothing but an overinflated blowhard. And you'd be out of your depth trying to take me. There are two paths before you: One is that you keep yammering on and eventually one of us gets so exhausted by your countless outbursts that we shut you up. Permanently. The other is that you keep quiet and do what we tell you to do. Hopefully we all get out of this mess alive."

"Or I could leave," said Malkyr.

"You could leave," said Ran. He gestured to the opening of the cave. "And you're welcome to do so."

Malkyr eyed him and then took a few steps toward the opening. As he did so, there erupted a ear-piercing shriek from outside and then a thunderous explosion as something slammed into the side of the hill they were in. All around them, rocks tumbled loose from the cave ceiling and crashed down. A huge cloud of dust issued up from the floor of the cave, and they all coughed violently.

When the dust cleared, the entrance to the cave was blocked by boulders and debris.

Malkyr looked at it and sighed. "Apparently, I'll be staying a little while longer."

Neviah shook her head. "Proof the gods hate us all."

Malkyr gestured at the entrance. "Now what? We can't very well go back outside."

Ran eyed the small fire he'd built. The flames continued to lick at the dry wood, burning brightly and illuminating the entire cave. But they weren't coughing from smoke. It was going someplace else. There had to be a way for it to escape or they would have noticed it filling the cavern by now.

Ran moved around the cave, exploring each and every nook and cranny. It took him twice around before he found it. He looked back at the others. "There's a tunnel leading out of here."

Malkyr hobbled over. "Is it big enough for all of us?"

"No idea," said Ran. "I only just found it."

"Well, perhaps I can be of service, after all," said Malkyr. "If you'll set me up with a torch, I'll go explore it."

Ran eyed him. "Are you sure that's a good idea?"

"You have a better one? You're going to be needed here to help tend Kancho and keep Jysal safe. Neviah needs your help more than she needs mine."

"Let him go, Ran," said Neviah. "Please."

Malkyr grinned. "There, you see? Give me a torch of some sort, and I'll be off. Once I've found my way down the tunnel, I'll come back and let you know if there's a way out."

"What do you know about exploring tunnels?"

Malkyr smiled. "I'm a ship's captain, boy. Not all of my voyages have been to carry passengers. I've done a bit of smuggling over the years, and I know my way around a tunnel."

Ran nodded. "Fair enough." He fashioned a torch out of some of the wood and few strips of Kancho's tunic. "Here, but there's no guarantee this will burn for all that long. I recommend you don't waste any time."

"I could use an extra weapon," said Malkyr.

Neviah came over and handed him a dagger. "I want it back."

Malkyr hefted the blade and nodded. "Hopefully I won't even need it. But good to have just in case." He bowed once. "See you all soon." And then he stuck his head into the tunnel and squeezed himself through.

Ran watched the flickering light from the torch dance around the tunnel and then vanish abruptly. He turned to Neviah. "Well, it's certainly going to be a lot more peaceful around here."

"One can hope," said Neviah.

A groan from behind her brought them racing over to Kancho who was seemingly awake now. Neviah looked into his eyes and frowned. "Can you hear me, Kancho?"

In response, Kancho retched once and then wiped his mouth on the back of his sleeve. "What the blazes attacked me? My shoulder and arm feel like they were dropped in a forge."

"We're not sure," said Ran. "It might have been a dragon of some sort."

Kancho frowned. "That's not good. I feel feverish. Is it infected already?"

Neviah nodded. "No sense lying to you. The wound looks terrible. I don't know if it's some sort of poison or if there was muck in the claws that ravaged your shoulder. Either way, you've got to get some medicine into you or it won't be good."

"You mean I'll die."

"Probably," said Neviah.

Kancho grunted. "This isn't the way I saw my end." He smiled at Ran. "You know what I mean."

"Of course. All warriors desire to die in battle. Better to go out with your hands around a sword then curled up in a bed somewhere longing for the time of old."

Kancho grunted again and waved Ran over. "You need to help me get better. I can't die here. Not with my daughter still missing. I promised my wife I would find her. And injury or no, I need to get out of this place and rescue her. You told me you'd help me do that."

"I did," said Ran. "But this is a bit beyond my skill."

Kancho shook his head. "I think there's more to you than meets the eye, Ran. As Murai, you know that I am duty-bound to our code of conduct. Some things are not possible for me that are for you. Do you understand what I'm saying to you?"

Ran frowned. He'd never doubted that Kancho might be able to work out his true identity, especially after picking the lock and scouting the castle. But it still shamed and angered him to have anyone know he was a shadow warrior. Members of the Nine Daggers never exposed themselves. In dealing with Kan-Gul, there hadn't been much of a choice. But what Kancho was now asking him to do was something he'd never attempted.

"I don't know if it will help."

Kancho laid a hand on Ran's arm. "I don't care what tradition you come from. You're an honorable man, and it's been my pleasure to fight by your side. Do me this one favor, and we will never again speak of who we are or what we might be."

Ran took a breath. "Very well. But I have never attempted this before. And if it fails, then it may well hasten your death."

Kancho smiled. "I do not fear death, Ran. I fear dying before I have had the opportunity to rescue my daughter and see justice served on those who took her away from me."

"I understand."

"Then do it," said Kancho. "Time grows short."

Ran looked up at Neviah and Jysal. "Help me lay him down on the ground."

Neviah looked at him. "What are you going to do?"

"What he has asked of me. But do not question me further. I won't talk about it."

Neviah and Jysal guided Kancho over to an area of the cave with the fewest bits of rock. The older warrior coughed as they settled him down on his back. He looked up at Ran one last time.

"I trust you."

Ran nodded. "Close your eyes."

Kancho did as he was told, and Ran waved Neviah and Jysal back. "I need some room now."

Both women moved away. Ran looked around him. The fire continued to burn, and its minimal heat cast a bit of warmth around the cave. Ran fixed his gaze on the dancing flames and allowed his breathing to relax and deepen. He slowly started a series of breaths, carefully timing his inhalations and exhalations until they were one seamless cycle that rose up and then fell in rhythmic focus.

Ran closed his eyes and let his focus drop to the point just below his navel. There he focused his attention, willing the energy that flowed in him to pool and circulate like a glowing orb. After several minutes, Ran sent the energy coursing into his hands, feeling the heat envelop them until they felt like they were being pricked with a million needles.

In his mind's eye, Ran saw Kancho's body before him, and he set his hands over the older warrior's still form. His hands rested a few inches above the wound to Kancho's shoulder. From there, Ran directed his energy into the wound. Ran saw energy spilling out of his hands and into the wound, filling it with a brilliant white energy the way he'd been taught back in Gakur.

Healing was an essential part of his training as a Shinobujin, but while he'd done it a number of times in practice, Ran had never used it on a mortal wound before. Certainly nobody from his clan went around advertising the fact that they could perform such a thing.

But Kancho had known about it.

Ran found himself wondering just what else Kancho might know about the Shinobujin.

He kept his focus on the wound and continued to pour more energy into it, willing the energy to drive away the infection and heal properly. For the next thirty minutes, Ran worked over Kancho until, at last, his hands felt cold and clammy. There was no more energy left to give to Kancho's wound.

Ran opened his eyes and saw that both Neviah and Jysal were sound asleep. No wonder, the cave was warm and the flames of the fire had dwindled. As tired as Ran was, he got to his feet, found the last few pieces of wood near the blocked entrance, and added them to the fire. The embers licked at the fresh fuel and flared back to life. Ran held his cold hands in front of the flames and tried to will some semblance of warmth back into them. If he'd had food and drink, he could have replenished his energy. But they had nothing. And until such time as they did, Ran would no doubt be at less capacity than he would be otherwise.

He couldn't let Kancho die, though. And as much as he worried the healing wouldn't help, he'd had to try. For Kancho to even ask Ran for such a favor was not something an ordinary Murai would normally do.

He leaned away from the fire and rested his back on the cave wall. It was difficult to tell how much time had passed. Malkyr had been gone for ages now. Surely he should have been back. Ran frowned. Perhaps the captain had found his own way out and was content to leave the rest of them behind.

His eyes drooped, and he realized he was exhausted. A few minutes of sleep would be the best thing. At the very least, they were safe from the outside world. And there seemed no way for Kan-Gul or his minions to reach them right now.

"Will he live?"

Ran opened his eyes to see Jysal kneeling beside him.

He smiled. "I don't really know. Only time will tell if I was successful or not."

Jysal rested her head on his shoulder. "It would appear that I'm not the only one here capable of magic."

Ran smirked. "There's no real magic in what I just did. All people have the skill to do it. It's merely a matter of recalling it. Dusting it off and being able to learn to use it again. That's all."

"What people don't know they possess looks like magic to their untrained eyes. You have done more for Kancho than any of us could have done."

"Maybe," said Ran. "Let's just hope that it's enough to stave off the infection."

CHAPTER TWENTY-ONE

Ran slept. When he awoke, Kancho was still unconscious. But that was to be expected. Properly healing him would mean that his body would be as inactive as possible while, hopefully, the energy cleaned his wounds. Only time would tell if Ran had been successful or not.

When he awoke, he found Neviah and Jysal deep in whispered conversation on the far side of the cave. Clearly they were trying to avoid making much noise and Ran appreciated that. Both he and Kancho needed the rest.

Ran stretched and felt some measure of strength returning to his body. He hadn't eaten in nearly a day, and his reserves had been pretty much exhausted by the attempted healing of Kancho. Still, he at least felt as though he had been able to manage some rest, and he yawned in spite of himself. Getting to his feet, he wandered over to Neviah and Jysal.

"Any sign of Malkyr?"

Neviah shook her head. "Not a one. Knowing that opportunist, he's probably found a way home and left the rest of us here to fend for ourselves. I swear if I ever lay eyes on that creature again, I won't hesitate to kill him."

"We don't know that he's left us here," said Ran. "For all we know, he could be finding out what is in the tunnel and possibly even bringing us back food and water. Or worse, he could've been killed or captured. I'm certainly not ready to say he's left us on our own just yet."

Jysal smiled at him. "Do you truly believe that Malkyr is going to bring us back food and water?"

"Probably not," Ran admitted. "But we don't have any proof he's doing otherwise."

"He hasn't returned yet," said Neviah. "For me, that's a fairly strong indication that we are going to be on our own. And without Kancho, we're effectively down to three."

Jysal pointed at Kancho's body. "How long will it take before you know if you were successful?"

Ran shook his head. "As I said, I've never done this before on someone as severely wounded as Kancho. It might take a day; it might only take a few hours."

"It's already been several hours," said Neviah. "You slept for about four if I judged the time correctly."

Ran frowned. "I was asleep for that long?"

"Yes."

He sighed. Clearly his strength had been taxed to the extreme in leading the party on its escape from Kan-Gul and then attempting a healing on top of that. Ordinarily, the best course for regaining his strength would have involved a huge meal, plenty to drink, and then about twelve hours of uninterrupted rest. Ran smirked. He wasn't getting any of those today.

"Jysal and I were discussing the possibility of discovery by Kan-Gul." Neviah pointed at the cave entrance. "I'm guessing it won't take him very long to track us down. Even with the rocks in front of the cave, those undead creatures of his could get through. And if they trap us inside, we're all as good as dead."

"So, what you're saying is . . ."

"We can't stay here," finished Neviah. "It was fine for a few hours, but we'd be pushing our luck imagining we can hide out here indefinitely. Jysal has already sensed a roving presence outside of the cave."

"The dragons? If that's what they were . . . " Ran shrugged. "Maybe they're keeping watch over the cave."

"I'm not sure what it is," said Jysal. "But it's getting stronger. That makes me think that Kan-Gul may well be close to arriving here. I have no idea what the limits of his power are, but it is certainly not beyond the realm of possibility for him to be able to manifest himself inside the cave with a band of Chekhal."

"We'd have no chance if that happened," said Neviah.

Ran frowned. He didn't want to leave the cave if at all possible. Not with Kancho's body in such a vulnerable position. "He needs more time."

"We may not have that time," said Neviah. "And since Malkyr hasn't seen fit to return as yet, we have to assume he's gone. One way or the other, we need to keep moving. It's the only way to stay ahead of Kan-Gul and hopefully get out of here."

Ran moved over to Kancho's body and laid a hand on his brow. He was still feverish, but less so. That was a good sign. Ran dearly wished the older warrior would wake up and show no ill effects from his injuries. But that seemed unlikely, at least right now.

"How are we going to move him?"

Neviah shrugged. "That's what we were discussing when you woke up. There's no easy way to do it. You and I can manage to some extent if Jysal wants to lead the way."

Ran cocked an eyebrow. "The tunnel isn't all that big. I don't know if it would even accommodate us trying to get Kancho's body through the opening."

"Well, we certainly can't leave him here," said Neviah. "If Kan-Gul breaks in and finds Kancho's body—"

"I'm not suggesting we leave him," said Ran. "If that were the case, we would have been better off letting him die." He glanced around. "Ordinarily, if we had access to the outside, I could fashion a litter from some saplings to haul his body around on."

"We seem to be a bit short on saplings right now, Ran," said Neviah. "And I don't see anything we could use as a substitute. It's down to you and me hauling him through. Jysal can spell us if either one of us gets too tired to continue. The important thing is we keep moving. I dislike the feeling of being trapped like a rabbit while the fox waits outside my den."

"Agreed," said Ran. He glanced at Jysal. "Are you comfortable with this plan?"

"I wish I was a bit stronger so I could help you," said Jysal. "But I will help any way I can."

Ran nodded and looked at Neviah. "How long?"

"The sooner the better. There's no telling how quickly Kan-Gul can get here and penetrate the cave. It could only take him seconds if he's as powerful as he's tried to make us believe he is."

Ran pointed at Kancho. "We'll need to move slowly with him. His body's extremely vulnerable right now. If he takes any more injuries, it may be beyond my skill to help him."

Neviah frowned. "I've never seen healing like what you attempted there. My skill is in herbs and potions. But it's obviously had some effect on Kancho. When you first fell asleep, his body twitched a number of times while the fever took hold. But he gradually seemed to relax and stayed still. Had I not checked on him regularly, I would have thought he was dead. As it is, he only breathes a few times each minute."

"That's normal," said Ran. "He's in a relaxed state, so his body requires less breath. The energy I poured into him will hopefully deal with whatever toxin is inside him. I'm hopeful he will awaken soon."

"That would be convenient," said Neviah. "But we cannot wait and hope it will happen."

Ran looked at the slowly dying fire and gathered up a few of the pieces of wood. He handed these to Jysal. "This is about as much as we have left for some sort of torch."

Jysal took the wood and smiled. "I'll be able to see regardless of the torch. Just make sure nothing happens to Kancho."

Ran eyed Neviah, but she was already busy positioning herself behind Kancho. "I'll get his arms if you can manage his legs."

Ran picked up Kancho's sword and laid it across the man's chest. There was nothing worse for a Murai than losing his sword. Undoubtedly, it would also prove a source of strength when Kancho reawakened. Its mere presence might infuse him with a bit of energy.

Ran handed his sword to Jysal. "You'll need to hold this for me. It will only get in my way while I carry Kancho."

"I will see no harm comes to it while it is in my care." Jysal tucked Ran's sword under her arm and moved toward the tunnel opening.

Ran positioned himself at the front of Kancho's body and then squatted down, his back to Kancho's torso, hooking his arms under the older warrior's legs. He glanced back at Neviah. "Ready?"

"On three," said Neviah. And then they lifted together.

Ran grunted. Kancho was significantly heavier than he'd imagined. Behind him, he heard Neviah take a quick breath.

"How much does he eat? I thought he would be lighter."

"I thought the same," said Ran. "Let's keep moving. We've got a ways to go before we can rest."

They moved toward the tunnel opening. Ran looked at it and turned to Neviah. "Let me go in first and then we'll ease him through. Then you come in and we'll resume our carry."

"Very well."

Jysal was already into the tunnel. The torch she held flickered and sent shadows sprawling across the tubelike cavern. Ran took a quick look around, trying to see how far it went on for. As far as he could tell, the tunnel snaked around and continued for some distance. Perhaps Malkyr hadn't abandoned them after all. If the tunnel was truly as long as it seemed, it might go through the entire mountain. Malkyr could still be walking.

Ran reached back into the cave and got a hold of Kancho's feet. Neviah fed Kancho's body through bit by bit until the older warrior was completely in the tunnel. He still showed no signs of waking up. *Good*, thought Ran. *If he continues to rest, that will bode well for his healing.*

Neviah entered the tunnel and looked around. "It's more roomy than I thought it would be."

"Lucky for us," said Ran. "I didn't fancy the notion of carrying Kancho in a cramped environment. We might be able to handle this, after all."

Jysal took the lead as they slowly worked their way through the tunnel. Ran's eyes constantly roved over the ground, trying to pick out any holes or stray rocks that would cause him or Neviah to tumble and drop Kancho's body. As they walked, he called out obstacles to Neviah, who maneuvered around them.

The tunnel, hewn out of rock perhaps by some long-forgotten spring, seemed to meander forever. It reminded Ran of how the water in a stream would simply take the path of least resistance and flow over and around everything. Ran supposed that was good. If the tunnel itself was unpredictable, their eventual destination would also be unpredictable. And perhaps even the mighty Kan-Gul would not know where they would end up.

Jysal led them around an outcropping of jagged rocks that looked able to tear open flesh with ease. Ran struggled to keep from dropping Kancho's legs as they made their way past it. Neviah grunted once and managed to keep her end up as well.

The deeper they got into the tunnel, the warmer it became. Ran was grateful it wasn't as cold as it had been in the cave entrance. He felt a line of sweat break out along his brow and nodded to himself. He wasn't dehydrated yet if he was able to sweat. But he also recognized the fact that it had been nearly a day without anything much to drink. If they kept up this pace and didn't find a ready source of sustenance or drink, Kan-Gul and his undead minions would be the least of their worries. Best not mention it to Jysal and Neviah. It'd only make them more aware of their own thirst.

Jysal stopped then. "I hear something."

Ran glanced at Neviah. "Let's put him down. If it's a threat, we need to be able to deal with it without being encumbered."

They lowered Kancho's body to the ground, and Ran took his sword back from Jysal. "Where did you hear it?"

"Somewhere up ahead," said Jysal quietly. "I wasn't sure if it was artificial or part of the tunnel itself."

"Stay here," said Ran. He moved out from where he had been squatting and maneuvered his way deeper into the tunnel. He didn't bother looking behind him, because he knew Neviah would be there to handle anything if Jysal had been mistaken and the noise was behind them. Ran had been in enough tight environments to know that sound could play with your senses.

He kept his jaw slack as he moved, opening his ear canals for the slightest noise to be picked up. Could it be Malkyr farther up ahead? Had they managed to catch up with him already? That didn't make any sense. Malkyr had been gone for hours. And they'd only been in the tunnel for perhaps twenty minutes.

Unless it was Malkyr returning.

Or someone else? Or something else?

Ran eased the first inch of his sword free of its scabbard, ready to spring into action the moment he sensed danger. He carefully picked his feet up and put them down again without making any noise. There were plenty of loose rocks on the tunnel floor that would skitter and echo deeper into the tunnel if he wasn't careful.

Then, ahead of him, he saw a large boulder off to one side of the tunnel. The rock looked strange, as if it had been dropped there by some unseen hand ages ago. But Ran appreciated its presence: it made for a great bit of concealment.

And now he heard the noise, too.

Slowly, aware that fast movement often draws attention, Ran lowered himself to the floor and stuck his head around the side of the rock to see what was making the noise.

CHAPTER TWENTY-TWO

The sight surprised him. Ran could see a small rivulet of water dribbling down the side of the tunnel rock and dripping into a small pool below. That would not have been a strange sound in and of itself, but what made the entire scene odd was that the water dripped onto a flat metal plate that reminded Ran of a shield. Where had that come from?

He crept ahead, scarcely able to believe their luck at finding a water source. He'd need to taste it and see if it was safe to drink, but if it had come through the rocks and mountain, then it certainly should be filtered by now. Ran slid out from behind the rock and crept down the tunnel. The dripping water was louder as he approached, and its rhythmic clanging sounded almost like someone beating their sword on a shield.

Ran knelt and put his hand into the dripping water. It was ice cold and clear. His mouth went bone dry and Ran smirked at how his body reacted to the sudden appearance of water. He waited until his palm was full and put it to his lips. As soon as the water touched his mouth, he tasted its sweet purity and marveled at how much it renewed his strength. Water was exactly what he'd needed, and here he had a ready source.

He checked the immediate vicinity and found nothing to suggest there was a threat. He dashed back up the tunnel and waved Jysal down. "There's water down there you can drink. I tried it, and it's fine. Slake your thirst, you'll need it."

Jysal rushed past him, and Ran moved to where Neviah waited.

"Are you sure it's safe to drink?" she asked.

He nodded. "As sure as I can be. It tastes amazing. Probably came through the entire mountain above us. As it traveled, the ground would have acted like a natural filter."

Neviah smiled. "I could do with a drink."

"We all could."

She pointed at Kancho's body. "Even him?"

"Especially him. Help me get him down there, and I'll see if I can wake him up long enough to try some of the water."

Together, he and Neviah managed to get Kancho down the tunnel to where the water dripped out of the rocks. Jysal was lapping up as much as she could. Neviah joined her and after a few minutes, stepped back so Ran could drink his fill. As he did so, Ran marveled at the existence of the water here in the tunnel. It had shown up just as they were becoming acutely aware of their lack of drink.

Timing, he decided, was everything.

He glanced over at Neviah. "Do you have a waterskin?"

She drew out a small pouch from inside of her tunic. "This is all I have. Most of my gear went down aboard the *Aqaria*."

"It will do," said Ran. He leaned back into the stream of water and waited for the small skin to fill up. Once he had it mostly full, he scooted over to Kancho's body and dribbled a small bit of water across the older warrior's lips. Then he leaned back and waited.

"Will that waken him?"

"I don't know," said Ran. "It's but one way to try to bring him out of his slumber. He really needs this water. No doubt it will help his body stave off the infection and replenish his blood loss."

Kancho coughed suddenly, and Ran helped him to sit up. "You need to drink this water."

Kancho's eyes barely opened, but he seemed to understand what Ran was saying, and his mouth dropped. Ran tilted his head back a bit and let the water slide down his throat. Kancho gulped several mouthfuls and then collapsed back down to the ground.

Ran frowned. This was not what he was hoping to see. He'd been expecting some sort of good sign that Kancho was recovering. But he was still warm to the touch. His body certainly seemed to be in the grips of whatever toxin had poisoned him earlier.

Neviah came alongside of him. "He still suffers."

Ran sighed. "I've done what I can. It is obviously beyond my skill to see him healed completely. Whatever happens next will depend on him. I hope his body is strong enough to fight off the poison. But there's no guarantee, unfortunately."

Neviah laid a hand on his shoulder. "No one could ask any more of you, Ran. You've done all you could and more. Kancho is lucky to have you here with him. I was able to do nothing."

"You helped Malkyr back on the beach."

"Do not remind me. I almost wish I hadn't helped him at all."

Ran grinned. "That he remained so annoying would seem to be fairly impressive testimony to your skills as a healer."

Neviah waved her hand. "It was but a trifling matter once we located the necessary herbs. What you were able to do no doubt slowed the mortality of Kancho's wound. There is much power in you."

"Thank you." Ran handed her back the waterskin. "Fill it up again. We'll need to get moving once we've all had our fill. I think it's imperative that we keep moving. The more distance we put between ourselves and Kan-Gul, the better."

"Agreed," said Neviah. "Will Kancho require any more water?"

"Not right now. But I suspect when he finally wakes up—provided he does—he will definitely want some."

"Then Neviah and I will drink our fill now and save the water in the skin for Kancho. Once we have drunk as much as we can, our bodies should be fine for another day or so. We have to be thankful for that, at least."

Jysal wiped her mouth and moved away from the water so Neviah could drink her fill. She smiled at Ran. "This was a lucky find."

Ran nodded. "Indeed. The timing of its discovery

certainly makes me feel better. I'm actually refreshed now. The quality of the water is excellent."

Neviah finally finished drinking and nodded at Kancho. "Let's get back on the trail and keep moving. This tunnel must end somewhere, and wherever it is, it's a fair bet it's away from Kan-Gul and his hordes."

Jysal turned then. "Did you hear that?"

Neviah smiled. "It's the water falling on that shield."

But Jysal shook her head. "No. There's something else." She put her hand into the stream and directed the water flow away from the shield. As soon as the dull tinging stopped, Ran could hear it, too.

Neviah stepped closer to Jysal and nodded at Ran. "Shuffling?"

"Definitely not natural," said Ran. He slid his sword out of its scabbard and then nodded at Jysal. "Stay back with Kancho."

Jysal moved to the rear while Neviah and Ran fanned out on either side of the tunnel. In the darkness, it was difficult to see much beyond the range of the torchlight. Shadows kept dancing along the rocky walls, and their movement left Ran unsure of anything. He took a breath and exhaled smoothly, willing his heart to slow down. Getting excited would only hurt his chances of being able to sense the attack when it came.

Neviah crouched and stayed close to the rock, trying to form her body into the rocky walls. "It must be the torch that is drawing them to us."

"Drawing what to us?" asked Ran.

Neviah smiled. "I think we'll find out soon enough."

Something moved deeper in the darkness. Ran

estimated that whatever was coming toward them was about ten yards away. He held his finger up to his lips, and Neviah nodded. Surprise was the best way to attack.

Ran wondered briefly if it might be Malkyr coming back, but quickly disregarded the notion. Malkyr would certainly have shouted some sort of greeting by now. He wouldn't simply continue walking forward.

The sound of the shuffling footsteps was slow and methodical. There was no rush to them. They simply plodded on, almost as if they had no choice but to continue to move forward.

Ran's nostrils caught a whiff of something now, and he winced. The stench of death hung heavy in the air. He wrinkled his nose in disgust but could do nothing about it. Whatever was coming toward them was getting closer with every step.

And then from the gloom, Ran saw it emerge.

It resembled one of Kan-Gul's Chekhal warriors, but it was larger. It wore armor, but the leather was faded and cracked. The dull gray skin seemed to ooze with some sort of goo, and the eyes were as opaque as those of the undead warriors they'd already seen. In its hand, the creature gripped a long, slender sword. Worms fell from its mouth and squirmed away once they hit the ground.

The fetid stench surrounding this Chekhal made Ran want to vomit, but he choked back on the urge. He'd only just had water, and the last thing he needed was to purge all the good water he'd just ingested.

The Chekhal stopped ten feet from them and sniffed the air. It let out a long groan and then started lumbering toward them again.

Ran stepped out and held his sword aimed at the center point between the Chekhal's eyes. As soon as he did so, the Chekhal focused on him and raised its own blade.

Ran feinted with a stab that made the Chekhal raise its blade to ward off the attack. Ran allowed his sword to be moved offline of the attack, rode the energy of the deflection, and then dipped under the Chekhal's sword. Ran cut up and stepped to the right before arcing his blade back and around, cleaving off the Chekhal's head from its shoulders. For a split second, the Chekhal stood motionless. Then it simply fell forward into the ground.

The single action had taken a mere second or two. Neviah came out from her spot on the wall and looked at the Chekhal on the ground. "You didn't leave me much to clean up."

"It was surprisingly easy to handle," said Ran. "Not sure if this is the same caliber of warrior that we dealt with back at the castle."

"It does not seem to be similar," said Neviah. She knelt and examined the armor. "This is old. Much older than that worn by the newer warriors at Kan-Gul's fortress."

"Do you think this was some sort of early creation of his?"

"Perhaps," said Neviah. "But it's disconcerting in its own right."

"How do you mean?"

Neviah gestured to the tunnel. "We thought we'd found a place where we could escape from Kan-Gul. But no sooner do we enter this tunnel than we find one of Kan-Gul's undead wandering around. And while he wasn't a threat to us, the fact he's even here means that Kan-Gul must know about this place. And if he does, then we are decidedly less safe than we originally thought."

Ran frowned. "Malkyr might have already stumbled into one of these things."

"He might also have bypassed them. It moved slowly enough to be avoided. But what worries me even more is what Malkyr might find when he finally does find a way out of here. It's conceivable that Kan-Gul knows exactly where this empties out. If that's so, then we are not running away from a trap, but heading directly into one."

"What choice do we have?" asked Ran. "If we stayed back in the cave, we would have been cornered. And while this still might lead us into danger, we at least control one key element."

"Which is?"

"Timing. Kan-Gul has no idea when we might arrive at the exit. That's somewhat valuable to us since it allows us to dictate when we engage."

Neviah smiled. "It's a bit of a stretch, but I agree. Kan-Gul could always surprise us, though, and choose to come in from the other end of this tunnel if he feels we're taking too long."

Ran nodded. "Impatience is something we can also exploit."

"I like the way you think," said Neviah. "Now we'll see if you're right."

"Behind you!" shouted Jysal just then.

Neviah wheeled around and cut out with her sword. Another of the Chekhal stopped its forward motion as Neviah's sword bit into its armor. But the old leather armor caught the blade and held it fast. Neviah jerked it back and forth as the Chekhal brought its own sword up.

Ran didn't hesitate. He launched himself at the Chekhal, bringing his sword up high and cutting down at the back of its exposed neck. His sword easily cut right through, and the Chekhal's head toppled free, bouncing off the tunnel wall as it did so.

"Two more!" called Jysal.

Neviah wrenched her sword free and turned to meet the new attackers. They moved as slowly as their comrades, and Neviah wasted no time launching a series of attacks with her sword. With her free hand, she drew a dagger and plunged it into the eye of the first attacker while she simultaneously deflected its sword strike. It groaned and fell to one side before finally going still.

Neviah kept moving and swept her sword down on the arm of the next Chekhal warrior, cutting it free near the elbow. Its sword dropped to the ground, and Neviah kept moving around to its rear. The Chekhal groaned and tried to grab at Neviah with its one free hand . She danced out of range and then waited as the Chekhal launched itself at her. Sidestepping, Neviah drew her sword up high and then cut down at the Chekhal's neck, chopping right through the leather armor of its helmet and through the dull gray oozing skin. The Chekhal dropped, and a fresh wave of rancid stench flooded the tunnel.

Ran bit back on the wave of bile at the back of his throat, willing himself to keep control over his desire to vomit. Jysal paled at the smell but managed to keep her gut in check.

Neviah waved a hand in front of her nose. "We need to

get out of here. The smell is almost worse than the physical threat these things posed to us."

Ran looked at Jysal. "Do you sense any more of them?"

"No."

Ran resheathed his sword. "Let's grab Kancho and get away from here."

Neviah hastily wiped and sheathed her blades and then resumed her position by Kancho's arms. "Ready."

They lifted together and then moved forward. Ran nearly tripped over a stone in his rush to get away from the undead Chekhal but managed to keep his balance. The sooner they were farther down the tunnel, the better he would like it.

CHAPTER TWENTY-THREE

"So Kan-Gul made some mistakes, apparently," said Ran as they continued down the tunnel. Jysal still led the way forward, her torch now dying and offering very little in the form of illumination. For Ran, the darkness wasn't much of a problem. Jysal also seemed unaffected by it, but Neviah struggled to make sense of where she was heading and kept telling Ran to slow down.

"What do you mean, mistakes?" asked Jysal.

"Those Chekhal back there. They weren't nearly as adept as what we faced at the castle. That tells me that Kan-Gul isn't the most powerful mage in the world, no matter how much he might wish it so."

"That might be another reason why he wants Jysal for himself," said Neviah. "If his magic isn't strong enough, then binding it with Jysal's power would certainly make him much more formidable."

"I'm not especially excited about the idea of binding anything with that lunatic," said Jysal. "And he cannot have my power. Or me, for that matter. If he's not as powerful as he wants us to believe, we can use that to our advantage. Hopefully it means we can kill him."

Ran looked back at Neviah. "Did you notice a bad smell when we killed the Chekhal at the castle?"

"No."

"Nor I," said Ran. "Perhaps those Chekhal we just dispatched were an experiment that went awry. Rather than destroy them, Kan-Gul placed them down here. Maybe they were the guardians of the water. I do not know for sure, but clearly Kan-Gul suffers from failures like anyone else."

"That doesn't really change our situation," said Neviah. "We still need to find a way out of this tunnel and find refuge from Kan-Gul. If the Chekhal we just killed are the easiest foes we face, then we'd be fools to assume that all of our encounters will be the same. I expect Kan-Gul has more in store for us than we know. Our escape from the castle felt almost too easy, looking back on it now."

Ran frowned. Neviah had a good point. Despite the combat, the Chekhal were handled easily enough. And Kan-Gul knew that Ran was intelligent enough to have noticed how to gain entrance to the castle. The same technique would work to get out. Were they simply going through the motions of an elaborate trap that Kan-Gul had devised for them? Or was that giving Kan-Gul too much credit?

"We've been walking for hours now," said Neviah. "When do we take some time to rest? My arms are aching from carrying Kancho like this."

Ran stopped. "I can still smell the Chekhal. Let's at least keep moving until that stench is far enough behind us. I'd love a good rest myself, but we can't stop right now.

I want to put some distance between us and anyone who might be tracking us."

"I can't even see," said Neviah. "And now I'm starting to sound like that fool Malkyr. Let's walk for another three hundred steps and then stop. Jysal needs her rest as well."

"Fair enough," said Ran.

"It doesn't help that we can't see a thing in this darkness," said Neviah.

Jysal called out from the front of the line. "I can make it so we can see."

Neviah grunted. "No using magic."

Jysal sighed. "It's the easiest spell in the world, Neviah. And we really need it. I can see fine but you and Ran are practically blind. Let me help us out a little bit, would you? You've both done all the fighting and carrying today, and I'm honestly feeling a bit useless."

Neviah sighed. "Fine. But nothing more extreme than that."

"Unless you can manage to conjure up a hearty meal," said Ran. "In which case I'd vote for that."

"Don't tempt her," said Neviah. "Jysal loves a good challenge like that, and her magic is probably potent enough to make it work."

"Really?"

Jysal shrugged. "I won't really know what I'm capable of until I reach the temple. Only they can tell me what my boundaries are."

"Is there such a thing as magic without boundaries?"

"An all-powerful mage?" Jysal shook her head. "I don't know, actually. If you believe what Kan-Gul says, then he's one. But I don't believe that for a moment."

"Why not?"

"Think about it," said Jysal. "If Kan-Gul was omnipotent, then this mountain would offer us no shelter or refuge. Kan-Gul would simply tear it apart until he got to us. The fact that we are still alive tells me that he can't do much to us while we're in here."

"Unless he's got some greater scheme we don't understand yet."

Jysal fell silent and then sighed. "That's true."

"Three hundred," said Neviah. "We're stopping. And Jysal, do us a favor and cast some light around here. Softly though. We don't want something incredibly bright bouncing off of walls and alerting anything else in this tunnel that we're around."

Ran lowered Kancho's body to the ground. As he did so, a pale blue light lit up their immediate vicinity. Ran blinked twice, but the light was easy enough on his eyes that he quickly adjusted. The tunnel came into stark relief, showing rough walls that had been worn smooth in some areas. Most likely due to water, Ran reasoned.

Neviah slumped against a nearby wall. "I thought my arms were going to drop off."

"I'm sure Kancho appreciates you hauling him around," said Ran. "And if it helps, his legs are even heavier."

Neviah grinned. "Thanks for taking that part."

Ran nodded and then glanced at Jysal. "Do you sense anything about our surroundings?"

"Like what? Enemies?"

"That would be a good place to start."

"Nothing," said Jysal after a quite moment. "It's

possible there are other things lurking out there, but right now, they don't seem to be anywhere around us."

"Good," said Ran. "I'd like to close my eyes for a bit and try to get some rest."

Neviah eyed Jysal. "Can you take first watch?"

"Certainly. But what should I do if I sense trouble?"

Neviah smiled. "Wake us, but do so quietly. And extinguish your light. If we fight something used to the darkness, a sudden burst of illumination might stun them temporarily and enable us to kill them faster."

Ran leaned back against the wall closest to Kancho. As he waited for sleep to overtake him, he looked at the older warrior's body and wondered if he'd done enough. Kancho showed no signs of getting better, although he didn't look worse, either. *At best*, thought Ran, *I may have only halted the advance.* If they could find a way out of the tunnel and manage to locate someone more skilled then him, there was a chance they could save him.

And what of Kancho's mission to rescue his daughter? He'd forsaken his code of honor and everything that the Murai held dear in order to find his child. Ran couldn't fathom it. He had no children of his own, and he'd never known his parents. For as long as he could remember, the compound deep within the fog-enshrouded peaks of Gakur had been his home, and the students and teachers his family. What must it be like, he wondered, to hold a baby and know it was your creation? Then to watch it grow and become its own person, only to have it yanked out of your life so suddenly?

Ran frowned. No wonder Kancho had gone against his clan. Ran would have probably done the same thing.

His eyes drooped, and he heard Neviah breathing deeply nearby. She was already asleep.

But as tired as Ran was, he couldn't drop off to sleep. Jysal sat motionless nearby, watching. Even from his position, she still buzzed with a faint energy. Ever since their initial encounter with Kan-Gul, it had been unmistakable Kan-Gul had awoken her power somehow. And now she wore it like an aura that surrounded her entire body, curving just so around her hips and breasts. Jysal was as beautiful as she was powerful. Ran smiled to himself. A woman like Jysal probably didn't even know how much power she could wield. He hoped the temple she was heading to could teach her to use it responsibly.

Ran's time in Gakur had taught him the same thing. Shinobujin were incredibly potent fighters, but his teachers stressed that sometimes the most powerful technique was doing nothing at all. Knowing when restraint and inaction were the appropriate techniques was at once the easiest and most demanding of all. Everyone wanted to be seen as the ultimate warrior—ego played havoc with perspective and rationale—so the teachers often set up assignments that would deliberately force the students to do nothing. Unlike more physically demanding assignments, these tests were mentally grueling and forced the students to confront the reality of their own ego and potential weakness.

Ran had hated those missions. But he'd managed to pass them all.

One of the toughest had been when he was sent into a local village to observe and report about a certain warlord's troops in the area. Ran had set himself up as a merchant selling tea at a stand near the center of town. On the second day, as the sun unfolded itself from the rain clouds that had bloated the sky for the past several days, Ran spotted a father beating his child in public. The boy had spilled a sack of rice, and his father had started berating the child. Ran watched as the man's rage increased to a fever pitch and he started beating his boy, pounding him with fists and kicks. Ran feared the young boy might die, and he wanted nothing more than to rush into the fray and defend the child. But the mission came first, and Ran was only supposed to observe the happenings in the town.

As the father continued to beat his son, Ran's own temper flared, and he found it harder and harder to restrain himself. Just as he thought the poor boy could stand no more abuse, one of the Murai stationed with the warlord's troops came striding out of a wine house. As Ran watched, the Murai drew his sword and cut down the father right then and there. Then he helped the boy up and carried him off to a local doctor.

The father's corpse lay where it was until one of the undesirables came by and collected it later.

Ran stayed another day and then returned to Gakur.

A trio of teachers awaited his report. "What did you see?" asked Noguchi.

Ran told them about all the troop movements he'd noted. He also told them about the father who beat his child.

"Did you want to help the boy?" asked another teacher named Muramatsu.

"More than anything," Ran had said. "I could hardly hold myself back."

"But you did. And that is admirable."

Ran had frowned. "But the boy suffered. I could have helped him."

"No," said the final teacher, Oguri. "You would have helped him and saved a single life. But by waiting, you instead now have information that can save many more lives. Had you waded into that conflict, the Murai that killed the father would have noticed you, and the mission would have been compromised. At the very least you would have been noticed. At worst, you might have ended up fighting that Murai. Neither outcome would have given us the desired result.

"But instead of giving in to your ego and the desire to mete out justice, you held yourself in check. And as a result, we now know that a certain Murai warrior is in that town. We've been tracking him for some time. And because you kept yourself from getting involved, we know his exact location."

It had taken Ran a long time to reason out that line of thinking. In the end, he came to an uncertain peace that while he might have acted properly in the eyes of his teachers, he wasn't so sure he was pleased with himself. Had it truly been ego that made him want to get involved? Or was it some long-forgotten memory of abuse at the hands of his own father that had made him so angered?

If the same situation happened again, Ran made a promise that he would carefully weigh the mission's importance with the well-being of the child. He had no love for anyone who harmed a child and could see no reason why such people should be allowed to walk the earth. He sighed, realizing that the sense of loyalty he felt toward his clan would often conflict with what he desired to do, or what he thought was the right path. He felt a small twinge of guilt for not leaving the others behind in order to more easily make his escape. He knew he'd done the right thing—he simply couldn't have abandoned them to have their souls devoured—but he had put them above the needs of his clan. He wondered how many more times in his life such a dilemma would arise? And how he would deal them? Would it always be so easy a decision to make? He doubted it.

"What troubles you?"

He opened his eyes and saw Jysal looking deeply into them. He smiled. "I wasn't aware you could also read minds."

She shrugged. "Some things are easier to see."

Ran stretched and placed one hand on her face. "Your tattoo, where does it come from?"

Jysal covered his hand with hers. "All the women in my clan wear one. Ours is a proud heritage. I was marked from an early age. I've never enjoyed it, however."

"It's exquisite," said Ran. "And it only enhances your beauty."

Jysal smiled and kissed him lightly on the lips. "Thank you. But you're dodging my question again."

Ran smirked. "I was remembering an old lesson. One I never felt comfortable with, but understood at the same time. If that makes any sense at all."

"It does." Jysal continued to look into his eyes. "It still plagues your conscience?"

Ran shrugged. "Not really. Although I worry about the consequences of rejecting the lesson."

"You never divulge details, do you?"

"Not if I can help it."

"Whoever trained you has done an admirable job. You are incredibly opaque and yet simultaneously very apparent in your role as a warrior."

Ran smiled again. "I'm not even sure I know what you mean by that."

"It's a compliment." Jysal kissed him again. "You should sleep. Our time here will be over soon, and we will be moving on down the tunnel. And we may all find that sleep is a forgotten luxury soon enough."

"You're making predictions now?"

Jysal shrugged and moved away. "One never knows what the future holds. I only see what I see. Nothing more. At least not yet."

"I'm not the only one being vague," said Ran. He settled himself back against the cave wall and closed his eyes. Taking a deep breath, he exhaled it long, fully emptying his lungs before taking another breath. Just as he was about to drop off to sleep, he heard Kancho's weakened voice.

"Does she kiss well?"

Ran opened his eyes. Kancho sat before him.

CHAPTER TWENTY-FOUR

"I only ask because it certainly seems like she has taken a liking to you."

Ran grinned. "Nice to see you back in the land of the living."

"Such as it is," said Kancho. "Where are we?"

"A tunnel that led out from the cavern we'd been in. We thought it prudent to move beyond there in case Kan-Gul showed up and was somehow able to gain entrance through his magic." Neviah began to stir at the sound of their voices.

Kancho nodded. "Is there water?"

"Neviah, bring over the waterskin." Ran looked at Kancho. "How are you feeling?"

Kancho shrugged. "As well as could be expected, I suppose. The fever appears to have broken, although I still sweat."

Neviah came over, looking sleepy, and handed the skin to Kancho. "It's good to see you awake at last."

Kancho sucked down the majority of the water and

handed the skin back. "Thank you." He looked around. "How did you manage to get me here? More magic?"

Neviah chuckled. "Not even close. Ran and I carried you the entire way. My arms have never felt heavier, thanks to lugging you around, you old coot."

Kancho bowed his head. "I owe you both a tremendous debt I fear I can never adequately repay. Ran, you saved my life. That is no small matter, and I am indebted to you."

Ran frowned. Obligation was one of the core tenets in the Murai code of honor. Once in someone's debt, a Murai would take incredible steps to repay the kindness he'd been shown. And since Ran had healed Kancho, the debt was greater than if he'd done him a simple favor. Having a Murai indebted to you wasn't necessarily a bad thing, Ran decided. But it could complicate things if Kancho ever decided that being indebted to a Shinobujin precluded his adherence to his code of honor.

Still, Kancho had pretty much broken that vow already by going against his lord's wishes. Perhaps there was some good to this, after all. Ran could cultivate Kancho as an asset and use him for information. Provided Kancho was able to extricate himself from the death sentence that would no doubt be hanging over his head if he ever set foot back in Nehon. Of course, there was the small matter of escaping Kan-Gul.

Ran chuckled and placed his hand on Kancho's shoulder. "We'll deal with that when we come to it, all right? For now, the biggest favor you'll be doing for both Neviah and me is to be able to walk on your own."

Kancho hefted his sword. "I am well enough to do just that."

"Good," said Ran. "We'll continue farther then."

"You haven't had a chance to rest fully yet," said Jysal. "You should wait until you've slept."

Ran shook his head. "No need. I won't be able to sleep. And we'd just be wasting time. Better to use this opportunity to move on ahead. And just in case Kancho's recovery is temporary, we're better served moving on."

Kancho frowned. "I don't think the recovery is temporary, but I'll go along with your decision. As long as you feel well enough to go on."

"I'm fine," said Ran. "I'll take the lead for a while. Kancho, you come next, and then Jysal and Neviah. We'll keep you in the middle until we're certain that you're better. That was a nasty wound to your shoulder, and I'm not sure if your body is finished purging itself of the poison."

Kancho rubbed his shoulder and winced. "It's still very tender."

"And likely will be for some time come," said Neviah. "The wound was grievous. I've bandaged it as well as possible, so it should be fine for now. But you should try to change the dressing every day if you can."

"Thank you," said Kancho. "I will."

Ran led them away from their resting place and crept down the tunnel. He rounded a bend carefully, checking first to see if there was anyone waiting to ambush them. As soon as he came around the corner, a new smell greeted his nostrils. He paused and then sniffed in and out quickly a few times. But he was certain he knew the briny smell of the ocean. Despite heading northeast, they appeared to be close to the ocean once more.

The others smelled the ocean as soon as they came

around the corner. Neviah frowned. "I thought we were heading inland."

"I thought so, too," said Ran. "But perhaps this tunnel has led us back in the other direction. I regret my sense of direction is not as keen as it would be if we were outside."

"It's not like we had a choice on where the tunnel led," Neviah said.

Jysal interrupted. "Is that light up ahead?"

Ran turned and looked. Perhaps a thousand feet down the tunnel there seemed to be a faint light source coming from somewhere close by. The light flickered and made Ran think of a torch.

"Malkyr?"

Neviah sniffed. "I doubt it. Knowing his luck, that little troll is no doubt halfway home by now, astride the wheel of a new ship."

"I don't think he would abandon us," said Kancho. "Malkyr's destiny is tied to ours, I think."

"We should proceed carefully," Ran said. "If there is light, and it's not Malkyr, then we could very well be walking into a trap of some sort. Let me scout ahead and see what I can find out."

"You want one of us to come with you?" asked Neviah.

Ran shook his head. "Me first. If there's trouble, you'll soon know about it."

He turned and crept down the tunnel. The light at the end would prove problematic, but Ran could work with it. He'd dealt with torches before and knew that they would throw his shadow behind him as he approached. But in a roughcut tunnel, he hoped there would be shadows to exploit.

As he moved down the tunnel, he held himself close to the tunnel wall, feeling the cool rough rock pass under his palms. He used the same cross-stepping technique he'd used back at Kan-Gul's castle, and it enabled him to look back at the others and up ahead. If the light source was some sort of trap, he could wave the others off quickly and deal with the trouble himself.

As he drew ever closer, Ran changed his stepping technique and faced forward, shrinking down until he was low-crawling along the tunnel floor. He could clearly make out the fact that the light came from a torch. But he couldn't yet see the torch. The smell of the ocean grew stronger with every step he took. And now he felt a breeze upon his face. It was as if someone had left a window open.

Fresh air, he thought. Being able to get out of the tunnel would be an incredible joy. As long as he wasn't in for a rude surprise.

He saw now that the tunnel ended and the torch must have been outside of the opening. Perhaps the opening was on a cliff of some sort? He couldn't yet see the ocean, but he supposed it would have to be somewhere up ahead. He kept moving, drawing his sword some length out of his belt keeping it close to his chest so that it didn't bump into the walls. Ran knew enough ways to draw the sword in confined locations like a tunnel.

His knees scraped the tunnel floor, but he kept moving forward. The presence of the torch made little sense to him. If the tunnel ended in some sort of cliff, then why would there be a torch there? He drew closer and then stopped right next to the entrance.

And understood.

The tunnel did not end in a cliff over the waves of the ocean. It opened up into an underground harbor. From his vantage point, Ran was able to look down and observe the scene before him. What he saw surprised him. Ships. Lots of ships. They were large and of the type he'd seen being used to carry troops around the waters of Nehon. But these ships weren't filled with troops. And there appeared to be only a few sailors down at the harbor proper.

Ran went back to the others and guided them forward. At the tunnel mouth, he spoke quietly and pointed out what he'd seen.

"Those large ships are used for carrying troops, right?"

Kancho nodded. "I've seen them before. But where are the troops?"

Ran shook his head. "No idea. It seems as though there are only a few sailors on duty down there. I don't understand what sort of place this could be. Does Kan-Gul control this harbor as well?"

"I would assume he controls everything in this region," said Neviah. "And that would include those ships. Remember what he said back at the castle? About the visitors from the north?"

She was right. Ran frowned. Combined with the presence of the barracks in the castle, it made perfect sense. Kan-Gul was allying himself with some large invasion force from the north. Presumably, when they first arrived, they would stay in the castle in the barracks area. From there, they would conquer the surrounding lands. And when they were finished wreaking havoc there, they would use these boats and sail for Nehon across the Dark Sea.

"This is worse than I expected," said Ran.

"Indeed," said Kancho. "If they are preparing to invade Nehon, then we will need to get word back to the lords across the Dark Sea. Since it is an island nation, they will never suspect they are being targeted for invasion."

"They've been invaded by a maritime force before," said Ran.

"True, but it was repulsed." Kancho frowned. "And that was long ago. I suspect they have grown complacent and think another such attack would never occur. These ships prove otherwise."

"Time will be of the essence," said Ran. "If an invasion is coming, then we will need to marshal some type of defense."

Kancho frowned and peered down at the harbor. "Do you see that ship? It's different from the others."

Ran looked where he was pointing. "It looks much smaller than the transport vessels. What do you make of it?"

"It's a coastal raider," said Neviah from behind them.

Ran turned. "Are you sure?"

She nodded. "I've seen plenty of them in my time. My family hails from a region known for piracy. The sight of those vessels always struck fear into my heart growing up. And when my parents were killed by raiders, the image of that kind of ship burned itself into my memory forever."

Kancho's frown deepened. "Your parents were killed?"

Neviah nodded. "It's not something I like to talk about. But when the raiders came ashore, my father and mother tried their best to keep the raiders from taking us prisoner." She took a deep breath. "They could not stop them, and they were killed for protecting us. Then the raiders took my brother and me anyway."

"What happened to you?" asked Jysal.

"They took us back to their land, where we were forced to be little more than slaves. My brother was strong at first, but fell ill and died during the first winter. I managed to fight off the illness, and, in the spring, I found a way to escape. That was when I made my way to one of the protector temples. I was accepted as a student and stayed for ten years."

"You graduated, obviously," said Ran.

Neviah nodded. "I did. And the first thing I did was head back to the town I'd escaped from. It was still a raider stronghold, but even the most impressive forts are not immune to a woman's wiles. Once inside, I found the men who had murdered my parents, and I killed them in their sleep. Then I laid waste to the entire town using pitch and fire." She exhaled as the memories played across her face. "I exacted my vengeance."

"Is this ship from the same clan that killed your parents?" asked Kancho.

Neviah shook her head. "No. It is from Nehon, judging by the flag it flies on its rear mast. See there?"

Ran looked and saw the simple black cloth emblazoned with a the image of a shark. "Raiders from Nehon? And they've found refuge here?"

Kancho tensed. "Look there."

Ran looked at the spot he pointed and saw several well-armed men leaving the raiding vessel. They came down the gangway and strode down the pier as if they were in command of the area. Why would Kan-Gul consort with raiders? At first it seemed unusual, but then Ran figured that the raiders were no doubt a convenient source of information for the sorcerer. If they were constantly operating near Nehon, they would have lots of information that could prove useful, especially if Kan-Gul was planning an invasion.

"They're definitely from Nehon," Ran said. He could clearly see the sloped eyes that marked his countrymen.

Kancho nodded. "These are men I want to talk to. They may have knowledge that would prove useful to me."

"Your daughter's whereabouts?"

"Yes," said Kancho. "If I can get them to talk, it will make my job easier."

"I could try to get down there," said Ran.

"You've done so much for me already," said Kancho. "No, this will be something I must undertake myself. Your job is to get Neviah and Jysal out of here and find them safe transport to the temple so Jysal can get her education. I will handle the raiders."

"You'll probably die if you go down there without any help," said Neviah.

Kancho grinned. "I have the penalty of death hanging over my head back in Nehon for dishonoring my clan. And death is something that a Murai lives with every moment of his life. I do not fear death."

"But you told me you feared dying before you got a chance to rescue your daughter," said Ran. "Surely there's no honor in throwing your life away when you have friends who can help you?"

Kancho took a deep breath and sighed. "I cannot ask you to do such a thing."

"You have not asked us," said Jysal. "We have volunteered to assist you. Two different things entirely."

Neviah laid a hand on Kancho's shoulder. "Your honor is intact, and you should fret not. As you have helped us, we shall help you."

"Thank you all," said Kancho. He looked at Ran. "How do you suggest we proceed?"

CHAPTER TWENTY-FIVE

From high above the underground harbor, Ran swung out over the edge of the tunnel and quickly hugged the sheer rock face leading down. This was the most critical part of the entire mission. He was utterly exposed on the rock face, and if anyone happened to look up, they would see him. His best option was to descend as quickly as possible and get down among the shadows where he felt more at home. Working in Ran's favor was the fact that most people don't ever look up, and if they do, they don't look much above the level of their head.

Ideally, Ran would have waited until dark to make his descent. But the underground harbor was immune to the darkness of the outside world. A small opening at one end of the harbor led out to the sea through a tunnel carved out of the rock. But the outside world still sat at least a thousand yards away from where the harbor sat lit up by torches positioned throughout the area. At least the early part of the climb, he'd have the cover of darkness. But the lower he climbed, the brighter it would become.

Ran clung to the rocks, aware that he had no safety rope. The strength of his muscles alone would determine whether he made it down successfully or whether he crashed to his death amid the gently lolling ships and the wooden piers.

Ran did not intend to die.

Working from the most basic tenets of always keeping three points of contact, Ran slowly came down the rock face. His eyes scanned constantly, alert for the movements of the few people milling out below. Ran knew there was a chance he hadn't spotted some of the guards that might be stationed around the area. But they needed to keep moving. Ran thought it might be possible to grab the raider ship and put to sea. It was probably their best chance to escape Kan-Gul.

A single path ran up to the tunnel, and Ran could have easily used that to descend. But that was also the most obvious path, and any guards stationed nearby would be alert to movement down the path. No one would expect a single figure to risk his life by climbing down nearly one hundred feet. This was another advantage the Shinobujin exploited—human psychology. Much like animals in the forest, humans would undoubtedly opt for the easiest path. As such, they couldn't conceive of anyone else going a riskier and more difficult route.

Mercifully, the rock face was pockmarked and filled with plenty of handholds and footholds. If it had been exposed to the sea, Ran could have counted on a much more challenging descent amid the smoothed surface. Still, Ran's muscles were on fire as he drew within twenty feet of the ground. It grew tempting to simply drop down among the wooden crates he saw below, but again, his discipline forced him to slow down and take his time. The most dangerous part of any mission was always when you felt like you were close to safety. During those times, the risk was always higher.

Finally, his feet touched the wooden docks, and Ran released his hands from the rock wall. He allowed himself to sink into the deepest shadows behind the crates. They were stacked two high and side by side for the length of two ships.

Up close, the transports looked even more massive. Ran couldn't help but marvel at their size. They could easily transport thousands upon thousands of enemies to the shore of Nehon. And the warlords in Nehon wouldn't even know about the coming invasion unless Ran was able to get word back to Gakur. The elders would know best how to proceed.

He crept along the dock with his back to the rock wall and his front toward the ships. Before each step, Ran checked to make sure he wasn't casting a shadow ahead of him. He noted the positions of the torches and where they threw their light. Then he moved into the spaces between that light. Gradually, he drew down the dock, closer to where the raider ship sat in its mooring.

He froze when he heard voices. He let one hand slowly fall to his sword. The voices spoke a brutish tongue he did not understand. Another seafarer language, he supposed. The voices spoke with urgency. Something must have been happening. The voices died away, and Ran waited another two minutes before moving again. The temptation to rush was always so great, but fast movement risked noise and was more readily noticed by the human eye, so everything Ran did was as slow and controlled as possible.

Ran knew that the eyes of the others would no doubt be searching for him amid the crates. He wondered if Kancho could see him stalking about. He knew the older Murai warrior must have guessed what he was by now. But Kancho didn't seem to care, at least not since Ran had saved his life.

Time would tell whether their bond would hold up over the constraints of Kancho's code of honor.

He stole farther down the docks toward the raider ship. While far smaller than the transports, the raider ship was nonetheless impressive. She must have run at least a hundred feet long and twenty feet wide at her beam. Heavy shields covered her bulwarks, and the double masts looked as thick as the thickest trees Ran had seen in Nehon. Her prow was lean and sharp, adorned with the visage of an angry demon called an Oga in his land. Ran heard more voices and paused in his assessment. Their suspicions of the raiders being from Nehon were confirmed by their language.

"We must leave by the next tide if we have any hope of making good time back," said one voice.

"Understood," said a second voice. "I will make sure the men are ready."

"Excellent. Kan-Gul does not want to waste the chance to position more of our men along the coasts."

"And what of the girl, my lord? Are we ransoming her back to her family? She claims her father is Murai. He would no doubt pay handsomely for her return."

There was a pause. "I'm not sure what I want to do with her. She is beautiful. Perhaps I will forego the ransom and keep her for myself."

"Your wife will not like that one bit, my lord."

"My wife doesn't have to know, does she?"

Both men laughed and soon passed Ran's hiding spot on the dock. Ran eased himself back away from the crates and took a few deep breaths. There was no guarantee that the woman the men spoke of was Kancho's daughter, but he wondered how many other Murai daughters these raiders could possibly have. Either way, it would bear looking into further. The question was: How to do it without attracting attention or exposing himself? And was the girl even on the ship itself, or was she being kept elsewhere in the harbor area?

Ran sighed. The only way to find out was to get aboard the ship.

He crept out and looked around the area. He still hadn't seen anything that led him to believe there were guards around. It was a fact he found peculiar. Unless the raiders felt completely protected here and the need for guards seemed silly to them.

Their mistake, thought Ran as he crept away from the crates. The gangway to the raider ship was a few steps away. Ran glanced around and then made his way swiftly up the gangway. He kept his forward momentum going with short, rolling steps that kept the boat from rocking and brought him up to the main deck as fast as possible.

He was exposed now and knew the others could clearly see what he was doing. Ran ducked down a hatchway leading belowdecks and paused halfway down the ladder listening to the ambient noises aboard the ship. The soft creaking of heavy, seaworthy ropes and the gentle lapping of waves against the hull reached his ears, but little else. Where was the crew?

Ran frowned. For an apparently busy harbor, there was very little going on. Nearly twenty heavy transports rested in the harbor, along with a raiding ship, and yet he'd seen perhaps three people the entire time he'd been there. Something was wrong. But he couldn't put his finger on what it might be.

Unless this whole thing was a trap.

The absence of the troops to fill the transport ships made sense. Clearly the army from the north hadn't arrived yet. But he would have expected the raiders to at least maintain some presence aboard their own ship. More so if they had a prisoner aboard.

Ran finished descending into the main cabin and regarded the doors before him. Two of them were open, and he could see into the simple galley and crew bunk area. The last door was barred with a simple lock.

Ran knelt in front of it and fished his wire from his tunic. Fitting it into the lock, he had it open in a few seconds. He stepped back and swung the door open.

What he found surprised him.

Malkyr.

The ship captain was curled up in a ball, apparently sound asleep. Ran glanced around and then nudged him awake. Malkyr stirred and groaned, putting one of his hands on his head.

Ran shushed him. "What happened to you?"

Malkyr's eyes widened when he recognized Ran. He looked around. "Where are they?"

"I don't know. Where have you been?"

"I followed the tunnel to its end and wound up here. I took the path down and bumped right into a guard."

"A guard? I haven't seen any."

Malkyr frowned. "There were a lot of people here when I arrived. They clunked me on the head and stuffed me in here. The indignity, I tell you. Here I am a ship's captain, and those wretches can't even be bothered to respect my rank."

"Raiders don't seem to care about much aside from themselves," said Ran. "Have you heard anything about the woman they apparently took hostage?"

"They have a hostage? I thought I was the only one."

Ran shook his head. "I heard two of them talking about her. There's a chance it could be Kancho's daughter."

"Sorry, no."

Ran helped Malkyr to his feet. "Can you walk? How's your leg?"

"Well enough, I suppose. Have you got a spare weapon? I feel naked without even a flimsy blade to protect myself with."

Ran fished one of Neviah's daggers out of his belt and handed it over to Malkyr. "Take care of that. Neviah is not a big fan of yours. If you don't bring that back to her, she'll probably track you down and slit your throat."

"I don't doubt it," said Malkyr. "Now what?"

"We get you out of here. The girl they were talking about has to be around somewhere. We need to find her and then get her back to Kancho."

"We're not even sure it's his daughter."

"We'll find out. In the meantime, what would it take to get this boat out to sea?"

"Why?"

"Because there's an army coming from the north and they mean to invade all the lands around here before sailing for Nehon. We need to get word back to the warlords so they can prepare an adequate welcome."

Malkyr looked around the boat. "She's seaworthy enough, but I'd kill for a few more crew to take her out. If I don't have help, it will be a troublesome thing to get out past the entrance to the harbor. Plus, I don't know what the tides are like. We've been underground far too long."

"An experienced captain like you ought to be able to tell how the tide's going as soon as you see it."

Malkyr grinned. "You flatter me."

Ran frowned. "You might be a pain, but you know your trade. Can you prepare to cast off? And can you do it without attracting attention?"

"Maybe. Where are you going?"

"Back ashore. I need to get the others down here and then try to locate Kancho's daughter."

"Forget about her, Ran. She's already lost."

Ran shook his head. "I told Kancho that I would help him find her. I don't have children, but if I ever did and one of them went missing, I'd move heaven and earth to find them."

"A noble gesture," said Malkyr. "But it's worthless if you can't find her." He poked his head around. "I can get the ship ready. Where are the others?"

"Up above at the tunnel entrance," said Ran. "I'll head up there now and get them sorted. Hopefully I won't run into any trouble."

"If you were able to get down here without attracting

attention, I doubt you'll have any problems on the way back up."

Ran grinned. "Now who's flattering who?"

"Just speaking fact," said Malkyr. "You go ahead and get them down here. I can be ready to leave as soon as you're back."

"You're certain of that?"

Malkyr nodded. "If the tide is going out, the current should at least carry us out to the entrance. If some of you don't mind manning the oars to get us beyond the entrance, we can raise sails soon after and be on our way. We could be back in Nehon in a little over a day if the winds are right and hold."

"Excellent," said Ran. "Don't do anything to make noise, and I'll be back as quickly as I can."

"Good."

Ran ascended the steps of the ladder and poked his head back above the main deck. The ship still lolled gently, and he could see no one nearby. He started to climb up, when he heard Malkyr's voice behind him. "Ran."

He dropped back down and started to turn around. "Wha—?"

But he never completed the turn before he felt something thunder into the base of his skull. Blackness swallowed him up.

CHAPTER TWENTY-SIX

"Tell us what clan hired you."

Ran's mind was filled with blackness. A strip of cloth covered his eyes, and he could not see a thing. Ordinarily this would not present much of a challenge, but the cloth had been so tightly tied that his head throbbed. For the last several hours, he'd been subjected to constant physical abuse. During the first round of questioning, they'd only shoved him around. But then it had escalated to punches and kicks aimed at his sides and ribs. His lower back felt like a side of beef after it had been pounded on.

He coughed. The cold air of the room they kept him in didn't help, either. In the time he'd been there, he'd developed a cough. He wondered if he was getting sick. Bits of phlegm and spittle shot from his mouth, but if he expected sympathy, he got none. For his trouble, they laughed at him.

"You can stop this anytime you want. Just tell us the name of the clan that hired you."

At times, they would ask him nicely. The tone of their

voices was soothing, almost hypnotic in its approach. And Ran desperately wanted to believe they were not going to harm him.

He knew better than that.

Other times, their voices were harsh and insistent. They played on these two extremes, trying to find a weakness they could exploit—one tiny chink in his mental armor they could worm their way in through and get him to spill his secrets.

When the psychological techniques failed, they resorted to the physical. Ran was stripped of his clothing and made to lean against a wall with his arms extended. This position produced severe muscle fatigue in only about a minute. As supremely well-conditioned as Ran was, the sleep deprivation and lack of proper food and drink had taken its toll. He could not hold the position for very long without lowering his hands. When he did, they got him back up, punched him a few times, and made him resume the position until he thought his arms were going to fall off.

Then the questioning continued.

"Just give us a name. Tell us who contacted you. Which clan hired you?"

On and on it would go. For hours. They were relentless. His silence never bothered them. They would simply come at him from another angle. No matter what they tried, Ran said nothing.

He wanted to, though. He desperately wanted to. Not during the violent times. He could use anger toward them as a defense against that. Fantasies of ripping off the blindfold and breaking all of their necks gave him enough spirit to endure those attacks.

The soothing voice, though, that was a real challenge. As much as he knew these were not his friends, he couldn't help thinking that maybe they liked him. That maybe they appreciated the way he'd been able to hold out and give them absolutely nothing. Perhaps they even respected him for it.

Would it be so bad to give them a little something? He could make up a lie. Tell them another clan had hired him. Would that be enough to get them to maybe give him some food and water? A little nourishment would help him fight off the sickness he felt certain he was getting in his lungs. It would cheer him up as well. And a morale boost would be an exquisite thing, indeed.

Maybe just a name.

A cold breeze blew in, and he shivered. Sitting on the stone floor, the cold seeped into his backside and right up his spine. His teeth chattered, and he coughed again.

"You are sick. We can hear it when you breathe. It sounds like a rattling baby's toy. Your body is losing its strength. Just tell us what we need to know and we will have a healer come see you. You will be allowed to rest. Perhaps even some food. You'd like that, wouldn't you? A warm bed to sleep in. Hot tea. Just give us a name. One simple name and it can all be yours."

He didn't believe them. He knew it was a slippery slope. Once they got into you, they would keep opening you up until they got what they needed. And even if he gave them a false name, a lie was just as bad as the truth itself, because then they had a dialogue with you. The problem with telling lies was that you had to remember exactly what falsehood you had constructed, because they surely would. And they'd keep asking you over and over again to confirm it.

If you forgot what the lies were, they had you. They could go back and say, "Well, no, that's not what you told us at all. You said this. Now, which is it?"

Then the beatings would start again.

Ran longed to feel the warmth of the sun on his face. To lie on the sand of the beaches to the south and soak in the seas, letting the healing waters carry away the last vestiges of this nightmare.

"What clan hired you?"

But the beaches were a long way away in the forgotten memories of his mind. The punch that followed slammed into his lower jaw, and Ran wondered if they'd cracked some of his teeth. He spat blood on the floor. They got him up into another stress position and made him hold it for three minutes before Ran collapsed.

"Would you like some water?" He said nothing, so they forced his mouth open and filled it with a spicy herb that set his teeth afire. He retched and spat it out, and they laughed at him.

More questions. More punches and kicks to his lower back. At one point, Ran felt his bladder go free, and he pissed all over himself. He wasn't upset, though. The puddle of urine actually warmed him up some. At least until it grew cold and wet. Then it was just as horrible as it had been before.

They laughed at him when they weren't yelling or beating him. Since he was naked and cold, the target of their scorn was obvious. They would invite women in and ask them if they'd ever seen one quite so small. The women would laugh along with them and say they couldn't even see that there was anything between Ran's legs in the first place.

Ran didn't mind those sessions. Anyone who had been cold and naked for as long as he had been would look exactly like he did. As far as he was concerned, their critiques were a fair assessment.

But that wasn't the point.

They were still trying to find a way inside his defenses. They wanted to know what made him tick. When they found out that something didn't work, they would change tactics and go at him another way. Always trying to find a way in. It didn't matter how small the hole was; once they found one, they had you.

So Ran worked to make sure they didn't find one.

While they questioned him, he practiced counting. First by ones, then by twos, fives, tens. Sometimes he'd count by hard numbers like intervals of twenty-seven. Anything to distract his mind from the pain at hand and force it to focus on figuring out what came after fifty-four and so on. He tried to create little refuges within his mind that he could escape to. If he could focus his mind there instead of on the pain, then he could hold out longer.

The problem was he was getting weaker. His lungs spasmed every time he coughed now. He knew he was caked in filth—urine, sweat, spit, phlegm, snot. If they'd caught him with a full stomach, he would have shat himself by now as well.

Lucky for them or he would've had some kind of weapon to fight back.

It would have earned him a severe beating, but the

thought made him smile, and that was almost as good as the real thing.

"Give us a name."

The soft voice had returned. It crept into Ran's mind like some type of nefarious ear worm. He could feel the syrupy tone of the words snaking their way through his head, nudging aside his desire to remain closed. He knew what was different about it this time, too. It was a woman's voice. He wasn't used to this. During this entire time, only men had questioned him. He had fended them off with relative ease.

But this was something new.

Her voice was like a warm blanket wrapping itself around his thoughts and hugging them into her bosom. And there, in that moment, a memory of his mother surfaced, bubbling up from the deepest, most protected area of his mind. He saw her face. Felt her embrace, her warmth. Heard her laughter. The soothing touch of her hand on his brow.

"Just tell me who hired you . . . my son."

He had blinked beneath the blindfold. He coughed again and he felt a cloth wipe away the spittle from his mouth. The soft caress of a warm hand against his cold, clammy skin. He felt something then beneath his beaten exterior, under his hardened heart and iron will to outlast them and their questions.

He felt hope.

And more than anything, he felt a desire to help his mother—to help her understand what he was and who had hired him.

If he could just give his mother the answer she wanted,

the answer she sought, then he could be with her again. She could hold him and rock him to sleep and tell him everything was going to be all right, that no one would ever harm him again.

No.

His mother was dead.

Years had passed since he'd seen her dismembered corpse bloated and twisted in the wake of the savage attack on his village that had left Ran an orphan. His father's body had been nearby, in even more horrifying condition. Blood spatters and streaks adorned their simple home. A fire raged in the back of the house and forced him to flee, leaving behind the bodies of his parents. Their home became a funeral pyre. The images of his parents were seared into his brain and locked away. He chose never to think about them for a reason: it brought back too much pain, too much uncertainty, too much of the world that he'd once been a part of before the Shinobujin took him in to become one of their own.

This wasn't his mother talking to him now. She would never speak to him again. This was another trick they were trying out on him to see if there was a chance he would crack under the pressure of an ancient memory.

Ran said nothing.

"Remove the blindfold."

Harsh light flooded his skull and made him wince. He blinked rapidly to acclimate to the abrupt change. He took several deep, rattling breaths and coughed again. Two pairs of hands helped him up and brought him over to a blazing hearth where the warmth was almost too exquisite to endure. A bowl of thin soup was held to his mouth, and

Ran greedily drank it down. If this was another tactic, he didn't care. He would take the warmth and the food and keep fighting them for as long as it took. He would never break.

"You did well, Ran."

He looked up and saw Akimoto, the head instructor for this part of the training, looking down at him. He wore a big smile on his face. "We very nearly got to you at the end there, though, didn't we?"

There was no point in lying about it. They knew everything about him by now. They had seen him under the worst pressure they could provide. All of his expressions had been noted. All of his reactions had been catalogued. To lie at this point would have been stupid and pointless. So Ran nodded. "Very nearly, sir. Yes."

Akimoto sat down next to him and helped him hold the bowl with his hands. Ran took several more mouthfuls of the soup. It had been days since he'd had any food, but they couldn't serve him a huge meal immediately or his stomach would vomit it back up after the extreme duress he'd been under.

"Just remember," said Akimoto, "that we cannot fully replicate the conditions you will face in the real world. The best we can do is what you have just endured. If you are ever captured in the real world, the torture will be far more horrendous than anything you have just gone through. They will stop at nothing to get the information they seek."

Ran coughed, and Akimoto placed one hand on his chest. "You have a bit of a cough there. We will give you a draught that should take away the infection in a few days.

You need to rest, obviously. You have been through a terrific ordeal and emerged from it a better student."

"Thank you."

"Do you understand why we have done what we did? Why we subjected you to this training?"

Ran nodded. "I understand."

"Then also understand this: everyone has their breaking point. Everyone talks eventually. The key is to hold out for as long as possible and make them work for the information. Death will undoubtedly await you after the torture, so you may ask why prolong the inevitable. But by doing so, you will save lives and hopefully render the information obsolete by the time you do give them what they seek."

"Death is a part of the path all men walk," said Ran. "Shinobujin, especially. I do not fear it."

"They will know you do not," said Akimoto. "So they will do everything possible to keep you from that final release, that final journey toward the darkness that waits us all." The old instructor paused, a frown creasing his face. "And as many ways as man has to kill, he has an even greater ingenuity when it comes to inflicting suffering on others."

Ran looked at him. "What then is your advice, sir?"

Akimoto laughed. "My advice? The same thing I tell every member of our clan regardless of how long they have been with us. My advice is always the same, because it is the simple unvarnished truth: don't get caught."

Don't get caught.

CHAPTER TWENTY-SEVEN

His head hurt.

Ran reached up and felt the base of his skull. A lump the size of a small teacup protruded and felt tender to the touch. He winced, aware of the memories of his past training that had just replayed in his mind. It had felt like a dream, but the training had been real enough. The final words of his instructor lingered in his head.

Don't get caught.

But he was caught now. Ran wondered why he hadn't been killed yet. Surely Malkyr wouldn't want to take a chance with him in captivity. He knew what Ran was capable of doing. He reached down and felt for the inside of his belt. The length of wire Ran had used to pick the lock back at Kan-Gul's castle was gone. Ran's weapons were also missing.

He blinked, trying to find his bearings. The last thing he could remember before Malkyr had attacked him was being on board the raider ship. He was halfway up the ladder when Malkyr had called him back down. Ran shook his head slowly. *Damn fool thing to do*, he thought. It wasn't as if Malkyr had been entirely trustworthy up until that point, either.

Ran sighed and rolled over. His feet bumped into the side of a wall. Wood. Ran looked and saw the bars on a door several feet away from him. He was in a cell of some type, but where? He stayed still and tried to get a sense of his surroundings. He still smelled the ocean, so they must be close to the harbor. And then he felt the sides of the cell shift slightly.

Ran smiled. He was on a ship. But whether it was the raider or one of the transports, he didn't know. But something told him he was on the same boat. Malkyr wouldn't have taken the chance that Ran would wake up and disable the raiders and kill Malkyr if they'd tried to drag him all the way to another ship.

No, he was still on the raider ship. Ran felt sure of it. His head ached, and Ran felt his stomach lurch. If he'd had anything in it, he probably would have vomited. But not eating turned out to be a small win in this case. Not that he was feeling especially pleased with how easily Malkyr had taken him down. He replayed the moment in his head. As he'd come down the ladder, something in his gut had made him suspect danger.

But it had been too late to do anything about it. Malkyr hammered him before his foot had even touched the lower deck.

Foolish.

Ran sat up slowly and tried to listen to any other ambient noises on the ship. He could hear footsteps above him, probably on the main deck. There were people about now. He wondered if the entire thing had been staged as a trap. Make it look like the harbor was deserted in order to entice Ran down. Malkyr certainly knew what Ran could do, having seen him in action at the castle. Perhaps they wanted him out of the way first.

Ran wondered if the others had seen him captured. If he was still on the raider ship, it didn't seem likely. But they probably knew something was wrong; Ran had been gone for a while.

Kancho would be the first to move, he decided. The older warrior would no doubt sense something amiss, and his sense of honor would get the better of him. They might be moving into position even now. Ran frowned. Although with more people clearly in view, that might not be an option. None of them would be able to scale the rock face the way Ran had. That left the path down as their only option. And Malkyr would send his men to meet them if that happened.

They could already be captured, he realized.

If that was the case, then Ran had little hope of rescue.

But he'd been trained for that as well. His instructors had stressed from the very first day of training that the life of a Shinobujin was a solo affair. No matter if the assignment or guise offered companionship, at the end of the day a Shinobujin operated alone. He lived in the murky grays that existed in the world. One day here, one day there. Never able to be pinned down for too long, he left no trail, no history, no past. Blink and he was gone.

If the unthinkable happened, the Shinobujin was expected to rescue himself. He was expected to find his own way out of whatever predicament he found himself in.

No other members of the clan would come to assist him, because that would risk exposing them all to the wrath of the warlords who despised them.

If rescue became impossible, there was but one option left: death.

Ran didn't fancy killing himself. Even when they'd taught him how to choke on his own tongue, or break his own neck, he had filed it away as a useless bit of knowledge that he would never have need for. He knew it was his ego talking when he convinced himself he would never get caught.

The real world apparently had other ideas.

Ran squatted and examined his makeshift cell. The door had steel bars set into it and looked solid enough. The hinges were on the outside, though, which Ran considered a silly mistake. It meant he could chamber a kick and bust down the door if it came to that. Further, the lock looked elementary. Ran didn't have his wire, but he knew other ways to open a lock. Then, the walls of the cell were wooden as well. Ran could effectively burrow through them if he needed to, and if he had a tool of some sort.

Overall, his predicament wasn't dire. At least not yet. But the sooner he got out of here, the better. His instructors had always taught him that escaping as soon as possible after capture was always preferable to staying put. The longer you stayed, the harder it would become to escape. Often times prisoners were moved to better and more secure locations. If Ran's cell was something he thought he could easily deal with, then he didn't want to take the chance that he might be moved to a stone-walled cell or something even more impenetrable.

He heard more footsteps overhead and then the sound of someone coming down the ladder. He pulled himself to the back wall of his cell and waited.

Malkyr's face appeared at the bars of his cell. "Wide awake are you? Good."

Ran stood and faced Malkyr. "That was a damned foolish thing to do."

"Why? Because I somehow managed to get the better of you?"

Ran shook his head. "Because you betrayed all of us. We should have let the sharks eat you back on the beach."

"I don't want you to think I'm not grateful for that. I am. It's the only reason you're still alive. Someone very powerful wants you dead, but I'm not so sure I want to hand you back over to him."

"Why? Out of gratitude?"

Malkyr smirked, reminding Ran of a pit viper. "Ran, my good friend, I am a man of few principles. Surely you know this by now. My motivations in life are fairly easy to discern. I don't adhere to some antiquated code that forbids me the basic liberties and freedom that I adore. My ethics are much more . . . fluid, shall we say."

"Get to the point."

"I can sell you back in Nehon to the highest bidder. And I'll make a terribly enormous pile of money off of your head."

Ran felt his gut ache. But rather than admit it, he frowned. "Why would anyone pay a lot of money for me?"

"Well, it's not so much you. Rather it's what you are. I'm well aware of the night demons. And you are without a doubt one of the most talented I've ever known of."

"I'm not a night demon. I'm a blade-for-hire. If I was a shadow warrior, why on earth would I have taken a trip abroad in your horrible boat?"

"The *Aqaria* was a good ship," said Malkyr. "Tragic that she had to be sacrificed the way she was. But then again, that was part of my deal with Kan-Gul."

"What did you say?"

Malkyr grinned. "Haven't figured it out yet?" He frowned for a moment. "Perhaps you're not a night demon, after all. I generally thought they were more intelligent than you seem to be." He clapped his hands. "No matter. Yes, well, I have a deal with Kan-Gul. You see, he's had his eye on the young sorceress for some time now. Kan-Gul has eyes everywhere. Dare I say he might even give you night demons a challenge when it comes to setting up spy networks. In any event, he learned that Jysal would be heading off to the temple, and he paid me to bring her to him."

"You wrecked your own boat to betray her?"

Malkyr shrugged. "The *Aqaria* wasn't really mine. I won her in a friendly wager with another trader. So I don't have much emotional attachment to her. She served a purpose and did it well."

Ran shook his head. "There was no guarantee that you'd successfully land us in his territory."

"Well, I'll be the first to admit things got a bit unpredictable there toward the end. And that business with the sharks was something I don't want to have to repeat anytime soon. But all's well that ends well, as they say. And now, not only do I have the opportunity to deliver Jysal to Kan-Gul and collect on my end of the bargain, but I also have a chance to auction off a real live shadow warrior. Surely the gods have smiled upon me this day."

"You won't be smiling when I get out of here."

Malkyr waved that comment off. "We have other things to discuss rather than your dreams of vengeance, which I assure you will never happen. Tell me something: Where are the other members of your party?"

"I told you where they were. Up at the tunnel entrance." Ran smiled. "They're not there?"

"You know they're not. I sent men up there to find them and they were nowhere to be seen."

"How unfortunate," said Ran. "I can't imagine that Kan-Gul will be pleased when he arrives and finds you don't have his treasure ready for him to take back to his castle."

Malkyr's demeanor changed. "You don't want to do this."

"Do what?"

"Upset me. I'm not a man who likes being mocked. I've asked you a question, and I expect an answer."

Ran shrugged. "I'm telling you the truth. When I left them, they were waiting next to the rock up at the tunnel entrance—or exit, whatever it is. If they're not there any longer, then they might have gotten impatient and left. Perhaps they thought I'd been captured and decided to abandon me."

Malkyr shook his head. "Kancho would never leave you behind."

"Wouldn't he? He's Murai. You know what that means."

"It doesn't matter. He's Murai, no doubt. But he's also

indebted to you. As such, he won't leave you. That would bring him even more dishonor than allying himself with a shadow warrior. And Kancho doesn't strike me as the type to easily sacrifice his honor. No, he's got to be around. And you know where they are."

"I do not," said Ran. "I wish I did, though, because I would urge them to skewer your worthless skin and hang you out to dangle above the hungry sharks we saved you from."

"That's not very nice, considering I'm thinking about denying Kan-Gul's request to hand you over."

"Where is the mighty sorcerer anyway? I'm a bit surprised he hasn't made an appearance yet. Surely he can transport himself across distances with ease if we're to believe he's such a powerful mage."

"He is on his way here with a force of his men. They ran into some trouble dealing with dragons or some such thing."

"The same dragons we had to deal with?"

Malkyr smirked. "Apparently Kan-Gul isn't the only master in this area. And the dragons were so upset about not getting to us that they attacked the Chekhal unit traveling with Kan-Gul."

"Interesting. I would have enjoyed watching that."

"Probably not," said Malkyr. "The dragons are apparently all dead. Kan-Gul wiped them out."

Ran frowned. "That would have taken some power."

"Indeed." Malkyr leaned against the door. "There's another way we could play this, you know."

"Oh?"

Malkyr shrugged. "I know a good man when I see one.

And you have an extensive array of talents I would like nothing more than to put to good use."

Ran smiled. "Good use in this case meaning what?"

"You travel with me, and when I spot targets of opportunity—be it a castle, bank, church, what have you—you sneak in and liberate their supplies of money, gold, and jewels. Any other treasure you find would be most welcome as well."

"And what do I get out of that deal?"

"You get your life back. Kan-Gul wants you desperately for his own sick purposes. Frankly, I think that's a waste of talent. We could make a ton of money together. Or I could auction you off back in Nehon and see which warlord wants to boil you alive in oil."

"Not especially fond of a death like that."

"Who would be?" Malkyr knocked on the door. "You've got a lot to think about and not much time to do it in. You know as well as I do that we will locate Kancho and the others. Jysal is going to Kan-Gul—there's nothing I can do about that. He's paying good money to have her, and I don't intend to stand in his way. Your welfare and that of the others is entirely in your hands, however. Agree to my conditions, and they will go free. You will stay with me in my employ for a period of ten years. During that time we will sail far and wide and rob whomever we wish."

"Do I get any of the treasure I steal for you?"

"You'll get a wage of sorts. And you'll have your life. When the ten years are up, provided you haven't been captured or killed, you will be free to go on with your life. I'll even give you a bonus at the end of our time together."

Ran looked at Malkyr. "You're being serious."

"Absolutely. I'm a businessman, Ran. Money is the only god I worship. So have yourself a think about it and let me know. Kan-Gul is due to arrive later tonight. I'll need a decision from you before then. Understood?"

"Understood."

Malkyr's face vanished, and Ran was once again alone.

CHAPTER TWENTY-EIGHT

Ran had no intention of accepting Malkyr's offer. As he listened to Malkyr's footfalls recede, he glanced around the cell and made his decision. He would not wait for Kan-Gul to show up and take Jysal for his own. Ran needed to get out of the cell and now. He had to find out where Kancho and the others were hiding, a fact he enjoyed because it meant more trouble for Malkyr.

He should never have trusted Malkyr at the start. That was one of the biggest mistakes he'd made. But even as he scolded himself for bad judgment, he reminded himself that this was what the wandering quest was all about. Shinobujin thought of it as a type of finishing school for recent graduates. There was nothing like being exposed to the real world and real consequences to impress upon you what worked and what did not.

Ran also recognized that he still had much to learn. Despite having graduated, he was still very new to the world at large. His ego had already tripped him up and he hadn't fully taken into account the possibility of betrayal by someone who had depended on him.

Malkyr's voice drifted down from above. "Baraz, get your butt below deck and guard the prisoner!"

Ran had precious little time. He ran his hands over the walls of the cell, searching for what he needed. On the second go-around, he found pieces of splintered wood and carefully extricated them from the planks they had been part of. They were both long and thicker than they needed to be, but Ran wasn't sure if the salt air had weakened them at all.

Ordinarily, lockpicking required metal tools to work properly. But Ran had also been shown techniques using stiffened wood with one acting as a rake and the other as a pick. If he was able to reach the lock, he could attempt it. He reached his arms through the bars, grateful they were set wider apart than he would have expected in a formal cell, and let them dangle down toward the lock itself.

Ran let his hands feel their way over the lock. He couldn't see it, of course, but he could picture it in his mind. Then he reversed the pieces of wood and inserted them one at a time into the lock. The simple padlock hung on a bolt that Ran could have easily kicked through if he'd needed to. But that would create a lot of noise, something he didn't want.

Footsteps echoed overhead. Ran forced himself not to rush. He worked the pick and rake into the padlock and felt the slivers of wood trip the pins. There were only three, and Ran quickly worked them into the correct position. Then he took the wooden pieces out and, using his free hand, pulled down on the lock.

It popped open with a thunk that Ran prayed hadn't echoed across the expanse of the ship. Then he slid the lock off the bolt and opened the door.

"Hey—"

Baraz. Ran didn't even pause. He stepped out of the cell and drove his front foot into the guard's groin, doubling him over. As his head came down, Ran's knee came up and crushed his nose. Ran kept moving and with his right hand cupped the guard's chin and yanked it around, snapping his neck. Baraz dropped to the ground. Ran dragged him into the cell, closed the door, and relocked the padlock. Let Malkyr wonder how he could have escaped a locked cell.

Ran smirked. Once again, the legend of the night stalkers might give him a psychological edge. If Ran could escape from a locked cell and take out a guard, did he do so using magic? The truth was he could not, but planting such a thought in the minds of his enemies could work to his advantage. And Ran was going to need every edge as he made his escape.

He crept across the deck, hearing footsteps above him. He headed toward the stern, back where he knew the captain's quarters would be located. He paused outside of the door and then pressed down on the handle, hoping it would not squeak when he entered. Inside, the small room showed a bed and a simple desk. A secondary door sat off to the port side. Ran opened it.

A toilet—little more than a seat over a large hole leading right out to the sea—greeted him. Ran frowned. He'd expected to find a closet or armory with weapons. He was still unarmed and didn't like his odds for confronting the other sailors aboard the ship.

His ears caught a sound. Ran turned. Someone was coming down the ladder.

Malkyr?

It had to be. Malkyr wasn't the patient type, and he would want an answer from Ran about his offer. When he found the cell empty, the ship would erupt into chaos, and they would search everywhere for him.

Ran felt his heartbeat quicken. He had no way out of the cabin. There wasn't a secondary ladder leading above decks.

"He's gone!"

Malkyr's voice reached his ears and Ran knew he had precious seconds to act. They would tear the ship apart looking for him.

Ran grimaced.

No choice.

He stepped into the toilet, closed the door behind him, and looked at the hole. It was barely wide enough, but fortunately the toilet looked to have been custom-made to accommodate a captain with a larger than normal backside. Ran jerked the seat up and looked at the hole. It didn't smell as bad as he thought it would, and he could see straight down into the water. Maybe ten feet. He heard footsteps running all over the decks now.

Ran positioned himself on the edge of the hole, aware of the filth caking its sides, took a deep breath, and then lowered himself down the short tunnel, carefully closing the seat over him as he did so.

As soon as he let go of the sides of the seat, he dropped. Ran tried to slow his descent, but the muck on the sides acted like a lubricant and shot him down the shaft and into the cold sea below.

Ran blew out as soon as he entered the water, trying his best not to make a large splash. He cracked his eyes and then kicked his legs, driving himself into deeper water. No doubt the sailors above on the raider ship had heard the splash and would be searching the depths.

As he swam away, several arrows zipped past him in the water. But they soon stopped. They wouldn't waste arrows unless they had a clear target.

Ran kept kicking and swimming away from the raider ship. He wanted to get closer to the transport vessels and use their massive bodies as cover. His lungs felt like they were going to burst, and Ran had barely cleared the first vessel when he needed to surface and steal a breath. As his head came out of the water, he could hear the chaos on the docks. Footsteps pounded across the piers and decks of various ships as Malkyr's men searched for Ran.

He allowed himself a quick grin, then stole another breath before submerging once again and heading for the last transport vessel. As he kicked, he heard splashes and then saw floating lanterns above him casting their light into the depths of the harbor waters. Overhead, Ran could see the roof of the cavern. He tried to stay deep enough that the lanterns would not illuminate him as he swam.

The bottom of the harbor was remarkably clean and sandy. Ran spotted a few fish, and fortunately he did not see any of the ravenous sharks that had marauded them at the reefs. Still, the sooner he got out of the water, the better. Malkyr would know there was only one possible way he could have escaped the vessel, and that was through the toilet.

Ran swam harder, aware that his lungs were straining again. He waited until one of the lanterns passed overhead and then surfaced when he thought the eyes of sailors would be on the lit area rather than the one the lantern had just passed over. He snatched a quick breath and dove down again. He pulled for all he was worth and swam beneath the keels of two more transport vessels. He estimated the depth of the harbor was roughly twenty feet.

A few more fish swam past him, but Ran paid them no mind. Beyond the last transport vessel was an outcropping of rocks that he hoped to use as a shield in order to gather his strength back after the exhausting swim.

Another lantern passed between the transport ships. Ran had to wonder if putting a lit candle so close to a wooden hull was a smart move. But Malkyr would be desperate, and rational thought was always the first casualty of hurried thinking. Ran kept swimming and passed by the last transport vessel. He had a hundred yards of open water to cross before he reached the rocky outcropping.

Just as he thought he might not make it, he pulled even harder and managed to surface directly behind the rocks. With only his head exposed, Ran sucked air into his lungs and took a moment to restore normal rhythm to his breathing. The chaos on the docks continued, and Ran leaned his head around just enough for one eye to see. Scrambling figures were running all over the place.

There seemed to be no reason to their search pattern. That was another psychological edge that Shinobujin had exploited numerous times in the past. A careful search pattern would have taken time to organize but resulted in a more thorough search. Rushed as they were, Malkyr's men were running here and there, scanning the water and thinking they had checked each place in turn. But in their rush to do so, they had obvious gaps. Ran had moved through those gaps and now rested away from where they were searching, somewhat secure behind the outcropping of rocks.

With his breathing back to normal, Ran scanned the immediate vicinity, trying to work out where Kancho, Jysal, and Neviah could possibly be hiding. The choices were limited to farther back in the tunnel or some place Ran could not see. Years of training had taught Ran to always watch for possible hiding spots as a matter of habit, so that at a moment's notice he could slip into one of them. But even he had to admit there were very few places three people could hide effectively from a thorough search.

The most likely answer was that they had retreated farther back into the tunnel. Perhaps they had managed to locate a branch in the tunnel. Ran frowned. They hadn't seen any branches on their way down. Although once Jysal had noticed the light, their awareness had been fixed on that. Even Ran had focused only on the light and not what else the tunnel might have held. He closed his eyes and took several deep cleansing breaths to focus his mind. He recalled the image of the tunnel as they approached the light at the end. There were several shadows along the rough wall that would have been large enough for him to hide in. Perhaps one of them held a small crevasse leading to a side passage.

Of course, Jysal had magic at her disposal. Was it possible she knew a way to turn them all invisible? Had she rendered them immune to sight? Could it be that Malkyr's men might be walking right past them? Malkyr knew that Jysal had magic power, but he didn't think she could do anything with it yet. She was, in his mind, on her way to the temple to learn how to use it.

Even if they were invisible, they would still need to be absolutely quiet. And just because they couldn't be seen didn't mean that some of Malkyr's men might not bump into them unexpectedly. Invisibility was no guarantee of safety, Ran decided. Better to try to make an escape or at least move back to a better defensive position.

But where?

While they were at the tunnel entrance, they held the higher ground. Kancho could have held off a frontal attack for some time and Neviah would have spelled him. But what would that gain them? Malkyr would simply throw more men at them until they were exhausted and easy to overwhelm.

And Ran would have heard the noise of battle. Kancho and Neviah were ferocious fighters. They would kill many of Malkyr's men before succumbing to the assault. No, he decided, they had to be elsewhere.

Something told him to duck back behind the rocks. As he did so, a brilliant burst of light flashed over the rocks he'd been bobbing next to in the water. Ran shrank back into the shadows of the nook he was in and waited. The light stayed on the area for another thirty seconds before moving off. Malkyr must have had some sort of huge candle and a reflector that could throw light into other areas.

Wonderful, he thought. *So much for being invisible in the shadows*. Ran would need to figure out a way out of the water and out of the harbor. He knew he could always swim out of the tunnel and head for open sea, but that meant leaving his friends behind. And the sea was no safer than his current predicament.

Malkyr would most likely assume he would make for the open ocean anyway. Ran would go where he was least expected—he would stay in the harbor and wait for his friends to arrive.

The water surrounding him chilled his bones, and Ran tried a rapid series of breaths to flush himself and generate some warmth. It helped momentarily, but then he heard several heavy splashes, and his heart started beating even faster. Something was wrong.

Ran sank into the water until just his eyes were out of it. Then he moved to the edge of the rocks and peered around back at the harbor itself. Sailors still ran around the docks, peering into the water. But they had added a new variable to the search. As Ran scanned the water, he could make them out easily moving against the current.

Malkyr had put swimmers into the water.

And two were headed directly for him.

CHAPTER TWENTY-NINE

They hadn't seen Ran yet, but judging by the direction they were swimming, they were coming to check out the outcropping. Ran had seconds before they reached the area, and he had a decision to make. If Malkyr was smart, he would have dispatched these men and then had one wait outside the location while the other went to check it out. If Ran tried to subdue one, the other could raise the alarm.

But as they approached, Ran could see they were both coming into the area. Even better, they appeared to be uncomfortable in the water. Their stroke technique was awkward and clumsy and produced more splashes than movement. Ran nodded to himself. He could work with that.

As they approached, he took a deep breath and dove deep. Once he hit the bottom, he kicked off and darted under the two men. Ran kicked over to the closest transport vessel and waited near the keel for the two men to scour his previous hiding spot and declare it free of nightstalkers.

It took them barely three minutes to do so, during which Ran surfaced exactly once to snatch a quick breath before descending again by the keel of the transport. It was too bad, he thought, that the transport ships didn't have an entrance under their keel that would grant him access. He could have hung out there while trying to formulate a plan to reconnect with Kancho and the others.

Eventually, the two swimmers exited the outcropping and floundered their way back to the dock, where two more men hauled them from the water. Ran surfaced and watched. As they stood there shivering, Malkyr stormed up and demanded to know if they'd found anything.

"There was nothing, my lord."

Malkyr backhanded the first man. "You are fools. How can one man disappear like that? He's not a wizard. He must be here somewhere."

The second man cleared his throat. "Perhaps, my lord, he swam out of the harbor and made it to open sea?"

Malkyr stopped and ran a hand over his jaw. "Perhaps. It would be a difficult swim, though. And the danger from sharks is great."

"They may have already devoured him, sir."

Malkyr nodded once. "It's worth investigating. You two get some warm clothes on and then take a skiff out of the harbor. See if you can find any signs that he passed that way. Better yet, see if you can find any sign that the sharks took him."

The two men rushed away, and Ran allowed himself to float in the gentle swells. The rest of the docks seemed to be quieting down now that Malkyr had assumed Ran was gone. But sailors still rushed around putting supplies on the transport vessels. Ran wondered when the army from the north might be due to arrive, but he guessed they were still some time away. The supplies being loaded were all dry goods and nonperishables. That meant the army was likely not due to arrive for a while yet.

Ran hoped that was the case, anyway.

Eventually, he heard a bell ring somewhere farther away from the docks. The sailors all stopped working and filed off through a tunnel leading away from the docks. Ran pulled himself out of the water, aware of how chilled he was. He squatted in the shadows of the remaining crates and used deep breathing techniques to rapidly flush heat into his body. The practice of doing so was an ancient one. The training for doing so consisted of sitting naked in a snow drift while cloth that had been soaked in icy water was draped over you. You then had to meditate and through deep breathing be able to generate enough heat to dry the cloth.

It had been so cold when Ran had undergone the training that he made a vow to himself that he would get it done the first time so he didn't have to suffer through it again.

He'd been the only one in his class to get it right the first time.

Now, as he dried himself, Ran felt his thundering heart inside of his chest and smiled. If Malkyr truly believed he was gone, that afforded Ran more opportunities. The first thing he had to do was get back to the tunnel and see if Kancho and the others were still there somewhere. So, after drying off, Ran stole out from the concealment of the crates and headed up the slope toward the tunnel entrance.

The torch still burned brightly. Ran was surprised there were no guards at the entrance, but then again, they were probably part of a search party following the tunnel back to the now-blocked entrance where they had entered. As Ran re-entered the tunnel, the first thing he saw was a small pile of stones that had been arranged in a peculiar way. Ran recognized it immediately as a Murai signpost meant to direct other Murai. Kancho had left it off to one side, and Ran read the direction as heading east, so he backtracked down the tunnel until he felt a shift in the air.

A branch? Ran let his hands trace their way over the rocks of a shadow recess and found the opening. It was barely large enough to squeeze through, but once he did, Ran was able to stand up and continue on. Twenty steps ahead, the new tunnel sloped downward and meandered left and right before widening out into a new cavern. Ran saw the faint blue light and smiled.

Ran came to an abrupt stop as bare steel hovered inches from his face.

"So this is where you all went."

Kancho's face popped out of the dim light as he lowered his sword. "He's back!"

Ran smiled. They had each whispered, but even so their voices sounded loud in the confines of the cave.

Kancho rushed over. "We thought you were dead. When we saw Malkyr emerging from the ship, we knew he must have done something to you. But then we saw you escape the boat and vanish completely."

Ran frowned. "You saw my escape?"

"We saw you drop off the back of the ship."

"I escaped by sliding down a privy shaft."

Neviah approached him and gave a sniff. "You don't smell any worse for having been down the shaft of a toilet. I'm surprised."

"Try spending a few hours in the sea after doing that, and you'll be surprised how clean you can feel."

"That must have been fairly awful," said Neviah.

"It was either that or stand there and wait for Malkyr to come for me."

"You could have killed him," said Kancho. "Surely that wouldn't have presented you with a problem."

"It wouldn't have been a problem," said Ran. "But I had good reasons for not doing that. At least, not yet."

"What reasons?" asked Jysal.

Ran eyed Kancho. "I heard two men talking about a hostage. They referred to her as the daughter of a Murai."

Kancho balled up his fists. "So they have her?"

Ran shook his head. "I do not know where they may have her. I came across Malkyr shortly afterward, and that's when he betrayed me."

"He's betrayed us all," said Neviah. "And he will surely pay for that with his life."

"I won't argue with you on that," said Ran. "But the priority has to be finding Kancho's daughter. The problem is, we do not have a lot of time. Kan-Gul is set to arrive tonight, and he intends to take Jysal with him. Malkyr deliberately wrecked the *Aqaria* so he could sell Jysal to him."

The look on Neviah's face reminded Ran of death. He had no doubt that she would find a way to kill Malkyr regardless of how many Chekhal stood in front of her. The thought that Jysal had been targeted like that no doubt made her blood boil.

Kancho wanted to leave immediately. "We must find her and then get out of here. I don't care about Kan-Gul. I just want to get my daughter back to the safety of her home. She is the only family I have left. My wife died three winters ago, and Yuki is my world."

"We have two priorities," said Ran. "Finding Kancho's daughter and then finding a way to get out of here."

"What about killing Malkyr and Kan-Gul?" asked Neviah.

Ran shook his head. "As much as I understand wanting to do both, the priorities are what I just mentioned. Killing those two is a luxury. And you still have to get Jysal to the temple."

Neviah frowned. "I dislike the idea that Malkyr will live to see more sunrises."

"And I hate the thought of Kan-Gul being able to cast more magic," said Ran. "But we need to get out of here. Only then can we reassess the situation. If it warrants coming back and killing them both, then we certainly will. But only after Kancho and his daughter are headed home to warn Nehon of the invasion, and Jysal is safely tucked away in the temple. I'm assuming that place would be pretty much unassailable?"

Jysal nodded. "The mages would never allow any invader to get close to it."

"If they could even see it," said Neviah. "The temple is cloaked in many spells, and only those who know how to find it will ever be able to see it. An invading army from the north would have no chance and would most likely wander right past it."

"Good," said Ran. "So, let's split up then." He looked

at Kancho. "You and I will go after your daughter." He eyed Neviah. "Can you and Jysal take Malkyr's boat down without too much trouble?"

Jysal smirked. "Only if Neviah lets me use some magic."

Neviah shook her head. "There's no need to use magic, Jysal. We can do it with cunning and force if need be. I don't want you casting spells. It's simply too dangerous."

Jysal sighed. "Fine."

Ran pointed. "Have you scouted ahead farther to see where this new tunnel leads?"

Kancho nodded. "It leads to the main ventilation shaft of a very large galley. Luckily, it's not in use, but we were able to steal some hardtack." He reached into his tunic and brought out a piece. "Would you like some?"

Ran took it and bit into it, chewing and swallowing as fast as he could. It was only some very dry stale biscuits, but he was ravenous. When he was done, Kancho offered him some water, and Ran drank deep. "Thanks."

"Thank you," said Kancho. "You've given me real hope that my daughter might be able to be saved."

"We don't have her yet," said Ran. "And we need to find her first."

Neviah took a breath. "How long should we wait after you leave before heading down to the boat? And how soon do you want it ready for sailing?"

"Malkyr said he could get the boat ready in quick time, that he would only need a few bodies for the oars. Each of us can take an oar if one grabs the tiller. So concentrate on getting the ropes undone from the docks and making sure the oars are fit into their locks. I'm sure you'll hear some commotion once we find Kancho's daughter. That will be your cue to start casting off."

"We are likely to be running very hard when we grab my girl," said Kancho. "Make sure you have the gangway ready to drop so others can't scramble aboard once we do."

Neviah nodded. "We'll be ready. Just go and find her quickly. The thought of Kan-Gul coming here is already making my skin crawl. I want to be far away by the time he arrives."

Ran nodded to Kancho. "Let's go. You lead the way as far up as you can. If they've got a galley down there, odds are good they must also have some sort of holding cell. My bet is we will find your daughter there."

"I agree it seems to be the most likely place for her to be held." He glanced at Neviah and Jysal. "Good luck to you both. I hope to see you again very soon."

Jysal smiled and then winked at Ran. Ran turned and followed after Kancho. The older warrior led them down a twisting path of dirt and loose stones that skittered and plopped away, bouncing against the walls. As quiet as Ran was able to be, Kancho simply could not help himself and continued to make noise.

Finally, Ran laid a hand on his shoulder. "Let me go first."

"Why?"

Ran smiled. "Because I'm quieter than you. And if they hear us coming, we will have no chance of getting your daughter back safely. They will simply kill her or use her to get us to surrender. Neither one of those options is acceptable to me."

"Nor I," said Kancho. "But it'll be fine until we get to

the ventilation shaft. It's just a crack in the ceiling, but the hoods for the stoves are but a short drop."

Ran nodded, and they moved off again. As they rounded another turn in the tunnel, Ran spotted a lot more light up ahead. It came from a long crack in the floor.

This is where it would get tricky, he decided. Up until this point, Ran had maintained the element of surprise. But they were about to go deep into enemy territory, and there was no telling what they might find.

Ran knew Kancho's daughter was still alive, but he had no idea what condition she might be in. Had they beaten her? Raped her? Ran hoped they had not done anything to her. If they had, then Kancho's rage would be severe, and all hope of a stealthy recovery would be gone. Kancho would most likely go insane with fury and kill anyone in the nearby area. The entire dock would be alive with enemies, and the girls would have to abandon them to Malkyr's men if they had any hope of escape.

No, decided Ran, it would not be a good thing if Malkyr had done anything to Kancho's daughter. Ran almost felt sorry for Malkyr. If he had roughed up Kancho's daughter, Kancho would not stop until the birds were pecking at the remnants of Malkyr's corpse.

Ran eased himself down in the shaft and onto the hood above a large stove. There were no torches or lanterns in the galley—all the light came through window squares cut into the double swinging doors of the galley. Ran eased himself to the floor and silently crept to the doors.

He drew in deep breaths to feed his body plenty of air as he lowered his jaw to allow himself a greater range of hearing.

He heard the muffled sound of many voices and the occasional loud clatter of dishes. The noises were quiet enough that Ran knew they weren't directly on the other side of the door, but rather off to his left.

Ran slowly leaned his head just far enough for one eye to see.

Directly across from him was a set of double doors much like the ones for the galley, but no light came from the squares cut into the doors. It was probably the main mess hall for expected army.

To his left there was a single door on the other side of the hall, and all the noise came from there. It was probably intended to be the officer's mess once the army arrived, but the sailors and raiders had availed themselves of the better digs in the meantime.

And between Ran and the officer's mess hall stood a huge man armed with a battle axe.

The guard was enormous. His muscles looked at least three times the size of Ran's, and the guard had almost no neck sitting atop his shoulders.

Luckily, his attention was on the entrance to the hallway, beyond the officer's mess.

Ran quietly eased open the door and prepared to take the guard out.

CHAPTER THIRTY

Ran carefully avoided looking directly at the sentry while his steps brought him up behind the guard. His instructors back in Gakur had stressed the fact that people often sensed the approach if you stared at them while you were moving in. The preferred technique was to use peripheral vision and then at the last minute make your strike hard and fast.

Ran lowered himself as he drew closer. As he closed to within six feet, he knew he'd entered the guard's area of lethality. If the guard turned now, he would see Ran and be able to take him down fast.

Ran struck first.

As he came up behind the guard, he kicked out the back of one the man's knees, buckling the leg. As the guard grunted and fell back, Ran reached under the man's chin and jerked his head to the side sharply. He heard the dull crick of breaking bones, and the man slumped over.

Kancho was there immediately, grabbing the massive axe before it had a chance to strike the ground and make noise. Together, Ran and Kancho dragged the guard back into the empty galley and laid him out. It would be impossible to conceal his absence for long, so they now had a time limit.

"Where are the barracks?" Ran asked.

"There?" Kancho replied, pointing to doors on the left side of the hall, closer to the open-end of the hall.

"And that door at this end? The one with a heavy lock."

Kancho shook his head. "No idea."

Ran nodded. "Head for that one."

They moved quickly, not running, but not walking, either. Ran kept his body level, his sword held low in front of him. Kancho, more used to the frontal attacking style that the Murai favored, nonetheless adopted a more stealthy approach like Ran. As they moved through the area, they could hear the sounds of diners, pots, dishes, and tankards of liquor being slammed on tables.

Ran eyed their surroundings. In the corridor they were in, if anyone spotted them, they'd have a whole lot of people to deal with. The best thing to do was get to the door and hopefully release Kancho's daughter before anyone was the wiser. If they could get her and get out without anyone seeing them, so much the better.

Ran doubted they would be so lucky. Things never went to plan, no matter how much you planned.

They approached the door, and Ran noted it had metal bars set into the wood. Just like the cell he'd been in on the ship. If this one was protected with another padlock, there might not be enough time to pick it.

Sure enough, as they came to the door, Ran clearly made out the heavy-duty padlock. He glanced at Kancho. "It's locked. I can pick it."

Kancho shook his head. "There's no time. I don't doubt you could do it, but if they come out and we're not through it, then we'll lose the chance to free her." Kancho looked through the bars and then back at Ran. "She's in there."

Ran nodded. Kancho's nonchalance was typical Murai mentality. He'd been missing his daughter for weeks, and yet the first time he saw her, he merely accepted it as fact. There was nothing emotional in it. Not yet, anyway. Perhaps when they were safely aboard the raider ship and heading out to the open sea there would be time for a warmer reunion.

Not now.

"I'll break it," said Kancho.

Ran frowned. "That's quality metal."

Kancho smirked. "Shadow warriors aren't the only ones with tricks up their sleeve." He stepped back and aimed a single kick at the lock. His heel slammed into the assembly and the lock sprang open, but did so like a clap of thunder. The entire frame shook.

Ran winced. He wished Kancho could have done that a lot more quietly than he had.

Kancho ripped the door open. "Yuki."

His daughter rushed into his arms. She looked all of sixteen. While she was covered in dirt and her clothes were tattered, there was beauty beneath all that filth. Ran stowed his assessment though when he heard a gap in the ambient noise of the diners close by. He tugged on Kancho's arm. "They know something is going on. We need to leave. Now."

Kancho nodded and pushed Yuki ahead of him. Ran took the lead, and they fled down toward the docks. Ran hoped that Neviah and Jysal were already in command of the raider ship and were getting ready to cast off.

The door to the officer's mess slammed open behind them and the first sailors came streaming out. As soon as they saw Ran and Kancho, they started drawing weapons. Ran didn't hesitate and bolted for the docks. Kancho followed behind, a bit slower than Ran and Yuki.

"Hurry!" shouted Ran. He wondered where Malkyr was; the captain hadn't been in the galley as far as he could see.

They hit the docks and headed straight for the raider ship. Ran could already see that Neviah was locked in a struggle with another sailor. He leapt onto the gangway and cut down another sailor who had started to come at him. The man toppled off the gangway and into the sea below.

Neviah used the distraction of Ran's attack to throw her attacker and then plunged her dagger into his throat. He gurgled, and blood erupted from his throat before Neviah jerked the dagger free and kicked his lifeless body overboard. Ran heard the splash and then fell aboard the ship. Yuki followed.

"Is that the last one?"

Neviah nodded, looking tired. "Yes. Jysal is at the tiller."

Kancho was back on the dock close to the gangway, locked in combat with two sailors. Ran watched them come at him from either side, but Kancho merely pinwheeled his blade and sliced them both apart at the seams. The men went down in a blossoming pool of blood, their knives clattering harmlessly away.

Kancho leapt onto the gangway. "The ropes!"

Ran cut through the thick hemp with his blade. Instantly, the raider ship started to pull away from the dock. Ran pointed at the oars. "We need to use them to get out to sea. Everyone grab a seat and pull for your lives!"

He slid into the closest rowing station and waited until Neviah was on the opposite side. "Ready?"

"Ready!"

"Heave!"

Both of their oars dipped into the sea, and they pulled as hard as they could. They were only two people, but Kancho and Yuki soon joined them while Jysal worked the steering. Fortunately, the current was slight, and their exertion brought immediate results. The raider ship's prow headed off to the tunnel leading to the sea.

Ran saw the hand coming over the bulwark and immediately abandoned his post to take on the attacker. Somehow, one of the sailors must have found a spare length of rope trailing the boat and climbed aboard. He was a massive fellow, and as he came up the rope close to the bow, he jerked a wide-bladed sword out of his belt, hopped over the bulwark, and faced Ran.

Ran eased his sword out of his belt and faced the man. The sailor grinned. He was much bigger than Ran, and Ran saw the gleeful look on his face. Big fighters always underestimated men who were smaller than they were. And while their size might well be an advantage in some situations, the ship would not be one of them. Even as he came down and launched a chopping attack aimed at Ran's head, Ran sidestepped and cut back horizontally, expecting his blade to cut deep into the man's torso.

Instead, his blade met the sailor's blade with a sharp

clang. The surprise jolted Ran. The sailor was quicker than he'd thought he would be. Ran immediately corrected his technique, flipped his blade over, and made another horizontal cut at the man's throat. The sailor ducked and kicked out at Ran, catching him in his upper thigh and barely missing Ran's crotch.

"Not so easy to kill, little man," grunted the sailor.

He drove in again, using his sword more like a shield to batter Ran back until they were both against the bulwark. Ran felt his grip loosening on his sword. He could see Kancho and Neviah both getting ready to come to his aid, but he shook his head.

"Keep rowing!"

He felt the sailor's weight against him and knew the man would easily overpower him. Ran took a breath and dropped his sword. The movement caught the sailor's eye, and he grinned.

Ran felt the weight come off just a bit, and that was all he needed. He jerked his hands up and over the sailor's, clapping them both on the man's ears and shattering his eardrums. The sailor shouted as the air pressure tore his eardrums apart and stumbled back. Ran followed up with a kick of his own to the man's stomach, knocking him onto his back.

The sailor started to recover and draw himself up, but Ran never gave him the chance. He grabbed the sailor's sword and brought the blade right down on his neck. There was a gout of blood, and then the sailor fell to one side. Ran dragged his body to the edge of the boat and dumped him over the side, listening to the huge splash the body made as it hit the sea.

Ran grabbed his sword and resumed his place on the rowing bench. They'd lost speed but were close to entering the tunnel that led to the sea. "Keep pulling," said Ran. "We have to make it to the entrance."

The oars creaked in their locks, rising and falling in steady time to the rhythm of their breaths. There was no need for anyone to call out the stroke. Desperation and a desire to escape drove them better than any drummer ever could. Ran looked overhead as the inner harbor receded and the tunnel leading to the open sea drew past above them.

Kancho grunted and kept rowing while Neviah glanced sideways at Ran. "I thought you were going to have some trouble dealing with that attacker."

Ran nodded. "Big man. He was strong as an ox as well."

"Your tactic worked," said Neviah. "I liked the way you distracted him."

"Sometimes all it takes is one moment to change the course of the fight."

Neviah nodded. "That is a lesson he learned too late."

"Better him than me," said Ran.

"Skiff ahead!" shouted Jysal.

The skiff. Ran had forgotten about the two men Malkyr had sent into the tunnel to look for him. Not that it would matter much. The skiff was a tiny boat compared to the raider's ship. They could simply sail right over them if they wished. But the tunnel was also narrow. If the men in the skiff managed to position themselves just so, there was a chance they could try to board the boat as well.

Neviah looked at Ran. "Let me handle this."

Ran nodded. "All right." He looked back at Yuki who

sat on Ran's side. "Ease off. Kancho and I will row for a bit."

Neviah abandoned her station and rushed up to the bow.

"Port side," called Jysal. "In the water ahead."

Neviah pulled two daggers free from her belt and waited. "Get me closer," she called.

Ran pulled hard on his oar and imagined the vessel cutting through the water as he did so, but with only two rowers, the sloop wasn't going anywhere fast. Behind him, Kancho also rowed hard. The ship moved ahead slowly, and Ran watched as Neviah pulled her arm back and took aim. She launched a single dagger, and Ran heard the shriek as it hit. He heard a splash soon after.

Neviah glanced back. "The first one is dead."

"Better finish them both," said Ran.

Neviah threw her other dagger and got a similar result. As she came back down from the bow and resumed her place at the rowing bench, she smiled at Ran. "I never cared for those knives, anyway. They're a far inferior blade to what I carried originally."

"If we get out of this alive, I'll buy you several new ones to replace the ones you lost when Kan-Gul took you hostage."

"I'll hold you to your word, Ran."

Ran glanced back at Kancho. "We should almost be at the tunnel entrance. A few more pulls on these oars and we will break out into the open sea. Then we raise the sails and make for home."

Kancho nodded. "Home would be a welcome sight."

But Ran wondered if it really would be. Kancho had

broken his vows to come and rescue his daughter. Would the Murai look favorably upon that? He doubted they would. In all likelihood, Kancho would be put to death for his crimes. The Murai did not tolerate violations like what Kancho had committed. Duty to one's lord always came first, and certainly always before family. Kancho had defied that, and he was certain to pay for his transgression.

He could have run away, of course, but being Murai, Kancho would face his punishment square on. Plus, he would warn the other warlords of the impending invasion. Ran couldn't fault him for that sense of duty, but he wished there were another way for Kancho to deal with the Murai.

The current picked up, and Ran could feel the boat starting to float faster now as the channel clearly deepened and the tide started to grab at the raider ship. A few more minutes, he thought, and they would be away from these terrible lands. The thought of freedom made him smile. There would be another time and place to deal with Kan-Gul and his undead Chekhal hordes. *Let the universe decide when and where*, he thought. *I will see to it that he meets his demise.*

"Ran!"

Jysal's voice snapped him back to the present. Ran glanced back. "What is it?"

"You'd better look at this."

Ran frowned but moved off the bench quickly and headed up to where Jysal stood at the stern. She had a view of the water ahead of them that they could not see from the rowing bench. As soon as he reached her position, Ran understood why she had called him up there.

"That's not good."

Ahead of them, Ran could see the opening that led to the open sea. Unfortunately, between them and freedom was a giant metal portcullis with thick steel teeth that descended from the rock above deep into the sea below. The wooden timbers looked as thick as trees, and the steel was as wide across as two hands.

"It looks impenetrable," said Jysal.

Ran nodded and then called down to the bench. "Stop rowing."

Kancho looked at him like he was crazy. But Ran pointed ahead. "There's a gate. And right now, it looks like there's no way we can get through it."

"No!"

Ran nodded. "We're trapped."

CHAPTER THIRTY-ONE

Ran tried to think.

The raider ship slowed to a crawl, drifting on the current that continued to carry it closer toward the huge portcullis. This far down the tunnel, the chaos of the scene back at the docks seemed distant. Ran could hear shouts and cries as the sailors tried to figure out how to give chase, but at least right now, he had some time to work through this particular problem.

The portcullis was not something he would be able to handle on his own. Obviously, the gate offered significant security to the ships it berthed in the inner harbor. That meant there must be some sort of trigger system for raising and lowering it. Ran couldn't remember seeing any sort of pulley system or pull-chain device that would have controlled the portcullis back on the docks. And he'd seen quite a bit of the place during his infiltration and escape from the ship—the same ship he now stood on.

So if the portcullis control wasn't back at the docks, then where would it be? Out here by the gate itself? Would that make sense? Not likely. Any invading ship could simply dispatch a few sailors to take control of the device and open up the harbor anytime they wanted.

No, he decided, it had to be elsewhere.

That revelation didn't particularly buoy his spirits. It meant that they were effectively trapped unless a miracle happened and the portcullis started rising on its own accord. Otherwise, they were going to have to abandon their plan of sailing out of here.

Kancho came up on the deck and stared at the huge gate. "I don't suppose there's any way to get through that?"

"I'm sure there is," said Ran. "But I haven't got the vaguest notion where the control is for it."

"Could we get through those gaps in the gate?"

"They're pretty small," said Ran. "We could maybe manage to squeeze through ourselves, but the ship's not coming with us. And once we get beyond that gate, we'd be bobbing in the swells and the coast is lined with jagged rocks. Any wave could cast us against the rocks and kill us. That is, if the sharks out there don't get us first."

"Or that beast we battled on the way in to the coast."

Ran nodded. "Fair point." He sighed. "I don't know what to do. If we stay here, Malkyr will send sailors and take us all prisoner. If we swim for it, we'll have other problems to deal with." He looked at Kancho. "I'd appreciate any wisdom you might have on this."

Kancho smiled. "One route leads to guaranteed capture and presumably death at the hands of a man with no honor. The other leads to probable death from dangerous beasts and the forces of nature." He shrugged.

"I'd rather take my chances with the sharks and waves than I would give Malkyr the satisfaction of killing us."

"So, overboard?"

"Overboard."

"Fair enough." Ran turned and waved Neviah up to the deck. "We're going to abandon the ship and swim through those gaps in the portcullis."

"You want us to get into this water and take our chances with sharks?"

"It's either that or wait here until Malkyr comes and kills us. He's got a lot more men than we can handle."

"I thought you were the clever one here."

Ran grinned. "Meaning what?"

"All we've seen you do is steal around places, move without making noise, disappear from sight almost at will. And now you're telling us to jump into the sea to avoid the enemy when another option seems perfectly viable to me."

Ran frowned. "You'd better explain."

Neviah pointed at the portcullis. "What if we make it appear that we followed your plan and swam through the openings in the portcullis, but instead we hide out belowdecks until they opened the gate and then reemerge?"

"There aren't many places to hide five people down there."

"You managed it."

"I'm trained to do it," said Ran. "And hiding one person is a lot easier than five."

"All the more reason why they won't suspect anything tricky. At least not at first."

Ran eyed the portcullis. "We could leave a scrap of clothing in the gap to entice them further."

"Yes."

"You know," said Ran, "you're a pretty clever warrior yourself."

Neviah shrugged. "I've been watching you. And learning."

"All right, let's do this. We don't have much time. You and the others head down into the cargo compartment and hide yourselves as best you can. It will be absolutely imperative that you make no noise. You need to be in a position that you can hold for a long time in case we end up waiting. So don't bother with crazy acrobatic positions and the like. Find some place you can lie down and rest if need be."

"What are you going to do?"

Ran pointed. "Tear off a strip of your tunic and I'll swim over and place it just so. It will be visible enough to lead them to think we swam out. Hopefully, they'll take the bait and raise the gate to pursue us. Once they do, we can come out of our hiding places and resume our escape."

Neviah tore a piece of her tunic and handed it to Ran. "You'll swim back once you place the cloth?"

"We'll see. It depends on how long it takes me. Also, if I come back aboard dripping wet, they might spot the water from my clothes. And we can bet that they will do at least a cursory inspection of this boat to make sure we're not hiding. So it's vital you are all well-hidden. Understood?"

"I'll get the others squared away." She turned and headed down to the decks below with the others.

Ran lowered himself into the water by one of the ropes at the bow. The sea water here was colder than in the inner harbor, but he wasn't too concerned about sharks. The portcullis looked like it extended all the way to the bottom of the channel, and its gaps would inhibit most larger fish from getting through unless they were really determined to squeeze through the gaps. Still, Ran didn't want to be in the water any longer than necessary.

He swam quickly toward the portcullis and positioned the strip of cloth to make it look like one of the nails had caught it and torn it free. He swam back and eyed it. It looked natural enough, he thought. Time to find his own hiding spot.

Ran slid through the water back toward the raider ship. The walls of the channel were worn smooth by the water and offered little in terms of concealment. Ran's best option was to either reboard the ship or stay in the water.

Noises behind him made him decide.

He turned and saw several skiffs racing toward the raider ship. He frowned, took a breath, and dove deep. He hoped Neviah and the others had taken his advice and hidden themselves well, otherwise they were going to be captured shortly, when Malkyr's men boarded the boat.

From the bottom of the channel, Ran peered up and watched the skiffs pass by him. He swam back behind the search line and surfaced around a small bend that afforded him a view of the raider ship and the skiffs. From his vantage point, Ran watched one muscular man with a thick beard directing several teams.

"You two get on that boat and see if anyone's there."

Two men from the skiff closest to the raider ship clambered up one of the ropes, taking their time on the approach. They were both armed with the shorter, broader swords that Ran had seen other sailors wearing. While they boarded the ship, another skiff approached the portcullis.

"Sir!"

"What is it?"

Ran saw one of the sailors holding up the strip from Neviah's tunic. Ran nodded. *Take the bait,* he thought.

"It looks like they might have gone through the gate and taken their chances outside the harbor."

"Fools," snapped the man on the skiff. "They'll be chewed up out there." He glanced back in Ran's direction, and the Shinobujin froze where he was, resisting the temptation to dive. A move like that would only draw the man's attention, and Ran doubted he was looking at the spot where he bobbed, anyway.

"Malkyr will want to know for sure. We'll have to go out."

Ran's eyes caught movement on the main deck of the raider ship. One of the two men who had boarded it hailed the boss in the skiff. "No sign of them anywhere on board here, sir."

Ran smiled in spite of himself. The timing of the discovery of the cloth on the portcullis had probably been overheard by the men searching the boat and would help to convince them there was no one on board the raider ship. So far so good.

The bearded boss pointed at the men in another skiff. "Raise the gate. We're going out." And then he looked back at the men who had boarded the raider ship. "Stand by on that vessel. We'll be coming aboard so we can search the waters outside here better. Grab the ropes!"

The two men on the raider ship scrambled to the stern

and bow and started hauling the ropes up. Ran felt a twinge in his stomach. Those ropes were his only way back on to the ship. If they hauled them all aboard, he'd have no way of getting on the boat, and he'd be left here in the channel.

Quickly, Ran dove back down and toward the bearded man's skiff. This was risky, he knew, but they weren't leaving him much choice. He surfaced directly at the rear of the skiff and stole a breath. As he did so, he saw another skiff approach the left side of the channel and press what looked like a huge boulder. The effect was instant. Ran heard the muffled grinding of gears and the rattle of chains as the portcullis slowly lifted free of the water. A massive amount of seaweed plopped off the teeth of the portcullis and fell back into the water with a resounding splash.

So that's how they did it, he thought.

"Come on, time's wasting!"

The skiff he was hidden near started to move. Ran quelled the panic in his stomach, allowed himself to sink below the surface, and then followed behind the skiff slowly so as not to disturb the water. As the skiff drew up alongside the raider ship, the bearded man ordered one of the men with him in the skiff to throw a rope up to the men aboard the raider ship.

"Let the ladder down, and we'll come up. Then tie the skiff to the stern."

"Understood."

Ran heard them lowering a ladder that clanked against the wooden sides of the ship. The bearded man and his two underlings scrambled aboard while Ran waited beneath the skiff. Then the skiff was led to the back of the ship and tied off. Ran placed a hand on the smaller boat and waited for

the raider ship to move out of the channel. At least he
could stay with them now.

The question was, how long would his good fortune
last?

The two other skiffs had already put out to sea,
although they seemed woefully unprepared for the surging
swells of the open ocean. Their boats were being pulled in
all directions by the volatile current. Ran could feel it
pulling on him and had to use both hands to hold on to the
back of the skiff. *I need to be out of this water,* he thought.
At any moment, he expected sharks to tear him up or the
jagged rocks to cut him open. Neither option appealed to
him.

He waited until the two skiffs were out of sight and he
didn't see anyone looking out over the stern. Then Ran
pulled himself out of the water and into the skiff itself.
Luckily, a small tarp lay on the bottom, and he scrunched
up underneath it. Anyone looking out from the ship
would see only the tarp, instead of a shadow warrior
sitting there.

Ran shivered beneath the tarp and started some
breathing exercises that would warm him up and keep his
muscles loose in the event he had to go into action
unexpectedly. At this point, Ran saw two problems.

The first was the fact that there were now four of
Malkyr's men aboard the raider ship. That evened the odds
with Neviah, Kancho, Jysal, and Yuki, but in reality, they
were outmatched. Yuki wasn't a fighter, and, worse, she'd
been imprisoned for some time and showed the strain of
captivity. She'd just exhausted herself rowing as well and
would scarcely be in shape to fight off an attacker.

Outnumbered as they were, the fight would be a brutal one if they were discovered.

Worse, Ran was in a skiff twenty yards away, and any attempt to shimmy up the rope to reach the raider ship would be seen in the midday light. The skiff bobbed on the swells and was now taking on a bit of water. While the tarp would conceal his presence, if the skiff took on too much water and started a slow sink, it would certainly be noticed and Ran exposed when they pulled the skiff in and tried to bail it out.

Both of these problems paled in comparison to what Ran heard next, though. The bearded man came to the rail and shouted out to the two skiffs that were still searching for the escapees. "Forget it. If they haven't been killed yet, they will be soon. Turn your boats about and head back in. We're going back into the inner harbor."

Ran frowned. If the raider ship headed back into the harbor, then they'd have no chance of escaping from Malkyr and Kan-Gul. Ran peeked out and noted that the two skiffs were already maneuvering their way back toward the portcullis, riding swells and steering with their oars to reach the relative calm of the channel. The raider ship was now also turning about. Ran felt the skiff lift and then fall as another swell nearly sent it aloft. His stomach lurched, reminding him of his seasickness when Malkyr first sailed them across the Dark Sea.

He choked back the urge to retch and steeled his will. They couldn't afford to have the raider return to the harbor. If they were going to act, they'd have to do so now.

CHAPTER THIRTY-TWO

As the raider swung about and headed back to the channel, Ran made his move.

He came out from under the tarp and reached for the rope that held the skiff to the stern of the raider ship. It was going to be risky for the first few minutes, but he gripped the rope and immediately started pulling the skiff toward the larger ship. Waves buffeted him and salt water lashed at his face as he hauled the skiff closer to the raider.

Ran kept pulling until the skiff was a few feet from the stern. Then he used his upper-body strength to haul himself off the boat. As soon as he cleared the skiff, he switched so that his feet took most of the weight. He wrapped the length of rope around the outside of one leg, passed it between his feet, and then wedged his feet together to create something of a stop-check. He would bend his knees and bring them up a certain length, then lift himself up as his feet tensed back together. The friction his feet created—even with the sea water making things a bit more slippery—was enough to propel him upward.

At the top of the climb, he could see over the back of the boat into the stern, where the bearded man held the tiller. His back was to Ran. Ran checked his position, then used his hands to bring himself up and over and onto the stern deck with hardly a sound. He crept up behind the bearded man and grabbed him from behind with the tip of his sword poking into the man's lower back.

"Carefully . . . very carefully now. Don't do anything stupid or you'll have a sword stuck through you for your troubles."

The bearded man raised his hands. "I won't do anything."

Ran cranked the arm he had around the man's neck and used his left foot to buckle the bearded man's left leg at the knee. "Just take it easy. Call your men and tell them to all stand at the bow. Do it now." Ran kept his voice level but firm. The sword at his back was motivation enough for the bearded man, and Ran doubted he would make a move while his life clearly hung in the balance like this.

The bearded man gave the order, and his confused crew did as they were told. The three men stood at the very point of the bow, waiting. When they saw Ran dripping from head to toe, the looks on their faces betrayed their surprise.

Good, thought Ran. *They ought to be surprised.*

"Kancho!" He hoped his voice was strong enough to penetrate whatever hiding spots the others had managed to find below decks. Ran waited several seconds before repeating Kancho's name. "It's Ran. Come out."

"Ran? Your name is Ran?" asked the bearded man. "Such a strange name."

"In my homeland it means 'storm.' Pray you never find out why they called me that."

Kancho poked his head out from belowdecks. The bearded man grumbled, "I thought I told those fools to search this boat."

"Apparently they didn't do a very good job," said Ran. "But I wouldn't be so quick to blame them. They probably heard you talking about how we'd supposedly swum out into the open sea and decided they didn't need to be thorough."

"This isn't my fault."

"We'll see," said Ran. "Malkyr may not feel as you do."

Kancho came up to the stern and grinned at Ran. "Glad to see you. We thought you might have gotten left behind or something."

"Luckily, no," said Ran. "But it was a little nerve-wracking there for a while."

Kancho drew his sword and leveled it at the bearded man. "What is your name?"

The bearded man spat at him. "Does it matter? You'll kill me anyway."

Kancho smirked. "I will kill you, but only if you give me reason to." He nodded at Ran. "I can keep him for you if you'd like."

Ran shoved the bearded man toward the stern of the boat. "Stay put while I get the others. This man is even better with a sword than I am. You'd do well to remember that."

Ran hurried below and soon had Neviah, Jysal, and Yuki up on deck. "We're going to make a run for Nehon."

Kancho called down from where he stood guarding the bearded man. "How about we use the crew to row?"

But Ran didn't want to do that. Keeping the enemy on board the ship would prove too tempting for them, and they'd be thinking about taking control back instead of focusing on the task at hand. "No, they can jump overboard."

The bearded man paled. "These waters are filled with sharks. They'll tear us apart before we reach shore."

Ran shook his head. "Then I suggest you swim faster. We're giving you the skiff tied up behind us. Get into that boat and stay there. Once we're away from the coast, we'll set you free. Understand?"

The bearded man frowned but nodded. "Very well."

"Tell your men that if they try anything funny—like untying the skiff before we reach open water—our mage here will turn you all into shark food by destroying the boat."

The bearded man passed the word to his crew. Ran had them line up at the stern and then jump into the water. The four of them splashed into the churning sea and swam for the skiff as quickly as they could. A triangular fin jutted out of the surf and closed in on one of the men, but at the last second he was yanked into the skiff just inches shy of being bitten by the ten-foot shark.

"Close," said Ran.

Kancho frowned. "I think we should have used them to help us row."

"We don't need them," said Neviah. "We're able to sail from here on out. Help me with the main sheet, and rowing will be a bad memory."

Ran eyed her. "You know your way around boats?"

Neviah shrugged. "Spare knowledge I acquired during my travels. I would never claim to be a captain, but I can get us going and on course. If things hold, we should be fine until we reach the coast of Nehon. I have no idea how to bring a ship into a busy harbor, so we may still have a swim ahead of us. But it will be a quick one."

"Fair enough," said Ran. "I'll turn the ship over to you then. Just tell us what you need us to do."

"Stay by the tiller for right now," said Neviah. She turned to Kancho. "Come with me."

Kancho shrugged and followed her belowdecks. Within thirty minutes they had the main sail fluffing in the strong winds. Neviah pointed at Ran. "Steer to the port side so the sail fills."

Ran did as she commanded, and the sail instantly took a gust that filled it. The raider ship responded by cutting through the waves with speed. Ran smiled. This was more like it.

But he was worried about the dark clouds gathering over the land to their left. A storm right now was the last thing they needed. And they were losing sunlight as well. *Neviah might not know enough to be a ship's captain, but she'd better know enough to navigate a storm,* he thought. *Otherwise, this is going to be a very short trip.*

Jysal stood at the bow, peering out to sea as the prow cut through the waves. The raider rose and fell as it carved a path through the Dark Sea. The wind tussled Jysal's hair, and Ran found it nearly impossible to look away from her. She faced forward, deep in concentration. Kancho came up to stand alongside Ran.

"What is she doing?"

Ran shook his head. "No idea. She looks beautiful, though."

Kancho grunted. "There is something eerily beautiful

about her. Such power, too. I wonder if she knows what sort of life lies ahead of her."

"Do any of us?" asked Ran. "Our destinies are known only to the gods. The best we can do is try to play the roles they set before us."

"Is that why you chose to become a shadow warrior for the Nine Daggers?"

Ran smiled. This was the first time Kancho had said the words. He knew that Murai custom was to never speak the name of his clan. But Kancho had demonstrated that he cared little for Murai customs if it did not suit his own agenda. Ran admired that.

"I didn't choose to become one of them," said Ran. "My parents were slain in a territorial dispute between two of the warlords in my region. I came home from playing in the fields one day—I couldn't have been much older than seven or so—and found them both dead. Slaughtered. We had no possessions, no weapons. It was a senseless act. But senseless acts are common, aren't they?"

"Indeed."

"The house was afire. I couldn't do a thing to rescue my parents. The house burned with them still in it."

"I am sorry for your loss. Their souls will have traveled on to a better life by now."

Ran nodded. "I hope that's true. In any event, I had nowhere to turn. I wandered by myself for two months. I begged for food from anyone who would listen. Gradually, I made my way out into the countryside and passed from temple to temple, offering to work in exchange for food. But one of the monks had a better idea and told me to go visit a temple hidden in the peaks of Gakur."

"Various clans of Murai have searched for that place for many years," said Kancho. "I believe they would destroy it if they ever managed to locate it."

"The temple is guarded by magic of a sort I have never known to exist elsewhere. I doubt any warlords would ever be able to locate it. No one knows how to get there unless you are given specific directions from one who knows. As it was, I nearly died getting there."

"But you managed to survive. Seven years old. Impressive."

"I was nearly eight by the time I found them. Getting there was part of the test," said Ran. "The temple elders who run the compound wanted only those who had the urge to survive no matter what. After being on my own for many months, I guess it was pretty well established that I wanted to survive. Not only that, but to prosper as well. Survival, after all, is not enough. You have to not just endure; you have to thrive."

"Did you thrive at the school?"

"I did. The lessons were tough, and there was no slacking. The teachers made sure of that. Complacency was ruthlessly rooted out of us through hard training. The only way to exceed expectations was to constantly challenge ourselves. The teachers made sure that we developed our own sense of discipline; that we never stopped challenging ourselves. Those who grew comfortable with their rank as they progressed were also dropped from the course. The attrition rate was severe."

"Sounds like a lot of people are wandering around Nehon with intimate knowledge of the shadow-warrior temple. I would think that a very dangerous thing."

Ran smiled. "They're not alive any longer."

Kancho raised an eyebrow. "The elders at your school killed them?"

"No. They sent them away on assignments. Those who returned were allowed to resume training. Those who failed inevitably died during the course of the mission. Their complacency effectively got them killed. The lesson was clear: never believe that you are the best or immune to critique. To do so is to be a slave to your ego. And ego gets people killed."

Kancho smiled. "There are many similarities between the Murai and Shinobujin."

"True," said Ran. "But members of the Nine Daggers are taught to rely upon themselves above all else. Murai are taught to depend on the structure of your code of honor and the service to your lord."

"Some would say such a thing isn't necessarily bad."

"It isn't," said Ran. "For professional soldiers like yourself. But it's the wrong approach for training spies."

Kancho considered this. "Murai consider the use of espionage beneath them."

"That doesn't preclude many from hiring us to do their dirty work, though, does it?"

Kancho grinned. "I suppose not."

"And your code of honor also precluded you from coming after Yuki, didn't it?"

"Indeed it did," said Kancho. "I guess you and I have more in common than I thought."

"We're two warriors tossed together in a bad situation," said Ran. "Both of us have our own paths, but while we're together, I'm honored to fight beside you."

"As am I."

Ran looked at the sky. The dark clouds were congealing into a rather terrifying sight. He could see the sheets of rain pounding the lands on the coast. And judging by the wind direction, the storm was headed right at them. "That's not good."

Kancho nodded. "The storm will be upon us very soon."

"Better get Neviah. I don't know what to do with this ship."

Kancho rushed down to the deck to get Neviah. Ran watched him for a moment, but then Jysal's voice rang out from the bow. She'd been unmoving for minutes.

Until now.

"Sail!"

Ran looked. Around a promontory ahead of them, he spotted the black sail of a narrow ship adorned with the head of a dragon at its prow. Another raider? Out here?

"Who is that?"

Neviah came back up on the deck and looked out across the sea. "They're on an intercept course with us. Same as the storm."

"Who could it be?" asked Kancho, coming up to stand with them.

But then he saw the lone figure standing at the rear of the boat a strange-looking helmsman gripping the wheel. There was something off about him. Ran peered closer and saw it.

Chekhal.

Kan-Gul had arrived.

CHAPTER THIRTY-THREE

The clouds opened up, deluging the raider ship with a torrential downpour that weighed heavy on the sails. Jysal came away from the bow and walked the length of the boat to stand next to Ran and the others. "He is using magic to control the storm." She shook her head. "I first sensed it back on the *Aqaria*, but I doubted myself. I thought I was being silly." Jysal sighed. "I know better now. His magic has a taint to it."

"You can smell it?" asked Ran.

"Not smell per se," said Jysal. "Even if we could outrun them, he would no doubt manipulate the weather to force us inland."

"Where did he get a ship?" asked Ran. "His castle sits in the middle of a plain. I didn't see any river leading out to the sea. Where did it even come from?"

Jysal shook her head. "Perhaps he conjured it. It's possible."

"Or else he has an agreement with Malkyr and the army to the north," said Kancho. "They may have supplied him with one. It is of a different style than the transport vessels or even this raider."

Neviah was watching the sails. "We're not going to last out here much longer. We'll have to make a run for it."

"We can't outrun him," said Jysal. "His magic will be too strong."

Kancho eyed Ran. "What do you think?"

Ran looked at the approaching ship. Its prow cut through the waves like a spear, and the Chekhal aboard numbered at least a dozen, perhaps many more belowdecks. Kan-Gul's ship's sails were blown out fully by the wind, and its path would bring it across the bow of the raider. They had the advantage of position. Ran considered reversing course, but the maneuver would take too long, and by that point Kan-Gul would be within striking distance.

A huge wave broke over the bow as the raider speared through the swell. Seawater drenched them all. Neviah frowned. "We can put in by those cliffs, but there's no guarantee it's going to be an easy mooring. We'll have to jump into the sea and try to make our way to land. That's about the only way I can see us getting out of this."

"What if we rammed him?" asked Ran.

Neviah shrugged. "We could try it, but this ship is smaller, and any damage would likely be on our end, not Kan-Gul's. Plus, he may have a reinforced hull that we can't see. If that's the case, then he'll turn us into splinters, and we'll be in the water anyway."

"Those Chekhal will try to board us as soon as we make contact," said Kancho. "They do not have any fear of the sea. And our attention will be diverted at that point, making the prospect of ramming not a good idea."

"Agreed," said Ran. "Jysal?"

"Yes?"

"Can you do anything to slow them down?"

Her brow furrowed, Jysal thought for a moment. "I don't know what I can do, honestly."

"It's too dangerous," said Neviah. "Jysal's power is untapped. Making her take on such a daunting challenge right now might lead to explosive consequences none of us might recover from."

Ran frowned. "We don't have a lot of options."

From behind the boat, they heard several shouts. Ran turned; their prisoners had untied the skiff and were trying to escape toward Kan-Gul.

"They're getting away," said Jysal.

Ran held up a hand. "Not for long." A huge wave crashed over the skiff and dumped the sailors into the water. They floundered in the swells, and then more waves broke over them. Amid the churn of whitewater, Ran caught a glimpse of the sharks. A few screams punctured the air over the thunder and lightning, but the ocean quickly claimed the men for its own.

Ran turned back around. "We'll head for the cliffs. There's no other way."

Neviah nodded. "As soon as we hit the rocks, everyone needs to get off of this boat as fast as possible. We'll need to claw our way up those cliffs if we're to make any sort of defensive stand."

Out of the corner of his eye, Ran saw more movement behind them. When he looked, he didn't know what to think. "Another boat."

Neviah turned. Sure enough, she saw the ship coming

out of the channel they'd left behind. With three sails, the ship was large and powerful, and it moved with a steady speed through the water, regardless of the storm's power and current. "I'll bet my last dagger that is Malkyr."

Ran nodded. "So would I."

"Two ships converging on us," said Ran. He grinned. "So much for a fair fight."

Kancho shifted his sword in his belt. "We'll take as many of them with us as we can."

"You can bet that Malkyr has a lot of men on that boat. Add that to the number of Chekhal that Kan-Gul will have at his beck and call, and we'll be facing impossible odds." Ran shook his head. "We might be better off taking our chances with the sharks."

Neviah shrugged. "We don't have any choice. Our best bet is to get to land and try to lose them there."

"But for how long?" asked Ran. "We keep running and they keep pursuing us. Kan-Gul won't let Jysal go free, and he won't stop until we're all dead. Sooner or later, he'll manage to get us into a situation where he will win and we will lose. I don't know about you, but I don't want my immortal soul eaten by the stuff of nightmares. That's not my destiny."

"Nor mine," said Kancho. "But I fail to see what other choice we have. As Neviah has said, there is little she can do when the storm is raging like that and Kan-Gul employs magic. If we try to run, he'll simply sink us."

Ran frowned. There had to be a way to even the odds. He looked back to see Malkyr's ship closing fast. Ran estimated it would be upon them within ten minutes.

Meanwhile, Kan-Gul's ship nosed ever closer, still on track to cut across their bow.

"Stay on this course," he said quietly.

"What did you say?" asked Neviah.

"Stay the course," said Ran. He nodded to himself. It would probably not work, but it was worth a try.

"If we stay this course, we'll ram into Kan-Gul's ship," said Neviah. "I thought we decided that was a foolish move."

"We did," said Ran. "But that was before we noticed Malkyr on our tail." He smiled at Neviah. "How fast can this ship turn?"

She shrugged. "I don't really know. If I can gibe the sail and work the tiller hard enough, we might be able to turn within one boat length. But I've never tried it, so I can't say for certain."

"Would you at least agree this is the most maneuverable of all three ships?"

"Without a doubt. These raiders are designed to be fast and agile. If we didn't have this storm to contend with, we could easily outrun Kan-Gul. He knows that. That's why he's had to resort to using magic against us."

Ran eyed Malkyr's transport vessel. "I'd wager that is the least maneuverable of the lot."

Neviah nodded. "He needs a lot of room to maneuver. Once those ships get moving, they're hard to stop."

"Excellent."

Kancho cocked an eyebrow. "What are you planning?"

"We're not going to ram Kan-Gul's boat," said Ran. "Malkyr is."

"You really think you can get him to commit?"

Ran nodded over his shoulder. "He's already committed to the path. We just have to make sure that he stays on our tail and thinks we're trying to get away from him."

Jysal frowned. "Kan-Gul may see that trick."

"It doesn't matter if he does," said Ran. "They can't communicate with each other, and I'd bet that Malkyr is so angered at having been bested by us that he is driving hard to get his hands on us before Kan-Gul. We'll use that desire against him. Keep us on the same path, and at the last minute we'll turn and scoot for open ocean. If they hit, neither one of them will be in any condition to give chase."

Neviah smiled. "I like it. It's risky, but it could work. We'll all need to work together, though."

"Just tell us what you need us to do," said Kancho.

Neviah pointed at the mast. "You'll need to stand by on that sail. The idea is to drop all the wind out of it, throw the tiller hard, and then get the sail into the wind again to gain separation from the two other ships. If we do it correctly, it should work. But only if we don't have any mishaps. With the weather this severe, there is no room for error."

Kancho and Yuki headed to the mast and started readying the knots on the sheet that held the mainsail. Neviah eyed Ran.

"The idea is sound. Risky. But sound."

"Let's save the congratulations until after this is all over. It could still turn out to be a horrible idea."

Neviah laughed. "I like you, Ran of Gakur. You don't get locked into only thinking that what you suggest is the right way to do things. It takes a strong man to be able to keep his ego in check and listen to others. You'd make a fine battlefield commander."

"Probably not," said Ran. "My path lies elsewhere. I'd rather leave the battlefield stuff to others who are more experienced in such things than I am. People like Kancho are suited to that life."

"Kancho is a professional soldier. He's not a thinker."

"He knows strategy."

"Strategy for individual and small-unit combat," said Neviah. "You have a better grasp of the bigger picture. Those who are able to do that are few and far between. Regardless of whether they are Murai . . . or not."

Ran grinned. "Thank you. Now, how can I help make sure this gambit has a chance of working?"

"Stand by the tiller," said Neviah. "I need to be up front to judge our distance better. Watch my hands. I'll point in the direction you need to move the tiller. You'll know how much by how far apart my hands are. Close together, small adjustment. Wide apart, big adjustment. Do you understand?"

"Perfectly."

"Excellent. When the time comes for the full turn, I'll raise both arms and bring them down at the moment of the turn. When I do, you move that tiller all the way over as if your life depends on it. Because it does." She eyed Ran. "Clear?"

"Yes."

"Good." Neviah dropped down onto the deck and headed for the bow. Ran watched her move across the ship. She might not have thought herself worthy of being a captain, but she certainly seemed capable enough to Ran.

"That leaves just the two of us," said Jysal over the howling wind. "Not exactly the best weather to try to talk to each other in."

"Certainly not," said Ran. "Are you worried?"

Jysal waved him away. "Why would I be worried? There's some creepy sorcerer who wants to make me his wife and do godawful things to me and force me to live in his terrible castle filled with the undead. What girl wouldn't want that?"

Ran chuckled. "At least you can joke about it."

"If I couldn't make a joke about it, I might get caught up in the fear I feel. And that might immobilize me, quite honestly. I don't want Kan-Gul to get his hands on me."

"Neither do I."

"So I'll try to keep fighting, and we'll see if this plan of yours works. Or not. Either way, it will at least prove frustrating for Kan-Gul. And I'm all for that."

"Good," said Ran. "Let's hope his desire to have you for himself makes him as predictable as Malkyr's ego back there."

At the bow, Neviah studied Kan-Gul's ship and glanced back at Ran with a nod. Ran smiled through the rain that spattered his skin. The plan could work if everything came together perfectly. Even still, it was better than simply making for the cliffs and hoping they could outrun their pursuers.

The sea kicked up more swells, and keeping the tiller from being jerked out of his hand proved more difficult than Ran would have imagined. But he gritted his teeth and kept to the course that put them on a collision track with Kan-Gul. He looked behind and saw that Malkyr's ship had closed some distance between them. It was still a good thousand yards back, though. Kan-Gul was roughly five hundred yards off their port bow.

And closing fast.

The raider ship bucked another swell. Ran wondered how much magical energy Kan-Gul must have been exerting to make this storm happen. Surely he couldn't keep this up indefinitely. It would prove too exhausting, even for a sorcerer of his skill. He didn't yet have Jysal to enhance his power. Perhaps he had bound other sorcerers in the past, but Ran had been able to see through some of his illusions. And if his power was so absolute, why had Kan-Gul worked so hard to impress Ran with his power when they first arrived at his stronghold? Ran knew this, but the sheer fury of the storm caused doubt to gnaw at him.

And Kan-Gul had plenty of Chekhal. They concerned Ran greatly. If the ships drew too close together, then the Chekhal would surely leap aboard and start killing anyone they found. Ran wondered if dying by their hand meant his soul would be devoured as well.

The challenge was going to be turning tightly enough that Malkyr couldn't turn and ended up crashing into Kan-Gul's ship. Timed correctly, the resulting impact could potentially send both enemy ships to the bottom of the sea. Bad timing would result in Ran's plan failing miserably.

The waves battered the raider as it rode another swell and crashed down into the trough. Another spray of salt water smacked Ran in the face, and he used his free hand to wipe it away. As dangerous a situation as this was, he still found it hard to complain. Back in Gakur, he could only dream of being out in the real world on an actual assignment for the clan. Now, here he was. He had several good friends to battle alongside and a large number of other people who wanted him dead.

He grinned in spite of it all.

A moment clearly etched in the timeless struggle between Life and Death. And he was a part of it.

Finally.

He surveyed the sea in front of him, trying to pick out his route through the next swells. The angry sea grew even more desperate to toss the smaller ship about, but Ran gave it no mind. His hand was set on the tiller, and the raider ship stayed glued to its course.

Then Ran spotted something that erased his smile.

Another variable. And it was one that he had not figured into the equation.

He just hoped it wouldn't be enough to throw his plan into chaos.

CHAPTER THIRTY-FOUR

Neviah saw the creature in the waves and yelled back to Ran. "Stay on course!"

Ran watched as the monstrous leviathan surged under the swells and launched one of its massive tentacles up through the waves closest to Kan-Gul's ship. A Chekhal warrior near the bow was too slow to react and got swept off his feet by the limb that snatched him overboard and yanked him beneath the waves. More Chekhal warriors on the main deck of Kan-Gul's ship brought out massive spears and started stabbing at the other tentacles that now threatened to overwhelm the ship. Kan-Gul stood calm in the midst of the chaos, directing his minions. While the tentacles came close to him, they never actually touched him.

But the Chekhal were having problems, and even as the ship kept its course to intercept the raider, more of the undead warriors fell overboard into the surf. As far as Ran could see, they weren't all that adept at swimming. Or else, as soon as they hit the water, the monster simply devoured them or drowned them. Ran couldn't tell which, and keeping the tiller on course meant his vision was limited to only what he could see standing on the deck.

Kancho rushed to the bow with Neviah. He had his sword drawn, but for the moment, the sea monster wasn't interested in attacking the raider. Ran nodded. If that beast kept them distracted, the chance of making this collision happen were better than they would be otherwise.

Something whizzed past his ear, and he ducked as he heard the dull thunk over the boom of another thunder clap. Ahead of him, a massive bolt had embedded itself into the main mast. There was a rope attached to it, and Ran felt the raider shift off course as Malkyr's men aboard the transport ship tried to gain control of the raider.

"Kancho! The rope!"

Kancho turned and immediately saw the problem. He leapt down from the bow and rushed toward the mast. Another bolt shot past Ran, and Kancho had to duck to avoid it as it fell harmlessly on the deck. It was about the size of spear and Ran wondered how much heavy artillery the transport vessel had aboard.

Kancho cut the rope, and it flew back off the ship into the surf.

Ran watched behind him as the transport continued to gain on them. If they kept their barrage up, the raider wouldn't be able to stand too much of it. The transport was now only a few hundred yards behind them. Whatever had shot that massive bolt had to have some serious draw power in order to get it through the wind and rain. Ran wouldn't have wanted to be on the receiving end of such a weapon.

The Chekhal warriors on Kan-Gul's ship were faring

better against the sea monster. Ran saw the sprays of blood as they chopped through the tentacles and sent pieces of limbs falling amid the ocean swells. Ran frowned. If there hadn't been sharks in the water before, all of this blood was certain to draw them like flies. And if Ran mistimed the direction change when Neviah ordered him to come about, they were all going to end up fending off the hungry sea predators.

Not good, he decided. *But better than having your soul devoured*.

Kan-Gul seemed to surround himself with a red aura, and then Ran saw him shoot an orb of energy at the sea monster. It hit and traveled down one of the limbs, sizzling even in the rain. Instantly, the tentacle shriveled and withdrew from the ship. Clearly Kan-Gul had decided to take a more active role in defending his ship. The sea monster was an unwanted distraction to his men.

Regardless, the sea monster continued its attack, and Ran made sure he kept the raider on course. Kan-Gul probably thought they were trying to outrun his ship and the transport behind them.

Neviah signaled another course adjustment with her hands and Ran adjusted the tiller until she nodded. The rain lashed all of them on the deck. Ran felt himself shiver in the cold spray. Between the sea and the rain, there was no part of him that wasn't soaked through to his bones. He realized that he hadn't been dry in many, many hours.

Another heavy bolt whizzed over the stern and hit the mainsail of the raider. Ran watched as it punched a hole in the top part of the fabric. The sail started to rip, but then held. Ran breathed a sigh of relief. They still needed to be able to move, and if they took out the sail, that would leave the raider dead in the water and at Malkyr's disposal.

Unless Kan-Gul reached them first.

Kancho was surveying the damage to the sail but just shook his head and looked at Ran. "It should hold."

Good, thought Ran. They only needed a few more minutes. With luck, they'd be speeding away from the wreck of two ships in a short time.

Neviah made another course correction, and Ran leaned on the tiller. The raider arced a bit more to the port side. Ran saw that she was setting them up to meet Kan-Gul's ship midway down its side. Too bad they didn't have an iron prow they could use like a battering ram. If they could have punched through the side, they could have sent it to the bottom in a few seconds.

He glanced behind them and saw the transport had course-corrected to stay firmly on their tail. Another heavy bolt flew by, but this one missed and splashed into the water, where it sank beneath the waves.

Neviah looked back from her position and shouted something to Kancho. Ran was too far away to hear over the fury of the storm.

She looked at Ran, and he nodded.

She raised her arms.

Another clap of thunder boomed overhead, and more rain poured down. On Kan-Gul's ship, Ran could see the wide smile the evil sorcerer wore on his face. It was like he was telling Ran that he would soon have his prize. And everyone else would be killed the way Vargul had been. Ran wanted to smile back, but doing so might have made Kan-Gul suspicious.

Surely Kan-Gul knew they were in danger of colliding now, but Ran hoped the sorcerer believed the transport had them hemmed in and that the raider's options were nearly depleted.

So Ran wore a grimace on his face and hoped he looked desperate.

The waves continued to grow in size. Each one the raider plowed through threw up a huge splash of water across the bow. Neviah shook it all off and refused to budge even as they entered another trough. Ran was amazed at her steadfast resolve to see this through. He waited for her signal and hoped it would come soon.

Another bolt shot past and embedded itself in the bulwark closest to Ran. The heavy archers on Malkyr's ship were getting a bit too close for his comfort. At least it would be a quick death if he was struck by one of those bolts. Still he gave thanks for the sea being as rocky as it was. The ocean made it tough to make an accurate shot.

Neviah shouted at Kancho and Yuki. They let the sheet go and drew on the ropes that lowered the sail. It quickly dropped. As the raider slowed, Neviah brought down her arms and shouted at Ran. Her shriek cut through the tempest. "Now! Turn now!"

Ran shoved the tiller hard to port, and the raider swung about, drawing parallel with Kan-Gul's ship within a few seconds, until they were on the same course.

"Now, Kancho! Trim that sail!" Neviah rushed to help them as Kancho and Yuki pulled on the sheet. The sail shot back up the mast, already starting to fill with wind.

The raider jerked forward as the wind took the sail, and they shot away. Ran watched behind them as he heard muffled shouts of orders on Malkyr's boat. The huge transport started to turn, but compared to how fast the raider had done it, the movement was slow and cumbersome. The transport didn't so much turn as slowly start to arc around.

Unfortunately, Kan-Gul's ship was in their way, and as the heavy transport's momentum continued to carry it forward, they were coming perilously close to Kan-Gul's craft. Ran could hear Kan-Gul shouting for them to heave away, but the transport was simply too large to respond fast enough. *Now*, he thought. *Let it happen.*

The heavy transport continued to arc, but just as it appeared they might not crash, a huge wave hit Kan-Gul's ship broadside and pushed the ship closer to the transport. Ran heard splintering wood shatter as the transport started to shear the starboard side of Kan-Gul's ship. The two ships looked like they were trying to push themselves together to become one, but the transport was at least double the size of Kan-Gul's vessel, and its size overwhelmed the smaller boat. Ran spotted several Chekhal warriors falling between the sides of the boats, smashed together as they were, and those who fell were crushed between the two ships. He grimaced.

The raider had responded well, and Ran kept a firm hand on the tiller. They had pulled away from the two boats behind them. If they kept on course, they could easily outrun them now that they had the advantage of position. Neviah looked pleased with herself, and Ran thought she had every right to be thrilled. The maneuver had gone perfectly.

Kancho came back to the stern to survey the damage.

He pointed at the water. "Kan-Gul's boat is taking on too much water. It can't survive the collision."

"Good," said Ran. "I hope they sink and the sharks get to them all. I don't know what sort of magic Kan-Gul could use against them."

"All things need to eat," laughed Kancho.

Neviah came up and patted Ran on the shoulder. "It worked."

"It did, indeed. Nice job calling the maneuver. I couldn't have done that."

"It was your idea," she said. "I just lent you my guidance."

"A team effort," said Ran. "And it worked well."

Neviah looked at the mainsail and nodded. "Even with that tear near the top, it should hold long enough to get us across the Dark Sea to Nehon."

"You think it will?"

"Most of these sails are designed to be able to endure attacks. Especially on a raider like this." She glanced behind them. "I just hope that Malkyr's ship has been damaged enough that he needs to stop chasing us. With three masts, he could conceivably overtake us on a straight crossing."

"I thought you said we could outrun them," said Kancho.

"If they were both seriously damaged in the collision." She pointed. "Kan-Gul's ship clearly has been damaged beyond repair. Look at it."

Ran saw that Malkyr's ship was taking on the survivors of the collision and had let down rope ladders that allowed Chekhal warriors to climb aboard. Kan-Gul was already at the bow of the transport, screaming at Malkyr.

"He looks extremely upset." Ran wanted to laugh at

the sorcerer's frustration. "I'll bet he wishes he could get us back."

Jysal pointed. "Look!"

Kan-Gul's hands were moving in a weird series of motions. Ran frowned. What was he up to?

"More magic," said Jysal quietly. "He's not going to stop."

"Well, what can he do?" asked Kancho. "We're already well away from him. And even the storm seems to be dissipating. See how the clouds are starting to break up?"

It was true, but Ran didn't feel as hopeful as he had before. Knowing that Kan-Gul was back there trying to cast spells made him uneasy. He glanced around. "Does this ship have any more sails on it?"

Neviah shook her head. "We've only got one mast to use. The mainsail is usually large enough to make a small ship like this zip through the water. If it had another mast, we probably wouldn't be as maneuverable, and that collision never would have happened."

"Fortunately," said Kancho, "it did. And now they're left picking up the pieces while we make our escape."

"Duck!" shouted Jysal.

They all hit the deck, and something whizzed over their heads. Another bolt? Ran frowned. They couldn't still be in close enough for that giant crossbow to hit, could they? He could have sworn they'd already pulled well beyond its effective range.

But it wasn't a crossbow bolt.

It was magic.

And as they looked up at the mainsail, they saw flames licking at the edges. Despite the continuing rain showers, the pale blue flames of the magic fire continued to eat the fabric of the sail.

"No!"

"Jysal, man the tiller." Neviah pointed at Ran. "Get some water on it if you can. Kancho, gibe the sail, and we'll try to douse the fire."

Kancho and Yuki brought the sail down while Neviah and Ran got buckets from elsewhere and tried to scoop water out of the sea to use on the fire. But as much water as they poured across the burning fabric, it did little good. The sail was burning, and nothing seemed capable of stopping it.

Ran looked at Neviah. "We need Jysal's help."

Neviah shook her head. "It's too late, the sail . . . it's gone."

Ran rushed back up to the tiller. Malkyr's transport vessel was pulling away from the sinking remains of Kan-Gul's ship. He watched as the hull of the sorcerer's boat slowly slid beneath the waves. Ran desperately wanted to kill the sorcerer. Malkyr's transport vessel started to pick up speed as it came about and aligned with the course the raider had been on.

Without a sail, the raider would flounder. Even if the tides carried them along, it would never be enough.

"They're going to catch us unless we manage to do something."

Neviah reappeared next to him. "I'm out of ideas."

Ran sighed and looked at Jysal. "Steer us toward the coast." He scanned the coastline and picked out an area that might serve them well. "See those cliffs? Head there. Let's see if we can get there first."

Overhead, the clouds opened up on them again.

"So much for the storm dissipating," muttered Kancho.

"It's Kan-Gul," said Jysal. "He's using the weather against us. He knows this boat is powerless. He's just adding insult to injury now."

A huge wave smacked the ship broadside, and they all stumbled to hold onto the rail. Jysal latched on to Ran's arm. Ran glanced around. The ship had moved a fair distance as the wave swelled under the keel.

"If we take many more hits like that, we won't have to worry about Kan-Gul killing us; the sea will."

CHAPTER THIRTY-FIVE

The sea swelled again as the transport vessel bore down on the raider. Ran took over holding the tiller, desperately trying to ride the swells to stay on course. But without a sail to power them through the waves, they had little hope of reaching the shore. More waves smacked the raider broadside. If this kept up, there was a good chance the ship would capsize.

All the while, Jysal stared back defiantly at Kan-Gul. "I won't give him the satisfaction of seeing me scared," she said. "And if he thinks he's going to pull the same stunt on me that he did back at the castle, then he's sorely mistaken."

Ran frowned. The raider drifted lazily toward the cliffs. Without the sail, they had no real hope of getting a head start on Kan-Gul and Malkyr. Chances were they would all arrive at the same time, which meant they would immediately have to start fighting again. And he was exhausted already. Ran wasn't sure how Kancho was holding up, but it was a fair bet that Yuki was tired. Neviah and Jysal had been on the run as well.

Larger waves lifted the raider up under her keel and shot her closer toward the cliffs. "Hang on!" Ran shouted. They had to reach the shore and get off of this boat. The sooner, the better, he thought as he gripped the tiller.

"Looks like they're arguing," said Jysal.

Ran glanced back at the ships. Malkyr kept pointing at the sky, and the expression on his face left little doubt that he wanted Kan-Gul to stop using magic on the weather. Kan-Gul looked exasperated, but at last he relented, and, with a single gesture, the storm abated somewhat.

But stopping the magic had little effect on the waves. More of them slapped against the raider and tossed her ever closer toward the shore. Trying to ride the waves in toward the cliffs took every ounce of his concentration.

Kancho came out from below deck and smiled. "Anyone hungry?"

Ran shook his head. "Where did you manage to find food?"

"There's a galley down here," said Kancho. "It's hardtack and dried meat, but it will give us some energy regardless." He climbed up and handed out the meager rations.

Ran took the dried meat with one hand and chewed it up. It had the consistency of hard leather, but his jaw was able to work it into a reasonable mess, and he swallowed hard to get it down. The salty aftertaste made him feel like he'd just swallowed the seawater that lashed his face. But the food would give them all energy. He bit in to some hardtack next and choked that down as well.

"More?" asked Kancho.

Ran held up his hand. "No. Too much and I'll be useless. That was just enough. Thank you."

Kancho chomped down some more of the dried meat and spoke around chewing it. "We're never going to get away from them."

"Maybe," said Ran. "The waves are pushing us toward the shore. But if we hit that coast, we're going to be in the fight of our lives."

"Are we all done with forming plans?"

"I think so. There doesn't seem to be much point in it. Those cliffs are tough going. If we manage to get to shore intact, and if we manage to get a head start on our enemies, I'd expect we head for high ground and try to make them pay dearly for any ground they take."

Kancho smiled. "I like it."

"I wish I had a better option."

Kancho shrugged. "Death stalks us at every turn, even when we cannot see it. A warrior's life is measured in how close we skirt that edge—at once so close to dying that it only makes our existence even more vibrant. Few will ever understand it. Fewer still will ever live it." He smiled and patted Ran on the shoulder. "I have been fortunate to do both, and with your help, I have found my daughter. As such, I will gladly battle my enemies, unconcerned with whether I live or die. I will exist in the moment and let the gods decide what my fate shall be."

"Let your sword decide your fate," said Ran. "There's no honor in giving control to the gods. They have far more important things to do than get involved with our affairs."

"You may be right," said Kancho. "I would like to return home anyway. If not for me, then for my daughter."

The raider heaved as another swell picked the boat up and tossed it closer to the coast. The sudden acceleration of the ship surprised them all, and Ran felt a measure of hope; he'd prefer to die on dry land. He pointed at where Neviah stood. "She is looking to see how deep the water is."

"Why bother?" asked Kancho.

"I don't know. I think we'll be smashed on the rocks before we can beach."

"I agree." Kancho shrugged and went back belowdecks.

Ran watched Neviah and then saw her jump up suddenly and come running toward him. "Try to aim the boat slightly starboard."

"Huh?"

"Just do it. I didn't shout the order, because I don't want anyone hearing me on the other ship. But adjust the tiller so we're a few degrees off our course right now. Hopefully, they won't even notice."

"What are you playing at?"

"Playing?" Neviah frowned. "Ran, I'm not playing at anything. I'm counting on this helping us survive. I know you and Kancho have these idolized views of what death is and how you're walking that line between both realms and all. That's great for you lot. But I still have a job to do, and that's to get Jysal to the temple. So forgive me if I'm still trying to work out ways in which we can take the advantage away from our adversaries. Now steer a bit more starboard, if you please."

"Fair enough," said Ran. He moved the tiller a bit to port, and the ship veered starboard. "How's that?"

"Ease back some, not too much. If I judged it right, the slight course direction should help us. It's fortunate we have a strong current, otherwise we'd be dead."

"But what good will this do?"

Neviah turned toward the bow. "There's a narrow channel between some nasty reefs on either side. If we can reach it and glide through the channel without taking out our hull, it's a pretty sure bet that the larger ship will not be able to avoid the reef. I'm hoping they wreck the ship on it. They'll see us go through first and assume everything is fine."

"Malkyr's been plying these waters for years," said Ran. "Won't he figure this out?"

"Maybe," said Neviah. "But I doubt it. Kan-Gul seems to have taken charge, and Malkyr is too busy arguing with him. For all of Kan-Gul's magic, it might be more of an annoyance at this point."

Even as she said this, the storm continued to abate. "I hope you're right," said Ran. "If we can get them to crash on the reef, we'll have a good lead on them when we get to the coast."

"It won't be a long one," said Neviah. "But at least we're in a different part of the land from where we first got shipwrecked with Malkyr. If we can get to the border and find some friends, that would be great."

"They'll be hard on our tails as soon as we leave the ship."

Neviah nodded. "And we'll make them pay for every step they manage to take off of that boat."

Another blast of magic sped past Ran's head and slammed into the main mast. A shattering crash tore through the mast and it came spilling down, punching a hole in the deck. Ran turned and saw Kan-Gul smiling.

"Someone's getting impatient."

Neviah frowned. "What I don't understand is why he's not using magic right now to kill us all."

Jysal shook her head. "That's not his way. He's milking this moment and he wants us to feel completely at his power. He knows that we're in bad shape, that we cannot do much to escape them. He's enjoying this. And when he gets us all where he wants us—most likely in front of him on our knees—he will take his time and inflict the maximum amount of pain upon us. Only then will he kill us and feed our souls to the Chekhal."

"Not you," said Ran. "He's got other plans for you."

Jysal nodded. "I know it. But I will make it as hard for him as I can. He will find that it is tougher than he may have imagined to bend me to his will. He tries even now to warp my mind. I can feel him reaching out, imploring me to do something to you all. He says he will reward me with things I cannot even dream about. Probably because they are too nightmarish for me to even fathom. But so far, I have rebuffed his efforts. That may be due to the distance between us, or it may be due to something else."

"And you can't use any of your magic against him from here?"

Neviah sighed. "How many times will you ask that? It's too dangerous."

"I'll ask as many times as I can," said Ran. "In case you haven't noticed, we're in a bit of a bad spot here. We could certainly use some assistance of the magical kind. Jysal is powerful, you've said as much."

"She is," said Neviah. "But that just makes her using untrained magic all the more dangerous."

"Eventually, it's not going to matter," said Ran. "Kan-

Gul will have us where he wants us. And if he successfully infiltrates Jysal's mind, it will be too late for her to do anything about it."

Neviah shook her head. "You don't understand."

"I don't understand why you would rather risk our lives when we have a potential weapon here."

Neviah sighed. "I won't risk Jysal's life. If she uses magic and it comes out untempered, there is a very real risk that she will die. And I cannot let that happen. Not now, not ever while she is in my care. You may see her as just a tool to help fight off the evil pursuing us, but to me she is someone special—a treasure—that must be protected at all costs. She has used small magic during the trip, and it has worked out. But in order to destroy the enemy behind us, she would need to tap into a dangerous vein of power. I will not risk her life."

Ran sighed. He understood that Neviah was protecting her charge, but what good was all that protection if you simply ended up dead? It made no sense. They had a real threat closing in on them, and Jysal potentially had the power to stop it. To Ran, it was worth the risk. Unfortunately, Neviah didn't see it the same way, and, worse, if she was right, and Ran pressed for Jysal to try it anyway, there was a possibility that Jysal would die as the unchecked strength of magic exploded out of her.

"Very well."

Neviah laid a hand on his arm. "I understand that you are trying to save us all, Ran. I get that. But you must also see things from my perspective. As long as we are not in the clutches of Kan-Gul, there is a chance the gods will see to us escaping. We are still free, and I will not have Jysal

endanger herself. Not yet, at least. And possibly not ever.
She needs to learn to control her ability before she can be
unleashed upon the world. It is my job to get her to the
people who can help her best."

"All right," said Ran. "I just hope we all live long
enough for you to make that happen. I think it's fair to say
that Jysal has some real ability at her disposal. And if that
can be harnessed for good, then all the better."

Neviah nudged him a little. "Let the tide carry us
starboard now."

Ran grinned. Back to the scheme at hand. He
wondered how he would feel if he was in Neviah's position.
Or Jysal's, for that matter. Surely it must be tempting for
her to try some of her magic? After all, she could probably
feel it bubbling within her veins. And maybe it felt strange
to have to hold back like this. In the tunnel, she'd used
some to cast a faint light. He wondered what it felt like to
use it. Maybe it felt like he felt during the flow of combat,
when everything just seemed to happen without effort. In
one instant you were about to die, but then your training
took over and you moved and responded in just the right
way with just the right technique. It was a heady experience
to come away from a struggle and know that your training
had won the day.

The raider ship bucked again as another wave rose up
under their keel. Neviah shouted, "Hold that tiller and pray
it doesn't heave us to one side of the channel."

Ran jerked his awareness back to the present and
leaned hard on the tiller as the ship came down severely
out of alignment with the course Neviah wanted them to
take. He tried to swing the ship around, but without the

sail, it was too much for the smaller ship to handle. "It's no good!"

"Keep trying!" Neviah swung down and ran to the bow of the ship, which now pointed away from the channel she'd wanted them to take, straight into the coast. Ran saw her shaking her head already. He guessed the news wasn't good.

And knew so when he heard the sound of shearing underneath the keel of the boat.

"We're on the reef!"

Kancho rushed out from belowdecks, with Yuki right behind him. "We're taking on water!"

Ran looked out at the coastline. It seemed incredibly far away—perhaps two hundred yards still. Jumping into the water at this point would be suicide. The sharks roving the waters would feast on them before Kan-Gul's twisted creations had a chance to. He wondered if the bodies and blood from the destroyed ship would be enough to draw the sharks away. He'd rather not bet his life on it.

He heaved on the tiller, but it was too late to do much. The raider ship wasn't moving while its keel lay on the reef itself. Behind them, the transport vessel still charged ahead, directly toward them. With only a few hundred yards separating them, Ran knew it was only a matter of time before they met in combat.

Perhaps they could board the transport vessel and take the fight right to Kan-Gul and Malkyr.

The raider ship rocked as another wave smashed into them broadside. The ship tilted, and Ran grabbed Jysal before she fell down. He helped her back up, and then they both fell as another wave buffeted them. Neviah sprawled across the deck as she tried to make her way back to the stern.

"We've got to get off of here!"

Before Ran could say anything, he gasped. Heading toward them was a huge wave, rolling in from far out to sea. It looked like it was at least forty feet tall, and even as he started to take a breath, the entire wall of water slammed down atop them. Ran felt his world shift and started to roll over and over again. Everything went black, and then he knew nothing more.

CHAPTER THIRTY-SIX

Ran's head broke out of the water. He gasped, sucking in watery mouthfuls of air. His chest heaved, his lungs burning from having been underwater for so long. The towering wave had collapsed on them, shoving the raider ship free of the reef, toppling it end over end while Ran and his friends were all trapped on the rolling cylinder of water, unable to break through to surface until the wave finally receded.

In its wake, the raider ship was stranded in about six feet of water along a strip of sandbar about fifty yards from the beach.

Hands grabbed at Ran. "Come on, we've got to move!"

He blinked the salt water out of his eyes and felt for his sword at his side. It was still there, thankfully. He glanced around and saw Neviah struggling with Jysal through the water. Kancho was on one side of him and Yuki on the other. Incredibly, they'd all made it through the giant wave.

Ran shoved the memory of the wave out of his head. "Where are they?"

Kancho grunted. "They hit the reef, too. They're about a hundred and fifty yards away, but Malkyr has already ordered men into the surf to chase us down."

"Chekhal?"

"Not yet. Kan-Gul seems to be holding them back for now. Not sure what his plan is, but we've got to reach shore and get up those cliffs so we can hold Malkyr's men back."

Ran felt strength returning to his legs. "I'm fine. Let me go on my own. You can help your daughter."

"She's fine," said Kancho. "I raised her to hold her own. It's one reason why she's held up as well as she has." He smiled. "She's made me a very proud man on this day."

Ran surged ahead, wading through the water until he drew up out of the surf. He turned and saw a force of ten men trying their best to swim through the breakwater and reach shore. Ran couldn't be sure, but he thought he saw the triangular dorsal fins of roving sharks out there. He nodded. Maybe those fish could help whittle down the numbers Ran and the others would have to deal with. That would be fine with him.

Neviah and Jysal reached shore and started climbing the bank toward the foot of the cliff. "How do we get up there?" called Neviah. "I don't see any sort of path."

Kancho frowned. "I might be able to help them."

Ran pushed him up the beach. "You go. I'll stay back to deal with them."

"Are you sure?"

"Yes. I'll make a note of how you get up there and follow along shortly. If I can cut a few of them down and make them nervous about following me, then so much the better."

"All right. Good luck."

Ran watched Kancho and Yuki head up the beach, with Neviah and Jysal following behind. Ran turned and watched as one of Malkyr's men screamed as he was attacked by a shark. A spray of blood flew up into the rainy air, and then the man was gone. But the effect of seeing their comrade taken only energized the remaining men, and they swam even faster.

Ran waited until they were fifty yards from shore and then drew his sword. He knew they would be tired from the swim. That would work to his advantage.

One of the men swam faster than the others. Ran frowned. He'd made a big mistake. By surging ahead, he was now alone and without any of his friends close by. As he waded through the water, he unstrapped a battle axe and took a few practice swings.

Ran didn't give him time to get out of the water. He knew about the battle-ax and its massive weight and strength. Ran also knew its weakness. What it had in strength, it gave up in speed and maneuverability. In the water, the man's footing would be less sure. Ran would use that to his advantage.

The man swung the battle-ax in a wide arc, and Ran stepped back as he did. The ax blade whistled past, and Ran cut down, aiming his sword at one of the man's hands. The sword nicked just above the wrist, and Ran saw the blood start to flow. It fell and mixed with the sand, staining it a deep red before the waves came in and diluted it.

The ax man flipped the blade back around and swung again. Ran hadn't expected the move to be as fast as it was and had to jump to the side to avoid it. As he did so, he let his sword come down and cut into the man's side. He heard the scream and followed through, plunging his blade deep into the man's back before cutting right to left. The man grunted once and dropped. The battle-ax slipped from his grasp.

Ran turned and saw another man charging ahead out of the surf. He had a smaller sword in each hand. Ran frowned. Two blades were always more dangerous than one, especially if the person wielding them was lean and light on his feet. This man was. He grinned at Ran and licked his lips. "I see you dispatched Revor already."

Ran said nothing. Talking was a waste of energy when there was killing to be done. He waited, and the man shrugged. Then he attacked.

He brought the two blades up, one higher than the other, and charged in, cutting down. If he'd expected Ran to try to deflect the blades, he was momentarily surprised when Ran merely avoided the cuts and then cut in with his own blade. This forced the man to retreat and parry Ran's sword. He backed up to the water's edge and then tried another attack. But Ran simply avoided the double strike by sidestepping and then arced a single diagonal cut down at the man's neck, cutting him open before leaping away. The look of shock on the man's face was the last expression he would ever wear. He slipped forward and then fell face-first into the waves that instantly sought to drag him back out to the reef, where the sharks could have him.

Good thing he wasn't better trained, thought Ran. The remainder of Malkyr's men were coming in together, slowly and already armed. Facing them as one would be foolhardy. Ran dashed up the beach and found the tracks of Kancho and the others. He followed these up and around until he came across a game trail that led upward.

He heard shouts behind him and knew that Malkyr's men would be giving chase. Seeing two of their comrades cut down would no doubt fuel their desire for revenge. Ran sprinted until he came to a corner where the trail banked around. Ran reached down, grabbed a handful of sand, and waited.

Less than thirty seconds later, he cut out from the corner horizontally and low. His blade impacted the thighs of the lead man and cut deep. Ran stepped out and threw the handful of sand in a wide arc aimed at the eyes of the men behind the lead man. As they struggled to deal with the eye-clouding sand, Ran finished off the lead man by dragging his blade up into his belly and finishing with a downward cut to the back of his neck.

Another man lunged forward. Ran stepped back, letting the man's momentum carry him forward onto Ran's blade.

Then he turned and bolted farther up the trail. As he ran, his lungs heaved. The ascent was tough on his legs and lungs, but Ran pushed on. He'd managed to take out four of the men. A shark had taken another. That left five more on his tail. Reasonable odds, he figured. And certainly manageable for Kancho and Neviah when they reached the top of the cliff.

Two hundred yards farther on, he reached the top of the cliff and saw Kancho and Neviah, armed and waiting. Behind them stood Yuki and Jysal. And beyond them, the sprawling Dark Sea glistened as more waves pummeled the coast. Ran thumbed over his shoulder.

"Five coming."

"You only left us five?" Kancho grinned. "Hardly worth the effort."

Neviah smirked. "He's so greedy."

Ran fell behind them and took several seconds to grab some air into his lungs. He looked out over the cliff and saw Malkyr's transport vessel lying on the reef. More men were coming ashore. And worse, so were Chekhal. He wondered why they didn't attack Malkyr's men and figured Kan-Gul's magic must have made them obedient.

But they would be here soon.

Ran's attention was drawn back to the top of the cliff. Malkyr's lead men had reached the summit and fanned out in front of Kancho and Neviah.

Kancho smiled at Neviah. "Would you mind if I took the lead?"

"Be my guest."

Kancho stepped out ahead of her. Ran knew the technique. Kancho would handle the first attacker and funnel them toward Neviah as he cut them first and she finished them off. A more experienced group of fighters would hold back and seek one-on-one combat with Kancho, aware of the trick, but these men didn't look all that experienced. Judging by his first two foes, these men were used to facing the weak and the panicked. They had all the technique of mindless butchers.

Two men rushed Kancho almost immediately. Kancho raised his sword high and brought it screaming down on the lead man's arms, then stepped to the side and shoved the man toward Neviah, who simply stabbed him in the heart and let him drop at her feet. Kancho engaged the second man with a reverse upswing cut that impaled him under the right armpit. Kancho drove in deep, severing the vital arteries there, before yanking his blade free and wheeling around to meet the next attack.

Another man stepped forward, holding a similar curved blade. Kancho paused, his eyebrows raised. The man might have held a Murai blade, but he was anything but Murai. Still, if nothing else, Kancho gave the blade more respect than the man.

"Where did you get that sword?"

"From an old man in Nehon who died by my hand. As will you."

Kancho frowned. "We hold our blades in high regard. That one deserves better treatment than at the hands of someone like you."

"We'll see."

Kancho nodded. "Yes. We will."

The man advanced slowly and then launched a searing downward cut at Kancho's head. He was fast, this man, but Kancho was faster. As the man launched the attack, Kancho simply stepped in and drove the point of his sword into the base of the man's throat, stabbed straight through and kept going. There was the briefest pause as the sword cut and then the man's head fell from his shoulders.

Kancho spun and faced the remaining two men. "Which of you is next?"

Neither man seemed ready to advance and meet the Murai warrior in front of them. Ran got back to his feet and watched the action unfold on the beach. More of Malkyr's men were streaming ashore, and the lead Chekhal had now made it to the sand as well. While the march up the cliff might exhaust Malkyr's men, the Chekhal wouldn't tire out. And the fact that they were now coming made Ran anxious.

"We're going to have a lot more visitors soon," he said. "Chekhal visitors."

Kancho let his sword blade dip toward the ground and that was the incentive the remaining men needed. They attacked from either side of Kancho. But the old warrior stepped back and simultaneously brought his sword up and over the first attacker's blade, cut down on his arms, and then flipped the edge toward the man's neck and cut through horizontally. The movement was so precise and fast the attacker never saw it happen. As his head and body fell in two different directions, the second attacker tried to correct his position, but by then it was too late. Kancho stepped around and delivered two sweeping cuts to the back of his legs and then back down into his chest. The second attacker went down almost as fast.

Kancho stepped back, barely breathing hard.

Neviah frowned. "Thanks for giving me so much work."

"I gave you one. Don't complain."

"He was basically dead when you handed him off."

Kancho flipped his blade and hit the back of the blade with the edge of his hand to clear the blood off of it. "Let's not fight over body counts. Ran tells us there will shortly be many more than we can both possibly wish for."

"Interesting choice of words," said Neviah. "Let's see how we do this time."

Ran came over. "They're going to keep throwing men at us until they overwhelm us."

"Most likely," said Neviah.

"In which case, we are dead," said Ran.

Kancho grunted. "But not until we cost them many lives. A good day's work, I'd say."

Ran frowned. "I don't want to die here on some lonely cliff. There's got to be another way."

Neviah eyed him. "I will not ask her to use magic. Jysal knows the risks."

"And what if she wants to help out anyway? What then?"

"She will not," said Neviah. "The danger is too great."

"If she doesn't help, then we are all dead and the point is moot anyway. But if her magic is able to help us, what's wrong with that? We need help or we'll be killed."

Neviah frowned and then nodded slowly. "Very well. Ask her while Kancho and I deal with our uninvited guests."

Ran moved back to Jysal. "You know what's happening."

"We are in a very bad situation."

"Malkyr is sending more men, and Kan-Gul has a unit of Chekhal proceeding up the hill toward us even now. We are only five and effectively only three. Unless you choose to help us."

"Neviah has told me it's too dangerous to use magic if I am untrained."

"But you did it in the tunnel. Remember?"

"That was only to light the area."

The first of Malkyr's reinforcements came around the corner at the top of the game trail. They engaged Kancho and Neviah immediately. And these men looked more like hardened veterans. Ran could already see that Kancho was moving more carefully than he had been before. Neviah was also taking her time instead of rushing. Ran resisted the urge to rush to their side and join the fray. Too many men were coming up the hillside for their blades to defeat.

"If you don't help us, we are all dead."

Jysal closed her eyes. "I'm afraid, Ran."

"You should be. If they manage to subdue us, we're all dead . . . worse than dead."

Jysal opened her eyes. "What would you have me do?"

"Whatever you can. I don't know any magic. So I trust you to do what's best. But if you can defeat these men, then I suggest you do so immediately. We need Kancho and Neviah for when the Chekhal arrive. And that will be soon."

Jysal took a deep breath and then exhaled. "Very well. I will try."

CHAPTER THIRTY-SEVEN

"Stand back."

Jysal said the words almost as if she were whispering, but Ran heard them loud and clear. He waved Kancho and Neviah back. Neviah wore an expression of alarm on her face, but Ran simply shook his head and she stayed quiet.

Jysal's entire body seemed to pulse for a moment. Then as Ran watched, a yellow aura broke out around her, sizzling and crackling in the air. He blinked and nearly missed the orb that shot from her outstretched hands directly at the men rushing onto the top of the cliff. It struck them and exploded, sending them all flying back down the trail, their bodies scattered like so many grains of sand.

None of them moved again.

Kancho glanced back at Jysal. "Impressive, young one."

Neviah sheathed her blades and rushed to Jysal's side even as Jysal started to slump. "I told you not to try it."

"I had to. You and Kancho would have been overwhelmed by the reinforcements. I couldn't let that happen. Not after all you've done for me."

Neviah cradled Jysal's head and looked at Ran. "You did this. You pressured her to use magic when she shouldn't have. If she dies, I will kill you."

Ran held up his hand. "You're not being rational, Neviah. There were too many of them. Jysal made the decision to try to help you—to help all of us. She knew we could never handle the enemy without her. And when Kan-Gul arrives with his Chekhal, you can bet it's going to get a lot worse around here. We'd be dead within seconds."

"If that's what is supposed to happen, then so be it."

"You're very cavalier when you say that," said Ran. "How would you reconcile that sentiment with the fact that Jysal would be forced into a life of pain and suffering? If you're dead, you certainly can't protect her."

Neviah frowned. "She still shouldn't have done anything."

Kancho walked to where the dead bodies of Malkyr's men lay. While Kan-Gul's magic storm had subsided, a persistent drizzle continued to soak the ground. Kancho glanced around the corner and then came rushing back. "You two are going to have to put this aside. Kan-Gul and his Chekhal are heading this way. Malkyr is with him as well."

Jysal stirred and looked up at Neviah. Her voice was a faint whisper. "I did what I wanted to do. Don't be mad at Ran. Without him, we wouldn't have made it this far. I just need some time to rest. That's all." Her head slumped against Neviah's chest and was still.

Tears streamed down Neviah's face as she laid Jysal down on the grass. Turning, she eyed Ran. "We're not done yet."

Was Jysal dead? Ran swallowed and hoped that she wasn't. There wasn't time to mourn her passing now. Not with so many enemies still to deal with. Ran nodded. "Fine."

Neviah drew her weapons. "It's time to finish this."

The lead Chekhal came around the corner of the trail and charged onto the cliff wielding a barbed spear. It wore leather armor studded with steel bolts, and its opaque eyes swept around surveying the scene. Neviah walked forward to meet it.

Brandishing two short swords, Neviah looked every bit as intimidating as the Chekhal she faced. The undead warrior spun the spear and thrust it three times before Ran even registered the first attack. These Chekhal were much faster and more adept with their weapons than the ones they'd dealt with back at the castle.

But Neviah was running on rage and her reflexes were even faster than the Chekhal. She twisted and leapt and dodged each attack, coming down on the balls of her feet before stabbing both blades into the midsection of the Chekhal. It grunted and staggered back, trying to free itself from being impaled. Neviah moved with it, wrenching her blades free before spinning and neatly severing the undead's head.

Another Chekhal rushed on to the scene. Ran drew his sword but Neviah moved faster, engaging and driving low with a sweeping cut to its unprotected legs. Her blades severed one leg, and the Chekhal toppled over. Neviah stepped behind it and drove the tip of one sword directly into its brain. It convulsed once and then lay still.

"Let's join the fray," said Kancho, drawing his sword.

He and Ran moved to opposite sides of the cliff as more Chekhal reached the cliff and started fighting with them. In the middle of the cliff, Neviah was a whirlwind of cutting action. She showed no signs of fatigue as she cut down three more Chekhal before Kancho had dispatched his first opponent.

Ran caught sight of Kan-Gul striding up the game trail. Malkyr hustled to follow, but he still walked with a bit of a limp. Ran smiled. It was good to know that his injury would slow him down. That would make him easier to kill.

The number of bodies around Neviah grew with each passing minute. As much as Ran and Kancho cut down more Chekhal, their numbers never seemed to wane. More and more of them were streaming up the game trail. Slowly, all three of them were pushed back, closer toward the edge of the cliff overlooking the tempestuous sea.

Overhead, the clouds still pummeled them with sheets of rain. The ground underfoot grew steadily more muddy and slippery. Ran was forced to widen his base of support and sink lower to avoid falling. Kancho adjusted easily enough, neatly cutting one of the Chekhal in two pieces. The Chekhal continued to move until Kancho cut his head off.

Neviah went airborne again, driving a flying kick into the chest of one Chekhal armed with a curved sword. The impact drove the undead warrior back into three other Chekhal. Neviah landed and ran directly at the four of them, her swords a whirl of mayhem that severed limbs and eventually heads. But as many as she continued to slay, more rushed in to fill the void left by their slain comrades.

Ran was growing tired, and he could see the toll on

Kancho as well. Kan-Gul and Malkyr hadn't come up onto the cliff top yet, apparently preferring to wait until the Chekhal had worn down their opponents. Behind him, Jysal's body lay still. Ran felt his heart drop. If she was truly dead, then this was not going to end well.

Not one bit.

Kancho was closer to Ran now. "We can't maintain this pace. There are too many of them."

Ran cleaved the head of another Chekhal off and watched it fall over the side of the cliff into the sea below. "What do you suggest?"

"We have but two options, really. One: keep fighting until we die. Two: jump over the side of the cliff and take our chances in the sea below."

Ran smirked. "I like how surrender wasn't on that list."

"Surrender would be suicide. We're dead anyway." He deflected another attacking Chekhal and cut it down with a low-high cut. He nodded at Neviah. "She's still going strong."

Ran shook his head. "It can't last. She's fueled by rage right now—or sorrow—at the thought that Jysal has died. Sooner or later, they'll overwhelm her."

Kancho smirked. "Youth. I miss it. Time was I would have had the energy to do what she's doing now."

"Regardless, it can't last." Ran dodged another attacking Chekhal and then cut it down with a backslash that severed its spinal cord. "We need to figure out what we're going to do here."

A trio of Chekhal rushed Neviah simultaneously. She couldn't handle them and they fell upon her. Ran rushed in, cutting two of them down while Neviah speared the third through its eye socket. She shoved the dead Chekhal off of her and glared at Ran. "This changes nothing."

"We're going to be overwhelmed here in a moment."

"We fight!" shouted Neviah. "We cannot leave her behind."

It was fruitless to argue with her. She rushed another pair of Chekhal and cut them down in seconds. But Ran could see she was beginning to tire. Her movements were slowing. It was impossible to tell if she was sweating given how much rain was falling on them, but Ran felt sure she was soaked as much by sweat as by precipitation.

More Chekhal strode into the fray. Neviah backed up, doing her best to ward them off, but there were more right behind them. Kan-Gul must have held some back and now threw everything at the trio on top of the cliff. Ran still hadn't glimpsed the evil sorcerer, but he felt his presence close by.

He glanced back, aware that he was being pushed perilously close to the edge of the cliff. He ducked under another attack and cut the Chekhal down. Then he moved ahead, trying to carve out an area where he could fight without fear of going over the side. Two more Chekhal came at him, and Ran struggled to maintain his breathing. Without it, fatigue would claim him more quickly. He ducked and dodged and sidestepped and then killed them both. His lungs heaved. The ground sucked at his feet. The corpses were piling up and starting to limit their mobility.

Kancho stepped over the corpse of one Chekhal and nearly tripped on another one. He frowned and cut down another attacker. "It's getting too crowded up here."

At that moment, the Chekhal stopped charging forward.

Neviah, Kancho, and Ran all paused, looking around for a new foe to dispatch. The Chekhal atop the cliff shrank back toward the game trail and then stood there. From behind them, Ran saw movement. The Chekhal parted and allowed Kan-Gul to pass through.

The evil sorcerer wore a big smile as he surveyed the scene. The smile faded when he saw Jysal's limp body on the ground.

"Is she dead?"

The look on Neviah's face could have made steel melt, Ran decided. But it had little effect on Kan-Gul. "She used magic before her body was properly prepared for it. It killed her."

"Where are my men?" asked Malkyr as he came onto the cliff.

Neviah nodded at Jysal. "They were her first and only victims."

"She used magic to kill them?" asked Kan-Gul. "Such a waste. But so much power. I can feel its residue even now." He glanced at Malkyr. "I told you not to rush too many men up here. If you'd followed my commands, we could have captured them and managed to keep the girl alive. Instead, this is a slaughterhouse. Worse, the girl is dead. Her magic is gone."

"We had to attack," said Malkyr. "After what they did to my men, to my ship."

"I don't care about your men," said Kan-Gul. "I only cared about the girl. That's what you were paid for. You were supposed to bring her to me."

"I did bring her to you, nearly at the cost of my leg, I might remind you."

Kan-Gul frowned. "Pity the shark didn't finish the job." He looked at Neviah. "You do realize this man betrayed you, don't you?"

Neviah nodded. "I do."

"Then perhaps you should kill him." Kan-Gul nodded, and the Chekhal behind Malkyr shoved him out away from their protection. Another Chekhal tossed a sword at Malkyr's feet.

Malkyr looked back at Kan-Gul. "We had a deal!"

"Exactly," said Kan-Gul. "We *had* a deal. You mucked things up by letting your ego make decisions for you. You've cost me the most precious thing I ever wanted. That girl's power would have made me the most powerful sorcerer in the land. Because of that, you will now face the wrath of her protector."

Malkyr snatched the sword up and wheeled to face Neviah.

Neviah took a breath and flexed her arms. She resheathed one of her swords and eyed Malkyr. "You're not worth two."

Malkyr screamed as he rushed in at her. The downward cut was off-balance and clumsy but still had a significant amount of force behind it. If he'd managed to connect, it certainly would have cut Neviah down.

Neviah sidestepped and smacked Malkyr on the back of the head with the flat of her blade. The solid clunk knocked Malkyr off his feet. He went sprawling and nearly impaled himself on his own sword as he did so. He slowly got to his feet and shook off some of the mud.

"Make this damned rain stop!"

Kan-Gul seemed ready to bark an order at Malkyr,

then looked at Ran and his companions and shrugged. "I suppose I could grant you one final favor." He snapped his fingers, and the rain simply stopped. No lingering drops or drizzle.

Ran sighed. He was certain Kan-Gul had meant to intimidate them with his show of power, but Ran didn't care. The absence of pouring rain was a welcome change.

Malkyr circled Neviah, trying to gain an advantage. He attacked again, this time attempting to cut her in half at the waist. Neviah backed up and let his momentum carry him past her. This time she used the tip of the sword to cut him under his rib cage as he went by. Ran heard the cut and saw Malkyr wince as the razor edge drew blood for the first time.

He wheeled fast and tried to cut back at her, but Neviah had already moved away. Malkyr's attack sailed through the air harmlessly. He doubled back and came at her with an overhead diagonal attack. Neviah leaned away and kicked Malkyr in the crotch.

Kan-Gul chuckled. "This is almost entertaining enough to make me forget about the loss of the girl."

Malkyr sucked wind on the grass as he tried to get his legs back under him.

Neviah spat at him. "You're pathetic."

Malkyr eyed her with hatred smeared across his face. "I will kill you, bitch."

Neviah backed up and used her free hand to wave him on. "Come on then and do your worst."

Ran watched as she backed closer toward where Kan-Gul stood. The sorcerer's face showed a mixture of glee and amusement. Ran frowned. If there was only a chance of killing him.

And then Neviah did the unthinkable. As she backed toward Kan-Gul, she abruptly changed direction and swung her sword horizontally right at Kan-Gul's neck. Ran's heart leapt into his throat.

Yes!

But it was as though Neviah's sword hit a solid wall right in front of Kan-Gul. The force of the impact knocked her back, stumbling.

Kan-Gul held up one finger and tutted. "Now, now, that wasn't very nice . . . "

Ran started to shout for Neviah to be careful, but then Malkyr was already rushing in from behind. Even as Neviah started to register the threat and turn to face him, Malkyr's blade plunged into her back, between her shoulder blades.

As Ran watched, horrified, the tip of Malkyr's sword erupted from Neviah's chest, spraying the ground with blood.

Neviah sank to the ground, her eyes already rolling white.

Silence descended over the cliff.

CHAPTER THIRTY-EIGHT

Malkyr yanked his blade from Neviah's corpse and let the blood drip off the end of it while he stared down at her. "Worthless bitch. I told you I would strike you down."

Ran felt his face go hot. His pulse pounded in his ears, drummed in his neck. He took several breaths, but it did no good. He gripped his sword tighter. Next to him, he felt the energy coming from Kancho as well.

Kan-Gul didn't move; the smile on his face stayed plastered where it was, and he started nodding. "Well, that was mildly entertaining."

Malkyr eyed Kan-Gul. "I should kill you for betraying me."

Kan-Gul chuckled. "As if you could. You exist at my whim, Malkyr. And unfortunately for you, I am about at the end of my tolerance for you and your stupid decisions."

"Then you won't mind if I kill him."

Kan-Gul turned to face Ran. "As a matter of fact, I wouldn't."

Ran nodded and stepped out to meet Malkyr. "Don't waste your breath talking. I don't intend this to take long."

Malkyr smirked. "You are as arrogant as you are young." He looked back at Neviah. "She thought she was good, too. So much for that."

"She was good," said Ran. "And she had more courage than you'll ever know in this life. You just took advantage of a moment to strike her down from behind like the coward you are. She would have easily defeated you otherwise."

"So what?" Malkyr shrugged. "In combat, everyone takes advantage of an opportunity. You're a dead fool if you don't."

"I guess you'll find out soon enough."

"Find out what?"

Ran stepped forward and raise his sword. "What it's like to be dead."

Malkyr attacked, cutting down with a savage blow meant to cleave Ran down the center of his body. As he stepped through, Ran sidestepped and cut at his hands. Malkyr dodged and cut back from the side, forcing Ran to parry the blade with his own. He twisted his blade and put pressure on Malkyr to hang on or risk losing his sword. Malkyr, to his credit, held on and then turned the blade, trying to cut at Ran's hands. Ran pulled his sword back, disengaging, and then flipped it over, cutting at Malkyr's head.

Malkyr backed up just enough to avoid most of Ran's cut, but Ran succeeded in scoring a line across his brow that produced an immediate flow of blood into Malkyr's eyes. Malkyr backed away and wiped his forehead.

"Cuts to the head bleed an awful lot," said Ran as he circled again.

Malkyr spat some of the blood out of his mouth. "You'll never win. Even if you kill me. Kan-Gul will have his Chekhal strike you down within moments."

"That's more time than you have," said Ran. "And that's enough for me."

Ran feinted with a stab at Malkyr's heart and then cut up suddenly, hoping to catch the underside of Malkyr's arms. But Malkyr showed a bit more skill than Ran had expected and jerked his arms away from the edge of the blade. He shook his head, flicking droplets of blood across the ground.

Ran stalked him, edging around and looking for the moment. Malkyr was heavier on his feet and slightly unbalanced. Twice he came at Ran, and Ran evaded the cuts, looking for the weakness in Malkyr's attacks. Malkyr snarled each time he missed, which only made him overcommit on the next attack.

"You can't avoid me all the time."

Ran allowed himself a small grin. "You think I'm avoiding you?"

"Aren't you?"

Malkyr attacked again, cutting from the left to the right and then back again. The two cuts were heavy and meant to overpower Ran. Ran sidestepped the first and parried the second.

"No," he said simply.

And then he swept Malkyr's blade over and up, flicking it away. The sword flew from his grasp and stuck point first in the ground ten feet away.

For a moment, Malkyr stood there.

Ran saw the indecision in his eyes. Should he try to grab for the sword?

Too late. Ran stepped in and brought his sword arcing in. The tip of his blade cut the juncture of Malkyr's neck close to his collar bone. Ran followed through and then drew back.

Malkyr laughed. "You missed."

Ran nodded. "Touch your neck."

Malkyr put his hand up to his neck and felt the surging pulse of fresh blood flowing from the severed artery. Even as his hand came away covered in sticky blood, he felt his legs buckle, and he sank to his knees.

Ran stepped in closer. "Neviah is waiting for you on the other side. I hope she gets her own chance to kill you when you get there."

Malkyr fell face-first into the bloody, rain-soaked ground and lay still as his life pumped out of him and into the sodden earth. Ran looked down and exhaled. "Good riddance."

Kan-Gul clapped his hands. "Marvelous. That was marvelous. Truly. I admire the way you led him around and only after you'd annoyed him sufficiently did you kill him. And that final cut, absolutely exquisite. But why didn't you cut his head off? Wouldn't that have been preferable?"

Ran shrugged. "Consider it a final insult. My way of showing him I didn't need to do all that much to kill him. He wasn't worth the extra effort."

Kan-Gul kept smiling. "You've got style, Ran from Gakur. I really must congratulate you on that."

"I don't much care what you think," said Ran.

"Well, you should. After all, I hold the lives of you three survivors in my hands. One nod from me and you'll have more Chekhal to deal with than even you and your talented friend there can handle. You might want to reconsider being rude to me."

"I wasn't being rude," said Ran. "I was simply stating a fact."

"You're tired," said Kan-Gul. "I can certainly understand that. You wouldn't believe how utterly exhausting it was trying to hunt you all down. And the troubles we had along the way. Honestly. But here we are. Atop this horrible cliff. My ship is wrecked. Yours is as well. And Malkyr's, well, that's a bit of a mess, isn't it?"

"I haven't really thought about the ships recently. We've been a bit busy."

"Indeed," said Kan-Gul. "Let me ask you something: who are you? Really. Because you most definitely are not some silly blade for hire. I've known mercenaries before. And I've known scum like Malkyr who would sell their own mother for the promise of a gold piece. You don't fit the mold. And I'm curious to know who stands before me."

"No one important," said Ran.

"You know, when I first met you I felt there was something about you that defied the appearance you've tried hard to affect. So I took to my library and consulted some of my books. I have so very many books, you know. Ancient texts on virtually every subject and culture known to us. And when I researched the region of Gakur in Nehon, do you know what the books told me?"

"I can't even imagine."

Kan-Gul smiled. "They told me that the region of

Gakur is known as one of the most remote places in all of Nehon. Towering mountains enshrouded with impassable fog, twisting mountain passes that are blocked virtually year-round due to the mountain snows. The people who live in this are are a most hearty folk who keep to themselves. Mostly, they're farmers who manage to eke out an existence only at the mercy of nature."

"They're good people," said Ran.

"I'm sure they are," said Kan-Gul. "But the books also spoke of something else. Apparently, Gakur is rumored to be the location of a training facility for a clan of mysterious fighters known as Shinobujin. So adept at combat, they are fearsome opponents. Their ability to steal through the night, infiltrate impregnable fortresses, and use virtually every weapon known makes them border on the supernatural."

Ran said nothing. He wasn't too fussed about Kan-Gul's revelation. Besides, Kancho already knew, so it wasn't like Kan-Gul was spilling his secrets.

"The legends that surround the Shinobujin clan rival some of the magic that sorcerers wield. It makes me wonder how much of what I read is rooted in truth and how much is the byproduct of the overactive imaginations of your enemies. Because it quickly became apparent to me that you are most definitely a Shinobujin. Especially when I saw the cell door in my dungeon so easily opened. Only a Shinobujin would have been able to pick that lock and fight as well as a Murai. And you did both as easily as drawing a breath."

I wouldn't say it was that easy, thought Ran. But he said nothing.

Kan-Gul folded his arms. "So, while I was busy pursuing you and dealing with obnoxious dragons, I got to thinking. Specifically, I got to thinking about how valuable it would be to have my very own shadow warrior. Someone I could send off to do some of the very dirty work that unfortunately tends to plague the existence of a sorcerer like myself. Honestly, so many enemies . . . it's quite tragic."

"Why would you need a shadow warrior to do your bidding? Isn't your magic strong enough to do whatever you need done?"

Kan-Gul sighed. "Well, ordinarily, I would say that magic would solve most of my problems. There are, however, certain situations that require a more deft touch. And solutions that once implemented don't necessarily point back to me."

"You're looking for someone who will kill for you such that it can't possibly be traced back to you."

Kan-Gul sighed. "Honestly, I thought the way I said it had a bit more finesse. But if that's what works for you, then fine. Yes, that's exactly what I'm looking for. It occurs to me that you would be the perfect person to fill that particular role."

Ran shook his head. "I'm not for hire."

"Not according to what I read. The books told me that night stalkers are often for hire. That they sometimes hire themselves out to the highest bidder and warlords all over Nehon utilize their particular skill set since the Murai are bound to a code of honor that precludes them from engaging in things they consider underhanded." He glanced at Kancho who had said nothing during the entire exchange. "Is that true, Murai? Does the notion of working with night stalkers disgust you?"

Kancho sniffed. "I don't presume to judge those who walk a different path. If they operate with honor and integrity, then I have no qualms with them."

"Spoken like a Murai with an identity problem," said Kan-Gul. "I should have expected that from you. You see, I also found it fascinating that a supposedly drunken warrior would behave as you did. It made me suspect you from the start. But you weren't a shadow warrior. I knew that much. But if you were Murai, then what in the world were you doing over here? The warlords of Nehon tend to keep to themselves, believing that pitiful island is immune to the whims of the world at large. There's no way they would send a lone Murai abroad. Unless that Murai went against the wishes of his lord. And to do such a thing would bring tremendous dishonor upon the Murai clan he was a part of."

Kancho frowned. "What would you know of my clan?"

"I know enough about Malkyr and his raiding tendencies. I also know of his associates who have been plundering local fishing villages on the coast of Nehon for years. A short time ago they came upon a sloop while at sea. And they took a hostage—let's call her a guest. Supposedly, this guest was a young and exquisite beauty rumored to be of Murai stock."

Yuki moved a little closer to her father. Kan-Gul nodded.

"Exactly. As soon as I thought it through, it made perfect sense. The Murai was alone in a foreign land because he'd come to rescue his daughter. Imagine the circumstances that conspired to place both of you on Malkyr's boat. Here he was, tasked with bringing me the delectable thing that was Jysal. Sadly, she is no longer with us. Such a shame. As such, I am forced to do what I do best: make the best of what I have at hand."

"Meaning what?" asked Ran.

"Meaning," said Kan-Gul, "that despite the shattering loss that was Jysal's death, I still have something to show for all of the trouble I've been forced to endure throughout this campaign."

Ran shook his head. "I'm not for hire. I don't know how many times I can say that before you'll get it."

Kan-Gul nodded. "That's fine. I understand. You don't much like the prospect of working for me. I can't say I blame you, given how we got off on the wrong foot when you first came to my castle. But that said, I could certainly make your employment worthwhile. I pay very well. And what I can't pay, I can supply in other ways. If you want women, I can have my minions raid the villages until they bring you back something that pleases you. If you have . . . other tastes, I can accommodate those as well."

Ran swallowed. Listening to Kan-Gul offer him a job was making him feel slightly ill. "I don't think there's anything you have that will convince me to come and work for you. If you know anything about the shadow-warrior clan, then you'll know that I am bound to them. Whether I am in Nehon or elsewhere in the world, my allegiance to the clan comes first."

"And how would they know?" asked Kan-Gul. "You'd still be free to do your spying and feeding information back to your clan. I don't have an issue with that. In fact, I might even be able to help you in certain regions through the use of my magic."

"I'm not for hire," said Ran. Ran knew some of his teachers wouldn't have approved of his being so quick to dismiss a potentially pragmatic solution. But the head of his clan would not want this monster left alive.

Kan-Gul paused, took a breath, and then exhaled it slow and smooth. "You can't say I didn't try to make this as palatable as possible."

"There's nothing palatable about you, Kan-Gul," said Ran.

Kan-Gul pursed his lips. "Very well. Let me put it another way, and then you can decide for yourself if this isn't an offer very much worth considering: either you agree to come work for me, or you will all die tonight."

Ran shrugged. "You'll kill us all anyway."

Kan-Gul let a thin smile creep across his lips. "Have I told you about my Chekhal? So much of magic remains a mystery, even to those who are trained in its use. Sometimes, you never know quite what the outcome will be. Surprises are not uncommon, especially when you attempt to cheat death."

Ran sighed. Listening to Kan-Gul talk was growing tiresome, but perhaps it would reveal an opportunity Ran could exploit.

The sorcerer continued. "Take my Chekhal, for instance. I've told you that they are reanimated warriors. They were dead, and I hauled them back out of the ground to serve me for as long as I need them. In exchange, I let them feast upon the souls of other living beings. In this way, they are . . . well, I suppose one could say they are reasonably content."

"How can anything that was dead ever truly be content? They belong in the afterlife, not forced to serve here with you."

Kan-Gul ignored him. "Being content is not really enough to keep warriors—alive or dead, for that matter—loyal to you. They need further incentive. A bonus, if you will, that will keep them only too happy to stay and serve me." Kan-Gul strode over to the closest Chekhal and placed his hand on the warrior's shoulder. "A curious effect of reanimating these dead warriors has been that they apparently have other needs apart from the ingestion of living souls."

"Such as?"

Kan-Gul's smile grew as he drew up the articulated armored plate that covered the Chekhal's lower abdomen and groin, exposing the flesh underneath. Ran was horrified to see the Chekhal's genitalia.

"You will note that for an undead warrior, death seems to have gifted it with an unusual physical ailment: nearly permanent rigidity."

Ran stared at Kan-Gul. "Nearly permanent?"

"There is a cure for it, albeit temporarily." Kan-Gul's eyes flicked over to Yuki, and his smile grew. "Perhaps I will see if Kancho's daughter has the ability to satisfy the unearthly cravings of my Chekhal warriors. She can start with the dozen I have here with me and later on attend to the thousands back at my castle." He sighed. "If nothing else, it will no doubt provide me with hours of entertainment."

Now Kan-Gul stared directly at Kancho. "Imagine that, Murai: your daughter's every orifice filled with the undead seed of my men. How much dishonor would that bring upon your house?"

CHAPTER THIRTY-NINE

Kancho's reaction was immediate. The older warrior lifted his curved blade and ran directly at the sorcerer, swinging his blade overhead and down, determined to cleave the evil sorcerer in two. Ran watched him rush Kan-Gul, and then it was as if time started to slow down. Ran felt himself breathing and his pulse quickening as the older warrior seemed to take a long time to close the distance between where he stood and Kan-Gul's position.

The sorcerer wore a nasty smile full of pleasure, and there wasn't a hint of surprise. Ran realized that Kan-Gul had deliberately baited the older warrior. He didn't care about Kancho or his daughter. He wanted Ran now that Jysal was dead. Everyone else was just a distraction.

Ran tried to shout a warning, but even the words took forever to spill from his mouth. It wouldn't have mattered. Kancho was beyond reason. Yuki had been the reason he'd dishonored himself in the first place. She'd been his entire reason for being. To hear the possibility of his only family being tortured in such a way had robbed him of common sense and any wisdom he'd gained from years on the battlefield.

The Murai adherence to their code of honor dictated that Kancho strike down Kan-Gul. The sorcerer knew this. And now he was exploiting it.

Kancho took another step in half-time and started to bring his sword down right at Kan-Gul. The sorcerer looked up at the descending blade; the smile he wore never wavered. For an instant, Ran wondered if Kancho would be able to carry through with this strike.

Then the sword simply stopped moving.

So did Kancho.

"Men are so often victims of their egos, wouldn't you say, night stalker?" Kan-Gul walked around the frozen Kancho. "Let us look at the example before us. Here we have a warrior who by all accounts is ferocious. He's a veteran of many conflicts, and his skill with the sword is obvious. Talented. Some would even say wise, filled with experience. And yet, despite all of his successes, he is still vulnerable to me playing his ego like a violinist plucks strings. It took but one little idea that his daughter would be ravaged by the primal lust of my undead warriors to get him to willingly abandon all restraint."

"It's his only daughter," said Ran. "She is the only family he has left."

Kan-Gul shrugged. "You're making excuses for him now? Surely you know the dangers of ego. Surely your masters taught you how to manipulate it to your advantage when it comes to gathering information or dealing with a warrior who would be, by any other standard, a formidable challenge?"

"They did. And I do."

"Those who claim to be immune from the vulnerability that ego infects us with are most often the first to fall prey to its insidious tendrils. They creep about the mind, destroy the spirit, and rob us of our ability to remain detached from vanity, idol worship, and whims of desire in all its forms. This is the advantage that sorcerers and other mages have over warriors: our minds need to be sharp, objective, and flexible in order to master the forces of magic. The art is demanding and full of traps and pitfalls that ensnare those of lesser discipline or lesser imagination. Most often it seduces them and blinds them with the promise of power and prestige while robbing them of everything they hold dear, until they are driven insane. This is how the lineage of sorcery protects itself; only the very best should ever be able to ascend to its highest peaks and wield power nearly equal to that of the gods."

Kan-Gul regarded the Murai in front of him. Kancho might have been frozen, but Ran could see that he was still trying as hard as he possibly could to bring the sword down on Kan-Gul.

The sorcerer continued to smile. "Even now—trapped as he is within the spell—the Murai is determined to strike me down. He has no hope of doing so, but his ego will not let him abandon the quest to kill me. To do so, he believes, would be giving up—surrendering—to a lesser foe, someone beneath his stature." Kan-Gul shrugged. "As much as he is trapped within my spell, he is simultaneously trapped within the cell of his own vanity. I find the human brain such a fascinating topic of study. Don't you?"

Ran shrugged. "Perhaps."

"Bah." Kan-Gul waved him off. "You do as well. It's one of the things you Shinobujin are so adept at playing with. You think I can't see through your legends? The ability to vanish in the night. The nearly supernatural physical abilities you are supposed to be able to do at will? Tell me, can you truly turn invisible? Can you really disappear in the blink of an eye?"

Ran smiled. "Why would I tell you my secrets?"

"We're making conversation." Kan-Gul leveled a finger at Ran. "Here's what I think: I think your invisibility isn't so much the idea that you are able to actually disappear as it is the subtle manipulation of physical boundaries of human awareness combined with an innate understanding of how the human brain works. Couple that with this discussion of ego and you have the perfect recipe for being able to vanish. And more importantly, *make* people think you can vanish. If their minds are already predisposed to the notion that you *can*, then when you employ your techniques, you are even more convincing." He clapped his hands. "It's rather ingenious, if I do say so myself."

"Thank you."

"Especially so, when dealing with warriors like our friend here—proud men who are convinced of their own imperviousness and skill. To be bested by a fighter like yourself, who refuses to limit himself to the parameters of some ancient code but rather utilizes anything necessary to get the mission accomplished—well, it would be rather insulting to them. So the very legends that you have created are perpetuated by your opponents as a means of explaining away their failure at being able to deal with you. Sheer brilliance!"

Ran sighed. "Glad you approve."

Kan-Gul's smile disappeared. "Can you imagine actual invisibility, though? Truly not being physically present? What would that be like."

"I didn't know that ability exists," said Ran.

"Oh, it does," said Kan-Gul. His body shimmered for a moment, and Ran frowned. He could see the landscape behind the sorcerer. He could see right through him. Then, in another blink, Kan-Gul's body was back and solid.

"I could teach you how to do it. Imagine that. You wouldn't have to rely on psychology and physical limitations. You could actually become invisible. You could become the most accomplished Shinobujin of the ages. And all I'd ask is for your help from time to time in dealing with the variety of unpleasant things I am distracted by. Your rewards would be extraordinary. Anything you desired."

"Attempting to appeal to my ago after a lengthy discussion on the very ills of it probably isn't the most compelling argument you could offer up," said Ran. "You're not dealing with a Murai, after all."

"Indeed," said Kan-Gul. "But even those of us who are aware of the pitfalls sometimes need to take a break from constant vigilance. After all, what good is treasure and fame if you can't enjoy them every once in a while."

"Perhaps I'm not motivated by those things."

Kan-Gul's eyes narrowed. "You're not, are you?" He paused. "So what does motivate you, Ran? Is it honor? A different form of honor than the yoke worn by your friend here. And what about friendship? Does that motivate you? Loyalty to comrades you've battled alongside. Is the Murai important to you?"

"Challenge," said Ran. "Challenge motivates me. When I was studying, all I could dream about was getting out into the real world and confronting the things I'd been training to fight against. The crucible of the everyday world is where I find all the motivation I'll ever need. It's through challenge that I expect to relish life to the fullest. Anything else—anything easy—wouldn't be living."

Kan-Gul stayed quiet for a moment. "You are an interesting specimen, shadow warrior. When others quest for glory and treasure, you only care about how strife makes you a better person. Intriguing."

"So you can understand why your offer of employment does not exactly tempt me." Ran eyed Kancho. The determination was still there, but he'd moved only a fraction of an inch farther on.

"Indeed," said Kan-Gul. "However, I still hold your friend and his daughter captive. Your decision will affect their fate. Are you comfortable knowing that turning me down will result in his death and her eternal suffering?"

Ran sniffed. "I've only known him for a few days. As for the girl, she means nothing to me."

"Easier said than done," said Kan-Gul. "And I don't know that I believe you anyway." The sorcerer waved his hand, and Kancho immediately sped up with his cut. A look of surprise and delight spilled over Kancho's face. But it was short-lived. Even as he resumed normal speed, his downward cut ran into an invisible wall. Inches away from Kan-Gul's face, the blade stayed where it was.

Kan-Gul laughed and moved his face even closer to the edge of the sword, taunting Kancho. "Do it, Murai. Make the cut. Strike me down, and all of your pain will vanish. All the Chekhal will go back to the afterlife. Do it now. Use all of your strength, all of your will. Cut me down!"

Ran watched the agony etched in Kancho's face as he tried to do what Kan-Gul commanded. But the exertion was futile. He could not move the blade any farther. Sweat erupted from Kancho's pores. His eyes winced, and he gritted his teeth.

"Yes," said Kan-Gul. "Do it. Kill me . . . "

Blood seeped out of Kancho's pores now. His lungs heaved as he strained to finish the cut. And still he could move the blade no farther. Blood ran down his face, spilling into his tunic and staining it a dark maroon. His legs started to buckle. And yet he would not give up. He would not quit.

Kan-Gul laughed. "You cannot kill me, Murai. I am beyond your ability. Your spirit is impressive, but no match for mine." He sighed. "Alas, our time is finished." He waved his hands and Kancho's sword suddenly moved again, but the momentum was so great it arced through the air and stuck right into the ground.

Kancho, surprised at being able to move again and unable to halt his momentum, stumbled forward and nearly impaled himself on the pommel of his sword. At the last moment, he avoided it by twisting and falling to the ground. He shifted and tried to stand back up. Reaching one hand toward his sword, he looked at Ran, and Ran saw only sadness. Resignation.

Kan-Gul eyed the man on the ground before him. "You are exhausted, Murai. There's nothing left to give. And you have nothing left to take." The sorcerer pointed a single finger at Kancho's chest, and Kancho seized up, clutching at his heart.

Yuki rushed to her father's side, crying as she tried to cradle his head in her arms. He reached one hand up and managed to stroke her face. Ran saw a single tear escape the side of his eye as he smiled at her. "Do not fear death."

Ran knelt next to him. Kancho's eyes turned to his. "It was an honor . . . to fight alongside you . . . " His head lolled to one side.

Still.

Ran placed his hand over Kancho's face and closed his eyes. Then he stood and faced Kan-Gul. "You didn't have to do that."

"Didn't I? What good was he to me? He would have tried to kill me if I had let him live. Better to slay your enemies than have them sneaking back into the cracks until a later date."

"He was a good man. And a brave warrior."

Kan-Gul nodded. "He was indeed brave. And I cannot fault him for wanting to rescue his daughter. In his stead, I would have done the same. But it still cost him his life in the end. Be thankful I at least granted him an afterlife. Even now my Chekhal are thoroughly displeased by that act."

Ran could feel the murmur of energy moving through the ranks of the Chekhal. Clearly they had been hoping to feast on Kancho's soul. "Thank you for not doing that."

Kan-Gul held up his hand. "There is a trade-off for everything, so don't be so quick to thank me. Kancho's daughter will have to atone for her father's sins."

"Meaning what?"

"Meaning she has a lifetime of agony ahead of her."

Kan-Gul gestured to the Chekhal. "They desire her. Can you feel their energy even now? It builds and builds. They need relief, and she is just the vessel for that relief."

Movement out of the corner of his eye caught Ran's attention. He turned and saw Yuki picking up her father's sword. Ran held up his hand. "Yuki, don't try to attack him. It won't do any good."

Kan-Gul laughed. "She is truly the daughter of a Murai. I admire her spirit as well. But the night stalker is right. Put the sword down. You know you cannot strike me down."

Yuki's eyes looked like dull stones. But she didn't try to attack Kan-Gul.

Instead, Yuki turned the sword over and in one swift move threw herself forward onto the blade. Ran heard the sound of the folded steel punching through her abdomen and into her heart. Blood spewed everywhere as Yuki's body slid farther down the blade. She gasped but once before going utterly still, falling into the trampled grass near her father's corpse.

For the first time, Kan-Gul looked shocked. "Why on earth would she do such a thing?"

Ran frowned. "You said it yourself. She is the daughter of a Murai warrior. Better death before dishonor. Had she consented to your twisted demands, she would have brought shame upon her family name. This was the only escape for her."

Around them, the Chekhal shifted and moved and grumbled. They had been robbed of not one but two victims.

Their displeasure was evident.

"Your undead minions don't look all that pleased with this most recent turn of events."

Kan-Gul shook his head. "No. They are not. I will have to come up with an alternative that will satisfy their cravings. In the meantime, I need to decide what I'm going to do with you. You're not going to be stupid enough to try to attack me the way the Murai did, are you?"

"No," said a voice behind Ran. "But I will."

CHAPTER FORTY

Ran knew that voice.

He turned and saw that Jysal stood behind him, her blue dress swirling about her in the wind that had suddenly kicked up. She was surrounded by tendrils of yellow gold energy that crackled and charged the air surrounding them on the cliff. Ran wanted to ask her a million questions, but now was not the time. Jysal's eyes blazed, and even the tattoo that decorated one half of her face seemed to pulse with life.

"How is it you've returned from the dead?" demanded Kan-Gul. "You could not have the power to do that. Especially one as inexperienced as you. Tell me how you accomplished it. Tell me!"

Jysal laughed, and there was a strength in it that Ran had never heard reflected in her speech before. Gone was the naive and hesitant novice that he'd known the past several days. In her place stood someone very much in possession of power—a lot of power.

"You are not in the position to demand anything,

warlock." Jysal surveyed the landscape. Her eyes lit upon Neviah's body, and Ran saw a crinkle of sadness creep onto her face. She glanced at Ran. "How did she die?"

"Malkyr," said Ran. "Neviah tried to surprise Kan-Gul. While her back was turned, Malkyr killed her."

"Where is he now?"

"Dead," said Ran. "I killed him."

Jysal nodded. "My thanks to you. Neviah did not deserve such dishonor."

"She did not." Ran bowed his head. "I wish I'd been able to save her."

"You couldn't have saved her," said Jysal. "We all fell victim to Malkyr's treachery. I hope wherever he is now, he is suffering at the hands of Neviah's spirit."

"As do I," said Ran.

Jysal turned her attention back to Kan-Gul. "You have tortured this land for many years. The time of your reckoning is at hand."

Kan-Gul smiled. "Then I welcome it." He raised his hands and blue orbs danced about him. Each one raced up and down the line of Chekhal, looking as though they energized the undead horde. The Chekhal started forward, their weapons drawn and intent on killing ran and Jysal.

"Stand by my side, Ran," said Jysal.

Ran needed no encouragement and moved to Jysal's left. Instantly, Jysal unleashed a wave of yellow energy that rocketed into the ranks of Chekhal. As they were hit, the dull gray skin of the undead warriors seemed to vaporize, leaving behind a line of skeletons.

Kan-Gul laughed. "It will take more than that to destroy my men." He waved his hands, and the blue energy crackled around the skeletal warriors. Once again, they started moving forward.

Jysal didn't hesitate and unleashed a volley of golden orbs that smashed into the skeletal Chekhal, blasting several apart. "I'll need help, Ran."

Ran launched himself at the closest Chekhal and cut from left to right with a brutal horizontal cut that severed the spinal cord of the skeleton. He used the momentum of the strike to bring his sword up and over his head, chopping down on another Chekhal, shattering through the collar bone and then into the rib cage and pelvis. The skeleton toppled apart and lay still on the ground.

Around him, Jysal shot more golden energy bolts at Chekhal, blasting them apart with relative ease. On the other side of the cliff, Kan-Gul kept up a steady stream of reinforcements, but as as each new Chekhal entered the fray, Jysal's magic reduced them to shambling skeletons as well. Then they were easy pickings for Ran as he smashed, cut, and kicked his way through their ranks.

Without their lifeless flesh, the Chekhal seemed much slower, but their weapons were still just as deadly. Ran had to evade and avoid swipes with their curved swords and spiked spears. But he felt energized by Jysal's reappearance and threw himself fully into the melee. Twice Kan-Gul shot bolts of crimson energy at him, but he managed to avoid them. If he and Jysal could manage to get through the Chekhal there would only be Kan-Gul left to deal with.

Kan-Gul sent another wave of his undead horde at them, but there were fewer of the Chekhal now. Kan-Gul might have had thousands back at his castle—unless he was lying, thought Ran—but he seemed to be running out of them atop the cliff.

"Keep the pressure on," said Jysal quietly. Even amid all the chaos, Ran could hear her voice as if it were inside his head.

He smashed through another Chekhal skeleton that tried to impale him with a thrust from a wicked-looking barbed spear. Ran chopped down, halving the spear shaft, and then flipped his blade and cut the head of the skeleton off. Bones littered the ground all around him, and he had to watch his step or risk turning his ankle as he fought through the mire of dead.

Ran glanced at Kan-Gul and saw sweat flowing down the sorcerer's face. It was the first time he'd seen Kan-Gul look concerned. The sorcerer kept throwing more spells into the air, but each one seemed to have no effect. He sent a barrage of brilliant red bolts at Jysal, but she was surrounded by a yellow aura that simply deflected the bolts and sent them careening back at Kan-Gul.

"The girl! Kill the girl!" Kan-Gul directed a trio of Chekhal to avoid Ran and turn their attention to Jysal.

Ran leapt in front of them, slashing side to side and driving the edge of his sword through bone and evil magic. Again and again he cut, swerved, cut, and evaded. Every fiber of his being felt like it was on fire, sizzling with an untapped energy that filled him with power despite his exhaustion. Ran had never felt this way during combat before and wondered if it was coming from Jysal or from somewhere even deeper within himself.

At the moment, it didn't matter. As more and more Chekhal fell to his strikes and fewer and fewer rushed into battle, Kan-Gul started slowly backing away. He still fired more and more deadly magic, but it had no effect. Even the bolts he shot at Ran were off-target and dissolved before they could harm him.

The ground around them was a seething mess of blood, slime, bones, mud, and trampled grass. Ran felt his footing slip several times and had to go with it to adapt to the environment rather than fight against it and risk a lucky strike from the Chekhal.

And then the Chekhal stopped coming.

Jysal looked around the top of the cliff. She seemed entirely nonplussed and not the least bit tired. Ran squatted down amid the bones of the countless Chekhal skeletons he'd slain and let his lungs heave as they flushed oxygen into himself. His muscles burned, and sweat glistened everywhere on his skin. It was if lightning had struck him and the energy had coursed through him like a liquid fire.

"Kan-Gul has left us, apparently," said Jysal.

Ran looked across the way. She was right. He was gone. Ran stood. "Where is he?"

Jysal closed her eyes for a moment. "Running back down the trail toward the shore. His magic is depleted. He has nothing left to give."

"Then now is a good time for him to die," said Ran. He rushed across the cliff and down the winding game trail. The wind still blew, swirling as if a fresh storm were coming to rest along the coastline. The air smelled cleaner, though, as if the impending rain would wipe the stench of Kan-Gul's magic from this inhospitable land.

Ran rounded another corner and then leapt into the

air to avoid a root. As he came down, something slammed into his chest, knocking him to the ground. All of the air in his lungs rushed out of him.

He threw himself to the side as he caught sight of the staff careening toward his head. The tip of the staff smashed into the dirt, spraying up dirt and gravel that flew into Ran's face. He jumped up and brought his sword up, but it was instantly swiped away by a strike to the back of his hands.

Kan-Gul stood before him, no longer dressed in the gowns he'd worn earlier but instead a simple pair of leggings and a threadbare half shirt of linen. Despite his obvious advanced age, Ran could see that Kan-Gul's wiry frame nevertheless possessed strength. Thin cords of muscle ran along his arms, twisting around his bones.

"You won't find me the easy opponent she thought I would be," said Kan-Gul. But the calm confident demeanor that had been a constant of his personality was no longer in place. And the beads of sweat told Ran that his opponent was much less a threat than he had been only minutes before.

Kan-Gul flipped the six-foot staff around and around, making a circular pattern in the air that reminded Ran of some of the techniques he'd been taught from one of the shadow-warrior schools. He glanced around, but his sword was somewhere off the side of the trail amid the tall, dry grasses. He wouldn't be able to find it. Not now, at least.

Kan-Gul launched a series of downward and upward strikes that swept in from all sorts of angles. Ran moved counter to them, fitting his body into the spaces they created, trying to draw down the distance so he could get inside the weapon's effective range. Twice he misjudged the distance and nearly got his head caved in for the trouble.

But even as he got hit, Ran kept moving. He knew it was tougher for Kan-Gul to hit a moving target than a stationary one. And as he moved inside the range of yet another attack, Ran threw an elbow into Kan-Gul's sternum, hoping to break the bones there and pierce the evil warlock's heart.

Kan-Gul grunted and drew back. Ran followed and grabbed the staff, breaking it out of Kan-Gul's grasp. Kan-Gul kicked him as he did so, and Ran lost control of it, dropping it. He watched it fall over the side of the trail.

Both men were now unarmed.

Kan-Gul ripped off his linen shirt. Sweat flowed from his pores and pooled in the crevices of his muscles. He wiped a hand along his mouth and regarded Ran. "Are you as gifted with your hands as you are with your weapons?"

Ran smiled. "It's the first thing we learn."

Kan-Gul rushed him, launching a massive arcing kick aimed at Ran's head. Ran dropped under it and waited for the limb to pass overhead before coming up with a series of punches into Kan-Gul's lower back. The sorcerer leapt away, surprisingly agile for someone as old as he was.

He circled Ran now, much more wary than he had been initially. "Impressive."

Ran said nothing, but kept his hands up, alert for the next attack.

Kan-Gul feinted with a punch and immediately went low, trying to tackle Ran around the waist. Ran stumbled back, taken by the head butt to his stomach, and then found himself falling onto his back. Kan-Gul snaked up his body, driving elbows and knees into all of Ran's crevices. Shots of pain riddled Ran as Kan-Gul used his body weight to keep in control.

Ran felt Kan-Gul's hands encircle his neck, squeezing and choking. Kan-Gul's face swam into view. Ran could smell his rancid breath. Drops of sweat spilled from Kan-Gul's face onto Ran's. And then the evil warlock leaned closer, so they were only inches apart.

"Tell me, shadow warrior, are you truly living right now? This is what you wanted, isn't it? The challenge? Well, here it is."

His bony fingers continued to crush Ran's trachea. Ran's vision melted into blackness. He could get no oxygen into his lungs. He heard the slowing pulse in his ears. Felt his muscles slacking.

Heard Kan-Gul chortling with glee.

"Time to die, Ran."

No.

Ran had tried with all of his strength to push back, but Kan-Gul had met him power for power. They were locked together, each pushing against the other, and Kan-Gul was slowly winning.

So Ran let himself go utterly slack.

The sudden release of power caused Kan-Gul to fall forward slightly. And there, in that smallest instant of possibility, Ran bucked his hips and brought his hands up behind Kan-Gul's elbows, smacking them off. Ran continued to roll, dislodging the warlock. Kan-Gul sprawled in the grass as Ran got to his feet, coughing and unsteady as he was.

He drew in several quick breaths and steadied himself. Kan-Gul was already on his feet and rushing back in at him. The sorcerer threw kick after kick, but Ran moved easily out of the way as each flew past. Kan-Gul's breath was audible now, and it came in stuttering spurts that betrayed his faltering strength.

Ran waited until he overcommitted on a chopping strike aimed at his neck. Then he stepped inside of the strike, drove another elbow into Kan-Gul's chest, and then straightened his arm, using the edge of his hand to chop horizontally into Kan-Gul's throat.

The effect was instant. Kan-Gul's hands flew to his throat, trying to free the pressure from the collapsed trachea. His torso convulsed as he vomited, but nothing could escape because his throat was permanently damaged. As Kan-Gul sank to his knees, still trying to work his bony fingers into his mouth in a vain attempt to open his airway, Ran stepped into the grass and searched for his sword.

As his hand closed around the handle, he looked back. Kan-Gul's eyes were already starting to roll over white.

Ran stepped out of the grass and stood before the sorcerer. Kan-Gul grunted as bile spilled from his lips. There was hatred in his eyes, but Ran never gave him the chance to utter a thing. With one sweep of his sword, the blade cut through the thin neck and severed it from the rest of his body. A small stream of blood shot from the neck as Kan-Gul's head dropped to the grass. His body slumped to the ground.

Ran picked up his head and walked back to the top of the cliff. He bypassed Jysal and stood near the edge. Below him, the sea churned. and the white froth of colliding waves called to him.

He hesitated only a moment before lofting the head as far as he could out to sea. He watched it tumble through the air, end over end, and then splash into the ocean. For a split second, it seemed to want to float. But then a wave swept over the grisly trophy, and it slipped beneath the waves.

Kan-Gul was dead.

CHAPTER FORTY-ONE

"I thought you were dead."

Jysal smiled. "I very nearly was. I'm still not entirely sure what happened. After that initial use of magic, my body shut down. It was as if I'd tapped into something so overwhelming that my body couldn't deal with it so it closed down. For the longest time, it felt like I was floating in darkness. I couldn't hear anything, see anything. Maybe it was like being suspended in time or something."

"What brought you back?"

Jysal frowned. "I don't know. Maybe if I was more experienced at using magic, I could answer that question. But something nudged me to wake up, and as soon as that happened, all of this amazing energy flowed into me. I felt more alive than I'd ever felt before."

"And apparently able to wield magic," said Ran with a smirk. "That certainly came in handy."

"I was always able to wield magic," said Jysal. "But I was held back by fear of the unknown. The consequences of using it scared me. It didn't help that Neviah filled my head with all of these crazy images and thoughts of what might happen."

"She was only trying to protect you," said Ran. "You can't blame her."

"If I'd used magic earlier, she might still be alive."

"Or she might not," said Ran. "You can't blame yourself for her death. Neviah never stopped trying to help us. The attempt she made on Kan-Gul's life shocked even me."

"She was a credit to the school of protectors she came from." She walked over to where the bodies of Kancho and his daughter, Yuki, lay. "Such a waste of life. I feel awful he is dead."

"He died in battle. He wouldn't have wanted it any other way. If he was unable to live, then death by this method brings him the most honor."

"And her? What does she gain by her death?"

Ran squatted beside Yuki and pulled Kancho's sword out of her. Then he arranged their bodies side by side and laid Kancho's sword between them. "She gains honor. Perhaps enough to offset the dishonor Kancho brought upon them by coming to rescue her in the first place."

"I don't understand," said Jysal. "She gave up."

"No," said Ran. "She refused to submit. There's a difference. Yuki was no warrior, but she was Murai. This was the only path open to her that would have enabled her to retain her honor and restore her family's name. Despite her youth, she understood this. And she displayed incredible courage by doing so."

"I still think it's a waste," said Jysal.

"It is a waste," said Ran. "But that is how the Murai think. I don't fault her for doing what she did. If I had been